THE BLOODSWORD SAGA

to: Chris
Best Wishes
Mark [illegible]
11-6-03

THE BLOODSWORD SAGA

The Trilogy

Mark Ventimiglia

ISBN: Softcover 1-4134-3188-7

This book was printed in the United States of America.

To order additional copies of this book, contact:
Xlibris Corporation
1-888-795-4274
www.Xlibris.com
Orders@Xlibris.com

21409

CONTENTS

BOOK I

Tulwryn and the Dragon

BOOK II

Trail of Vengeance

BOOK III

The Flesh Merchant

APPENDIX

PREVIEW OF CHAPTER ONE BOOK IV

For Logan Michael Morelli
The beautiful son of Michael and Spring Morelli
Born on 10/16/02

In a mythical world of wizards and warriors, damsels and dragons, pirates and plunder, one man stands alone as the Hero Supreme, and that man is Tulwryn Bloodsword. This is his story!

Whether fighting his way across the blood soaked snows of the frigid northern battlefields, or sailing the skies in a magical windship, or chasing pirates on the high seas, you will always find Tulwryn, sword in hand, teeth clenched, and ready for battle.

Set sail for the adventure of a lifetime and embark with him on a fantastic odyssey as he travels through Phantasodyssea, a world filled with magic and heroic adventure!

This trilogy contains the novels:
Tulwryn and the Dragon
Trail of Vengeance
The Flesh Merchant

REVIEWS

Exhilarating, spellbinding! The Bloodsword Saga has it all: Action, romance, horror, and magic. Mark Ventimiglia has outdone himself once again! From tender love scenes to heroic fights, the pace never slows down. This saga is truly a Harry Potter for adults!

-A. C. Morgan, St. Louis, Missouri.

Thrilling adventure! The Bloodsword Saga, I feel, is a modern literary masterpiece. Not since Gulliver's Travels has a contemporary fantasy author created such a dramatic adventure. The colorful tapestry of Mr. Ventimiglia's world, and his unparalleled poetic means of conveying that world, is truly a delight to modern readers of fantasy fiction. In my opinion, the Bloodsword Saga is destined to become a contemporary classic!

-Andrea Michele Voke, Jerseyville, Illinois.

Intense emotion! I am impressed by the vast array of emotion on each page. This emotion seems to spill over from the author's other writings, of which I have read most. Mr. Ventimiglia has an uncanny ability to put the dark side of humanity into the written word and I look forward to many more literary contributions.

-Brian Bollinger, Brighton, Illinois.

ACKNOWLEDGEMENTS

I would like to take this time to thank the following people for helping me keep my sanity whilst working on the manuscript for this book. Without their support, this novel would never have materialized: Andrea M. Voke, Scott Davis, Tracy Randall, Mike Purcell, Mike Morelli, and my wonderful parents, Walter and Sandra Ventimiglia.

A very special thanks goes to Rachel Davey of Xlibris.

My deepest apologies, if through my ignorance, I have left anyone out.

A LETTER TO THE READER

Dear Reader:

First, I would like to thank you for purchasing this novel, the trilogy of the Bloodsword series. The production of the entire Bloodsword Saga depends solely on your continual and undying support. I thank you all sincerely.

The concept for this series of novels actually began over fifteen years ago when I created a storyline for what I hoped would become a fantasy adventure video game. Back in 1989, when I designed the world of Phantasodyssea, it was looked at by a number of video game producers including Premier Technologies and Nintendo. Inevitably, since I was no PC game designer and could not produce a working prototype on computer disk, the idea for a video game was rejected. After months of trying in vain to find a manufacturer for the project, I shelved the idea.

It wasn't until November of 2000 that, due to seriously devastating events in my life, I got the idea to re-write my game and turn it into a novel series. I dug out the manuscripts from my den's closet, blew the dust of the ages from the box they slept in for over a decade, and then began the task of converting the game idea into a workable Saga.

Over the years, of course, my thinking matured and changed, as did the idea for the series. There were a number of character changes, as well as plot changes. In fact, it wasn't until December of 2000 that I reworked the entire map of Phantasodyssea, and started delving deeper into the Mysteries of Caiwryn (Caiwryn is the Nuvian word, in spelling and meaning, for the entire world of Phantasodyssea. In essence, Caiwryn is the word Tulwryn himself uses when he is speaking of the world at large).

What I do want to stress here is, unlike J.R.R. Tolkien's Lord of the Rings, Phantasodyssea, Tulwryn's world, and the entire Bloodsword Saga in general, constitutes not an entire age, or a number of ages, but merely catalogues a man's life. While some attention to detail is necessary to any story, I have kept most to a minimum, opting to concentrate more on Tulwryn's adventures rather than the world in which he lives. In this manner, the Bloodsword Saga more closely resembles Robert E. Howard's Conan Saga than Tolkien's Lord of the Rings epic. Even so, there will be, I am certain, a great number of individuals that will adhere to the thought that I created the Bloodsword Saga after the Lord of the Rings trilogy. Nothing could be further from the truth, for the entire Bloodsword Saga is much more than simply three novels! While I am a great fan of J.R.R. Tolkien, the idea of Tulwryn (mainly in name only) evolved, not from the Lord of the Rings, but from one of the Master's earlier works.

J.R.R. Tolkien's character, Turin Turambar, was introduced to our world in the twenty-first chapter of the Silmarillion by Tolkien's son Christopher, working as editor to that production. Originally, the Silmarillion was never even meant to be published, but rather was used by J.R.R. Tolkien as a working guide to the writing of the Lord of the Rings trilogy. Or so I am told.

Once again, in the second volume of Tolkien's Book of Lost Tales, we find an earlier version of this same tragically heroic character in the second chapter of that book: Turambar and the Foaloke. Likewise, the entire first part of J.R.R. Tolkien's Unfinished Tales is again comprised of Turin's adventures as documented in the story: Narn I Hin Hurin.

I believe that the earliest version of Turin Turambar's character development is found, not in prose, but in alliterative poetic verse, in J.R.R. Tolkien's third book on the history of Middle-earth titled the Lays of Beleriand. Herein we find the poem, Lay of the Children of Hurin (Turin's father), which was first penned in the year 1918.

To the best of my knowledge, no other character possessed

Tolkien's mind as did Turin Turambar. Even though he wrote often about hobbits and elves, dwarves and men, orcs and wizards and gnomes, still it was Turin that was the driving force behind the ultimate shaping of Middle-earth in the First Age. Certainly no other character touched me as did Turin, and for this reason alone, when crafting the Bloodsword Saga, I used his name as a template for the hero in my own story, mainly to honor the man from whom I have drawn most of my literary inspiration, J.R.R. Tolkien. In truth, the name Tulwryn (pronounced tool-rin) is merely my attempt to spell the name in a Gaelic-like (or possibly Welsh-like) fashion, hoping to bring a little romance and nostalgia to the body of the story.

Even though Tulwryn's name comes from the inspiration I gained from J.R.R. Tolkien, his personality did not. Certainly, there are many similarities betwixt the two characters, and this again, is most likely why Tolkien's Turin hit home with me so much. He reminded me of myself, to a degree. The moodiness, the melancholy, the quick to anger, all of these negative personalities I find in myself. Hence, I related to the character. Therefore, when I created Tulwryn, I instilled in him my own weaknesses, but unlike in our modern world, whereas these negative traits are considered major weaknesses and blatant character flaws, in Tulwryn's time they are strengths. In Tulwryn's world, a passive man could not survive. This is what makes the story interesting, I believe. Even though the character is somewhat predictable, the degree of savagery and his unrelenting willingness to violence keeps the pace of the story moving and exciting.

Also, there are a few passages in the present work that some might feel were culled from the works of Robert E. Howard, Ursula LeGuin, Tolkien, H.P. Lovecraft, etc. Yet this is simply not the case. It is a fact that I am a huge fan of the afore mentioned authors, and I deeply respect their work. They are amongst the best in the fantasy literary genre, and I have gained much inspiration from them. I give full credit and praise to those fine writers that have came before me, for it is from their *Well of Inspiration* that I continue to drink.

Another thing that needs to be addressed is the manner that the novel is formatted. After the first novel was released, I noticed some grammatical and structural errors. After checking my disks, as well as the original manuscripts, I discovered that these errors where mainly due to inconsistencies in the formatting of the book, since my disks and manuscripts did not contain any of these errors. After speaking with my editors at Xlibris, we discovered that the PC program I used to write the book, and the PC program that Xlibris used to format the work was not 100% compatible.

While most readers will inevitably ignore these inconsistencies, focusing mainly on the story rather than the formatting structure, I am certain that some will most likely be annoyed. I can assure you that the utmost care was taken in the formatting of this novel so that none of the afore mentioned errors appear herein. Even so, human nature being what it is, errors do occur in even the best-edited works by the greatest of authors, and I am sure that this work is no different.

Currently, there are six novels planned for this series, although the entire Bloodsword Saga will most likely contain at least ten separately bound volumes (and a few collector's hardbound editions as well, of which this volume may be one).

Books one through six will consist of the Bloodsword Saga itself, which chronicles the life and adventures of Tulwryn Bloodsword. Books seven and eight will contain the Unremembered Tales. These are the legends and yarns told around the campfires and ale halls throughout the Saga, as well as some of the pre-history of the world and events leading up to Tulwryn's birth. Book nine is comprised of the poetry of Caiwryn, and laid therein are all the poems, lays, and songs, of the Bloodsword legend. Book ten, possibly the last volume in the series, is the tale of Tulwryn and the Dragon, which incidentally, will be the complete and unedited hardcover version of the first book, the Adventures of Tulwryn Bloodsword the Warrior. The novel appears in this work as the first book of the trilogy!

Of course, due to reader demand, I might yet uncover further lore and, putting quill to parchment, add to this ever-growing Saga. Only time will tell. Perhaps the Book of Selah will materialize? Or maybe the Sacred Scroll of Covensted, which was penned by Mimir himself over a millennium ago, will be discovered. But alas, let us cease this needless speculation and get on with the present tale!

The trilogy that you have before you, is only the first part of the Bloodsword Saga. This story has been a long time in the making, and I hope that you enjoy reading the fantasy as much as I did in writing it!

Sincerely,
Mark Ventimiglia

BOOK I

Tulwryn and the Dragon

Running at full pace, heart pounding to the point of bursting, Tulwryn hurdled the ashwood fence that surrounded the main house, and seconds ere the bandit turned and caught sight of him, he screamed a war yell and hewed the villain's head in twain with one mighty blow from his hand axe. A crimson arc of blood and gore painted the sky red before him as the axe cleaved home through skull, brains, and teeth, until becoming lodged in the thick of the victim's collarbone. Instantly the man crumbled lifeless to the ground and then Tulwryn wrenched his weapon from the carcass. Tulwryn looked down at the dead man that lay at his feet. He would never forget the glazed look in those dead eyes. It was the first time that he had ever killed; it would not be the last.

SYNOPSIS OF BOOK ONE

Born to a family of alfalfa farmers in the tiny village of Nuvia, Tulwryn was a bright and cheerful lad, and grew into a strong and resilient man with high moral virtues and a strict code of honor more akin to a soldier than a farmer. But a farmer he was through and through, and a family man as well.

Nuvia was located just south of the Plain of Kem, east of the River Phaedron, and on the main trade route that criss-crossed the length and breadth of Phantasodyssea. Yet, Tulwryn established his farm far to the south of the village, deep within the Azure Wood, to protect his family from the marauding bands of Kemite river pirates and plains outlaws that constantly plagued the area.

The village of Nuvia's main export was agriculture in the form of alfalfa, barely, corn, oats, and wheat, but some of its inhabitants farmed the illegal herb Wormwood, used in the manufacture of Absynth, a highly addictive and toxic social drug, for it demanded an extremely high price in places like Covensted and Baezutu.

Being of black hair and medium build, with the olive skin and the dark eyes of his people, Tulwryn prided himself on an honest days toil. He trafficked naught in the growing of illegal poisons, as did those around him, but worked hard to provide for his growing family, his wife Durayn and his four young sons. Tulwryn was always light of mood and in good cheer, even though he was but a poor farmer, for his family gave him much joy. But alas, this was to change, for a dark cloud of doom would soon settle over his life and his heart would darken and become grim.

As a farmer, he was an unlikely candidate for warriorhood,

yet a warrior he did become, and a strong one at that. Perhaps it was the doom that over shadowed his life, or perhaps it was the will of the gods, who often twisted the fates of men for their own fell purposes. Perhaps none will know for certain, for all that remains of Tulwryn's life is this account, a mere collection of his travels and adventures across the whole of Phantasodyssea.

During the dark times, his wrath had become great and entire nations rose and fell at the wave of his hand, and so it seemed that he was of the land and the land was of him, for their two destinies had merged and become one. Yet, through all the wars and the bloodshed, his heart had hardened and he wanted none of it, save only to throw down his sword and return to the simple life of a farmer, and to his family. But that was not to be his destiny.

In the thirty-eighth winter of his life, Tulwryn found himself at the dawn of a New Age. Eighty thousand turnings of the great wheel of the seasons had passed since the forgotten Ice Times and all had remained quite ere now. But a great darkness emerged far to the north and laid over the whole of Phantasodyssea threatening a grim thralldom to all that breathed, yet there was one last hope, and that hope lied in Tulwryn the Warrior, but he himself was over shadowed by a heavy burden, difficult to bear.

An ancient and archaic prophecy foretold that a stranger from the south, the Bloodsword, would assume the throne of the House of Rexor and unite the warring northern tribes against Darkoth, the evil Frost Dragon, and his minions, the Frost Giants.

More than sixty winters past, Darkoth executed his plan and birthed a minion, in the form of a Volva, an evil sorceress, to the clan of Heidmar with the hope of thwarting the prophecy of the Bloodsword.

And here begins the heroic saga of Tulwryn Bloodsword, the Warrior of Nuvia. Embark with him on a fantastic journey as he travels through Phantasodyssea, a world filled with magic and heroic adventure!

ONE

A Darkness in the North

Standing on an outcrop of rock, Tulwryn gazed out over the cold bleak tundra of the frozen north. He had grown accustomed to the harshness of this life, yet his mind wandered back to a more peaceful time; back to Nuvia and his farm, his family, back before the doom had come and shadowed his life.

It was a beautiful memory and he recalled it often, but the horrors of that memory came as well, and so he was also filled with gloom. Tulwryn's stead was a quaint farm snuggled in a quiet valley east of the Obsidian River in the eastern reaches of the Azure Wood, just south of the Plain of Kem. The fields were small, yet fertile. His main crop was alfalfa, but he also maintained a tiny grove of oak, from which he would harvest mistletoe in autumn, since it was in much demand in places like Covensted and Baezutu.

His mind then traveled back even further and he remembered his family, his wife and his four sons. Tulwryn thought of the day he met Durayn, his wife. She was but a mere child of sixteen. Yet in Nuvia, girls wed young due to the harsh nature of the village, for Nuvia was poor and a farmer's life was hard. She was beautiful. Her long black hair tumbled down over slender shoulders and her green eyes blazed with a hidden passion, a zest for life. Perhaps, somewhere down in the depths of his mind Tulwryn knew, even then, that she was not to be satisfied with the life of a farmer's wife. Even so, her sinewy build and wide hips produced him four healthy sons, which was unheard of in

Nuvia, where often babes perished in childbirth along with their mothers.

All seemed plentiful and good, even by poor Nuvian standards, and the wheel of the year turned many times. The harvests were good and Tulwryn's sons grew. Still, it would be many more seasons ere they could join him in the fields. He smiled as memories flooded back to his mind.

"Father, can we come to the fields today," they would ask, as they tugged at his breeches when he was leaving for work early in the morning. He would simply pat their heads and mutter, "soon, my sons, very soon." But alas, those days never came. And Tulwryn's brow furrowed deep as he recalled the shadow that settled over his stead and destroyed his family, his life.

It happened in the eleventh year after his handfasting. Tulwryn was yonder working in the oak grove collecting his yearly take of mistletoe. He had no interest in magic, yet he earned more by his small yearly harvest of this bitter herb, which he would then sell to the witches of Covensted for their potions and philters, than all his alfalfa fields combined. It was odd, he often thought, why some people would work twice as hard at getting out of work than just buckling down and working an honest living. Anyhow, that was how Tulwryn viewed magic. It's not that he didn't believe in it, for he realized that there were forces at work beyond the mere boundaries of the human eye, but still, the ability to control such forces was beyond his simple comprehension. It didn't make sense to him why an herb as useless as mistletoe would bring more at market than alfalfa, which was one of the best crops for fattening livestock. He shrugged, for he concerned himself naught with the lunacy of unscrupulous people as long as their gold fed his family and his mind rested in the fact that he earned his keep by legal and respectable means.

One afternoon, after collecting more than his normal take, he felt the hair on the nape of his neck prickle up and his stomach churned with a nauseating feel. Glancing over his right shoulder, he caught a wisp of dark smoke curling skyward in the crisp autumn air; it was coming from the direction of his stead and he felt his heart jump as he thought the worse. Dropping his bushel basket and grabbing his heavy hand axe, Tulwryn turned and ran at full pace back towards the smoke, towards his stead and his family, and whatever disaster that had overtaken them.

As he ran, scenes of horror tormented his mind. Life at the stead was comfortable, but it had its risks. Even though he built the farm in the Azure Wood and east of the Obsidian River, it was still close to Kem. Long had the river pirates and bandits that hailed from that sleazy bowery town plagued the area, but for eleven turnings of the great wheel of the year, his small farm had been overlooked. Perhaps the poverty of his stead was not appealing to thieves; or perhaps the farm had simply been overlooked due to its isolated and hidden location. There was no way of knowing, yet it would seem that the black hammer of doom finally caught up with Tulwryn and his family. An icy hand gripped his heart as he ran from the oak grove and through his fields.

When the stead finally came into view Tulwryn could see that the main house was aflame. There was a pungent scent of charred human flesh floating on the air and his stomach heaved at the thought of his loved one's within its black walls.

Tulwryn was still a few hundred paces away when he caught sight of the first bandit. The man was of medium height and stocky, and carried a cutlass, the symbol of Kemite river pirates. But what was a river pirate doing this deep in the Azure Wood? He did not care; all that mattered was extracting his vengeance and salvaging his family, whatever was left to salvage.

Running at full pace, heart pounding to the point of bursting, Tulwryn hurdled the ashwood fence that surrounded the main house, and seconds ere the bandit turned and caught sight of him, he screamed a war yell and hewed the villain's head in twain with one mighty blow from his hand axe. A crimson arc of blood and gore painted the sky red before him as the axe cleaved home through skull, brains, and teeth, until becoming lodged in the thick of the victim's collarbone. Instantly the man crumbled lifeless, and then Tulwryn wrenched his weapon from the carcass.

Tulwryn looked down at the dead man that lay at his feet. He would never forget the glazed look in those dead eyes. It was the first time that he had ever killed; it would not be the last.

Suddenly, the sound of horses took his attention from the dead man on the ground to the barn beyond the main house; he spied a group of six men riding away from the stead with his wife, Durayn, accompanying one rider. Anger and rage welled up within Tulwryn's veins because he could tell that the way Durayn rode she was not riding against her will.

He noted the direction in which they rode, then turned and entered the burning house. The scene was a grisly memory and Tulwryn tried hard to blot out the visions of his four sons lying dead in scarlet pools of their own blood. Their throats had been slashed, and their young faces were charred and twisted in hideous grimaces of unrelenting pain. No matter how hard he tried to banish these dark scenes of death, they remained and fueled his bitterness. He carried the four small bodies out of the burning house and buried them in the high pasture, in the custom that was his people.

"I vow, my sons, that I shall avenge you, even if it takes the whole of my life; I shall avenge you." Tulwryn then gathered some provisions from the barn and set out in the direction after the Kemite pirates. As he rode past the razed stead, he took one final glance back at the farm that was his life; a single tear creased his cheek, it was the last tear he would ever shed.

For eight days, Tulwryn tracked the marauding band of pirates. Often he would come upon abandoned camps and ransacked farms. The band never left a witness alive and great carnage was spread in their wake. By the signs left at one abandoned camp, he discovered that Durayn was still among the group, and by the looks of it, she had taken a lover. Rage swelled in Tulwryn's heart at this betrayal, and he knew that he would kill seven more times ere his vow was complete.

Tulwryn's mind raced; he remembered the scenes so vividly as he relived them. They haunted his days and nights, as they had for the past three years. Armed with only his heavy hand axe, a gift from his friend Dillwyn Anvilhand the smith, and astride Blackthorn, his trusted mount, he tracked the group past the village of Nuvia, over a score of burned out farms; he tracked them through the Azure Wood and across the Obsidian River and over the Plain of Kem. Blackthorn heaved as the corded muscles of his heavy body strained at the pace, yet still, his heart was strong and he lusted for the run.

On the night of the eighth day Tulwryn came across the gang camped in a grotto. It was located on the western bank of the Obsidian River, just across the waters from Kem. It was apparent that the group was about to make their way across the river at daybreak and melt back into their cesspool of villainy, as they undoubtedly had done countess times before. Vengeance stirred in Tulwryn's veins as he tethered Blackthorn to a rowan tree and crept within a stone's throw from the encamped bandits. The moon was at her peak and its wide silver face illumed the entire camp whilst Tulwryn waited in the shadows.

"My, it was amazing to watch ye slay your own kin, Durayn," said a big man with heavy thews and a thick red beard. "I realized that you were tired of the farmer's life, but to kill the very cubs ye bore, well, I must say you are cut out for the life of a cutthroat indeed."

The woman, once beautiful but now soiled with the filth of betrayal, glanced up and gave the big man a scornful grin.

"Yes, you knew quite well Shamael, that I had no love for Tulwryn," she said. "Indeed, it was lucky for me to have met you last season on your autumn raids. The long years in Tulwryn's stead had grown difficult to bear and had I not fell in with your band I surely would have gone mad. Living on that farm was more than my stomach could take."

"Yes, wench," said a dark man. He spoke naught in the Kemite tongue but another, strange and harsh. His features were black as coal, yet his hair and beard were the brightest yellow and Tulwryn recognized him to be from Knob, a cannibalistic tribe of savages located in the far western reaches of the Golrin Prairie. "It was good of you to give us the information we needed over the past few moons. It was by your words that we knew which of the Nuvian farms to hit, and when. Much of the plunder you will enjoy."

"All I need enjoy is the adventure of this gang and Shamael's love betwixt my thighs," she said with a snickering grin, and the entire camp broke out in lustful laughter.

From his vantage point, Tulwryn could hear the conversation. His heart grew cold as he listened to how his wife slashed out the necks of his sons and burnt their young faces with a white-hot branding iron. How a mother could brutally slay her own flesh and blood he knew not, it was more than he could readily comprehend. He waited, for hours it seemed; he stalked there in the darkness, just beyond the glow of the firelight, waiting for the time to extract his vow of vengeance.

What happened next was a blur, even in the scenes of his own mind. Filled with unsurpassed anger and rage, Tulwryn could restrain himself no longer, and he leapt from his hiding place brandishing his heavy hand axe and nothing more. He screamed his mighty battle yell, a yell that was to become legendary in the years to come, as the shocked bandits struggled to their feet groping for their swords. Normally, a single man with nothing more than a woodsman's axe would not have stood a chance against six men armed with steel blades, but Tulwryn was fueled by the passion of vengeance and he had surprise on his side as well.

Before the men could come to guard, three of their numbers lay dead, their heads hewn from their necks. Amidst the screams and confusion, Tulwryn, in a mighty maelstrom of red violence, cut through his enemies as a warm knife slices butter. Lastly, when all six men lay dead at his feet, he came upon the shivering wreck that was once his wife.

"Praise the gods, I knew you wouldst come for me Tulwryn, and rescue me from this vile band of villains," she said as she stood to embrace him.

"Hold your tongue, wench," he answered contemptuously, as he raised his axe. "I know how ye slew my sons and soiled yourself with the likes of this scum. Thy treachery is beyond forgiveness and thou shalt get no mercy from me."

Durayn's face paled under the light of the bright harvest moon. She spat in Tulwryn's face and saw the rage in his eyes; it was the last thing that she would ever see, for she closed her eyes hard as his axe fell, and she knew nothing more.

Tulwryn was brought back to the present by the sound of approaching feet, and he spun around, axe in hand, and glared daggers at the man behind him. The man that approached was a dwarf, short and stout, and dressed in the golden chainmaile and battle gear of the western dwarves of Carthus. He had a full beard the color of tanned leather and his face was criss crossed with deep lines; his skin was burnt a bright red from many days exposed and unprotected from the burning northern sun and the harsh crisp winds of the frozen tundra. On the dwarf's head sat a heavy helm of gilded steel, yet he carried no weapons that could be seen; his hands were covered with heavy bronze gauntlets that were studded with large round steel bolts.

"Heilsa, Tulwryn," said the dwarf, raising a large hand in friendship; Tulwryn relaxed his grip on the axe. "I see that ye have grown bitter with age. "

"As wine to vinegar. Ha! So what of it? Does the world seem better through your eyes, Dillwyn?" The dwarf looked hard at his friend, ere he answered.

"Probably no," said the dwarf, "but I carry not the baggage that burdens you, my friend. Are ye still plagued with the visions?"

"Aye, methinks that these horrors are burnt in my brain and I shall have no rest whilst I breathe. Only does the act of slaying my enemies give me but a brief rest from this torment," Tulwryn said, and he sighed heavily.

"I wish there t'was something I could say or do to relieve you from this doom, my friend. The loss of sons and the betrayal of a wife, dearly loved, is not an easy weight to bear."

Dillwyn Anvilhand was a dwarf of middle years that hailed from Carthus, a dwarven town far to the west, over the vast Golrin Prairie. For the past five years, he had been a good friend to Tulwryn, and often gave ear to heed Tulwryn's pain. They had met two years ere Tulwryn's doom had befallen him, when the dwarf was adventuring in the east. After the kinslaying, he had taken up with Tulwryn and become his traveling companion.

They spent time in the Ymir Mountains, north of Kem, hunting and slaying outlaws, but not for profit. Both men, it seemed, had dark clouds cast over them by the gods, and they exiled themselves from their native lands and rode north into the vast frozen wastes.

After crossing many leagues and fording many rivers, they had arrived in the misty northern territories; a land clouded in myth and legend, and peopled by nomadic barbarians. One such tribe, the clan of Heidmar, after a dreadful battle that turned the frozen ground red, accepted the two foreigners into their kindred since it was decided that such fierce warriors would be a mighty asset in future days. And for certain, these two unlikely warriors, who were not warriors to begin with, but a mere dwarven smith and a simple Nuvian farmer, were indeed forged into great warriors by the very hand of doom. It was for this tribe that Tulwryn had taken up as sentry this day and perched himself on an outcrop of rock to survey the northern frontier, for in the north, battles between clans were frequent and fierce.

"Any sign of movement," Dillwyn asked, changing the subject.

"Nay, mine heart grows heavy with no sign of combat in the near future. What brings ye hither?"

"The council is gathering and they request our presence. It seems that the Volva has foreseen a great darkness forming in the north; there is word that she has advised the council to amass a small war party and trek north of the frozen lake to intercept it," Dillwyn said, in a low and muffled tone.

"A great darkness?" Tulwryn's face twisted in a grim frown. He was not fond of magic, and his faith of the tribe's soothsayer was questionable; whilst he held no contempt for the old woman as a person, he often wondered about her motives, and the intelligence of a race of people who put their trust in the ramblings of the aged. "What is this great darkness of which she speaks?"

"I know naught, mine friend," answered the dwarf, "only that the Volva has requested the council to gather at once. She says the signs are clear and that she will reveal all this eve."

"Signs," Tulwryn huffed. "I have been perched on this rock for the better half of the day and I have seen no signs!"

The dwarf laughed. "But ye are not a Volva, mine friend! Thy sight is limited but to thine mere eyes. This old woman has sorcery as her ally. But rest assured, I share thy reluctance in putting my trust in the senile. Come, let us go and hear what she may say. At least we can fill our bellies with food and drink ere we retire for the eve. I have sent for Urgan to replace you at sentry. See, he comes now."

On heavy loins did Urgan stride, yet he was a mere seventeen years grown. He was a splendid example of his people, sturdy and tall, with light skin and pale yellow hair. He wore the furs of his tribe, and carried a long pole of ash topped with a slender spear of bright polished steel. On his left arm, he wore the Circlet of Bravery, a golden torque of polished brass that terminated with the interlocking heads of the mighty ice boar, which he had earned during the Battle of Volsung when he was but fifteen. The Circlet, as it was called by the tribe, was a symbol of great courage and only the most skilled fighters boasted such honors; Urgan wore the badge with great pride.

Approaching the two warriors, Urgan proudly thrust out his chest and spoke:

"'Tis I, Urgan the Brave. May I have the honor of relieving ye from your post?" For the past three years, Tulwryn never ceased to be amazed at the degree of pride these savages displayed. According to many of the southern legends of Phantasodyssea, at least where the northern territories were concerned, was that the entire area was peopled with savage barbarians. Yet contrary to these legends, Tulwryn had discovered that this was far from the truth. Yes, the many tribes of the north were extremely warlike, barbaric even, and they fought with a battle rage few had ever witnessed. Still, they lived by a strict moral code, and honor was held in the highest regard. A father often instilled these high values to their sons, where it was taught that a man's life is the only thing of any real value that he possessed, that and his honor. Gold and jewels were not even held comparable. Also true, was the fact that they despised any sort of civilization. Their steads were comprised of simple hide tents yet these were not organized into any sort of city or village. Tulwryn had often thought that he was more savage than even these northern barbarians, for who could slay a wife in cold blood, even if that slaying was justified, and consider himself not a savage. The weight of his dark secret he kept hidden from most. Although many of the north had grown to fear his wrath, even those whom he called friend.

"Well met, Urgan," said Tulwryn, and he gripped the youth's thick forearm with his large calloused hand. "Keep a keen eye yonder, we do not wish our necks cut whilst we sleep."

"You can sleep soundly this eve, Tulwryn, knowing that the keen eyes of Urgan the Brave guard this stead."

"Aye, my friend, this I know for certain." Tulwryn then turned to the dwarf and said, "Come hither, Dillwyn. Let us go and hear from the lips of the old one of this darkness that encroaches upon us."

Urgan stood as a stone sentinel on that outcrop of rock as the two men left him; he did not sleep at all that night.

Thus ends the First Chapter of Book One

TWO

The Council Fire

Tulwryn entered the council circle, with Dillwyn close at his heels; he glanced about and then took his seat. He and the dwarf were the last to arrive, and there was a slight mumbling as the two foreigners took their places amidst the kindred.

"What keeps you, Tulwryn," whispered Vogelmir the Bold, "from a meeting of this magnitude. Have ye heard naught of the Volva's prophecy?"

"I am here now, let us get on with this nonsense," he said, grumbling.

"Nonsense? Ye have been among us for three snows and still you are alien to our ways. Yet, you are a bold warrior and a strong asset to the tribe indeed, but often times I am concerned why ye stay and fight amongst us, if you cannot accept our lore."

Tulwryn gave a hard look at the barbarian and said in a low tone, "Vogelmir, you of all persons should know why I stay and fight. Are ye not a warrior? I slay not for you or your tribe, but for the pleasure of the kill. If this pleasure benefits the tribe, so be it. Now be still, for I have come to hear the old woman, not your questions."

It was no secret that there was no love between Vogelmir and Tulwryn. Ever since the strange foreigner had been accepted into the tribe, Vogelmir had protested. Never did it matter that Tulwryn had proved himself in more than three score of battles since joining the kindred, there was something in the southerner's disposition that troubled the barbarian. Perhaps it was Tulwryn's raw savagery. Even though Vogelmir had been born on a battlefield, the son of a great barbarian warrior, and he himself possessed the natural combat skills of his tribe, he had never, in all his battles, witnessed the ferociousness that Tulwryn possessed, and that worried him.

Ere any further words were exchanged betwixt Vogelmir and Tulwryn, a great horn was sounded to signal the beginning of the meeting. A sturdy thegn tossed a few more logs of cedar onto the council fire and the flames rose high into the crisp night air. Sparks flew and the fragrant wood sputtered and popped as the old woman made her way to the center of the circle.

The entire council was present, all seven and twenty; strong warriors of the clan of Heidmar they were; yet, not all were men. Grimthor the Strong, the chieftain of the kindred, was present, as was his wife, Halgr Manslayer. Gunnar Trollsbane was also present, as was his three brothers, Uther the Courageous, Luther the Daring, and Omar Giantslayer. Halgi Mansbane, the daughter of Grimthor the Strong, was there as well. Long had she kept hidden her feelings for Tulwryn; for her heart stirred at the mere sight of him and she longed to call him husband. But she bit her tongue and spoke naught her feelings for him, for she knew he was troubled by a great burden, although she knew naught the cause of that burden.

Grimthor the Strong rose from his place and announced the Volva.

"Kindred," he said, "mighty warriors of the clan of Heidmar, well met and welcome to this council fire. The Volva has summoned us here for she has seen in a vision, a great darkness amassing in the north and wishes to give us council ere this shadow fall upon us. I ask that all here present heed her words and return good council, for the decisions we make this eve will preserve our clan, or destroy it. May Odhinn look favorable upon us." The entire council, save that of Tulwryn, gave a hearty cheer.

"Heilsa, Grimthor the Strong, and hail to Odhinn and the northern gods. May our battles be pleasing to them that we shall not fall from their favor!" Grimthor then stepped down and once again took his seat amongst the council members.

Tulwryn rolled his eyes. All this talk of sorcery and visions and gods was nauseating to him. Who cared from whence the gods came, or for the gods themselves, for that matter? Not he, that was for certain. The gods may be many, but where were the gods when Durayn was slaying his four sons? No! Long ago Tulwryn abandoned all hope of divine intervention in mortal affairs. He came to realize that the gods care naught for what happens to a babe after it is born. They do not concern themselves in the affairs of the flesh, save for the delight they take from watching battles and seeing men slay one another. And, where the prayers of men are concerned, Tulwryn deemed that the gods care naught for the prayers of mortals. Ere the birth of an infant, the gods breathe into the flesh a strength to face enemies, and endure; that is the most any man can reasonably ask of his gods, who take their own council. It is bad enough that mortals concern themselves in the affairs of the gods, who are then blamed for all that goes wrong in one's life, and are yet all but forgotten during the times of plenty. Tulwryn heeded naught the will of the gods, but the strength in his own thews, and that of his steel.

Shadows danced about the council circle as tongues of flame from the central fire licked skyward and the entire area was scented with the sweet fragrance of burning cedar. The Volva stumbled slowly to the center of the circle and all was silent, eagerly awaiting her council. For more than sixty snows, she had given good guidance amongst the kindred, and her words were etched in stone. Many of those present revered her as a great seer and sorceress, one who guided the clan in wisdom and ancient lore. But she was also feared, for even though she herself was a blood member of the clan of Heidmar, her powers and sorceries were alien among the members of the tribe.

Her body trembled as she spoke, and her words were harsh, as if uttered by a cawing raven rather than by a mortal human. Her white hair, long and unkempt, hung limply over bony shoulders and her tattered robe and dark cloak covered all but her face and one emaciated hand. As she lifted a gnarled finger in the air she spoke thus:

"I have seen a great doom, a darkness, which will fall over the whole of the land, not just our northern home, but the entire world in which we exist. We, the clans of the north, are merely the first defense."

"What care we, old mother, if a doom takes the southern reaches of our world? For what have we to care, we who never leave our frozen home? And why say ye clans; are we not at constant war with all other tribes of the north? Surely ye do not wish for us to make peace and band together."

The old woman lifted an eye, and the grimace on her lined and aged face was that of wrath.

"Who spoke thus?" She asked. Vogelmir the Bold stood up tall and proud, yet all else present bowed their heads and shielded their eyes.

"Nay, mine kindred, fear naught mine wrath, for I shall smite naught Vogelmir. For true, he is bold as his namesake, and I feign he speaks for the benefit of the clan, even though he knows naught the need of which I speak." The group relaxed and the Volva continued her council.

"Ere the creation of our world, there was silence. And yet, the silence was alive; and space moved. Out of the silence came also darkness, cold and eternal, and so it is said by the ancients that this silence is the First Cause, the beginning and the end of all existence, and of all things." She paused to look about the circle; a dry tongue licked dry, cracked lips. The Volva pushed her sight into the hearts and minds of those there present, and then continued.

"And the silence was intelligence, but it possessed neither form nor substance. So therefore, the silence folded itself upon itself and gave birth to itself. Out of the chaos that was the silence, form and substance arose and became as flesh, so that it could walk upon the land. And in the walking, the thing that the silence had become surveyed the whole of the land, which was its new domain, and was pleased." Again, she paused for a moment, glancing around the council circle, gazing deep into the eyes of all present.

"Now, in time, the thing that the silence had become had forgotten its origin, and it had become troubled. It sought answers to questions it did not remember; truths it thought it had never seen. With a heavy heart, it sat. In deep contemplation it sat, dreaming. Countless slow turnings of the great wheel of the seasons passed and still the questions were not answered, and the thing began to fall. It fell back into the darkness; into the icy silence, whence it came. And all was still once again. Centuries passed over the land, uneventful; and mortals of all forms began to slowly crawl from their caves at first dawn. With sleep still in their eyes, they slowly evolved, and with it, did their arrogance and ignorance evolve as well. They were cunning and evil, a cancer upon the land. Vile and treacherous they were, and murderous. But from this loathsome scene came forth a shadow, and this shadow is the great destroyer, and it has come forth to purge the world of the disease called humanity."

After she finished speaking, the Volva went slowly back to her place in the circle and sat in silence. The entire circle was clothed in quiet for some time, and then Dillwyn broke the silence and spoke.

"What is the meaning of this vision, old mother? It sounds as a grim creation myth rather than a prophecy, yet it is none that I have ever heard, and I have heard many during my travels."

"Aye, what does it mean, for your words are utterly cryptic and surely to be shrouded in mystery," asked Gunnar Trollsbane. Many others around the circle also voiced their concern, and finally the Volva raised a finger and all were silenced.

"This is a creation myth, for true, but a prophecy as well," she said. "'Tis not the legend of our race. It is the creation myth of the frost giants. But know this, the myth is still unfolding and has not yet come to full fruit. These beings, mortal as are we, but more akin to gods since their lives span eons rather than mere seasons, are stirring once again, and they see all lesser mortals as an illness to be stamped out as one extinguishes a flame with wet fingers. All races will suffer, not just humans; dwarves and elves, halflings and woodwights, and all other peoples as well."

"But what can we do to stop a frost giant," asked Luther the Daring, "or even an entire race of such beasts?"

"Slaying giants is no problem," spoke Omar Giantslayer, Luther's brother, "one merely hamstrings the beast and then hews it down with mighty blows."

"As ye know," spoke the Volva, "many of the northern clans do not traffic in the arts. Most of our race, as noble as that race may be, are concerned with survival in our harsh, frozen world. Our people, and those of our kind, are fearful of the wrath of the gods and the terrible powers they unleash. Yet, it is our small kindred that have always kept the ways of the gods alive. You have not shunned me as a senile old fool, but have kept me within the fold and cared for me utterly. I, in return, have given you good council for more than sixty turnings of the great wheel of the seasons. This is my last council, for the gods have shown me my doom and the end of my days draw nigh."

There was a slight murmur among the council members, but the old woman silenced them with a glance and continued.

"As my time hither draws to a close, my sight dims as well. I cannot see as I once did, yet I can still see further than most. My council is this: Choose four amongst you, brave and strong, and form a scouting party to travel north, beyond the great frozen lake, and espy for yourself the doom of which I speak. More I cannot say. Ye must take your own council whence ye faces your doom, for 'tis your decisions that will shape the future. But I will not send you into the wilderness alone; with ye I shall send magic."

The council erupted with talk and questions, and Grimthor was forced to raise his voice over all others and regain control of the council. As the members grew quiet, he focused his gaze on Tulwryn, then glanced to each and every member there present ere he spoke.

"We must choose, as the Volva has counseled us. The four we choose shall hold the doom of our clan, nay, the doom of the world in their hands. We know naught what this doom is, therefore once confronted, we must act and act swiftly ere the doom destroy us all."

Tulwryn stood and said, "I shall go my lord. Give me leave, but allow me to choose my own companions. I have not tasted combat for a fortnight and am ready to wet my axe in the blood of foes, be they mine or my kindred's."

"Aye, master Tulwryn, why are ye so eager to draw blood?" cawed the old woman. "Are ye so bitter at the loss of your sons that you must slay even strangers and beasts to compensate for their blood, three seasons in the grave? So be it, the visions have foretold that you shall lead this party, but I fear that you will be its undoing."

Tulwryn stood in shocked silence for a moment, and the others there present were also confounded at the words of the witch. How could this old sorceress know the secret of his burden, thought he? In all his time amongst the northern people, he had told no one of the kinslaying, save Dillwyn, and the dwarf had given his word to keep the secret as well. Truly, her magic was powerful.

"Why loose thy venom on me, old woman," he asked; his brow furrowed as he stared at her.

"Ye are a stranger, and an alien to our land, yet ye slay our enemies, who are naught your enemies, for the sheer pleasure of the kill. Blood flows freely from the blade of your axe, yet your bitterness remains. How many more will die to appease your thirst?"

"The reasons I slay are mine alone and no other need concern themselves of my motives. As long as my actions benefit the clan, I see no reason to question them. Leave me be, old woman!" He then looked again at Grimthor and asked: "Send me, my lord! I beg of you, release me from the bonds of this stead and let me go forth and slay this darkness."

After some time, Grimthor asked the council of their thoughts on the matter and all, save only Vogelmir, voiced that Tulwryn was the best choice for captain of the mission. Therefore,

Grimthor the Strong, Chieftain of the clan of Heidmar, stood and proclaimed:

"Tulwryn the Warrior, ye who hails from the un-named south and foster son of our great clan, I do hereby send ye forth to meet your doom, and ours. Choose three that shall go with ye."

Tulwryn stood and gazed into the faces of those there present, and with a menacing look in his dark eyes he chose the fate of three fell warriors. Tension was pulled tight as a bowstring ere he spoke.

"My lord, I choose only Dillwyn the Dwarf, Omar Giantslayer, and Urgan the Brave."

A great protest then erupted from the other council members at Tulwryn's request, and Vogelmir voiced his contempt that Urgan was chosen over the other council members.

"Urgan," cried Vogelmir, "is indeed brave and strong, but he is a mere child of seventeen snows, and he is not even of the age to stand at council! He should not go. I shall go in his stead!"

"Nonsense," shouted Tulwryn. "It is true that Urgan is young, but he has achieved in his short span of winters more heroic deeds than many twice his age. And as for him being too young to stand at council, that rule is lunacy. Whilst we are here discussing the fate of the world, Urgan stands sentry and guards this very stead! What are we to be guarded by his vigilance, yet deny him the glory of combat? He should accompany the party northward. I have spoken my mind, yet I shall heed the words of our mighty chieftain. It is Grimthor that shall decide this matter, not Vogelmir nor I."

Dillwyn sat quiet as the entire council argued amongst themselves. He knew that the heavy weight of Tulwryn's words would carry all the way to Grimthor's heart, for he knew how Grimthor loved Tulwryn, as blood kin and as a son he did not have. Even so, he hid this knowledge deep and spoke naught of it, for Tulwryn was a man of grim emotions and his burden was not to allow himself another wife or a father-in-law.

Finally, Grimthor arose and spoke.

"Enough! The Volva has given council, and the circle has

answered. This is a fell day that a darkness shall enshroud our people and our land, yet I feel that Tulwryn and his choice of companions are the best for this mission. Therefore, I grant him and his party leave. Ye may depart when ready, Tulwryn. This meeting is now closed! May the gods favor us with victory!"

The Volva raised a bent and twisted hand and said, "A final word before ye part this circle; there must be a forging of a new sword, and this sword must be carried north by the party's leader. On the morrow, send forth Dillwyn the smith to my hut and I shall instruct him in the forging. After the sword is made whole, only then shall the party depart for the north."

"I am a dwarven smith of Carthus," spoke Dillwyn, banefully. "I am surely able to forge a sword, but I need no woman to instruct me in the workings of my craft!"

"Tis not the craft I seek to instruct thee in, Dillwyn, but the empowerment of magic into the blade ye shape."

"I want no part of thy sorceries, old woman," the dwarf protested.

"Enough," said Grimthor. "The Volva has spoken and it shall be done as she has commanded."

The thegn then drowned the center fire with buckets of wet snow and the entire circle was blanketed in darkness as the members of the council departed for their own tents.

Tulwryn made his way to Dillwyn through the dusky night and bade him to follow.

"I fear a great shadow will engulf us, old friend," he whispered.

"Aye," answered the dwarf, "yet, what happens to you happens to me. I shall follow ye into the pits of hell if need be."

"I fear that is were we are headed." And they disappeared into the night.

Thus ends the Second Chapter of Book One

THREE

Of Gods and Men

It was dark in Tulwryn's tent when the two men entered. Tulwryn lit a taper and the dim orange glow illumined the enclosure. It was a small area, sparsely furnished and the interior of the tent reflected Tulwryn's frugal way of life; the floor was a beige woven rug of course wool, aged and tattered; a few blankets and pillows were piled in one corner, and in another corner, a simple round shield of oak. In the center of the floor was a small fire pit and a few cooking utensils.

Tulwryn placed a few small bundles of kindling into the fire pit and lit the faggots with the taper. The two men each grabbed a pillow and sat facing each other, opposite the pit. It was midwinter and the night was brisk, and for a few moments, the two just sat there and quietly warmed themselves by the fire.

"What thinks ye about all this talk of gods and doom and such," asked Tulwryn.

"I am as confused as you, old friend. When I was a boy, my father taught me the lore of our people. Yet, that lore learned so long ago is vastly different from what these northerners tell. I have been among them for three snows now and still I understand them naught."

"Tell me of your people's lore, Dillwyn," asked Tulwryn, as he placed a few larger logs on the fire.

The dwarf sat quiet for a moment, his mind searching the thoughts of his memory. Dwarves live doubly the length of that of mortal humans, and their memories are great storehouses of lore, yet recalling these many tales is no easy task and Dillwyn strained hard to recall the old legends of his people; tales his father taught him more than ninety years ago.

"From what little I remember, the elements of fire and wind come from Ymir and the other sky gods," he said, "yet Morab and Tuc, Hem and Lectite, the dwarven gods of iron and steel, live in the rock of the land. Giants also live in the dirt and the rock and the ore. I was also told, by my father, Nillwyn the Smith, that in the shadows of chaos, the giants fooled the gods and a great battle arose. The gods were angered, and the land trembled, and they slew the giants and tore their bodies asunder. From these pieces, new beasts arose, more hideous than the first; beasts such as demons and dragons and other damnable creatures that have yet to be named."

"Do ye suppose these frost giants, that the Volva spoke of, could be such beings as are named in the lore of your people," asked Tulwryn?

"Nay," answered the dwarf, as he accepted a wineskin from his friend, "my people hail from Carthus, as ye already know. The lore of mine people is that of the arid mountains and barren lands and burning deserts of the west, not the frozen wastes of the north. Of these beasts, which the old woman speaks, I know naught."

Tulwryn erected an iron tripod over the fire that by now had become a small, but warm, blaze. He hung a cooking hook from the center of the tripod and from this hook, suspended a small iron pot full of warm gruel. Shadows danced about the tent and the scent of oak mingled with the fragrance of the simmering food.

"Do ye trust the old woman," Tulwryn asked, apparently changing the subject. Dillwyn gave Tulwryn a look of apprehension, then answered.

"Nay, I trust no one. If there be one thing that I have learned in all my travels 'tis this: No one in this world can ye trust, not gods, not men, not women, not beats, no one."

"I trust naught but mine steel." Tulwryn grinned and patted his axe.

"Good council indeed, mine friend," answered the dwarf, "good council, indeed."

The two men softly chuckled to themselves and Tulwryn handed Dillwyn a bowl full of warm gruel. The dwarf passed the wineskin back to Tulwryn and took some hard bread from his knapsack; he then passed the sack to Tulwryn as well. Tulwryn took some bread and the two ate in silence for some time, both contemplating the evening and wondering what the future held.

Tulwryn finished his bowl and refilled it, broke more bread, and then spoke thus:

"What thinks ye of this magical blade that the Volva will have ye forge on the morrow?"

"Ye know I have no use for wizardry, Tulwryn. Even so, do you know how to wield a sword? All I have ever seen ye slay with is your axe."

"I suppose I can wield most anything; 'tis not the skill of the warrior in the weapons he uses, but rather the strength of his thews and the rage in his heart. I have no shortage of rage, and my wrath knows no bounds. Even still, the axe that ye gifted me has always been dear to mine heart and has served me well."

"So, do ye have a plan for this mission?" The dwarf smiled a grim smile.

"At the moment, my mind is a blank," answered Tulwryn. "More I will know after you forge the sword. Perhaps the old witch will speak further to us. I am sure she has more lore to tell ere we depart. Still, the three I chose should fare well."

"Aye," said Dillwyn, "Omar Giantslayer is a stout fighter and a cunning warrior, and I also would have chosen him, as well as Urgan. He may be young of age, but he has fire in his heart. He will prove us a great asset, I am certain."

The dwarf finished his meal, took another draft of wine from the skin, and said, "Well then, my friend, I shall go now to my own tent and sleep on this. In the morn, I shall go straight to the Volva and begin the forging. Well part."

"Well part, old friend," answered Tulwryn, as he watched the dwarf leave. For many hours, he sat there by the fire, his mind reeling with thoughts of combat, and the haunting visions of his dark past. Soon, very soon, he thought, his axe would taste blood and his torment would be appeased, if only for a while. Finally, his heavy eyelids shut and he fell into a deep sleep, still seated by the fire.

* * *

The next morning, Dillwyn was greeted by a bright red sun and thoughts of the upcoming battle ran through his mind. He stirred from under his thick woolen blankets and grumbled at the frigid conditions of the frozen north. The air in his tent was bone chilling and he glanced at the fire pit near his pallet; it had burned itself out sometime during the night and the pile of coals were black and cold. Even though he had spent the past three snows with Tulwryn amongst the northern tribe he had not adjusted to the harsh climate; he was a western dwarf through and through, and he missed the hot sun of Carthus on his brow and the warm breezes of the Golrin Prairie upon his face. His mind then recalled the Volva and he lay on his pallet for some time remembering his meeting with Tulwryn the previous night.

Dillwyn finally roused himself from under his blankets and rolled out of his bedding; he sat up and reached for his knapsack, retrieving a small package of dried meats and a lump of stale cheese. He then took his bone knife and cut a small chunk of mold from the cheese, discarding the tainted piece into the dead ashes of the fire pit.

As he sat there in the quiet of the morning eating his sparse meal, he noticed the silence of the camp and realized that he was among the first to rise. The night had been cold and his sleep, unusually deep, considering the circumstances. All this talk of prophecy and battle and doom would have normally kept him awake for hours with his mind reeling for the thrill of combat. Perhaps it was his age, he thought. He knew he wasn't the warrior he used to be, but even so, he was more than a match for a man half his age. He chuckled silently to himself.

"Half of a wine skin and I sleep like a babe," he mused to himself ruefully. "I must be getting too old for this sort of thing, I guess." Shrugging his thick shoulders, he disregarded the notion of weakness and sloth and banished the thoughts from his mind.

Normally, the dwarf would rise and dress in his battle gear, but today would be different he realized. This day he was to spend toiling in the forge under the watchful eye of the tribe's sorceress. He rued the idea that she would infuse his steel with her wizardry, but in the clan of Heidmar Grimthor's word was law and he knew the sword would be forged, either by him or another smith. Since it was Tulwryn, his friend, that would be destined to carry the enchanted weapon he deemed it best if it were he that created it, since he was the most able smith amongst the tribe. Therefore, he rose and donned his boots, leather breeches and a short-sleeved woolen shirt. Over this, he tied a thick canvas apron that covered the whole of his wide chest and hung down past his knees. Lastly, he strapped on a heavy tool belt of darkly tanned leather, took one last bite of cheese and left his tent, heading off in the direction of the clan's forge.

Dillwyn squinted his eyes as he emerged from his dark tent. Even though the day was young, the sun was surprisingly bright. His heavy boots crunched through the snow and frozen ground as he made his way through the meandering paths that wound past the various tents of the clan. The fragrance of burning oak and ash was lingering on the air as the tribe's people began to kindle their small cooking fires to break their night's fast in preparation for a new day. Even though the clan of Heidmar was blood kin and a tightly knit unit, they were also highly individual. Each member of the clan was independent of the others and often ate alone, or in the company of wives and immediate children.

As the dwarf walked past the tents, he took notice of the looks that were cast at him. He was a foreigner in this land even though he had lived with these people for the past three snows, but still, that was not it. The glances he received this morning, he realized, was of apprehension and fear. These northern barbarians feared magic of any kind, and they knew this morning he was to be employed in the forging of a magical weapon that would ultimately shape their lives, yet in which way that shaping would take place they knew naught. Dillwyn often wondered why these people, as fearful as they were of magic and the supernatural, would keep a witch so close in their midst. He questioned the sanity of their decision, and then pondered whether the Volva had cast a spell of domination over the entire clan years ago to insure her place in the tribe. The tales of his people were full of evil sorceries and he knew that most, if not all magic workers, had some form of self serving motives behind their seemingly pious actions. The possibility of a spell of domination was not out of the question, it was a grim reality. Ultimately, he did not trust the witch.

When the dwarf arrived at the forge, he entered the small log and stone structure and looked about, then yelled for the assistant.

"Boy," Dillwyn roared in a severe and agitated tone, "where art thou?" From a room behind the furnace a small male child appeared, already covered with soot and grime. He was a fair lad, with pale skin and light yellow hair, wearing the attire of an apprentice. Standing barely to the dwarf's chest in height the boy was small for a northerner and it was apparently for this reason why he was chosen to work as a smith's assistant rather than be trained as a warrior. The child was at least ten snows grown and Dillwyn thought it a sad destiny for this lad to be confined to the smithy when others of his age were being instructed in the manipulation of weapons and the honing of battle skills. Still, the skills of a blacksmith were honorable and had served him well throughout his long life, so he deemed not all was lost. Today, we shall forge a sword, he thought, there would be time enough to learn combat later.

"Yes, Dillwyn," spoke the child. "I rose early and have already stoked the furnace. The bellows are working and I have placed three billets of iron on the anvil; your tools I have also put in their required place."

The dwarf's heavy brow furrowed deep. "How didst thou know to rise early and enter the smithy," he asked.

"I stowed away near the council last eve and overheard the Volva's instruction to forge a new sword for Tulwryn," said the boy in a shaky voice. "Didst I do wrong, Master Dillwyn?"

For a tense moment the boy stood still as a stone statue, sweat beading on his pale brow, as Dillwyn looked hard at him. Slowly a smile stretched across the grim face of the aged dwarf and he laughed.

"Nay, Ian," said Dillwyn, "Ye did well, mine boy. Ye did well. From this moment on, you shall be known as Ian the Eager, for ye are more eager to forge than most are to slay. Someday I shall show ye how to use the weapons we shape, but until that day comes, let us forge mighty weapons by which our clan shall be strengthened." The child smiled and sighed heavily.

"I am off to find the witch," Dillwyn said, "remain hither and mind the forge. I shall return shortly." The dwarf turned and left the smithy; Ian sat on a log stool near the anvil and patiently waited for his return.

Thus ends the Third Chapter of Book One

FOUR

A Sword is Forged

It was still dark in Vogelmir's tent, and he lay fast asleep, when the witch appeared to him, almost as if in a dream.

"Wake, warrior," she whispered in his ear. "Fear naught, for 'tis I, the Volva."

Vogelmir stirred and terror gripped his heart. He knew not how the old woman had slipped past his two bodyguards, posted at the entrance of his tent, nor the reason why she was there, yet he felt some evil at work and was unsettled in his thoughts. Slowly and cautiously he sat up and wrapped his woolen blanket about himself. "What brings ye hither, witch," he asked.

"Ye guards sleep more sound than you, Vogelmir. Do ye wish to be slain in the night? Only babes and fools sleep so deeply. It dose not make for a grim warrior," she said in a mocking caw of a laugh. He was about to ask again his unanswered question but was silenced by the wave of the Volva's gnarled hand, which had materialized from under her dark cloak and then disappeared in a blink of an eye.

"There is evil afoot this day," she whispered, "and I fear that that foreigner, Tulwryn, will bring doom to us all ere we intercept it."

"Yes, yes, you have spoken such last eve at council," replied Vogelmir, apparently growing tired of the old one's riddles and twisted words.

"Nay," she said. "I have kept some things from your people, for I believe that many here cannot comprehend the truth." She paused for a moment then stooped closer to the warrior; the rancid breath escaping from her black toothless maw was unbearable, even for a seasoned slayer like Vogelmir, yet he summoned the strength to listen. He turned away from her as she spoke. "Last eve I made a comment that the great shadow amassing to the north is none other than the sleeping frost giants, awaking from their long slumber. This is not entirely true. Whilst the giants do stir, I feel that the true shadow is Tulwryn himself."

Vogelmir sat up, eager to hear this new piece of information, and many lucid thoughts ran through his mind. "Speak on, old woman," he said.

"This morn I shall go with the dwarf to his smithy and shall work an enchantment whilst the dwarf toils over the anvil. As the weapon is wrought, certain future events will be made known unto me and I shall discover for certain if these visions I have been granted are true."

"But why have ye chosen to confide in me," Vogelmir asked.

"I have known for some time that ye have no love for Tulwryn. If my visions hold true, then 'tis you I shall employ to do my bidding. When Tulwryn and his companions rides thither to the north, ye will accompany them and at the required time, will slay the lot of them and return hither."

Vogelmir leaned on one stout elbow and drew his blanket tighter around him. The air in the tent had become unbearably cold, yet the sweat of fear formed on his body like summer dew.

"Tulwryn has already chosen his companions, old woman," he said. "How can I accompany them?"

"By means of my sorcery, I will weave an enchantment about you. Ye will take on the shape of a great war wolf and you will pull the party on a mighty war sleigh. When you are beyond the reaches of the frozen lake, many leagues to the north, you will strike!"

Even though Vogelmir was a seasoned veteran of war and had seen many bloody battles, the very idea of being physically transformed into a great war wolf by means of magic instilled a terror in him that he had never experienced.

"Are ye certain of this, witch," he asked, trying to conceal the fear in his trembling voice.

"I will know for certain only after the forging of the weapon. The color of the blade will determine the outcome. If the blade be black or brown or of a bluish tint, then Tulwryn truly is the evil of which my prophecy speaks, and we must make hast to end his reign of terror." She paused, looked around, and then removed a small cloth pouch from the folds of her cloak. Opening the pouch, she sprinkled a few grains of powder about the interior of the tent.

"This powder will protect ye, Vogelmir. Fear naught the evil that enshrouds this camp. But at the required time, strike first, strike fast, and strike hard, without mercy!"

Vogelmir felt a strange sensation wash over his being and his fear left him. He took a deep breath and stood up, towering over the old witch.

"Know it shall be done, master," he said. She laughed a raven's laugh and disappeared into the darkness of the night. Vogelmir slept like an infant and remembered nothing more.

* * *

When Dillwyn finally caught up to the Volva it was nearing the noon of the day. He had been to her tent but had found nothing, and so then decided to make a survey of the camp to locate her whereabouts. After failing this, he stopped into his own tent, had a small lunch, and then returned to the smithy. Meanwhile, Vogelmir slept throughout the day, his two bodyguards standing sentinel near the entrance of his tent, oblivious to all around them, their glazed unseeing eyes staring off into a dark and bleak eternity.

Upon arriving back at the forge, Ian ran out to greet the dwarf with dire news. "Dillwyn," he cried, quite hysterical, "she is here!"

Looking quite surprised, the dwarf grabbed the boy by both arms and tried to calm him down. "Who's here," Dillwyn asked.

"The Volva, Dillwyn. She's here and she has been swearing oaths and such all morning. She arrived shortly after you left. She is quite upset that we have not begun the work on the sword ere now."

Dillwyn released the boy and frowned at the news. "Ye never mind that old woman, Ian. Leave her to me. Come; let us see what doom has befallen us this day," he said, as he walked past the boy and entered the smithy.

Cautiously, Dillwyn eyed the witch as he entered the room. She was near the anvil, huddled down beneath the many folds of her dark cloak. Her hands were waving madly in the air over the three billets of iron, while chanting in an unknown tongue. Without looking at the smith or his apprentice, nor breaking her intense concentration, the Volva said in a low and raspy tone, "Where have you been smith? We have work to do!"

"I have been searching ye out, old woman."

"Now ye has found me! Man the anvil and let us begin this work. Make haste, time is running out!"

Dillwyn, quite taken aback by this intrusion in his smithy, shot a glance at the boy and instantly his apprentice disappeared into the bellows room as he himself approached the anvil. The Volva backed away into a far corner of the room as the dwarf took up his hammer and began to smite the iron billets. For many hours, Dillwyn toiled over iron and anvil as the old woman sat and chanted archaic incantations. His mind reeled with visions of dark death and bloodshed and his stomach became nauseated as the scent of charred human flesh wafted past his nostrils and deep into his lungs. His tongue and mouth became parched with the coppery taste of blackened blood, yet he continued through this onslaught; hammer pounding, iron glowing, fire roaring. All the while, Vogelmir stirred naught in his tent, for he was dead to the world.

Slowly the magical process of turning iron into steel was all but complete. This was the extent of Dillwyn's belief in magic, although he knew it to be the blacksmith's art and not magic at all, yet it seemed mystical at times. He was proud of his ability in shaping tools and weapons of great strength, and this day was no different, save for the old woman chanting in the background of his mind.

Suddenly, the dwarf regained his complete consciousness and a fear washed over him as the likes that he had never known. Somehow, the forging of the sword was complete, but how could this be? Normally it would take many days at the anvil to shape the weapon, next would be the tempering, and then the polishing and sharpening of the piece. All would take the better part of one full turning of the moon, yet this day the work was completed in all but a few hours. Yet, this was not what created the fear in Dillwyn's heart; something was amiss and he knew it to be sorcery, a dark and betraying sorcery. As he looked down at the sword, it was not the hue of freshly wrought steel but rather the tint of wet blood. He grabbed a polishing rag and scrubbed the blade dry but the hue remained. Turning to the old woman, he roared.

"What sorcery is this, witch? What have ye done to mine blade?"

"It is another prophecy revealed, smith," she said trembling, her face white with fear. "'Tis the sign of death. From this day onward, Tulwryn shall be known as Tulwryn Bloodsword for he carries a blade of grim death. More I cannot tell ye at this time." As she spoke her final words, she vanished in a blinding flash of white flame, which all but blinded Dillwyn for a moment.

Ian emerged from the bellows room rubbing his eyes. "I am sorry, Master Dillwyn, but I must have fallen asleep. Please beat me naught." He hid his eyes and whimpered.

"I shall no more beat you that slay my own self, young Ian. This day we have both been entangled by a dark sorcery. I am as much to blame as you. Be off to your own tent and rest. Tell no one of these strange happenings."

The boy ran from the smithy and as Dillwyn watched him leave as thoughts of treachery ran through his mind. He felt that the witch was plotting evil, but to what extent, he could not be sure. Taking the sword, he left the forge and walked toward Tulwryn's tent.

* * *

The following morning the entire clan of Heidmar, save that of Vogelmir, assembled to bid the four warriors farewell and wish their mission success. The day had begun pleasant enough, with a bright sun and crisp fragrant air. Each of the warriors had feasted to their heart's content, and were eager to be off, for adventure was as intoxicating as fine wine and the thrill of combat ran wild through their veins.

Tulwryn, wearing the Bloodsword forged by his friend, Dillwyn the dwarf, leaned close to Urgan and asked the whereabouts of Vogelmir. The youth shrugged his massive shoulders.

"No one has seen him since the eve ere yester eve," he whispered. This puzzled Tulwryn. He realized that Vogelmir despised him, yet he felt that something was wrong. For surely he would not miss the opportunity for one last try at gaining admittance to the group, unless treachery was afoot. He knew Vogelmir to be a brave and cunning warrior, but he possessed no honor that Tulwryn knew of, and he trusted him naught.

At the appearance of the witch, Tulwryn was brought back to the conversations of the clan. There was much talk of valor, and of combat, of bloody battles and honor. Much cheering and merry making permeated the group until finally Grimthor the Strong, Chieftain of Heidmar, raised aloft his mighty war hammer and spoke. "Clan of Heidmar, mine people, strong and proud in the ways of the north, hear me!" His voice was loud and unwavering, and the sun reflected brightly off of his heavy helm, his eyes blazed with a fierceness most had never seen. "This morning ye shall stand to witness a great turning of events, for Tulwryn, our adopted and beloved son shall ride forth with those of his choosing to slay an unknown doom that threatens us all. May the gods go with him and be pleased with his carnage. May the clan of Heidmar live long enough to slay its foes ere our last warrior lay down his own life in battle!"

The entire group then broke out in a frenzied cheer, but was instantly silenced as the Volva raised a twisted hand in the air and began muttering strange words and incantations. Meanwhile, Vogelmir tossed in his tent, apparently tormented by dark dreams and hideous visions. Still, he remained unconscious to the world.

"As I promised at council," she said, in between her mumbling and chanting, "I shall now weave a magic more powerful than you have ever seen ere now. It will protect ye on your journey."

With strange gestures of her gnarled hands, waving violently in the cold northern air, her voice growing louder and louder with each spoken word, a thing of immense size began to take shape in front of the bewildered crowd. Particles of golden light assembled from beyond the veil of sight and, coming together magically, formed a large war sleigh. The crowd gasped as the sleigh materialized; large and heavy it was, fully wrought through and through in fine steel armor, with running blades as keen as the stoutest sword. Surrounding the upper echelons of the sleigh were twelve great war shields, four on each side with two fore and two aft; the entire vehicle was the hue of fresh snow.

Tulwryn glanced at the three other members of his group with apprehension. He did not like sorcery and something in his guts told him things were not as they seemed. Dillwyn nodded back, signaling he understood and agreed with his friend's feelings. They would talk soon enough, but now was the time to remain silent and keep their thoughts hidden.

Slowly, in front of the sleigh, a great ball of red pulsating light appeared. The light grew brighter and brighter until all present had to shield their eyes from the intensity. Screaming at a frenzied pitch, words and phrases none had ever heard ere now, the Volva summoned her last bit of remaining strength to complete the enchantment.

In his tent, Vogelmir began to fade from existence, his body first growing lighter and lighter until his flesh merged with that of the air around him. The fabric of time and space was torn asunder and then he was no more.

When finally the light subsided, standing amidst the clan of Heidmar was a beast of unsurpassed size and ferocity. It was taller at the shoulder than the largest man, and its heavy body was covered with thick corded muscles over which was laid a bristly layer of grey fur. The creature's claws and fangs were the length of daggers and looked as if wrought in iron rather than the matter of living flesh.

"Behold," screamed the witch, "I give ye, the war wolf!" All gasped as the beast roared and the entire clan broke out in a mixture of cheers and confused screams of horror. Grimthor tried to regain control of the assembly, but in vain. The berserker rage was alive amongst the clan and only bloodshed, or magic, could relieve them of their appetite.

"Fear naught," she whispered to the four warriors. "This beast already knows the route, and it will harm you naught. In combat, it will be a great asset, and will return ye hither upon the slaying of the doom that awaits."

"You speak as if we are already victorious, old witch," Tulwryn grumbled. "Ye have been amongst the people for more than sixty winters, yet ye know naught the ways of war! Perhaps this beast will devour us ere we reach our destiny."

There was a murmur that passed through the clan as Tulwryn spat words of discontent and rage at the old woman. Never before had anyone questioned the Volva with such disrespect, yet they all knew this was Tulwryn the Warrior, strong and bold, and he cared naught for formalities but for combat. All bit their tongues as the dialog continued.

After some time, the Volva then commanded Tulwryn to unsheathe his sword and hold the blade aloft for all to see. As he did this, she spoke thus to the kindred in a loud and commanding voice:

"Behold, people of the clan of Heidmar," she said. "Hither stands naught Tulwryn the Warrior, but from this day forward he shall be known as Tulwryn Bloodsword, for he carries with him yonder the sword that drinks blood and whose thirst canst naught be appeased! He shall be your savior or bring ye doom; only time will reveal all."

The assembly began cheering great oaths of victory and much

commotion spread over the entire clan. The Volva then turned to Tulwryn and his men and disclosed the route the war wolf would take. For safety, she declared to the warriors in confidence, that no one save the wolf, herself, and them, would know the path toward their northern doom.

"The planned route," she whispered amidst the confusion, "is south by twenty leagues then west by thirty leagues, around the great un-named mountains. The war wolf will then pull the sleigh northwest by fifteen leagues unto the banks of the frozen river. You will ford the river and continue northward by twenty-five leagues to the frozen lake itself, then traveling westward, you shall circumnavigate the lake and enter the realm of the frost giants beyond the northern reaches where no man has yet been."

Unbeknownst to the four warriors or the witch, Halgi Mansbane, Grimthor's daughter, listened to the words of the old woman as she spoke, and she heard aught even though the words were meant naught for her ears.

Finally, the Volva turned her attention from the war party to the clan itself. A gnarled hand appeared from beneath the many folds of her dark billowing cloak and all was silenced. In somber consternation all there present watched as the four brave warriors climbed aboard the great war sleigh. The Volva uttered a single word and the large grey beast began running forward, pulling the sleigh behind its massive loins. The strength and speed of the beast was impressive, and in a matter of mere moments, as if wearing the wind itself, the sleigh disappeared from the sight of the clan. A dark, cold fist gripped the heart of Halgi Mansbane and she sighed a heavy sigh; in silent desperation, she wondered why she had revealed naught her feelings to Tulwryn ere he departed. Sadly, she walked back to the privacy of her tent and wept.

Thus ends the Fourth Chapter of Book One

FIVE

The War Wolf

Tulwryn stood holding the reigns as the frozen tundra flew past him in a blur. The massive body of the great war wolf heaved as it strained under the heavy burden of the sleigh yet still they lost no speed. A great spray of white foam spewed forth from the creature's mouth and nostrils, occasionally groaning and bearing its yellow teeth.

"This is not the way warriors should travel," commented Omar Giantslayer, one large hand gripping tight on the wall of the sleigh, his other on the hilt of his sword.

"Aye," answered Urgan. "I would agree with you, Omar; this wizardry reeks of evil. Yet what do I know, being but a mere lad amidst great men." The large youth laughed a hearty laugh hoping to conceal his fear; the other men concealed theirs likewise.

Dillwyn, gathering strength and banishing his own fear, leaned over to steal a look past the edge of the sleigh. He saw the speed at which the vehicle was traveling and then his eyes traveled down to the long running blades. His face, white with terror, snapped back and he stood as if frozen in time, blind and dumb. Tulwryn saw the look in the dwarf's eyes.

"What did you see," he asked. It was some moments ere the dwarf answered, and when he finally did, none there present could believe even though they witnessed it with their own eyes.

"Look men," he said, "we touch naught the land, but float over it!" And indeed, the sleigh, as large as it was, sped past the frozen tundra as a wind born seed flies across a spring valley.

"This is treacherous evil," cried Urgan, and Omar agreed, swearing oaths and cursing the gods.

"Be silent, warriors," Tulwryn commanded. "For certain there are things in this world that are strange and unknowable. Whether they are good or evil is naught for mortal men to decide. Regain your strength and steel yourselves! We have a duty, now let us get on with it."

It took some time for the men to grow accustomed to their present manner of transportation, but all tried diligently as Tulwryn commanded, and by the noon of the second day they were comfortable and relaxed.

The mighty wolf had showed no sign of tiring, and he slowed naught his pace. Tulwryn had grown concerned about the beast's endurance. He discussed the matter with his men and the group decided it best to bring the sleigh to a halt just beyond the frozen river and make a camp for the remainder of the day and on through the night. They would allow the beast to rest throughout the night and regain the trek north in the morning. Interesting, Tulwryn thought, was the fact that the old woman had not informed him in caring for the creature, nor had she revealed why she commanded the dwarf to forge the Bloodsword or bade him to carry it; it was all a dark mystery and he enjoyed it naught.

"Behold, men," Tulwryn cried, "yonder stretches the frozen river. I shall reign this beast on the far side and we can rest until the morrow." The men cheered. With a great leap the war wolf took to the skies, sleigh following smoothly behind. Far below, the warriors could see the frozen river, a thin thread of silver winding its way through deep ravines and tall mountains. In moments, they were over the river and descending, and once again, the great beast heaved under its burden and sped forward, neither slowing its pace nor showing any sign of fatigue.

Pulling hard on the reigns, Tulwryn brought the war wolf to a halt. As the four warriors climbed down from the sleigh, he commanded Urgan and Omar to tend the area and build a camp whilst Dillwyn and himself made ready to tend to the great beast. The dwarf grumbled at the thought of ending his days in the belly of a monster, but the other two were quite relieved and began to scour the area for dry firewood.

* * *

It was early in the morning when Omar was roused from his slumber by the hot breath of the war wolf on his face. The sky was black for the sun had not yet risen, but a faint blue haze could be seen on the far eastern horizon. It was the last thing that the great warrior would ever see for the large beast pounced upon him and in one mighty bite tore him in twain just above the waist.

Tulwryn and the others heard a bloodcurdling scream and came instantly to arms. Shaking dreams from their hair, and with sleep still in their eyes, they came to face their reality; standing before them was the mighty war wolf, its grey fur speckled with the fresh blood of their fallen comrade, dripping entrails hung from the creature's gaping maw and the entire campsite reeked with the stench of offal and death.

"We have been betrayed," cried Dillwyn, as he stood there shaking with rage. The wolf circled the three, careful to keep the campfire between itself and his prey.

"So, beast, what treachery is this," screamed Tulwryn. "It seems that ye have missed your mark, for certain, the way to win a battle and destroy an army is to slay the leader, not a mere solider. Come, feel the bite of the Bloodsword!"

The long blade hissed as is leapt from its scabbard. Urgan raised his spear and circled deosil as the other two paced widdershins, hoping to back the beast up and corner it betwixt them and the sleigh ere it strike again.

From deep inside the wolf came a hideous laugh. "I see no army here, foreigner," taunted the beast, "but mere fodder for mine feeding."

"What kind of evil is this, that gives speech to a beast," asked Urgan.

"Deceitful and . . . ," Tulwryn's answer was cut short as the wolf lunged at him, fangs bared. Tulwryn squatted and rolled as the large body passed over him. As he came to his feet, he was knocked back to the ground by one mighty blow form the creature's massive paw; its claws ripping across his thick fur tunic and opening a seething wound across his deep chest.

As the beast closed in on Tulwryn for the kill, Urgan pounced from behind and drove his spear deep into the wolf's right flank. The dwarf leapt up from the darkness to smite the beast's great head with a mighty blow from his right fist, heavily concealed within the sturdy confines of its bronze gauntlet. The beast screamed as Urgan's spear ripped through its vitals and blood poured forth from the wounds inflicted by Dillwyn's many blows.

Turning with blazing speed into his aggressors, the creature's flank slammed into Urgan, knocking him to the ground and wrenching the spear from his grip, and then it came around to face the dwarf nose to nose. Urgan fell to his knees, shook the stars from his head, and then unsheathed his broadsword for another attack. The beast rose on its thick loins, its maw still dripping with the blooded remains of Omar Giantslayer, and howled with pain and rage. But seconds ere the wolf was to strike its deathblow at Dillwyn the mighty beast shuddered and dropped unconscious at the dwarf's feet. Lodged betwixt its thick shoulder blades was the Bloodsword.

The three warriors stood in amazement as the dead creature shrank in size and was transformed into the form of an armored man. Over the dead man's armor was a thick fur tunic, and on that tunic was the seal of the clan of Heidmar. Dillwyn and Urgan glanced in wonder at the body that lay before them. Tulwryn walked to the corpse and lifted the visor of the dead man's helm; the face that stared back at him was that of Vogelmir the Bold.

"For certain that vile bitch never revealed this evil in her prophecy," cried Dillwyn, spitting foul curses into the morning sky.

"There is more here than has been revealed, friends," Tulwryn said. "Perhaps we will discover the answer to this dark riddle on the far side of the frozen lake."

"Are we to continue northward then," asked Urgan.

Twisting his blade from Vogelmir's body, Tulwryn wiped the blade clean using the dead man's tunic. He looked hard at the dry blade, still appearing wet, then answered Urgan.

"Aye, Urgan, northward we go."

"And what about Vogelmir? Shall we not bury him?"

Tulwryn looked hatefully at the corpse.

"Vogelmir is a traitor to the clan of Heidmar, Urgan. Let his rancid flesh feed the ravens; he shall get no burial from me!"

"But Tulwryn," spoke the dwarf, "our destination lies many leagues hither, and we have no steeds."

Sheathing the Bloodsword Tulwryn laughed. "Then we travel afoot, my friends." The two warriors watched as Tulwryn removed a few war shields from the sleigh. He then slung a large knapsack over his shoulder, then strapped one shield to his back and bid the others to do the same. He then headed away from the camp on foot, paying no heed to the severe gash in his chest.

* * *

Nine days after the slaying of Omar Giantslayer and Vogelmir the Bold, the three made camp in a small spruce grove a few leagues south of the frozen lake. Tulwryn's deep chest wound was healing nicely and he dispatched Urgan as sentry whilst he searched for firewood and the dwarf prepared a sparse dinner.

The sun was setting low on the horizon and the silvery steel sickle of the crescent moon was beginning to show her face when Urgan the Brave noticed a rider far off in the distance. Raising his horn to his lips, Urgan sounded the alarm. Moments later Tulwryn and the dwarf were at his side, peering at the distant rider.

"What thinks ye, Tulwryn," asked Urgan. Dillwyn strained hard and then cursed his dwarven eyesight. "Had I been born an elf or a woodwight, I could tell you who follows yonder. But mine eyes are useless at this distance."

"Let us then lie here amongst the trees until he is closer,"

Tulwryn said. "Once we know who he is we can then either let him pass or slay him in ambush. His intentions will seal his doom." The three nodded then melted back into the spruce grove.

The next morning Tulwryn woke the dwarf and Urgan with a gentle kick to the ribs. All three had chosen vantage spots from where they could watch the incoming rider, yet Tulwryn was the only one who had not slept.

"Has the rider passed us in the night," Dillwyn whispered as he crept to where Tulwryn sat.

"Nay," answered Tulwryn, pointing southward with the tip of his short dagger. "He camps yonder."

The dawn was paling and through the chilling mist and tendrils of fog Urgan and the dwarf could see the makings of a tiny camp. The horse was in plain view but the rider was nowhere to be seen.

"He must be on our trail. Why else would he stop and camp downwind of us if he knew naught of us camped here," said Urgan.

"Tis possible," answered Dillwyn, "still, until we know who he is, we should wait him out."

Tulwryn stood, unsheathed the Bloodsword, and began walking from the grove into the open.

"I grow tired of this cat and mouse game. Let the rogue come to us if he hunts us," he said, looking back at his two companions still seated beneath the spruce boughs. He walked a stone's throw into the open and then began to shout grim oaths in the direction of the encamped rider.

Urgan and Dillwyn looked at each other and laughed. They both knew Tulwryn to be rash, as often his rage alone kept him alive when lesser men would have laid their lives down and perished.

"Well boy," grunted the dwarf, "seems that Tulwryn is bent on combat this morn. Bloodshed before we break our fast is one way to put hair on your chest. Come and let us accompany Tulwryn. We should naught allow him all the fun."

"There are worse ways a man can throw his life away," Urgan

said laughing, as he and the dwarf rose and walked to were Tulwryn stood.

By the time they reached Tulwryn, they could see that the warrior had mounted his steed, broken camp, and resumed the path northward on their trail. They were clearly exposed yet the rider gave no heed as he rode toward them. Suddenly, Urgan smiled.

"Tis Grimthor the Strong that rides yonder," he said. And surely, the rider was clothed in the armor and tunic of the chieftain of the clan of Heidmar.

Dillwyn's brow furrowed deep and he clenched his big fists in a tight ball.

"Grimthor would naught have abandoned the clan lest some evil befell the camp," he said.

"Aye," spoke Tulwryn. "I feel something is amiss."

Moments later, Grimthor cantered up to the three warriors. Dillwyn and Urgan bowed their eyes, yet Tulwryn stood tall and proud.

"What brings ye hither, woman." He said. Dillwyn and the boy glanced in amazement at Tulwryn's address and then looked at Grimthor, still mounted atop his horse. Raising the visor of his war helm, the three looked naught into the face of Grimthor the Strong, but Halgi Mansbane, his daughter.

"Heilsa brave warriors," she said, as she dismounted.

"Why have you donned your father's armor, Halgi? And why do you track us," asked Tulwryn. The other two stood in confused amazement as Tulwryn spoke to the girl.

"The eve after ye departed, my father, Grimthor the Strong, chieftain of the clan of Heidmar, was found slain in his tent; his head cleaved in twain whilst he slept. The entire clan is now in an uproar and crying for blood vengeance as a Rodmarian battle-axe was found near my father's body. I disguised myself thusly to prevent ambush since I traveled through the mountains rather than around them. No clan would dare to attack Grimthor the Strong, riding alone, and bring down the wrath of Heidmar!"

She paused and removed her father's helm; long golden locks

tumbled down over her armored shoulders. Tulwryn noticed her raw rugged beauty, but disregarded the feelings that were stirring in his loins. Never, he vowed, would he enter again into the company of women; they were simply not to be trusted. Still, there was something different about Halgi Mansbane. She was not the typical female, as are bred in the southern reaches of Phantasodyssea. Halgi Mansbane was large for a woman of her years, standing fully as tall as her slain father, and she had proven herself in more than two score of battles. Whilst most women were content in bedding men and bearing children, Halgi was concerned only with the slaying of her clan's foes.

"Furthermore," she said, "the Volva and Vogelmir are missing. I feel something is afoul and this is why I follow you in pursuit."

Tulwryn agreed that he too felt evil at work and told her of the events that had befallen them over the past few days. The three warriors then accepted her into their party and they sat down to make plans for a return to the Heidmar camp rather than to continue north on their mission. To save time, Tulwryn decided that they should hike across the un-named mountains rather than trek around them.

"We will sleep hither this eve," he said, "for on the morrow, we shall begin a long and hazardous trek and will need all the rest we can steal. Once we enter the mountains, we will be at the mercy of the snow beasts as well as the hill clans of Gerdmor and we will know no rest until we emerge on the far side of the range." He looked at Halgi Mansbane and smiled.

"The armor of Grimthor the Strong protected ye once as you passed alone through the mountains. On the morrow we shall see if it will do so again."

Thus ends the Fifth Chapter of Book One

SIX

Blood Runes

Early in the afternoon, a heavy snow began to fall, and although the large northern sun was high in the heavens and bright, a dread cold scoured the land. Tulwryn and Urgan quickly constructed a makeshift windbreak and shelter of pine boughs while Halgi built up a warm fire; Dillwyn diligently went through their meager supplies locating edibles for a possible meal. He found a few loaves of hard bread, some packages of salted and dried meats, and three wine skins. Not much fare to feed four starving warriors, he thought, but it would have to do.

By the time he had gathered the food, Halgi's fire was a nice blaze and so the dwarf erected a small tripod of lean saplings, freshly cut by Tulwryn, over the fire pit whereas to hang the small cast iron pot that was amongst their sparse belongings. Dillwyn then added liberal amounts of snow to the pot, time and again, allowing it to melt until the pot was filled almost to the brim with water. Once the water began to boil, he added the meats. Two wine skins he buried in the snow, the other he passed around to his companions that were already seated, warming themselves by the fire.

For the next few hours, the four warriors relaxed at their small camp, each silently contemplating what the future held. The old dwarf plopped himself down on a frozen log near the fire and retrieved the tobacco pipe from his ditty whilst Urgan sat quietly to his left sharpening his spear and sword, a fell look etched across his young brow. Seated across the fire from Dillwyn was Tulwryn. He was troubled over the recent turn of events. The slaying of Grimthor the Strong, Heidmar's chieftain, weighed heavy on his mind and his unfortunate duty to look after Halgi Mansbane, Grimthor's daughter, was another burden he cared naught to carry. Surely she was capable of looking out for herself, for she was a Heidmar warrior through and through, but still, Tulwryn was in command of the group and its members were his sole responsibility.

Halgi seated herself to the left of Tulwryn and wrapped her father's woolen war cloak around her armored shoulders. She turned her love for Tulwryn over and over in her mind and pondered if it were best to keep silent or reveal her feelings to him. Ere now, the decision was an easy one, for she was first and foremost a Heidmarian warrior and her father's only heir; her primary duty was to her clan and she had not the luxury to take a mate. But with Grimthor slain, and her tribe in an uproar for blood and vengeance, her situation was complicated. Even though her mother, Halgr Manslayer, had assumed her father's position as chieftain, she could not hope to lead the clan to victory in war against the Rodmarians. What Heidmar needed, she realized, was not only a fell warrior but a strong and powerful leader. While Halgr was indeed a stout fighter, she lacked the leadership skills needed to safeguard the clan and bring about their ultimate victory. In Tulwryn, Halgi witnessed the leadership abilities the likes of which Heidmar had never seen. Still, he was a foreigner and not from the House of Rexor. She had no way of knowing how he would be received by the clan had she revealed her feelings for him openly and taken him as a mate. Since Grimthor had no sons, it was a grim possibility that violent infighting would erupt, tearing the clan of Heidmar asunder, until a suitable leader would emerge from the blooded snow. Such had not happened for over three hundred turnings of the wheel of the year, when Rexor the Merciless, her great grandsire fifteen generations removed, slayed Nexus Irontongue and assumed the role of Heidmar's chieftain. Now, with Grimthor dead, the long line of warrior kings begat by Rexor the Merciless might come to a close, and with it, possibly the end of the entire tribe. She realized that for the good of the clan she must reveal to Tulwryn her feelings, but that time was not now and so burying her emotions deep she bit her tongue and remained silent.

The hours passed and the sun dipped low on the horizon as the large flakes of snow continued to fall. With the sky as their canvas, the gods began the task of streaking the heavens with various hues of crimson and orange and yellow. The sent of cedar intermixed with the fragrance of the food simmering in Dillwyn's iron pot caused the warriors to stir, eager to fill their bellies ere turning in to their blankets for the night.

"Sup is ready," spoke the dwarf, motioning all to grab a small wooden bowl and an iron spoon and help themselves. Dillwyn spooned out a healthy serving of his make shift stew into his own bowl, grabbed a chunk of bread, and returned to his log stool.

Urgan passed the wineskin to Tulwryn as Halgi filled her bowl with stew. Within moments, all four were seated around the fire, steaming bowls nestled affectionately in their laps.

"So," asked Dillwyn, "what is the plan?"

All remained quite and Tulwryn shrugged his thick shoulders.

"All day I have been pondering our return to Heidmar," he said, "yet, I cannot think of a way to ford the frozen river. For certain, the shortest route to Heidmar is through the un-named mountains, but ere we enter the mountains we must cross the river, and how to do that I cannot decipher."

"Aye," said Urgan, "on the back of that fell beast, bounding over the waters was but an easy task, but afoot is a different story. A river as wide and as violent as the frozen river, I know naught. Many grim warriors have thrown their lives away trying to ford it. Never has it been done in the dead of winter, where the great sheets of ice buckle and shift constantly; their sharp edges as keen as the stoutest sword."

Halgi accepted the wineskin from Tulwryn and took a long drink. She looked hard at the grim warriors in her company then passed the drink to Dillwyn.

"Many leagues back I found an ice bridge over the river and whereby I was able to dry ford the waters," she said.

"So, ye have become our sole salvation, Halgi Mansbane," snorted the dwarf. She shot him an angry glance, but he smiled back in jest and cooled her heart.

"Aye, ye are a fiery one," he said, laughing.

"Mine father has just been slain, Dillwyn, and my clan readies itself for war. I am not in a light mood for your jokes."

"I beg your forgiveness, for I knew naught the extent of your grief. Ye hide your sorrow well, Halgi Mansbane," Dillwyn said.

"Perhaps I hide my grief well 'cause I have naught a target for mine wrath," she said angrily. "'Twas a cowardly assassin that slew mine father, and I know naught his identity. But rest assured, someday I will uncover the villain ere I throw my own life away, and when I find him, I shall cut the blood eagle in his back and extract mine vengeance tenfold!"

"Halgi," Tulwryn said, hoping to stop a fight ere it start. "Tell me what befell the tribe after we departed." She turned her attention from the dwarf to Tulwryn but took another bite of her dinner ere she spoke.

"As I have already disclosed," she said, "My father was found slain in his tent and a Rodmarian battle-axe was found near him; the clan accuses the Rodmarians of the slaying and is planning war. Mine mother, Halgr Manslayer, has assumed my father's role as chieftain, but I fear some will loath being led by a woman thus a bloody coup could erupt ere the war against Rodmar even begins."

"I may be a stranger to your tribe, Halgi," said Dillwyn, "but I am certain your mother can force down a coup ere it starts. A bold warrior she is indeed."

"For true, but still she is only a woman. And she lacks experience in leading troops in combat." Halgi paused and passed the wineskin back to Tulwryn, took a bite of bread, and then continued.

"What Heidmar needs now," spoke Grimthor's heir, "is a new chieftain, strong and powerful, to step into my father's boots ere any infighting begin. Someone like . . . like you Tulwryn." Immediately she shot her gaze to the other three and took note of their reaction to her suggestion. Tulwryn frowned but said nothing.

"Indeed, Halgi, Tulwryn would make a strong and powerful

leader," answered the dwarf, "but he is not of northern blood. I certainly would follow him to hell and back, but how many of your people would remain loyal in his service?"

"I would remain loyal," said Urgan, proudly. It was only the second time he yet spoke at the meal and his youthful voice was but a shocking interruption to the already interesting conversation.

"Enough of this talk," growled Tulwryn. "What more can ye tell us of the past events at camp, Halgi?" Whilst it was true that Tulwryn was a fell warrior and an able leader, he was also a humble man and could accept naught the idea of himself in a royal position, if chieftain over the Heidmar barbarians could actually be considered a royal seat.

Changing the subject, Tulwryn asked about the missing witch, and the possibility of her magically transforming Vogelmir into the war wolf. The group also speculated about the reason why the witch wanted them to travel north of the frozen lake into the land of the frost giants. They deemed that the Volva was scheming something, but what she was scheming they knew naught. Yet, they all felt that the prophecy she foretold at council to be a ruse, and revealed for her own evil purpose.

After the meal was consumed, the talk around the fire all but ceased. The sun had long ago disappeared behind the jagged teeth of the mountains and the crimson art of the gods had been replaced by a thick sheet of ebony draping the northern sky; for some time the four sat quietly warming themselves by the fire. In time, the flames sank into glowing coals and the warriors, wrapped in their woolen blankets and fur cloaks, nodded off into an ethereal world of dreams and bloody battles. The snow continued to fall throughout the night.

It was early when Halgi Mansbane woke and rolled out from under her blankets. She looked about camp and noticed that Tulwryn and the dwarf were still asleep in their pallets but Urgan was gone. Curious, she rose and walked about searching for the boy. The ground was blanketed with many inches of freshly fallen snow and therefore his tracks were easy to find.

Far to the east, a bright red sun was waking to the new day

and raising its noble head over the tall mountains. About an arrows shot from the parameter of the camp she found Urgan. He was squatting in the snow with his back toward her apparently working on something. Quietly Halgi crept, hoping to espy what the lad was doing; if there was treachery in the air she would perform her duty and dispatch him quickly for in the frozen north no one could be trusted.

Diligently Urgan worked, his concentration so intensely focused on the task at hand that he heard naught the crunch of snow under the girl's boots until she was upon him. With a start and a lithe movement as graceful as a mountain cat, he sprang to his feet with spear in hand and spun around facing the intruder. Halgi Mansbane was surprised at the youth's speed and agility, yet her own sword leapt from its scabbard instinctively with a hiss.

"Why do ye stalk me," grumbled Urgan, looking at the armed woman standing before him.

"I rose this morn and found ye gone from the camp. There is treachery in the air, young Urgan, and no one is to be trusted. I came hither seeking the reason why ye were missing."

"So ye think I am made to betray mine own people as well as mine dear friends," Urgan asked contemptuously. "Come, woman, and see what treachery lives in mine heart."

Lowering his spear, he stepped away from where he had been working. Lying in the snow was a long white stone about as large as a man's leg and as thick as one's torso. Next to the stone lay a makeshift stone hammer and a few stone chisels. Inscribed in the stone was a runic inscription, written in the manner of his people, the clan of Heidmar. The inscription simply said:

Omar Giantslayer, brave warrior of the clan of Heidmar, betrayed by a friend and slain by a traitor whilst he slept. Brother, ye will be avenged.

Halgi looked away from the stone and glanced back at Urgan, who had already turned away and had begun walking back toward the camp. She ran to catch up with him.

"Urgan," she called out, "wait."

The young warrior stopped and turned, waiting for the woman.

"Are you naught going to erect the stone?"

"Nay," he said. "There t'was nothing left of Omar to bury, therefore I leave the stone where it lay. 'Tis naught a memorial stone, but a blood stave." She was the daughter of Grimthor, and knew well the manners of her people. This was no enchantment of the Erulian's craft, but a simple gesture of honor from one warrior to another, and she could see the fire in Urgan's young eyes; she knew he would spend the rest of his life, if need be, to avenge his friend's murder. No further words were spoken. The two simply returned to the camp in silence.

Tulwryn and the dwarf were already up and dressed when Urgan the Brave and Halgi Mansbane entered the camp. More than a few curious glances were traded at the youngsters but naught was said.

Dillwyn had tended to the fire and was once again spooning out a portion of the hot stew into his small wooden bowl. The four once again seated themselves around the fire and ate the warm meal to break their night's fast. They then began their duties to break camp soon afterwards.

Halgi's horse, a proud Heidmarian war steed, was converted into a humble pack animal and was loaded down with their meager supplies. Halgi gave good council as to the direction of the ice bridge and the four set out afoot, trudging through the deep snow towards their destiny. Off in the distance, a raven cawed loudly as the large bird landed on a stone, half buried in the snow. Fresh blood dripped from its wet beak and colored the runes of Urgan the Brave.

Thus ends the Sixth Chapter of Book One

SEVEN

Battle of Gerdmor Gorge

It was nearing the noon of the day when the four found the ice bridge that Halgi Mansbane had used to dry ford the river just days prior. The party stood at the western gate of the enormous structure, in awe of its sheer size. And Halgi herself made notice that the bridge seemed to have grown larger than she had remembered it. The span of the structure was great, at least three leagues across, and the sheer cliffs supporting it on either side dipped steeply to the rocky banks of the river, at least a league below.

The men also looked upon the river with amazement, their mouths gaping open at the sight before them. Never had they seen such a formidable adversary ere now, nor had they ever stood on its mighty banks. Surely, this was the river they had crossed, safely nestled within the confines of their war sleigh. But the war wolf had magically went aloft, and from their vantage point high in the heavens, gliding over the great frozen valley many fathoms above the river, it seemed like merely a slender thread of wrought silver. Never in their darkest nightmares could they believe the immensity of the great frozen barrier of deadly water and ice they now saw before them.

The bridge, ancient beyond imagination, was clearly the work of gods yet there was signs that mortals had, throughout the ages, apparently worked the ice and carved barracks and vast storehouses within its frozen ramparts and glassy towers. Caution washed over the party in a rush, for they were about to cross the threshold and enter into the forbidden domain of the clan of Gerdmor, sworn enemies of Heidmar, and there was no way of knowing if the many towers and barracks were occupied by armed warriors.

Uncertain if the barracks and storehouses were occupied, but sensing that the men were reluctant to pass, Halgi Mansbane, summoning the strength in her heart, grabbed the leather reigns of her warhorse and pushed through her companions. Her bravery was inspiring and it could be clearly seen that she was indeed the rightful heir to Grimthor the Strong, chieftain of the clan of Heidmar, descendant of the House of Rexor. Boldly, she passed under the western gate and trekked out onto the bridge. The midday sun was warm and bright and the silver armor of her father sparkled like diamonds in its reflection.

Tulwryn, wrapped in a great cloak of fur, the Bloodsword hanging at his side, was the next to step out onto the bridge and Urgan followed closely behind, spear in hand, his long woolen cape billowing in the crisp air of the frozen north. Dillwyn, wearing his gilded Carthusian battle armor, took up the rear position.

The cold wind whipped down from the mountain passes and over the bridge with a great force, yet the warriors steeled themselves and pressed on. Like proud heroes entering a conquered kingdom, the four boldly tread across the expanse showing naught weakness nor fear.

Within the better part of two hours, the party had successfully passed under the eastern gate and found themselves on the frozen ground of the east bank. Looking behind them naught, they continued on their trek. The path was rocky, and with less snow than they experienced on the western side, yet the grade wound steeper as it left the frozen river behind and ascended into the vast and foreboding un-named mountains.

"May the gods be with us in this desolate land of frozen death," said Urgan, shuddering at the thought of a Gerdmorian ambush behind every rock and crag. He unfastened the shield that was attached to his back and slid it over his thick left forearm.

Tulwryn turned to the young warrior and smiled. "We shall need more aid that the gods would give us, young Urgan, if Gerdmor caught sight of us on their land. They are fell warriors, cunning and wrathful."

"As long as I keep mine visor down," said Halgi, interrupting, "they will attack us naught. My father's wrath is feared throughout the whole of the northern world, and they would not risk unleashing the wrath of Heidmar upon themselves."

"Still, Halgi," grunted the dwarf, "we are but four against many, with dwindling supplies and no possible reinforcements. Perhaps Gerdmor would attempt to capture the mighty Grimthor the Strong rather than slay him, and use him as a pawn for their own bidding. How would we fare then, as they would discover that ye are not Grimthor, but his daughter?"

"'Tis best if we creep softly and kept silent, methinks," said Tulwryn, "so as not to draw unwanted attention from wrathful eyes." The others nodded in agreement and continued on in silence, their hawk-like eyes scouring the mountain cliffs for any sign of movement.

For three bitter days and nights, the four warriors from Heidmar traveled unhindered through the meandering trails and passes of the un-named mountains. The sun rose and fell, uneventful, as it had done since the beginning of the world. On the eve of the third day, Halgi led the party to a deep gorge. Tulwryn, realizing that the gorge may hold unseen dangers, called the group together for council. After some quiet discussion, the four agreed that there was little hope of crossing the range any other way for the crests of the mountains were high and the walls of stone increasingly steep.

"Methinks we should wait it out hither, near the mouth of the gorge, till dark," spoke Dillwyn. "Under the cover of night we are less likely to be seen by Gerdmorian eyes." The other three agreed and each chose a secluded position against the cliff wall where they could sit, concealed from wrathful eyes until the sun dipped behind the jagged peaks and clothed the range in inky blackness.

It was nearing dusk and the setting sun was washing the white cliffs of the gorge a ruddy scarlet red, a seemingly eerie omen for the coming eve, when Dillwyn the dwarf crept near where Tulwryn was seated.

"Tulwryn," he whispered, "what thinks you?"

The warrior turned to his friend and frowned. "We are found out, methinks."

"Why think this, mine friend?"

"Listen," Tulwryn whispered. Both men sat quiet for sometime, diligently listening to the serene silence of the frozen air. The sun was impaling itself on the peaks in the far distance and there was a solemn stillness that reeked of like an ancient Vodmarian tomb.

"I hear naught," spoke the dwarf.

"Precisely," whispered Tulwryn, with a frown. "All the days of mine travels in the wilderness with ye I hath never heard such quiet. No sounds of any kind permeate this gorge. Even in the most remote valleys of the Ymir Mountains, there was the music of birds and the snorting of beasts. But hither, there is naught. I can only assume we have been found out. If there is an amassing army about, it wouldst account for the lack of nature sounds. What thinks ye?"

"Aye, mine friend, ye may be right," grumbled the dwarf under his breath. "Shall we continue onward then?"

"I fear we have no choice. We have come too far to turn around; and even if we did retreat, it would take too long to circumnavigate these desolate hills. Even so, this is the only way through the mountains that Halgi knows, and she is the only one of us that has been this way prior. If we change our trail now we risk being lost forever."

"Well then," whispered Dillwyn under his breath as he crouched even closer, "what about the magic in the sword? Do ye remember what I told ye when I presented the Bloodsword to ye in your tent?" There was a mixed look of fear and excitement in the dwarf's round face yet Tulwryn just shrugged his shoulders and shook his head.

"Aye, I remember what ye told me. You revealed unto me how the Volva had been present during the forging, simply seated in a corner of the smithy, chanting incantations. Perhaps you are correct in the assumption that the sword is imbued with magic, but if so, what kind of magic I wonder? Do ye remember the evil sorcery that has already befallen us with the deception of the war wolf and Vogelmir? Perhaps this sword is of a similar evil. At times, I fear to wield it, but so far the weapon has served me well so I will continue using it for the moment. As for magic, I have seen no evidence that the blade is magical; at least it has naught revealed any unseen power into my hands."

"I am as reluctant as you to wield magic, Tulwryn, but in these dire times we must utilize every weapon at our disposal."

"This may be true, but I cannot believe that vile witch would give us a tool of her own destruction. If there is any magic in this accursed blade I am sure it will be our undoing!" Tulwryn grabbed the scabbard of the Bloodsword tightly and frowned.

"May the gods curse that bitch, and us too for accepting this evil!" Suddenly the sun disappeared behind the mountains and the entire gorge was clothed in darkness.

"Summon Urgan and Halgi," ordered Tulwryn, "'tis time. We needs make our departure through the gorge at once. To tally longer will mean our deaths." The dwarf nodded and vanished in the night.

He returned a few minutes later with Urgan the Brave and Halgi Mansbane leading her warhorse, in tow. Without a word spoken, the four warriors from Heidmar silently entered the darkness of the gorge.

Shrouded in the inky blackness of the night, the party hid their fear well and wore the badge of courage proudly. If they were to die this eve, then so be it, for they were soldiers of Heidmar and welcomed death in its myriad forms, yet they would not die easy and their wrath would be felt ere the last one threw their life away.

As they entered the dark canyon, their hearts grew cold. The sides of the gorge rose steeply and their height could not be judged by the naked eye. Perhaps the summit of the cliffs were more than a league above them, thought Tulwryn, but alas, the cliffs were not the danger here, but rather, what secret death the cliffs held hidden in the form of Gerdmorian warriors.

Tulwryn and his party were barely three hundred paces into the gorge when the first wave of the attack came. In a shower of flaming arrows and spears, raining down on them like a plague, the Gerdmorians unleashed hell and the entire canyon was alight with the fire of death.

"Retreat," roared Tulwryn and the dwarf, in unison. There was no cover, and the four were in the open and exposed to the enemy's fiery missiles, therefore they retreated about a hundred paces to a grotto carved in the cliff's face, shields held high. Halgi's horse fell during the retreat, a Gerdmorian crossbow bolt piercing a lung.

"What now, Tulwryn," asked Urgan, apparently outraged at the thought of running.

"For certain we are cornered, and our retreat is sure to be closed to us as well. They knew we were coming and set the perfect trap! Either we wait it out hither, with the cliff to our backs for a straight fight, or we climb the cliffs."

"I may be young," said Urgan, "but I know this much, if we stay pressed up against this wall much longer, out of reach from the Gerdmorians arrows, they will sooner than naught send their warriors down upon us to hew us down man to man."

"For true," said Halgi, "we are outnumbered and a straight fight would be suicide!"

"Well then, let us climb!" roared Dillwyn, and he fastened his shield upon his back, then turned and began climbing the frozen face of the rock wall behind them. Tulwryn and Halgi followed the dwarf's lead. Urgan grunted oaths as he strung his shield on his back.

"I am no mountain beast," he said to no one in particular, "but no fool either." Into the darkness, he reached for the cliff and began his ascent behind Halgi and the others just as more flames poured down around them.

The fiery rain of flaming arrows and spears continued to fall for some time as the four groped up the cliff's sheer face, their bodies pressed hard against the rock and the frozen wall biting into their hands and making the ascent even more unbearable. From the far end of the gorge, a mighty war horn was sounded and the four climbers heard the unrelenting sound of growling snow beasts off in the distance.

"We are caught betwixt the raining fire from above and the hell that awaits us below," cried Tulwryn. "We must obtain a footing above those mounted warriors that come for us astride them fell beasts and out of the reach of their grim blades."

"For certain we have our shields," yelled Halgi Mansbane, "but even if we avoid the flaming missiles from above the Gerdmorians on the ground will smite us with arrows. We are doomed!"

"By the gods, I will naught die alone," roared Urgan the Brave, and he reversed his position and began climbing back down the cliff.

Riding atop fierce snow beasts, a dozen mounted warriors came into view. The gorge was still lit by the raining arrows of fire and the entire canyon continued to be illumined with an ethereal glow; some of the cedar and spruce trees clinging to the canyon walls began to catch the flame and alight, adding to the brightness of the night. "Truly we are in the maw of hell," grumbled Dillwyn, to himself, as he turned to witness Urgan stumble and fall. The boy disappeared into the dark undergrowth below.

"Tulwryn," yelled the dwarf, "Urgan has fallen from the cliff and I can see him naught!"

"Then we must needs descend," answered the warrior. "If it is our destiny to perish hither, let us extract our vengeance ere we expire!" At once, the three warriors from Heidmar began their descent into the fray.

Urgan hit the frozen ground with a thump, knocking the air from his lungs. He was instantly surrounded by three Gerdmorian warriors mounted on fierce snow beasts. Shaking stars from his head, Urgan sprang to one knee, coughing.

"Die ye Heidmarian dog," screamed one warrior, and charged at the fallen youth. Urgan, clearly in awe of the massive beast bounding toward him, and still somewhat out of breath from his fall, managed to remove the shield from his back and slide it over his left forearm in one smooth motion. Waiting for the exact time to strike, he steeled himself until the beast was almost upon him, then, with the lightning speed of a mountain cat, he dodged to the right and smote the large beast in the left flank with his spear. The beast screamed in pain as the spear pierced flesh. The mounted warrior reined the injured beast and spun around for another pass.

"Is that the best ye can do," roared Urgan. "I am Urgan the Brave, warrior of Heidmar, in the service of Grimthor the Strong, come and taste death!" With a hiss, Urgan unsheathed his mighty broadsword and attacked the other two warriors surrounding him.

From behind a cluster of small bushes, Halgi, Dillwyn, and Tulwryn appeared, blades in hand and ready to join the fray.

"Nice ye could join me," spat Urgan at his comrades jokingly.

"We shant allow ye all the fun," yelled Halgi, smiling. A dozen more mounted warriors suddenly came into view and the confusion of the battle was increased tenfold.

"Look," she cried, "company!"

Two riders charged Tulwryn yet he cut their mounts from beneath them with a mighty stroke of the Bloodsword. Screaming, they went down in a heap of blood and entrails. Urgan was assaulted again by the mounted warrior he had speared, and at the fighter's approach he could see that his spear had not only sank deep into the beast, but had penetrated the man's thigh as well, pinning him to his animal. A heavy blood trail poured forth from the wound, and even though the man was not mortally wounded, Urgan could clearly see that the beast was. It would not be long ere the beast fall and take its rider to his death.

"I shall take Grimthor," cried another stout warrior as he dismounted his snow beast and unsheathed his sword, running madly toward Halgi. Other warriors screamed and yelled and the sounds of battle and death echoed throughout the night.

Halgi seen the man looming toward her, blade in hand, and she laughed silently to herself. As the warrior attacked, Halgi blocked and counter attacked. The fighting was fierce; slash, parry, thrust, cut, slash, parry. Steel rang off steel and sparks leapt from the singing blades.

"Know this Grimthor of Heidmar," spoke the fell warrior in the heat of battle, "'tis I, Monan the Stout, first general of the clan of Gerdmor, that will take your life." Without an answer, Halgi continued her unrelenting attack. Cut, thrust, parry!

"Will ye speak naught to me, Grimthor," asked the man, angrily. "I have never known ye to fight thus. For ye are known throughout our land as a boisterous one!"

Laughing, Halgi lifted the visor of her father's great war helm for a mere second, exposing her beautiful face. The moment the visor dropped she sprang forward, taking full advantage of the man's surprise. The warrior stumbled back against the cliff wall as she swung her broadsword with both hands. Monan's head hit the cliff and bounced back toward Halgi's blade. The man screamed his last as his neck was severed by the steel of Grimthor's heir and he fell gurgling on his own blood. Halgi, paying no heed to the fallen warrior, turned to face another.

Urgan easily dispatched his assailants and ran to assist Tulwryn, who had already slain four and was presently fighting two more.

"It seems there is no end in their numbers," cried Tulwryn. "At this pace, we will slay for eternity, and still win naught the battle."

"Aye, Tulwryn. They are many, but their skills are weak. Soon we will tire and then they will hew us down."

As the two continued to fight, they were joined by Halgi. The three, fighting back to back, clove a great wound in the mass of Gerdmorian warriors approaching them. Suddenly, they heard a loud cry far off in the distance. It was Dillwyn; he had taken an arrow in the calf, but unbeknownst to them, continued fighting.

"That sounded like Dillwyn," yelled Urgan. "I will go yonder and see if I can help."

Halgi and Tulwryn were still in the heat of battle when the youth vanished behind a burning shrub. The raining fire from above had all but ceased, yet the ground and trees were still alight giving the canyon the gloomy atmosphere of a dream.

"Tulwryn," cried Halgi in the heat of battle, her long broadsword ripping through the armor of the fell warrior standing before her and spilling his blood and entrails on the white snow, as another attacked to replace him. "Even though we hail from Heidmar, and brave and strong we are, we cannot keep up this pace of slaughter ere we be slain ourselves. We must needs retreat to higher ground."

"Aye," Tulwryn yelled, "dispatch that Gerdmorian dog and follow my lead. I have a plan!"

Two warriors then attacked Tulwryn, but in one fell swoop he hewed them both in twain and then disappeared into the gloom of the night. Within seconds, Halgi too had killed her assailant and vanished.

Urgan ran through the darkness of the night to where he believed Dillwyn lay wounded. As he rounded a trail in the canyon floor his heart great stronger as he witnessed the dwarf, surrounded by six mounted Gerdmorians, in the heat of battle. The fierce dwarf, still burdened by the thick shaft in his calf, was amazing to behold, for he brandished no weapons save for his fists clothed in studded bronze. As a beast would attack, and its rider thrust down a great lance at the dwarf, he would block the attack with one gauntlet while smiting the beast with the other. More than once did Urgan witness the death of a massive snow beast by means of the dwarf's heavy hands; its innards beat to jelly by heavy blows. Crying a loud war cry, Urgan charged into the fray with sword in hand, its wet blade still dripping from past foes.

As the riders attacked, Urgan cleaved armor and rent flesh whilst Dillwyn landed mighty blows breaking bones and smashing steel. The battle continued for some time, and there seemed to be no end to the numbers of the Gerdmorians. For every one that Dillwyn and the youth cut down, two seemed to appear in their place.

"We cannot keep up this pace," cried Urgan, slaying a man before him.

Ducking under the blow of a heavy battle mace from a mounted rider, Dillwyn smote the warrior's mount in its right flank with his bronze fist. As the beast shuddered under the blow its knees buckled and the large body fell to the ground, tossing the rider over its head and into a granite boulder. The man fell dead from a broken neck, but the beast moaned, regained its strength, and once again rose to its feet.

"I agree, young Urgan," hollered the dwarf, still battling with the riderless snow beast. "It seems we are separated from the others. Keep those mounts busy, whilst I try to subdue this one. Perhaps, once on its back we can ride thither and retreat."

Although the plan was a desperate one, it was all they had. Urgan, fearing that Halgi and Tulwryn were lost, felt the anger well up in his northern veins. Shrieking in a berserker rage, he attacked the warriors riding towards Dillwyn.

The snow beast growled and attacked the dwarf, but Dillwyn rolled sideways past the charging monster and grabbed the reins hanging from the creature's thick leather harness. The beast, feeling his enemy's grip on the reins, pivoted around and tried to gorge Dillwyn in the side with a razor sharp tusk. Dillwyn dodged the snow beast's slashing tusk and, still gripping the reins, blasted a fist into the creature's ribs. The animal coughed, pausing just enough to allow the dwarf to jump up into the saddle. Shrieking, the monster bucked and kicked trying to throw Dillwyn from its back. Another blow, this one an open palm to the ear of the beast, all but dropped the monster. Dillwyn then bit down hard on the creature's ear, drawing blood and yelling oaths.

Urgan was knee deep in gore when he saw a large snow beast galloping toward him with the dwarf of Carthus in the saddle and holding the reins. From atop the creature, Dillwyn could see the look of surprise in the youth's eyes; all about the boy lay the severed bodies of at least five dead Gerdmorian warriors, his sword still dripping with their blood.

"Sheath that blade, boy, and grab my hand as I pass," Dillwyn screamed. Three more riders came into view, and Urgan slew one with a heavy diagonal slash and then sheathed his sword. Running from the other two riders, he crossed in front of Dillwyn's beast, grabbed his thick hand as the monster passed him, and was effortlessly lifted into the saddle behind the dwarf. Urgan was dumbfounded at the immensity of the dwarf's strength even with the loss of blood from his wounded leg, but shook it off. No time for hero worship, he thought silently to himself, and Dillwyn reined the beast about and made for a quick retreat. The two rode hard for the better part of the night, not slowing their pace until the bright rays of the rising sun greeted them at the dawn of the new day.

Thus ends the Seventh Chapter of Book One

EIGHT

Of Herbs and Dwarven Magic

Dillwyn and Urgan rode west astride the massive Gerdmorian snow beast. Far behind them, they could still hear the deafening roars of enemy beasts and the rueful orders being screamed at foot soldiers by angry commanders. It was apparent that their sudden disappearance had left the Gerdmorian army in confusion. The dwarf laughed under his breath at his resourcefulness of the theft of the creature, yet the burning sensation in his calf reminded him of his injury and he realized that it required immediate attention. Still, he knew they could not stop and make camp until they were far from the ambush site and out of reach of the Gerdmorians. Therefore, they rode on all throughout the night slowing naught their pace.

The bright rays of the rising sun warmly greeted them at dawn of the following day like an old friend and the two battle weary warriors smiled. Once again, they had cheated death to witness the miracle of life in the rebirth of the sun god early in the morn; indeed, thought Urgan the Brave, life was good.

They rode due westward, meandering at times hither and thither in order to hide their tracks and lose any unwanted pursuers. When the day reached its noon, and Dillwyn felt confident that their trail had been lost, he reined the snow beast and slowed the creature to a canter. Coming upon a large aspen grove, which was dotted sparsely with giant cedars, he brought the animal to a halt.

"We shall camp hither for a few hours," he said, casting a

glance back at Urgan. "My leg needs some attention, and by your looks ye needs rest as well."

"Aye," answered Urgan, "riding atop this great bouncing beast is more exhausting than mortal combat! It would do me well to rest mine sore back side from the onslaught of this accursed Gerdmorian saddle."

"Well, mine friend, our work is not yet finished. First, we must hobble this steed ere we rest lest he run off and return to the enemy, for he would certainly return hither bringing a horde of Gerdmorians back upon us to finish the job they started yonder. Anyhow, we can still use him."

"For true we will cover more ground astride this beast than on foot," said Urgan, "but the stench is intolerable and he is a most disagreeable creature. The Gerdmorians have taught it well to hate their enemies."

"Perhaps we can domesticate it and turn it to our own needs," pondered the dwarf. "Yet, if it becomes too much bother I will slay it and we will enjoy much meat on our journey home." The two laughed and Dillwyn patted the beast gently on its thick neck. Even though the creature had been bent on their murder when they captured it, the long ride through the cold night seemed to have weakened it and it had become placid, at least for the moment.

They approached a large cedar whose girth was easy that thrice a man's chest and Urgan dismounted, holding the reins in his hand, whilst the dwarf maintained a death grip on the beast's head. When Urgan had the tether secured tightly to the tree Dillwyn released his hold and dismounted. At once, the beast began snorting and bucking, trying to break free. The large cedar creaked and moaned but was not uprooted, and surprising enough, the reins held fast without breaking attesting to the near legendary strength of Gerdmorian leather. Finally, the beast calmed down and became quiet, seeing that freedom would not be his this day.

The two removed themselves about fifty paces from the beast and began working to pitch a small makeshift camp were they could have a short rest whilst Dillwyn tended to his wounded calf.

The dwarf soon had a small fire built. He then removed a tiny burlap pouch of dried herbs from his belt and dumped the contents into the leather jack he kept tied about his waist. Then he put some large stones into the fire, added a liberal amount of snow to the jack, and then placed it onto the stones.

"What is that for," asked Urgan, curiously?

"'Tis an old remedy for battle wounds, mine friend," answered the dwarf. "Mine people are earth dwarves, not cave dwarves. I hail from Carthus, far to the west. 'Tis the only dwarven settlement above ground in the whole of Phantasodyssea. We have long cultivated healing herbs for use in salves and ointments."

"Aye," said Urgan, as he watched the dwarf stir the concoction with a stick making it into a thick and fragrant paste. "I have heard of that remarkable place. Carthus, ye say?"

Dillwyn paused for a moment, looked up at the boy, and smiled. He then noticed that Urgan had evidently taken a solid blow to his left upper arm, for his Circlet of Bravery was missing, apparently cleaved from his bicep during the battle. There was a gaping wound covered with dried and crusted blood where the cherished badge once sat.

"Seems as if your badge of bravery has protected your arm, young Urgan," he said, pointing at the wound.

The boy frowned.

"Well enough, methinks, that I should lose the Circlet and keep the arm. In the heat of battle I never even felt the blow, but now my arm aches most heinously."

"There is enough salve hither to patch us both, my friend. Come, let me take a look at that wound."

Urgan scooted closer to the dwarf and turned his shoulder toward him. Dillwyn examined the gash; he then took the stick and heated it in the fire. Once the stick was blackened through and through, he shoved it back into the jack and scooped out a liberal amount of herbal salve, which he then smeared into the wound on Urgan's arm.

"Now bandage that with an old rag," he said. "Ye should be good as new in a day or two."

The dwarf then turned to his own wound, and Urgan watched intently. Whilst he had seen severe battle wounds, and even witnessed them patched in the field, he had never seen one patch one's own self. He was amazed at the dwarf's high tolerance to pain, which seemed to match his inhuman strength. With a grim tenacity, Dillwyn grabbed the shaft that had penetrated his lower leg, and with one great thrust, he pushed it clean through the thick muscle of his calf. His other hand grabbed the bloody point protruding from the wound and pulled, yanking the entire shaft from the muscle. He then took up another heated stick and scooped out more herbal salve, and then, with a grunt and a groan he shoved the stick into the wound and through his leg as he had just done with the arrow only moments prior. Pulling the stick clean of the wound, he then ripped a patch from his breeches and bound his calf tightly.

Clearly exhausted, sweat beading upon his brow, he relaxed back and let out a sigh of relief.

"Ye stand the first watch, Urgan. I must needs some rest. Wake me just before sunset and I will watch whilst ye sleeps." He then closed his eyes and drifted off. Urgan walked a few paces off into the distance between the camp and the tethered snow beast and sat down, his hawk-like eyes scanning the horizon for anything that moved.

It was early the next afternoon when Dillwyn woke Urgan from his slumber. Nothing had stirred through either of their watches; both were well rested and so it was time to finally break camp and move on. The two mounted the snow beast with little effort; the creature had become surprisingly docile and Dillwyn wondered if it was some sort of trick taught to the beast by its previous Gerdmorian owners. He kept on his toes concerning the handling of the animal. Two days later they passed back over the ice bridge and pitched a small camp on the far side, attempting to make another short rest before trekking the long way around the mountains back to the Heidmar encampment. As hardy as the two warriors were, they were beginning to feel the ravages of hunger, as they had eaten naught since ere the ambush. With Halgi's steed slain, and their supplies lost, they would eat naught until their return to Heidmar since neither were in any condition to hunt.

Seated around the fire, both men wondered about the ambush and battle, about Tulwryn and Halgi, and about all that had befallen them over the past few weeks. Perhaps Halgi and Tulwryn were captured; that could account for their own easy escape. There was no way of knowing; all that could be done was to ride to Heidmar as fast as they could and hope that their two lost comrades would be there waiting. Only then, could they piece together this dark riddle and hopefully salvage their broken world from the grip of the horrendous evil that had ensnared them.

Facing west, the two warriors from Heidmar watched the sun dip over the far horizon and disappear. Dillwyn's mind then drifted to Carthus and the warm plains of the Golrin Prairie, to the beautiful places of Phantasodyssea, and to a more peaceful time. Slowly his eyes closed and he was fast asleep; Urgan once again slept naught but kept a keen eye open till dawn.

Thus ends the Eighth Chapter of Book One

NINE

A Face in the Smoke

The alarm sounded loudly and ran through the Heidmarian camp like a plague. Grimthor the Strong, the clan's chieftain had been slain in his tent whilst he slept and a Rodmarian battle-axe, still wet with his royal blood, was found near the body. Confusion gripped the entire tribe, which was screaming for vengeance at the thought of a Rodmarian assassin amidst their numbers.

Sorcery was assumed the culprit. And since no tracks were seen entering or leaving Grimthor's tent and the clan's soothsayer, the Volva, was nowhere to be found, she was considered a prime suspect. Vogelmir was also discovered missing, and even though he was a trusted member of the tribe with a long list of valorous deeds in battle, he could not be overlooked as a suspect as well.

Two days after the murder, Grimthor's wife, Halgr Manslayer, assumed the position as chieftain of Heidmar and rallied the council members to meeting. Earlier that day it had been discovered that Halgr's daughter, Halgi Mansbane, was also missing. Firestar, Grimthor's mighty warhorse, was also gone. So, Halgr assumed that her daughter had set out on her own to find Tulwryn and his party and inform them of the gruesome deed that had befallen Heidmar, since Firestar's tracks lead thither in the direction that Tulwryn took some days earlier. Therefore, Halgr Manslayer charged the clan's three strongest warriors to pursue Halgi and guarantee her safe return to the camp. Gunnar Trollsbane, Uther the Courageous, and Luther the Daring, accepted the duty with pride and departed at once. Then Halgr, as acting chieftain, petitioned the council members to amass a great war machine and move on Rodmar. Even though the clan was in an uproar for blood, Halgr declared that they should attack naught Rodmar until Halgi's safe return. Begrudgingly, the members agreed to hold off on their assault although the clan's generals and troops were assembled and held at the ready, should Rodmar attempt to thwart Heidmar's plans and attack them first.

After many days on the trail, the three warriors sighted a small camp far in the distance. The midday sun was to the south of them and they rode at a cautious pace until they saw that the two vagrants posted no threat. Still a ways from the camp, it was Uther who first recognized the two men seated by the small fire.

"That is Dillwyn and Urgan," he said to his brothers. At once, the three spurred their steeds and rode like the wind. In a blink of an eye, the heavy Heidmarian warhorses covered the nine hundred paces separating them from their comrades. They entered the camp with heavy heads and somber faces.

Luther, Gunnar, and Uther quickly dismounted and approached the fire. They were shocked to find Dillwyn and Urgan weak and starving. Equally shocking was the fact that a domesticated snow beast had been tethered to a tree, apparently in their care. Luther noticed Dillwyn's injured calf, healing nicely, no doubt to the quality of Carthusian herbal lore and the dwarf's skill in patching battle wounds. Gunnar quickly retrieved some dried meats and hard cheese from his saddlebag and the five sat down around the fire to consume the cold meal.

After some time, Dillwyn regained his strength and thanked his gods in his rough Carthusian tongue. The sun was sinking low on the horizon and the creatures of the frozen north were beginning to stir for their nightly hunt when the conversation finally began. In the distance came a shrill cry and then all was silent as a northern marmot made the acquaintance of a hungry eagle.

Finally Gunnar spoke, breaking the silent tension. He told the two of how Halgi Mansbane was discovered missing and that he and his two brothers were charged by Halgr, Halgi's mother, to search her out and return her to Heidmar. He then asked the whereabouts of Tulwryn.

"That is a long story, mine friend," answered Dillwyn. Through glassy eyes, the dwarf looked at the brave warriors seated around him at the fire. Pride welled up in his veins knowing that even though he was not of their Heidmarian blood, he was still an intricate part of a very noble clan. He was happy.

With a shaky voice, the old dwarf recounted how Halgi arrived to warn them of the slaying of Grimthor. He also told how his party was returning to Heidmar, being led through the un-named mountains by Halgi herself and was attacked by a fierce force of the Gerdmor clan. It was not as vicious a battle as that of Volsung, he laughed, but still it was grim as they were vastly outnumbered and many Gerdmorians were astride ferocious snow beasts. He then continued on, telling of how he and Urgan became separated from Halgi and Tulwryn sometime during the battle. At last sight, he informed them, both were alive, but there was no way to know for certain if they still live. Once they were atop the stolen snow beast he and Urgan retreated with the hope of attempting to circumnavigate the mountains and to rendezvous with Tulwryn and Halgi at the Heidmar encampment, but fate was not on their side since Grimthor's horse was slain in the fray and they lost all their supplies of food. Without food, and being a fortnight from Heidmar, they realized that their mission back to the tribe could fail in starvation and death.

"Indeed," he said with a cheer, "'tis good fortune that ye have found us!"

There was much back patting and bragging, and then more serious talk as the three men informed Dillwyn and Urgan of the happenings at the Heidmarian camp after Halgi departed.

"Halgr has assumed the role of chieftain," said Uther, "and Vogelmir is also gone. Magic is suspected since tracks in the snow lead to his tent, although none lead away. His bodyguards are missing as well and the Volva too is gone." There was a deafening silence and Gunnar then spoke to change the subject.

"Tell us, Dillwyn," he asked, "how our brother was slain? On our journey hither, we came by way of a blood stave carved in stone and were grieved by our loss. The runes of the stone claimed that Omar died in his sleep by the hand of treachery, and that he was refused the noble death of a warrior. Tell us how this came about."

Taking another bite of cold food, the dwarf paused and then answered:

"For true, Gunnar, Omar was slain in his sleep, and by a dread sorcery! He was given no chance to fight back!"

The brothers rued the thought of Omar, their brother, being robbed of a warrior's death and they vowed vengeance, swearing oaths. Dillwyn and Urgan took turns telling the three brothers how Omar Giantslayer was slain, and all that had befallen them on their journey north. Dillwyn then explained that the war wolf was Vogelmir and told how Tulwryn had slayed him with the Bloodsword. The men, frowning and grinding their teeth, were appalled at the evil that had ensnared them.

The three warriors then retold their tale to Urgan and the Dwarf. They told how they came across the abandoned war sleigh and witnessed the aftermath of a great battle. There was no sign of Vogelmir's body, apparently devoured by ravens and wolves days prior. They told how they then spied tracks leading still north and gave heart to follow them. Five days on the trail the brothers were besieged by a terrible blizzard lasting three days and so they lost their path north. For two more days they traveled, blind and lost amongst the great frozen plains with the mountains to their east. On the eve of the second day after the blizzard subsided, a great raven came a cawing.

Uther told how Luther was about to fire an arrow at the pest, but seeing the creature dripped blood from its black beak they gave chase and followed the bird. Gunnar told how the creature cawed loudly, and thereby allowed them to track it even throughout the night.

"We slowed our pace naught," he said, "and the following day ere noon, we came upon a small and abandoned encampment. Some paces to the northeast of the main camp we espied the blood stave lying half buried in the snow that had been carved in Omar's honor and there we were grieved at our loss."

"Well," spoke Uther, trying to lighten the mood, "if Halgi is with Tulwryn then she fares better with him than with us, if in fact they lived to escape the Gerdmorians. Methinks we should return thither to Heidmar with our two new found comrades."

"Halgr will like it naught if we return without her daughter," Luther answered, and Gunnar seconded the idea.

"But they are on the other side of the divide by now. Certainly, ye thinks naught to pursue them through Gerdmorian country."

"Uther is right," spat the dwarf. "As much as I would like to re-enter them mountains and slay more Gerdmorian dogs, 'tis best if we travel back the way ye came and return to Heidmar yonder. If Tulwryn and Halgi still live, I am certain they will arrive in Heidmar ere us."

The night was upon them and the fire had shrunk into the coals. Gunnar passed around a full wineskin of cold Heidmarian ale and Urgan was happy to wet his lips on something other than melted snow.

The five agreed to rest throughout the night and break camp at first light returning south toward Heidmar. Luther took first watch as the other four closed their eyes to sleep; it was the first night's sleep Urgan would enjoy hence a fortnight, and he shut his eyes to dreams of combat and bloodletting, and he smiled.

* * *

Far to the north, many leagues past the frozen lake, in a great castle of ice older than mortal imagination, an evil frost dragon sat on his dark throne. Before him hovered a censer of black smoldering coals. A taloned hand emptied itself of bitter herbs onto the coals and a thick cloud of pungent fumes rose high into the air of the throne room. Moments later, the face of a terrible evil emerged from within the billowing smoke. "Master, what is thy bidding," asked the face?

"Did thy do as I have commanded," asked the dragon?

"Aye, master. I revealed the false prophecy to the council of Heidmar and sent the four northward; Grimthor is also slain as ye has commanded."

Darkoth smiled a grim smile and his great leathern wings unfolded to their full width, casting a gloomy shadow throughout the whole of the throne room.

"Then the true prophecy is unfolding," he said, but then a frown creased his heavy brow. "But Vogelmir struck too soon and so failed his mission!"

The Volva sensed the wrath in the dragon's voice and fear poured over her in a wave.

"Yes, master, I know. Tulwryn and the others still live. Please, I beg of ye, forgive this failure." She lowered her eyes to him and he turned away to ponder a distant thought. For a moment, he sat quiet, dead to the world, and then looked back at the face in the smoke.

"But the sword," he asked, "was the forging complete?"

"Aye, master, the forging was complete," she answered, her voice shaking with fear. "Yet the blade was not of a dark color as ye had hoped, but that of wet blood."

Darkoth growled.

"The prophecy foretold that if the blade be of a dark color, then the one who wields the blade would be of evil and the powers of evil would work through him. Yet, if the sword be of any other hue, the one who wields it would be pure of heart and would vanquish evil . . ." The dragon left his sentence hanging in the air, the thought not yet completed. Pausing, he bit his tongue and thought for a moment.

"But Tulwryn carries the grim burden of the kinslaying, master, and he reeks of evil; how can he be pure of heart? Perhaps he can he be turned for our bidding?"

"My darkest fear has emerged and the legend of the Bloodsword is upon us," he said, ignoring her previous question. "Yet, 'tis good that ye slain Grimthor and made it to look like a Rodmarian assassin! The confusion may bide us time."

Working hard to conceal her panic, the Volva spoke thus:

"My Lord, Halgi Mansbane, the virgin daughter of Grimthor the strong has stolen away from the Heidmar camp and has made her way into the wilderness to find Tulwryn and the others; she suspects me of evil treachery and will surely inform him."

"Fear naught, my servant," laughed the mighty dragon, "for the bitch of Grimthor's loins can be made to serve us! If we can trick Tulwryn into slaying the wench, all power in the Bloodsword will be destroyed, for the prophecy has also foretold that if the blade drinks the pure blood of a virgin it will then lose its strength henceforth! Our plan is not yet usurped!"

The smoke billowed and rose and the Volva's face grew distorted in the fumes.

"Can we persuade Tulwryn to slay the wench, master?"

"Aye," he said. "Ye must devise a plan. I have foreseen that the party has ceased to trek to my abode in the north. They have turned east into the un-named mountains on a quest to return to Heidmar. Yet they were attacked by the Gerdmorian clan and their numbers have been parted. The dwarf travels west with the boy and is of no concern to us; yet, Tulwryn treks east with the bitch of Grimthor. Ye shall make certain they reach naught Heidmar! Fail me naught!"

"But master," answered the Volva, "I grow weary of this ruse. And the body of a mortal is stifling!"

"Fail me naught this time, lest I relieve ye of thy worthless life itself," roared the dragon in anger, most heinous. "Ye shall have thy reward only after Tulwryn and the Bloodsword are in my service, or destroyed!"

"I have served ye faithfully for more than sixty turnings of the great wheel of the seasons, master. I shall do as ye commands."

The face in the smoke faded into nothingness; Darkoth then closed his eyes in deep thought, evil dreams of tyranny running though his black mind. Far to the east, in a small hide tent hidden high in the un-named mountains, an old witch knelt over a cauldron of boiling oil. Smiling, she already knew she had devised the perfect plan to turn Tulwryn to the service of evil, or destroy him.

Thus ends the Ninth Chapter of Book One

TEN

The Ice Cave

The tiny cave was dark and cold; a reeking dampness permeated the still air not breathed by human lungs in over a millennium. Tulwryn and Halgi sat motionless, listening to the roaring snow beasts and the screaming Gerdmorian generals barking commands at dumbfounded foot soldiers a mere stone's throw from the mouth of the cave where they hid. It was a gift from the gods that Tulwryn had spied the cave's entrance, a dark shadow behind a small yew bush, and allowed the two exhausted warriors a quick escape from the fray and a secure hiding place.

"'Tis sorcery," cried one of the Gerdmorian generals, "that four helpless Heidmarian dogs could just vanish from our sight."

Tulwryn held back a laugh and Halgi grinned. For the moment, it seemed they were safe. But for how long, they knew naught. It was only a matter of time ere some keen eyed Gerdmorian tracker would pick up their scent and track them to their hidden lair.

Silently, Tulwryn poked Halgi in the ribs motioning her to crawl to the rear of the cave. Within an hour's time the outside commotion quieted and the cave took on the air of a deserted Vodmarian tomb.

Far to the rear of the cave, Tulwryn and Halgi groped in the inky blackness to build a small makeshift camp. They removed their weapons and shields and each felt their own body, making certain they suffered no wounds. Tulwryn, finding no serious injury, took off his boots and massaged his aching feet.

"Methinks they have given up on us," whispered Halgi. Tulwryn said naught but merely reclined in the darkness.

"Shall I search this wreck of a tomb for some timber, Tulwryn," she asked, but still the warrior before her spoke no words. As was her nature, and the nature of her people, Halgi quickly grew agitated at being ignored.

"Ye speak very little, Tulwryn," she spat through clenched teeth.

Tulwryn looked grimly at her. Through the opaque darkness of the cave, he could barely make out her form, yet his instincts told him that her patience was wearing thin. He silently swore an oath to one of his grim Nuvian gods for allowing him to fall into this predicament.

After the kinslaying, he swore to have nothing more to do with women; they simply could not be trusted. He was not like other men, who manipulated women for their own pleasure, and who likewise, were manipulated in return. No, Tulwryn was not like that at all; he would not use a woman simply to satisfy his own carnal lusts. Yet all the same, those lusts were still present, still coursing through his hot blooded Nuvian veins, even though the curse of Durayn had wounded him deeply.

"I see no reason to waste time with useless words," he said.

"I can see that ye are truly a callous warrior, my lord," answered Halgi, her tone changing from bitterness to that of compassion. "Yet, I can also see that ye does carry a grim burden, though I know naught what that burden be. Can ye naught confide in me and allow me to share thy burden? Surely, it would be easier to bear if two carried it rather than one." She scooted close to him and placed a warm hand on his knee.

"Why would thou seek to aid me, woman," he said, as he pulled away from her touch. "I am not of thy blood, but rather, a foreigner and a stranger to thine people."

"Ye may be naught of my blood, and a foreigner, but you are naught a stranger. Ye are a bold and cunning warrior and have shed much blood for mine clan, and from the first time my eyes looked at ye love stirred in my heart, but I bit mine tongue and spoke naught, for I knew ye carried a dark burden."

"My foreboding, ye cannot aid me with, Halgi Mansbane," he grumbled under his breath. "'Tis my burden to bear."

"Perhaps t'would be easier to bear if t'was carried by two rather than one. Have thee naught confided in thy gods, Tulwryn? Canst they naught aid thee?"

"I know of many gods," he said. "Some are said to be good and bring benefit, others are quick to wrath. He who refutes them is as ignorant as the one who completely depends upon them. I seek naught beyond death's gate. That doom will befall me soon enough. Blethno lominpye mortu, lythno lominpye panyanu." The warrior paused for a moment, but he realized Halgi understood naught his native tongue.

"Birth guarantees death, life guarantees suffering," he said. "After death, there may be the blackness of the Void, or it might be Odhinn's icy realm. Perhaps 'tis even the snowy plains and high domed halls of Athrum's dominion? Who am I to know? Anyhow, I care naught. I shall live intensely while I yet live. I will taste the cold ale and the sweet wine of Caiwryn in mine mouth, and I will feel the hot passions burning in mine veins. Even will I endure the lust of battle when mine grim blade finds its way to the entrails of mine enemies! And I am content. Even with the pain of mine burden, I am content.

"Let the truth-seekers, and the theorists, and even the dreamers, dwell on the problem of reality and illusion. I know only this: if life is illusion, then I too am illusion! And being so, the illusion is real to me. I live, I am ablaze with life; I can feel the pleasure of the flesh, or be consumed by the weight of mine burden. Either way, for me, there is no hope. Neither hither nor after death. I find peace only in the act of slaying mine enemies. After mine death, likewise, I shall know no peace, for I am cursed to endless wandering. And drearily I shall pass that time wandering through the misty realm of ice and snow for all eternity. 'Tis Athrum's will. This I know. You canst help me naught, dear Halgi."

"But I just thought, if we were to handfast . . ."

"Enough talk of love!" Tulwryn was losing his patience and

he wished to quickly change the subject, for he had no use for idle talk of gods or demons or love or handfasting. "We must needs speak of a plan to steal past that devil Gerdmorian clan and make our way back to Heidmar. There, we can rendezvous with Dillwyn and Urgan, if they still live, and salvage what is left of this riddle. I feign that Rodmar will soon strike, if they were truly responsible for the slaying of your father. Still, a battle-axe is not the weapon of an assassin. I feel treachery is afoot!"

"So ye thinks that Rodmar slayed naught my father," she asked.

"'Tis possible that Grimthor was slain by one of the Volva's enchantments and the murder was made to appear like a Rodmarian killing. There is only one way to know for certain," he said, pausing, and losing Halgi's shape in the shadows of the cave. He looked around, and then spying her form in the darkness, he continued:

"We must needs trek to Rodmar and hold council with their elders."

"But we are of Heidmar, my lord," she said, a slight tremble in her voice. "They will slay us ere we enter their camp."

"That may be true, but 'tis a chance we must take; for as ye have already forespoke unto me, your clan amasses a great war machine to attack Rodmar, and under thy mother's leadership. Would ye have thy clan murder unjustly?"

"We are a warrior race, Tulwryn. War is all we know, justly or unjustly," she answered. "Yet what of Gerdmor, Tulwryn? We must escape their wrath, and that of these evil mountains ere we make plans to even enter Rodmar."

"For true," he said. "The Gerdmorians are a fierce clan whilst in the hills, but they will soon lose their spirits once we make our way to the flats. They will pursue us naught if we make it that far, yet I see much bloodletting in our future."

"Aye, Tulwryn, I was born to shed blood, for I am of the clan of Heidmar. Never have I known anything but war."

For some time all was silent and no words were spoken, then in haste, Tulwryn asked:

"Have ye known no man?" As soon as the words escaped his lips, he bit his tongue and wished them back in his mouth.

"Curses," he cursed silently to himself, "this wench has tricked me and I fell for it." Again, the conversation turned to love.

"Nay, Tulwryn," answered Halgi, "I am a warrior through and through, sired by a warrior and birthed by a warrior. My spirit and flesh has been soiled naught. How else do ye think I came by the name of Mansbane?" Halgi smiled a devilish smile yet in the darkness of the cave, Tulwryn saw it naught.

"Only to thee will I submit," she said, "for I have loved ye from the beginning."

"It has grown cold this eve, and we can risk no fire for it would bring the entire clan of Gerdmor down upon us," he said, fidgeting.

"Then come to me, and allow my love to warm thee this night, my lord," she said as she crawled to Tulwryn and wrapped her arms around him. He reached out to grab her and felt her lithe body press hard against his; warm and naked she was, and he wondered when in the gloom of the cave had she removed her armor. Silently, she buried her face in Tulwryn's neck and wrapped herself in his great fur cloak.

Thus ends the Tenth Chapter of Book One

ELEVEN

A Ghost in the Night

The five warriors from Heidmar had been on the trail for a few days, trekking homeward bound. The weather had been surprisingly good considering that it was only a fortnight past midwinter, and the bright northern sun felt warm upon the frozen faces of the five as they traveled. Gunnar, Uther, Luther, on proud Heidmarian warhorses; Urgan and Dillwyn still astride their stolen Gerdmorian snow beast.

The dwarf's calf was all but healed and Urgan's left bicep had a permanent badge of honor where his Circlet once sat. Time and again, the youth would glance down at his bulging arm and smile at the site of the wicked scar that would forever remain a constant reminder of the Battle of Gerdmor Gorge, as the ambush would come to be known in the years to come.

As was their habit, the men stopped every third day just ere sunset to make camp, allowing themselves and their mounts a much needed rest. Presently, they were camped in the open, just on the downside of a large snow dune. From the north, the direction they had just rode, their camp could not be seen since it was strategically placed on the southern side of that high ridge of snow and ice, but they were completely exposed to anyone traveling up the trail from the south. This did not seem to trouble the warriors much, since the plain that stretched south before them was broad and flat and they could see any oncoming riders long ere they would be in any danger of attack.

The camp was sparsely furnished, in the manner of their

northern barbarian clan; a small fire was crackling within a tiny circle of stones and each man had made a small pallet of woolen blankets around the fire whereas he would greet the night's sleep. The three warhorses were set free to roam the frozen plain and munch the sweet tundra, as they were faithful to their masters and would return hither as quick as the wind at the sounding of the small reed whistle that each man carried, a pitch too shrill for human ears to hear.

Surprising enough was the behavior of the Gerdmorian snow beast. The creature, once unmanageable and extremely aggressive, had mellowed considerably and seemed to have grown quite fond of its new owners. Six days prior, at their last campsite, Dillwyn had dropped the tether whilst trying to hobble the beast and to his surprise, the animal ran naught, but gathered the tether in its mouth and returned the reins to the dwarf's hand. Dillwyn, as an act of faith, tethered naught the animal that night and was happy to discover the beast still near camp the following morning. Since that day, the dwarf had allowed the creature to roam free throughout the night whilst they camped, and this seemed to benefit the beast well, since the dwarf nor any of the other four understood neither snow beast husbandry nor what the creature ate. For the first few hundred leagues on the trail, the beast seemed to weaken, apparently from the lack of food, but since Dillwyn had refrained from hobbling the creature at night, it had quickly regained its strength and likewise, its mood lightened.

This eve, Luther stood first watch whilst the other four crawled under their warm blankets to shake the fatigue from their tired minds and exhausted bodies.

The night was dark and moonless and even Luther's massive form, standing but a mere arrow's shot from the small encampment, could not been seen. Soon the fire shrank into coals and the winds across the plains abated and all was quiet; silently, four warriors from Heidmar drifted off to sleep.

"Urgan, wake up," spoke a familiar voice, and a strong hand reached out to shake the young warrior from his slumber. "Shhhhhh. Wake naught the others."

Urgan sat up wiping sleep from his eyes. Startled at the face looming over him, he wanted to cry out, but his tongue was stilled and he was all but mute. He was no longer lying round the small fire of his camp deep amongst the frozen plains of his northern world, but found himself in some great hall of a seemingly powerful warrior.

The man standing over him was none other than Omar Giantslayer, yet the warrior was clothed naught in the traditional garb of Heidmar's warriors. He wore plate maile of bright silver over which was draped a great purple robe of thick velvet. The warrior's hands were gloved with steel gauntlets of the same quality as his armor, a large two handed broadsword hung loosely at his hip. Omar was holding a full-faced war helm, a sugarloaf of polished silver, yet over his head was draped a maile coif of wrought silver.

"Omar?" asked Urgan in a whisper, dazed and confused, and wondering if the shade before him was an omen or a dream.

"Aye," said Omar, "'tis I, your friend; come to warn ye of the doom of the world and reveal unto you your destiny."

"But brother, I seen ye slain," said Urgan, still believing naught the man standing ere his eyes. "Am I dead as well? And what is this hall? Where are we?"

Omar pulled up an oaken stool and sat beside Urgan, who was still half covered with a dark green woolen blanket and seated on a high cot. He placed his helm on one armored knee, smiled, and spoke:

"No Urgan, ye are not dead, but you are in the mighty Hall of the Slain, Odhinn's Hall. For true, ye did witness me murdered. Although I died naught in battle, my past deeds of valor on the battlefield won me access to paradise; that, and the blood stave that ye erected in mine honor. For that act of love, I thank ye."

"The blood stave," whispered the youth, "but how . . ."

The shade of Omar lifted a finger to Urgan's lips, silencing him.

"'Twas also the stone that ye carved in mine honor that swayed the gods to grant me this one visit. Listen, for even though they allow me to speak to thee, mine time is short and I must needs return thither to the eternal battlefield."

Urgan's eyes glowed with excitement and wonder and his body trembled at the icy cold permeating the hall. Glancing down at himself, he saw that he was likewise clothed in the same silver maile that Omar wore and his heart leapt.

"Ye spoke of mine destiny," he said, "and the doom of the world."

"Aye," answered Omar, "as ye have already comprised, the Volva is evil. For sixty turnings of the great wheel of the seasons, she has been portraying a great act as the loyal sorceress of the Heidmarian clan. But unbeknownst to the kindred, she is actually an evil minion of Darkoth, a dread frost dragon residing in an enormous castle of ice far to the north of the great frozen lake.

"Darkoth created the witch from the seething entrails of dying Gerdmorian infants, babes that he stole from their dead mothers soon after slaying the women long ago. Over that vile gore, he cast a horrendous enchantment, empowering it to breathe life with a dread lust for the death of others. From this mass of blood and offal came the Volva; the dragon then clothed it in mortal flesh and set it within the womb of Kath, a simple Heidmarian girl. Darkoth then wove a false prophecy about the primitive minds of our Heidmarian people. When the child was born she was revered as a great enchantress, and was appointed the title and rank of a Volva.

Kath perished in the birthing, unable to survive the dread venom stirring within her virgin womb, and was all but forgotten from the memory of our people. The Volva has lived a secret life amongst our clan ere now. She has betrayed our people and is working to enthrone a terrible evil upon the world. This, the gods have shown me, and now I have shown you." Omar paused, looking deeply into the youth's heart.

"Ye must forsake returning to Heidmar, but rather, journey far to the south, through the Darkwood and across many rivers, to the village of Covensted. There ye must needs find an old he-witch named Mimir. He is a good man and the keeper of many secrets. From him you must recover the Dragon Shield. Only after the shield is recovered can ye return to Heidmar."

"But what can I do with a shield? Am I to enter into combat with this frost dragon," asked Urgan.

"Nay, mighty Urgan," spoke the shade, "'tis not thy destiny to battle Darkoth, but to bring forth the shield from the south. For many eons has the Dragon Shield been in the trusted care of the witches of Covensted. The stars are now aligned aright and the prophecy is unfolding. Ye must unite the shield with the sword. That is thy destiny."

"Sword? What sword?"

"The sword of the north must be reunited with the shield of the south, for only then is the world made whole. Only when he who wields the Bloodsword carries both, the sword and the shield, can the great beast be defeated. 'Tis thy destiny, young Urgan, to return the Dragon Shield into the fell hands of Tulwryn the Bloodsword, mighty warrior of Heidmar, the foreigner from Nuvia, stranger, and friend to our people, so that he can meet his destiny and unite the warring clans of the north.

"Only united can we hope to engage the dragon and his army of frost giants and countless evil minions in a bloody war that will turn the northern snows red with blood and defeat his evil tyranny." Slowly, the shade of Omar Giantslayer began to fade, and with him did Urgan's consciousness fade as well.

The following morning, Urgan woke to the scent of boiling coffee and warm gruel simmering over a crackling fire. The sky was grey and overcast and a slight breeze blew from the west warming the plains. Around him, already eating were his four companions.

"Look comrades," laughed Uther boldly, "Mighty Urgan wakes from his slumber!"

"Urgan, you sleep like an infant, dead to the world," said Gunnar. "For true, we feared that you were under some strange enchantment, for ye tossed and turned all night long but woke naught."

Frowning at their jests, Urgan rose from his pallet and joined the men around the fire. Dillwyn handed him a warm bowl of gruel and smiled. He sat down and ate quietly for a few moments ere he spoke.

"A strange enchantment," he said? "Perhaps so. Last night I had a dream. Gunner, Luther, Uther . . . I was spirited to the Hall of the Slain and took council with thy brother, Omar Giantslayer."

The three brothers looked at the youth in amazement, yet Dillwyn ignored all and kept to his bowl, greedily. The wind whistled over the tundra and a raven cawed in the distance.

Urgan then turned to the dwarf and spoke to him thus:

"Dillwyn," he asked, "have ye ever been to Covensted, in the far south?"

A white pall washed over the dwarf's aged face when he heard the name of that accursed village of black witches. With much effort, he swallowed his mouthful and tried hard to suppress his superstitious fears. He could tell that the three brothers had never heard of that village before and he wondered by what dark sorcery Urgan had come to know its name.

"Nay," answered the dwarf, "but I have heard of that evil place, and I do know where it lies. Why do ye ask?"

"Covensted may be peopled by dark sorcerers, but the man I seek is not evil. We four have never been away from our frozen world, but ye are well traveled in your adventures. We must needs a good guide if we are to embark on the quest Omar has charged me."

"What says you," asked Gunnar? "We are on our way thither back to Heidmar. Why speak ye of southern quests given by some shade in a dream. And how can ye be certain if it was our brother Omar that has charged ye? Perhaps this is yet another trickery of evil sorcery." Luther and Uther likewise voiced their concern in the matter, but Urgan quieted them both with a lifted hand.

"Omar it was," he said, "this much I know. He revealed much to me as repayment for erecting the blood stave in his honor, yet I need your help to fulfill my quest. If you will aid me naught, then so be it, I will ride south alone."

"Perhaps it would be better to embark on Urgan's quest rather than return to Heidmar empty handed without Halgi," said Dillwyn, jokingly, still trying to hide the fear in his stout heart. Whilst the dwarf was a fell warrior and feared no mortal enemy, sorcery was a different matter altogether, and he liked it naught.

"Halgr may be a mere husbandless wench now," he said, "but without Grimthor alive to curb her appetite for bloodletting I would fear her wrath if we return to Heidmar without her daughter in tow."

The three brothers laughed a hardy laugh but deep down they knew the dwarf was right. Halgr had received the title Manslayer many years ere she handfasted with Grimthor, and even after taking him to husband she retained the title whereas most other women of Heidmar assumed their mates namesake. Halgr was a strong woman and her wrath was measureless for she knew naught mercy nor compassion. Once she cut the blood eagle in the back of a man simply for insulting her father.

"So then, we ride south, to Covensted," asked Urgan.

"Let us not make haste," answered Uther. "First, we needs make a plan or two. Please, Urgan, tell us thy dream." The other four nodded in agreement and began to discuss the details of a possible plan.

First Urgan told them of his dream, in as much detail as he could remember. The three brothers informed Urgan and the dwarf that they had only brought enough food for themselves, and only for enough time to find Halgi and return to Heidmar. For a journey as long as what Urgan was proposing, would take them many days, perhaps a whole turning of the moon, or two. And then there was the problem of mounts. Whilst the three brother's warhorses could easily make the trip, Urgan and Dillwyn's snow beast could not be forced to leave their frozen world, for it would surely perish in the stifling heat of the south. Somehow, they would have to steal two more horses and release the snow beast back into the frozen wilds of their northern lands ere they cross into the southern reaches of the world.

Dillwyn, being the only one of the group to have ever

adventured outside of the Northern Territories, informed them that the journey to Covensted would cover at least one hundred leagues, one way. They would have to travel around the un-named mountains and across many rivers, through the vast frozen plains of the northern tundra, until finally leaving the northern territories and entering the Phaedron Wood. After passing through the Phaedron Wood, he then told them that they would then find themselves at the threshold of the Ymir Mountains and would need to find the Balor Pass in order to successfully cross over that seemingly impassable wall of granite. If the Balor Pass could be found, and successfully negotiated, they would then enter into Darkwood, a vast stretch of densely canopied forest believed to be inhabited by savage beasts created by the witches of Covensted. Dillwyn then told them that the Phaedron trade route was the only safe passage that cut through that expanse of Phantasodyssean wilderness. But due to the expense of that toll road, he advised it best if they bypassed it and tried their luck through the wood itself, since northern barbarians carried no coin but rather took what they needed from the bounty of the land. In any case, he told them, the trade route was routinely traveled by Phaedron troops and their northern appearance would raise much suspicion. Their quest would be for naught if they were captured and left to rot in some Phaedron dungeon. Traveling due south through Darkwood, he told them, they would soon pick up a tributary of the mighty River Agu and could easily follow it eastward all the way to Covensted.

Finally, the dwarf ceased talking and reclined back, with a frown. The others sat quiet for some time absorbing all Dillwyn had said. Urgan, glancing at his stout friend and noticing some perturbation on the dwarf's grim face, he asked:

"What is it, Dillwyn? Do ye fear the sorcery of Covensted and the outcome of our quest?"

"Ye know quite well young Urgan that I am no friend of magic, but that is not what ails me."

"Well then, what is it," asked the brothers in unison.

The dwarf looked about with a gruff, then growled.

"It seems that sometime during the battle, or on the trail thereafter, I have lost my tobacco pouch and pipe. Yuck!" Great laughter erupted from around the campfire and the heavy mood quickly lightened. Soon the five were boasting of past glorious battles and battles not yet fought. After a time, they quenched the fire, rounded up their mounts, and rode off south toward their destiny.

Thus ends the Eleventh Chapter of Book One

TWELVE

A Thief in the Dark

A few hours ere daybreak, Tulwryn woke from his slumber and dressed. Looking about the cave, he saw naught; it was still entombed in pitch darkness and he shuddered at the thought of leaving Halgi there unattended. Reaching for his sword, he paused, a million scenarios running through his brain. Finally, he decided to leave the Bloodsword and take his trusted hand axe. "This mission, he whispered silently under his breath, "needs naught reckless heroics but stealth."

Whilst Halgi still slept, he stole away from their cave and located a Gerdmorian camp a mere few hundred paces downwind of their cave, on the far side of the gorge.

Outside the cave, still under the cover of night, only a few hours ere first light, Tulwryn smelled the scents of charred wood and burnt human flesh, evidence of the massive carnage from the battle earlier that eve. Silently, on cat feet did he creep into the enemy camp.

The walls of the gorge were exceedingly steep, and even if there were a bright moon this night it would shed no light into the deep crag where the Gerdmorians slept. Only shadow haunted mystery lurked in these desolate northern hills, and Tulwryn was among them.

On hands and knees Tulwryn crept, groping through the burnt underbrush as silently as a slithering serpent, hoping to attract no unwanted attention. He crawled past a corral of sleeping snow beasts. The animals stirred slightly, but woke naught. With a gleam in his eye, Tulwryn espied two Gerdmorian sentries posted at watch. One man, standing with his back against a tree, was clearly asleep at his post, and Tulwryn chose him as his first target. The other sentry, an arrow's shot downwind from the first man, seemed to be awake and so he realized that much care would be needed in dispatching him quickly and quietly ere he could sound the alarm and bring the entire wrath of Gerdmor down upon him.

Without a sound, Tulwryn slithered up close near the sleeping guard. Slowly he removed his weapon from his belt and within a blink of an eye he struck with the speed of an angry tiger. With a mighty blow from his hand axe he clove the man's head in twain betwixt the eyebrows and clean down through his chin to lodge the blade deep in the meaty portion of the dead man's collarbone. The man died without uttering a word, dead ere he knew he was dead.

Tulwryn caught the body as it crumbled lifeless to the ground. Gently he laid the corpse on the blooded dirt and crept away silently toward the other sentry. On quiet cat paws he crept to his prey, silent, like a ghost. Then, with the speed of a striking cobra, he dispatched the second Gerdmorian in the like manner of the first.

With both sentries removed, Tulwryn made his way unhindered through the sleeping camp. Like a dark angel of death, he walked amongst the sleeping warriors. Taking note of their numbers, his muscles tensed at the thought of combat and he was ready to extract his vengeance at a moments notice.

Finally, and after some time, he saw the quartermaster's tent. Off to the east the sky was turning from a dark black to a hazy blue and Tulwryn knew that dawn was near. He must needs enter the tent and be off with his bootie ere sunup, he realized, lest he be caught in the midst of the Gerdmor camp, alone and without his sword.

Noiselessly, he entered the quartermaster's tent. There he quickly slayed the quartermaster, stole a few day's supply of food, stuffed the food into a large canvas bag, and snuck back out of camp as silently as he entered. With a smile etched across his darkly scared face, Tulwryn Bloodsword, warrior of Heidmar, quickly hiked back to his hidden cave.

Halgi woke from her slumber and was angered at finding herself alone. She hastily dressed in the darkness of the cave and was strapping on her sword when Tulwryn finally entered. In the blink of an eye, she spun, her sword hissing from its scabbard and leveled at the intruder in the dark.

"Who goes there," she said.

"'Tis I."

At once, Halgi recognized Tulwryn's deep baritone voice and lowered her guard, returning her blade to its sheath.

"Where didst thou go," she asked, her tone clearly informing him of her moody disposition.

"We needed food for our long journey, so I went and got some." He tossed the large bag onto the ground before her. She knelt down and rummaged through the bag, removing a chunk of hard bread like a starving child. Taking a bite, she looked back at him glaringly.

"Ye crept into the Gerdmorian camp thither and stole this? Are ye mad? If you had been caught, you would have surely been slain!"

"Better to be slain by noble enemies than to die starving in the wilderness like a beast," he answered, jokingly.

"Noble," she scoffed, "the Gerdmorians are anything but noble."

"Enough," spoke Tulwryn, strapping on the Bloodsword, "we must needs make our escape from these mountains at once; we lose precious time, for the sun will be up in a matter of moments and soon the enemy camp will awaken and find those that I slayed in the night as payment for this grub. Come; let us be off quickly."

The two left the safety of their cave and hiked, unseen, through the gorge. The sun was poking its head through the overcast morn and sending shards of light deep into the crag. Climbing a high ledge on the canyon wall, Tulwryn and Halgi could see the entire floor of the gorge.

Tulwryn pointed out to Halgi the camp that he assaulted ere dawn and in time, they passed over five other Gerdmorian encampments. Halgi informed Tulwryn that at the far end of the gorge was a pass, and once through that pass, the trail descended to the frozen plains and meandered east out of the mountains.

A wily thought passed though Tulwryn's dark mind and he decided to attempt another theft. This time, he told Halgi, that he would sneak down and steal two Gerdmorian warhorses from the last Gerdmorian camp. Halgi shuddered at the thought of another daring maneuver and the possibility of failure.

"Ye have not to do this to impress me," she said, looking hard at the warrior. "Last night's love was well enough to ensnare my loyalty. Never will I bed another man, for ye are my one and only lord."

"I do this to impress ye naught," he answered, ruefully. "If we are to travel forth all the way to Rodmar, we need mounts. The distance is too far to trek afoot, and anyhow, time is on our side naught since your mother already amasses an army to march on Rodmar. We must make our way thither ere Heidmar engages them in battle. Stay hither and await my return," he said, and with that, he disappeared in a flash. Halgi, swearing oaths to her grim northern gods, sat waiting.

A little less than an hour later, Halgi was greeted to the thundering hooves of large Gerdmorian warhorses. "Quick," screamed Tulwryn, "jump aboard and ride like the wind for the dogs are close at our heels!"

Looking east, Halgi could see Tulwryn riding hard, and leading another horse in tow behind his own. He led the animals close to the cliff wall just below the ledge where she stood. Gracefully timing the leap, she jumped into the saddle of the horse trailing behind his.

Instantly he released her reins and she quickly caught them up. Although the theft had been successful, Tulwryn was spotted riding off from the camp and a chase had erupted. Spurring the animals onward, Tulwryn and Halgi rode hard under a barrage of missiles and did all they could do to dodge the many arrows, spears, and crossbow bolts that were being hurled at them from the angry Gerdmorians.

Ere they rode a league, Tulwryn's mount was shot from beneath him by a Gerdmorian crossbow bolt; he tumbled from the dying horse in a heap. Halgi circled around, and Tulwryn jumped up onto her steed and the two rode off like the wind.

As Tulwryn had predicted earlier, once free of the mountains, the Gerdmorians ceased the chase. Howls of rage and screamed oaths echoed through the pass behind them, and the two riders laughed at their escape.

On through the day, they rode, and due east. For many leagues, all the way to the shores of the frigid North Sea, for on the coast of that frozen sea lay the realm of Rodmar, the sworn enemy of Heidmar.

* * *

It was quiet in the tent of Halgr Manslayer. The entire enclosure was shrouded in a dusky blackness as still as a somber tomb, save for the soft orange glow of a single burning taper, all but extinguished. Soft warm wax gently poured from the dripping candle and spilled out over the holder onto the oaken table in the far corner of the tent. Halgr, almost as if in a daze, slowly dipped a finger in the soft wax and raised it to her eyes. Gazing at the clump of wax, quickly cooling and hardening on her finger, she was brought back to the present by a cough outside the flap of her tent. Pausing for a moment, then wiping her finger on her byrnie, she turned and walked to the other end of the tent, then seated herself on a scarlet cushion.

"Enter," she called out in a gruff tone.

A large Heidmarian warrior cautiously entered the tent. He was a big man, even for northern standards, and his hawk-like nose and strong square chin gave him an almost inhuman appearance. Long blazing red hair tumbled loosely over his broad shoulders and his long scarlet cape hung to the ground. A large Heidmarian broadsword was strapped to his thick waist yet he carried no shield for his left hand was missing. His closely set smoldering blue eyes blazed with the fierceness of a hungry lion, yet he spoke in a soft and revered tone.

"Lady Halgr, there is no word of the brothers and it has been more than four days since their departure. The council fears the worst and the people cry out for justice."

She nodded her head in silence, clearly turning over the options in her mind.

"The army grows anxious for bloodletting, I presume."

"Aye," answered the warrior. "And the council would have me urge ye to loose the army on Rodmar for the slaying of Grimthor the Strong, thy husband and our chieftain."

"I am chieftain now," she snorted with contempt.

"Aye, and I will follow ye faithfully to hell and back. Give me thy words and I will inform the council of your wishes, whatsoever they may be."

Halgr, thinking the worse, that Halgi her daughter, and the others were all dead, paused for a moment, thinking. Angered and outraged by the murder of her husband, the loss of her daughter, and the treachery extracted by the Volva she was as quick as any of her tribe to scream for justice, yet she was no general. She realized that even though she was capable of slaying men with ease, arranging battle lines and commanding men in war was another matter. Oh, how she wished Tulwryn were here to relieve her of this unwanted burden. Tulwryn, the stranger of the south, taken to the bosom of Heidmar only three snows prior, had become the favorite son of Grimthor, the strong warrior king that had no male heir. And now, with Grimthor slain and Tulwryn lost, what was to become of Heidmar. Under her breath, Halgr cursed the gods. Equally outraged was she at the fact that the council was heeding naught her orders but trying to force her hand to unleash the Heidmarian war machine ere she wished. For true, her own wrathful vengeance would be extracted and blood would flow, but in her own time; she was acting chieftain now and would bow naught to their pressures.

Finally, she turned to the fell warrior that waited patiently before her, and spoke:

"One more day we wait. If the brothers return naught ere the eve of the morrow, then give the command to assemble the army; we march east toward Rodmar the following morn. Ye have leave to go, General Tyr."

Bowing, the warrior turned and left the tent. Halgi slowly rose from her cushion and walked back over to the oak table. Moistening her fingers with her wet tongue, she pinched out the candle's fragile flame and the entire tent was consumed in darkness.

Thus ends the Twelfth Chapter of Book One

THIRTEEN

To Find a Wizard

Two days on the trail south and the weather turned drastically bad. In all of Gunnar's thirty-three years, he had never seen a storm so wicked and he readily agreed with the other four when they suggested that sorcery was the culprit. The day had started as any other, but ere noon they were besieged with low hanging clouds that poured torrents of frozen rain down upon them and pelted them with first sized hail. There was an extremely cold wind blowing fiercely from out of the north and the sun was all but completely blocked out by the thick overcast. Whilst the mailed warriors were protected from the relentless hail, their steeds took some damage and Dillwyn insisted they must needs find suitable cover ere the animals perish.

Cutting west, the men rode hard for a small stand of pine that Urgan espied through squinted eyes. For six hundred paces the animals thundered through the cold wet snow, as scores of whelps were raised on their heaving bodies by the jagged shards of hail assailing them. Luther's mount took a grave blow to its left shin and a deep laceration opened wide spilling thick red droplets onto the frozen ground. The animal whinnied in pain but continued on at a breakneck pace trying to outrun the falling menace.

Dillwyn and Urgan, riding astride their snow beast, were the first to reach the pines, followed by Gunnar, then Uther, and Luther bringing up the rear with his badly injured horse. Urgan and the dwarf quickly dismounted and the snow beast disappeared into the bush. They yelled for the brothers and aided them in hobbling the steeds under the boughs of a group of very large trees. Whilst the pines did very little to break the severe bite of the cold northerly wind nor keep them dry from the frigid rain their boughs did serve as a minor protection from the pelting hail and the panting animals knelt down in the snow and huddled together for warmth.

Uther and Urgan used their swords to hew large blocks of ice from the tundra whilst Gunnar and Dillwyn assisted them in building a makeshift shelter. Luther tended to the animals. Soon, the horses were secure, the shelter was built, and the five warriors were safe inside, away from the elements.

"That was the most damnable storm I have ever experienced," said Dillwyn. "Surely there is evil in the air this day."

"Luther, is your steed alright? I saw that he took a nasty blow to the shin," Gunnar asked, tightly pulling his great cloak about himself.

The big man nodded.

"He shall live. The cut was long and deep, but he has seen worse in combat."

"Aye," commented Gunnar, "methinks I agree with Dillwyn. For true, this storm must be some sort of enchantment from evil. Never have I seen one so violent, nor whip up so fast without warning. Do ye think that some evil attempts to bar our way south?"

"'Tis possible, I would guess," said Dillwyn. "The Volva was surely behind the treachery that slayed master Omar, and methinks that the elemental wizardry of controlling the airs and rains is beyond her naught."

"If this be true, Dillwyn," said Luther, "then what kind of demon do we fight? Surely she can know naught that we ride south for Covensted rather than north for Tulwryn and Halgi."

"Perhaps we fight not one demon, Luther, but a legion," answered Urgan. The four looked at him in amazement, for the tone in his voice was mature and serious.

"That grim thought never crossed my mind ere now," said

Dillwyn to Urgan. "It could be that the Volva is an emissary of evil employed by an even greater evil. But what that may be, I can say naught."

Luther had removed his maile shirt and was nursing small bruises on his arms sustained in the hailstorm whilst Gunnar rummaged through a large knapsack of food.

"We might as well have some grub if we are to wait out this storm," he said, as he distributed some loaves of hard bread and even harder cheese.

The men then discussed further plans and Dillwyn told them tales of his adventures with Tulwryn whilst they ate their sparse meal. Many seasons, he told them, he and Tulwryn spent in the Ymir Mountains, south of the great Phaedron Wood, slaying bandits and outlaws, and living under the rule of no man, king, or chieftain. There was much boasting and back patting but soon the talk died down and their thoughts turned back to the fell evil that gripped their world and their faces became grim.

"I shall go thither and check on the animals," said Luther, donning his maile shirt and woolen cloak. The others nodded as he wrapped the cloak about himself and left the shelter.

"There are many free ranging steeds south of the Northern Territories. Once we pass into the Phaedron Wood it should be no problem to capture a few," Dillwyn said, "but we should turn the snow beast out ere we cross into the south. I can walk many leagues afoot . . ."

"Nonsense," answered Uther. "Ye can ride with me on my mount till we snag ye a stallion."

"And Urgan can ride with me," said Gunnar, with a smile. Urgan and Dillwyn smiled at the brothers and finished their meal in silence. Luther returned from checking the horses and soon all bedded down for the eve. No sentry was posted due to the severity of the storm, for the warriors comprised no enemy would be afoot this night. Within moments, all five, exhausted but with full bellies, were fast asleep.

Sometime during the night the storm's wrath ceased and the five were greeted the following morning to a pleasant day. The wind was dry and crisp, birds were singing, and there was a strange freshness in air. Dillwyn and Urgan looked for their snow beast but he was nowhere to be found. It seemed that the creature had finally abandoned them and returned to the wild.

A few hours after sunup the horses were saddled and the warriors were once again off and riding, Dillwyn sharing Uther's steed and Urgan riding along with Gunnar. Luther's mount, with its shin bandaged, heaved and strained through the deep snow but kept his pace up with the others proving to the superiority of Heidmarian warhorses; their physical strength legendary, their spirits unbreakable.

For ten leagues, with the frozen river to the east of them, the warriors rode. The deep snow had abated and turned to tundra, and then to bare ground. The further south they traveled the warmer the day became and soon the frozen river began to break up. The five searched for a suitable crossing point whereas to ford the river and in a short time they were riding hard with the mighty river behind them. Stretched out before them were the gently descending slopes of the vast northern steppes and twenty-five leagues further was another barrier of water that would need be crossed, the Basalt River.

Other than the intense storm three days earlier, the journey south had been a relatively uneventful one. Luther's horse was all but healed and the men were in good cheer at the prospect of a successful adventure. The days became longer the further south they rode, and warmer.

Riding south from the northern steppes, the four barbarians looked to Dillwyn with horror and excitement. "What is that," proclaimed Gunnar.

"My friends," answered Dillwyn, "behold the Phaedron Wood, the great forest of the city-state of Phaedron and under the glove of the High Elder, the crowned King of the known world."

The four barbarians shuddered in awe at the majesty of the forest. A frightful barrier the woods made, such in contrast with the flatness of their northern world, for the steppes abruptly ended at a wall of towering green that stretched as far as the eye could see. From horizon to horizon, the forest spread it massive arms, deep and luscious and green. The trees were taller than any in the frozen north, and quite different. Nowhere could be seen the needled pines or cedars or spruces that were so common to the barbaric warriors, for the trees before them were massive, with great outstretched limbs larger than the torso of a man and with broad leaves as big as one's open palm. The horses were slowed to a canter and the warriors entered the wood reluctantly, and with great caution. Moments later, as they entered the dark foreboding embrace of the wood's thick eaves the daylight winked out as they left their bright and shining lands behind.

The canopy overhead was thick, but not so much as to block out all sunlight. There was a filtering of rays through the branches and countless dust motes and insects could be seen floating in the haze. A thick scent of decay permeated the air and the northerners, not familiar with southern forests, held their noses at the stench. The deeper they traveled, the more humid the day became, and the northern warriors quickly begin to shed their furs due to the warmth that they were not accustomed. The dwarf simply smiled to himself as he seen the discomfort and uncertainty of his companions. Ere long, he realized, they would get used to these conditions, for they were a hardy breed and quickly adapted to many adverse circumstances.

For thirty leagues, they meandered through the thick underbrush of the Phaedron Wood. Their pace was slowed to a crawl, yet still they lost no heart and trudged onward. The second day after entering the great forest, the group espied a pack of wild horses foraging on some fresh shoots in a clearing and made haste to capture two of them. That scene became quite humorous, as Phaedronian horses, wild or domestic, prove to we a wily lot, and that tale could very well have been a saga in itself. In time though, the warriors had managed to lay hands on two very healthy specimens and ere long the five were once again riding south on their quest to Covensted, each man seated on his own steed.

With the majority of the Phaedron Wood to their rear, the party finally came upon the rugged and majestic Ymir Mountains, tall, cold, and grim. Dillwyn slowed the warriors to a halt. He had them dismount and creep behind some giant boulders whereas they would be well concealed yet have full advantage of surveying the ravine below. The dwarf then pointed out the Phaedron trade route downwind and just an arrow's shot away.

"Yonder road cuts through the very heart of the Phaedron Wood," he said, "coming all the way from the walled city itself, making its way through the Ymir Mountains at the Balor Pass, and goes all the way to Nuvia and beyond."

The road was surprisingly plain for such a grandiose reputation, for this portion of it was merely a wide dirt path without pavement or shoulder. It wound its way through leagues upon leagues of forests, deserts, and plains, over rivers and through villages and towns and cities throughout the whole of Phantasodyssea. In legend, it was said to be paved with gold and silver, yet in this desolate spot it was simply a muddy trail slithering though a steaming wood permeated with the overwhelming scent of forest rot.

"We seek naught to travel the toll road," Dillwyn quietly whispered. "We shall climb to higher ground, up yonder on that high ravine and follow the trail to the pass. That way we shant draw unwanted attention." The others nodded.

A gentle, misting rain began to fall and he then motioned them that their spying was finished and so they followed him back to the horses. Slowly, they climbed the steep face of the ravine all the way to the summit and continued to ride its crest, following the toll road below.

It took the better part of the afternoon to reach the Balor Pass. Dillwyn then suggested that they hold up in the high country until the sun disappeared behind the peaks, since it would be easier for them to sneak past the toll guard's booth after sundown.

The rain had subsided but the wind was fierce and it whipped over the jagged peaks. Even though they were far to the south where the sun stayed long in the heavens and burnt men's flesh a ruddy crimson, the air was cold and bitter. The Ymir Mountains were exceedingly high, a lasting remnant of the ancient Ice Times and after sunset the five warriors from Heidmar retrieved their fur and woolen cloaks from their saddlebags and donned their northern attire once again.

Everything went as Dillwyn had planned. After the sun had sunk low behind the peaks of the mountains and blanked them in darkness, the five crept past the toll guard's booth, which was situated in the center of the Phaedron trade route at the mouth of the Balor Pass. And, leaving the mountains behind them, they entered Darkwood.

There was no moon this night, yet the darkness revealed a myriad of stars poking through the black firmament. Urgan took a deep breath and absorbed the excitement of his first adventure away from his frozen home. He glanced up at the shining heavens and thought it odd to see no northern lights, just countless pinpricks of light beaming through the black curtain of eternity. Had the party descended from the mountains into Darkwood during the daylight hours they would have witnessed that vast wood stretching forth from the foothills in a seemingly endless web of horror, where the limbs and branches and boughs of those accursed trees interlock with ferocious seething, waiting to lash out and imprison the unsuspecting traveler. But this night no fear was felt, for no horror was seen, yet as the warriors entered the forest they all sensed an ethereal consciousness that permeated the atmosphere around them; in Darkwood, death was more often heard ere it was seen.

Dillwyn commanded that swords be unsheathed. At once the hiss of blades leaping from their scabbards filled the night air as hungry serpents searching for prey and eager to strike. Urgan looked up at the night sky again but a cold hand gripped his heart as the entire sky was all but blotted out under the dense canopy of Darkwood.

"Surely this place is the gateway to Odhinn's seven hells," commented Luther, "for I can see naught my own horse that I sit upon."

"For true, Luther," answered Urgan, "this darkness appears to be more than it seems, for it gives the impression that it devours light."

"Aye," spoke the dwarf, "there are many that say the witches of Covensted birthed magical beasts and monsters to roam the reaches of Darkwood ere the coming of civilized men, yet others believe that the wood itself is the most malevolent spawn of all, alive and constantly searching out prey. But on the contrary, I highly doubt whether your fine Odhinn would tarry in a place such as this, for he loves the cold of the north. Ride on comrades, yet keep a keen eye foreword and loose not the grip on your hilt!"

Tension was high as they trekked a bit to the east and left the Phaedron trade route behind them. A few leagues later, they resumed their course due south, and fifteen leagues further, made their way to the River Agu. They then follow the river east all the way to Covensted. Many strange sounds did they hear, and more than naught the hair was prickled on the nape of their necks, yet the gods, or luck, was with them, for they saw no evil beasts and were molested naught.

A silver sliver of a crescent shone its face high in the heavens on a dark and cloudless night and the five travelers from Heidmar entered the second moon of winter, though they knew it naught for they journeyed under the eaves of Darkwood and its roof was dense and opaque. A wolf bayed in the distance and the haunting cries of ravens and the hooting of owls filled their imagination with horror, yet the warriors steeled themselves and rode on, but cautiously.

Suddenly, and without warning, the thick tangle of undergrowth parted and the men came upon a clearing. Reining their steeds to a halt, the group paused momentarily to survey the village that sprang up before them. Swords were sheathed and the five entered the town, warily.

Covensted was a village of witches located on the eastern border of Darkwood. No roads lead thither and visitors have long been discouraged from travel within its magical boundaries.

The town that stood before them was an assault on the eye and mind and imagination of mortal man. Houses and buildings of assorted sizes and shapes sprouted from seemingly impossible foundations, their walls and roofs and awnings, many of strange hues and angles, looked as if to defy the very science of architecture. Dillwyn, the dwarf from Carthus, was more appalled than the others, since he hailed from a city and a people that took pride in building and craftsmanship, whilst the men from Heidmar, at home in their hide tents, were simply amazed at the strange geometric shapes and myriad of colors that played havoc on their primitive minds.

Cautiously, they cantered though the winding dirt paths that meandered in and out amongst the strange dwellings. Curiously, thought Dillwyn, there was no living person to be seen. It was if the entire village was deserted, although tiny wisps of smoke from chimneys and the pleasant scent of wood burning on the heath told him otherwise.

"How are we to know for certain where this Mimir lives," asked Gunnar, apparently thinking aloud, not directing his question to anyone in particular.

"If the wizard, indeed, still lives," answered Luther, to his brother's question.

"Mimir indeed lives," answered an unfamiliar voice, and the warriors reined their mounts to a halt and spun their heads around frantically seeking the one who spoke thus. With a start, the men looked upon a small child of no more than ten years old, yet there was a fire of intelligence in his young eyes.

"What says ye," asked Dillwyn, looking down on the lad from his saddle.

"You seek Mimir? He lives thither, around the bend and at the end of this trail, in a small stone cottage the hue of dried blood," said the boy.

The dwarf nodded his thanks to the child and spurred his horse forward, the others followed. Urgan wondered why a child so young was allowed to wander the streets of such a town so late in the eve, and with that thought, he turned to take another look at the child behind him but to his surprise the boy was nowhere to be seen. He had vanished as quickly as he had appeared.

The five rode on down the trail, around the bend and even further onward, until the path ended at the decaying porch of a small brown dwelling, just as the child had said. All remained in their saddles but Urgan. "This is my destiny," said the youth, "I shall summon this sorcerer. Wait hither."

Urgan, with long strides on thick loins, mounted the porch and boldly rapped on the wooden door. It creaked open and a tall figure, darkly clad in a course robe emerged.

"I have been waiting for ye, mine friend, please enter," said the wizard to Urgan. And with a long finger, he motioned for Urgan's companions to enter as well.

The men dismounted and followed Urgan inside the dwelling. Once inside, the five shielded their faces from the bright candlelight, allowing their eyes time to adjust from the inky darkness that they had grown accustomed to since entering Darkwood five days prior.

Amazingly, the interior of the cottage was immense compared to its external appearance, and the wizard could sense their wonder.

"In Covensted, dear friends, things are naught always what they seem," he said with a chuckle.

It was apparent that the old wizard found these five warriors from the north quite entertaining in their naive and primitive way. Dillwyn could sense that the old man was quite able to handle himself and he knew that the wizard feared them naught, which was strange since the dwarf had grown accustomed to instilling fear in men, especially when he rode in the company of grim warriors.

The group was led down a long narrow hall to a quaint oval room with a warm hearth situated on its far wall. The room was littered with candles, wooden stools, and low oaken tables. Over the fire hung an iron pot, which was emitting the fragrance of a tasty stew and the five immediately remembered their stomachs, which were empty and had began to growl.

"Please friends, sit and sup with me as we discuss our plans," said the old wizard as he sat on a stool near the fire.

"How did ye know we were coming," asked Urgan.

Mimir began filling bowls and handing them to the men. When all were seated with a warm bowl of piping stew before them, he then turned to address Urgan's question.

"I am Mimir, the oldest he-witch in Covensted. I am older beyond the imagination of mortal men, and the keeper of the Dragon Shield. Many things do I know, many things." He paused, looked around at the five fell warriors seated about him, and drew a long and raspy breath akin to the hiss of a serpent.

"Long ago," he said, "ere the coming of men to this world, a race of dragons and giants walked the face of the land. Evil and terrible these creatures were, yet they were powerful beyond comprehension. Where they were spawned from, none can know, but their appetite for destruction and cruelty was legion. The gods sprinkled them with magic thus causing them to fall into a deep slumber, but slay them they did naught, for 'tis not the will of the gods to slay their own creation, whether they be good or evil. Time passed and the centuries wore on, and with it, so did legends begin to appear amongst the lore of men. Amongst such legends was the saga of the Bloodsword and the Dragon Shield. A grim prophecy that was, so old and forbidden that many have heard it naught. Those that do know of the legend know naught whence it began, nor whence from it came. Only I, Mimir, the Keeper of the Dragon Shield, knows the truth, yet reveal it, I will naught, for to do so would be a grave injustice to your mortal minds."

Urgan looked deep into the folds of the hood that hung dark and low over the wizard's head shielding his face from the five. Never had they been in the presence of such a man, if indeed this wizard was a man of mortal flesh. Grim were the Wizard's words, but they were spoken with a serene kindness and displayed no malice and the warriors were at ease and feared naught.

"So tell me, Mimir," spoke Urgan, "what am I to do? How shall I fulfill mine destiny?"

"That is easy, my boy, that is easy."

Standing, the old wizard languidly walked to a closet at the far end of the room and opened the door. He disappeared for a moment and then re-emerged holding a large circular shield of odd construction. Never before had any of the men seen such a fascinating piece of work. The shield was as wide as a man and embossed around the edges with a metal that shone like gilded steel, yet its face was a profound scarlet, deeply etched in the likeness of the scales of a fish.

"Behold my dear friends, the Dragon Shield," said the wizard as he turned to Urgan. "Simply reunite this shield with the Bloodsword and thy destiny is complete."

"That sounds simple enough, yet in mine experiences, often times the simplest plan turns out to be the most dangerous. What is this ruddy metal," asked Urgan, pointing to the scarlet face of the shield.

"That is no metal," laughed the old man, "that is the tanned and stretched hide of Zakkabod, a dragon of antiquity slain by Iyengar the Strong eons ago. A mighty warrior was he, and a dispatcher of vile beasts, and valiant. Iyengar was the sole heir to the Throne of Machthorr, and crown prince of the House of Yenengrad. Yet some knew him as Panyano-mortu or Suffering Death in the common tongue, for his wrath was great and his strength unmatched in all the world. But his dearest comrades guarded his true name, for he was Garthor, the king's son and that name carried a heavy price. Some say that fell warrior was of the siring line of the Bloodsword even ere the Bloodsword was prophesied. Ah, the legends and myths of mortal men . . ."

The five sat quiet for some time, consuming their meal and thinking about all that Mimir had revealed unto them. In due time, the wizard stood and bade them follow, for his work was done. He showed them back down the long narrow hall and out through the front door. Urgan and the others bid the old man farewell and thanked him deeply for his help ere they turned and left the cottage. The dwarf was the last to leave when he heard the wizard speak.

"Oh, Dillwyn," spoke the old man.

Startled, the dwarf spun around and looked at the tall wizard standing before him.

"I want you to have this; to replace the one you lost," he said with a smile and a gleam in his eye, as he handed the old dwarf a small tobacco pouch and a long stemmed smoking pipe. Dillwyn's eyes perked up like a child on Yule morning. He knew naught how Mimir knew that he had lost his pipe, but it mattered little, and so he bowed his head and thanked the wizard profusely.

Grinning, the old wizard patted the dwarf on his stout head as if he were a mere child rather than a fell warrior seasoned in the art of spilling blood.

"We old timers must stick together," Mimir said, laughing. "Now be off, your companions must needs your strong hands in the coming days, for there is bloody battles in your future, but much glory as well. Make haste my friend!"

Dillwyn left the house, mounted his ride, and trotted off after the others down the trail, heading back through the pitch blackness of Darkwood, towards the north. Smiling, he remembered a poem he penned in his youth and began humming its melody softly to himself.

"Under a tree I sat sitting, dreaming of many things.
Of coffee on the fire and mine heart's desire,
had I some leaf 'twould be fitting,
whilst I sat 'neath this tree sitting,
dreaming of pipeweed and blowing smoke rings."

Thus ends the Thirteenth Chapter of Book One

FOURTEEN

Of Blood and Snow

Tulwryn and Halgi, on one horse, and with only one bag of food betwixt them, rode towards Rodmar. On through the day they rode, and due east. For many leagues and over many mountains and across the barren northern plains, all the way to the shores of the frigid North Sea, for on the coast of that frozen sea lay the realm of Rodmar, the sworn enemy of Heidmar.

'Twas their quest, or Tulwryn's, to petition the elders of Rodmar and hold council with them to find where their heart sat concerning the slaying of Grimthor the Strong. Deep in his heart, Tulwryn believed naught that the Rodmarians were responsible for the heinous act. The reason was simple; a battle-axe is no weapon for an assassin, yet a Rodmarian battle-axe had been left in the chieftain's tent. He realized that there was no love betwixt Rodmar and Heidmar, the reasons he knew naught but he speculated it reached far back into antiquity, when both clans were young and spawned from the same blood. Even so, he was the enemy, representing the entire Heidmarian nation and their dead chieftain, and the meeting would naught be without its risks.

Although the sun was high in the firmament a great misting rain fell gently over the tundra and a chill was in the air. Tulwryn draped his great cloak about himself and the girl, and with his arms surrounded Halgi, seated afore him in the saddle, and protected her from the chilling drizzle. Although she was a fierce Heidmarian warrior, in the safety of his arms she became all woman. They had been riding nonstop for better than a day and a half and Halgi swooned in and out of a trancelike slumber. She lustily remembered the night of love she and Tulwryn had spent in the cave; she relived the soft passions of the fell warrior over and over again, and smiled to herself in ecstatic joy, for she had never known any love but his. Likewise, Tulwryn's mind toyed with his emotions as well, although he was plagued with visions from his haunting past and was torn betwixt the new feelings that he had for Halgi.

He shook his head and a spray of water showered Halgi's rugged beauty, hidden beneath his dark cloak. Straining hard, he tried to banish the thoughts of love from his tormented mind. Women and love, he told himself, was not in the keeping of a grim warrior, and that was what he had become, a grim warrior that bathed daily in blood and carnage. No longer was he the farmer from Nuvia. That life was over, for Tulwryn the farmer was buried with his sons up on that high Nuvian pasture so long ago. Now he was a warrior and had no time for a wife, or love. But yet, Halgi's lust for life, her rugged beauty, and her indomitable spirit spoke to him intimately; more than any other woman in his life, he trusted her, and this from a man that came to trust no one.

The two rode on throughout the day. The rain ceased after noon and the sun showed its face from time to time from behind the low hanging grey clouds, heavy with snow. A few hours after the noon of the day, they came upon a small outcropping of rock; a circle of large granite boulders littered the area and Tulwryn suggested that they make camp ere nightfall. Halgi agreed.

They dismounted and turned their horse out to graze on whatever sparse tundra it could find whilst they began work at pitching a camp. Tulwryn scouted the area for suitable firewood, all the while keeping a keen eye out for Rodmarian scouts, which he felt might be in the area since they were getting closer to the boundaries of Rodmar. Halgi gathered their meager supplies and began working at clearing an area to build a small cooking fire. Tulwryn returned after a time and within minutes they were warmed by a crackling flame, the scent of cedar and ash and juniper lingering on the frozen air.

The sun sank low on the horizon and off in the distance a wolf bayed for its mate. Across the darkening sky, a large eagle soared and dipped on frozen arctic thermals and then disappeared over the crest of distant mountains far to the north. There was tension in the air as the two warriors sat eyeing each other opposite the fire. Halgi looked deep into Tulwryn's dark eyes and pondered the burden he carried, silently wishing she could relieve his pain; Tulwryn gazed back, his mind a void, not wanting to contemplate the grim future of his tribe, or his possible future with the female he sat looking at.

"What thinks ye," Halgi asked, handing Tulwryn a loaf of hard bread. Taking the bread, he spoke thus:

"I think naught but of the death of thy father and the outcome of this mission. Why?"

"I, myself, have been wondering such things," she answered. "Perhaps 'tis not proper to ask thus, but what of our handfasting? Has such a though crossed your mind?"

Tulwryn thought he heard an owl hoot off in the distance and his mind reeled with the words that had just come from Halgi's lips. The fire caused shadows to dance about the stone circle and Halgi's face shone like a Wight. He squinted his eyes hard trying to push out the words from his mind, yet he wondered why he fought his feelings so hard.

"Truly, the night was wonderful, that we shared in yonder cave, but a future is uncertain for us. Perhaps we were fatigued from the battle and needed comfort rather than love, for how can a grim warrior be a passionate lover if naught for the fatigue of battle?"

"Ye claim to be concerned for Heidmar, and worry of its fate, yet you love me naught? Tulwryn, I am Heidmar! To love Heidmar is to love me, for I am heir to Grimthor the Strong and the only daughter of Halgr Manslayer. If we were to handfast, my mother would eagerly step down from father's office and you could assume the position of Heidmar's chieftain. Ye could lead the clan, our clan, to victory and I will fight by your side all the days of my life!"

"Have ye naught seen enough bloodshed for one lifetime, woman? We travel east not for vengeance but to prevent a war."

Tulwryn spoke the words with contempt in his voice. The thought of marriage ran through his mind and it angered him. The position of chieftain he was interested naught, nor did he wish to be hobbled like a slave to a woman, even though he had feelings for her, feelings that he believed had died with Durayn.

"So ye laid with me, yet you love me naught? And now we travel to the home of my father's killer and ye have naught fury in your heart. Tulwryn, you confuse me."

"Halgi, you confuse yourself. I am a warrior of Heidmar, but am not of blood kin to your tribe. No one would follow me if I assumed the position ye offer, whether we were handfasted or naught. Perhaps in another time or place things would be different, but here, there are complications."

There was a long silence and the two finished their dinner and sat long into the night, listening to crackling flames and the cries of timber wolves. After a while, Halgi fell into a deep slumber and Tulwryn kept a hawk-eye open for enemy scouts whilst his mind drifted to the night he spent in the cave with the daughter of Grimthor. He though of the future, of a possible future, then he thought no more for fatigue consumed him and he fell to sleep.

Through the realm of dreams Tulwryn walked, empty and alone; he waded through blooded fields of scarlet and crimson where warriors lay dead or dying, crying out in torment and gnashing their teeth, their bodies rent from the clash of combat. Then he was transported to a great hall under a high vaulted ceiling, and stood ere a throne, large and gilded. Upon that throne was no man, but a shadow of a man with a fell countenance that mirrored his own. The man was dressed in shining battle gear over which was draped a cape of royal purple of the deepest velvet that he had ever seen. Slowly, Tulwryn approached the man but he bowed naught, for pride overtook him, nor did he bow his head or lower his gaze.

"Tulwryn Bloodsword," came a fell voice from out of the ethers, "approach my throne, but with caution."

A wave of anxiety rushed over Tulwryn and he grasped quickly at the hilt of his sword but the sword was no more, and his anxiety turned swiftly to fear and his blood froze in his veins and his marrow was as ice. Ere he could mutter a word, the voice spoke again, and this time Tulwryn saw that it was the shadow that spoke, and he bent an ear to listen for he was vulnerable and without arms.

"Why seek the sword at thy hip, Tulwryn? Know ye naught that I am the Bloodsword? I am ye and thou are me! Come and hear thy destiny."

Cautiously, Tulwryn approached the throne, not understanding the cryptic message unfolding before him. He gazed into the flaming eyes of the shadow and became one with the shadow. No words were exchanged, but visions were given unto him and he saw the whole of his life in the flash of time. He saw himself a great warrior, a great king, yet he knew naught where his kingdom lay. He then saw his castle, made from the suffering of men and built on the bones of his foes, and he heard much lamentation. Then he saw himself, old and alone and fearing death, yet he walked with death all the days of his life. Finally, when the visions became too heavy to bear, he felt the weight of his burden crushing him and he fell to his knees. Reaching out before him, he grasped at the shadow's cape yet grasp it he did naught for the shadow disappeared and in his hand was the Bloodsword, and he collapsed, his mind heavy with guilt.

Although it was the second moon of winter and the night air was bitter cold, Tulwryn woke bathed in a thick lather of sweat. The fire had disappeared into coals and a dim orange glow was cast from the fire pit barely illuminating the small campsite. No moon shone this night yet shadows roamed his mind, shadows too large and real to be cast from the glowing coals of his tiny fire, shadows he knew could only come from the dark depths of his mind, or from sorcery.

Suddenly, the shadows thickened and he espied the evil Volva standing over the sleeping body of Halgi Mansbane, her dark robes billowing in the cold night air. The old witch was chanting sorceries and waving a long dagger of wrought silver wildly in the air over the sleeping girl's bare throat. In an instant, Halgi vanished in a wisp of scarlet smoke and Tulwryn, rubbing his eyes, struggled to his feet, not believing the scene unfolding before him. His body, bound as if by iron fetters with evil magic, responded slowly to his command as he lumbered toward the witch, every muscle straining for strength and speed. The Volva turned and saw her adversary; a dread frown ran across her already aged and lined face. Hissing like a wrathful serpent bent on death, the Volva quickly cast an enchantment and transformed herself into a seething demon of unimaginable size. Gripping the hilt of the Bloodsword, the spell was instantly broken and Tulwryn leaped up as fast as a striking tiger to do combat with the beast.

"What have ye done with the girl," he screamed as he unleashed all his fury, the crimson blade of his sword lashing out at the monster before him. The beast was exceptionally fast for all its bulk and time and again Tulwryn's blade found naught flesh nor bone.

Slashing madly, the warrior fought in a crazed frenzy, his strength empowered by anger and lust. The blade shown in the night like a great red comet jetting through the black curtain of night, sending out arcs of angry fire in all directions. Tulwryn seen the supernatural attack, but slowed not his own, for he was caught up in the visions of the Bloodsword and he was focused on vengeance.

The beast dodged and parried, but the dancing fire from the sword surrounded it and finally its keen edge found flesh. A shrill scream filled Tulwryn's ears and curdled his blood. Never in all his days of combat had he heard the sound of such suffering, and he cringed at the thought of the evil that surged through his veins at the moment of the kill.

The sword penetrated the chest of the monster to the hilt and two feet of its crimson blade protruded from between the demon's shoulder blades. The creature writhed in agony as the Bloodsword's venom coursed through its body, its form spitted on the steel shaft of death the grim warrior held in his hand.

Suddenly, Tulwryn cried out in horror for the beast suddenly disappeared and Tulwryn found himself gazing into the dead eyes of Halgi Mansbane impaled on the bloody end of his sword, and the seething sounds of combat were swallowed by the darkness.

Unexpectedly, a hideous laugh rolled out over the plains and shattered the silence of the night. Wrenching his blade from his dead companion's body, Tulwryn spun around to face the direction of the laugh. Standing before him was the Volva, grinning a great toothless grin. In a fit of rage Tulwryn screamed and charged yet ere he could smite the witch down she vanished in a haze. Tulwryn attacked the air repeatedly, his blade flashing in the night yet biting no corporeal thing. Exhausted, he fell to the ground shaking in rage!

* * *

Far to the north, the Volva appeared in the smoke over the dragon's fuming censer. In a grim voice, the witch told Darkoth of the slaying of Halgi Mansbane, yet the dread beast smiled naught for the Volva struck too late.

"Fool," hissed the dragon, "the warrior and the girl had loved throughout the night, and she was not a virgin at the time of her death, therefore the Bloodsword lost no power. Tulwryn has now grown even more wrathful and dangerous unto me due to this last bit of thy treachery. Ye struck too late and have failed me again, and your failure shall be your undoing!"

Utterly angered at the witch's incompetence, the dragon stood and unfurled his mighty wings, shrieking curses. The face in the fumes turned an ashen grey and vanished; many leagues to the east, in a dark cave nestled in the foothills of death, an old woman breathed her last breath and laid herself down to die, cold and alone. At her side was a Rodmarian battle-axe stained with the noble blood of Grimthor the Strong.

At that instant, Darkoth ordered his army of frost giants and evil minions to amass and he took up reigns and lead them himself in a desperate frenzy across the barren tundra to crush the northern kingdoms in a reckless march south.

Thus ends the Fourteenth Chapter of Book One

FIFTEEN

A Cairn of Stones

Far to the north, many leagues past the Frozen Lake, Darkoth sat brooding in his throne room as the aurora borealis swirled and shimmered, casting an eerie mood of melancholy over the vast frozen tundra of the dragon's icy realm. No eagles flew this day, nor ravens, and even the baying of wolves had been silenced as well, for an evil was stirring in Phantasodyssea under the dark midnight sun; an evil that had slept undisturbed since the beginning of time.

Angered at the Volva's failure, Darkoth quickly dispatched the witch and then summoned the whole of his dark strength and weaved an evil enchantment over the land. From the blackest regions of the netherworld, the dragon summoned an army of four hundred thousand preternatural troops. This immense war machine, peopled by the blood spawn of hungry minions of evil, loyal unto their own death, slowly grinded its way across the snow covered rocks of their dark frozen world. Ten thousand cruel frost giants, acting as the dragon's generals, commanded the insidious army on its trek southward, consuming everything in its path, and leaving a wide trail of carnage and death in their wake. Like a great seething ocean of blood, the army of Darkoth, the evil frost dragon, ebbed and flowed, choking the life from the land and staining the shimmering snows a bright crimson. There was much wailing and grinding of teeth as clan after clan fell to the power of the dragon, and the lamentation was deafening.

Fearing the prophecy of the Bloodsword, Darkoth planed his strategy well. His generals were ordered to attack and assimilate the weakest tribes first, then, after gaining much strength, march onward to the larger and more dangerous clans. The great siege engines of Darkoth rolled across the tundra, spilling blood and lighting the dark skies under the midnight sun with missiles of fire and brimstone. His horsemen thundered angrily over the wastes riding down all in their path, and his troops marched on and fought hand to hand slaying northlanders by the thousands, yet the dragon still was uncertain of victory, and there was fear in his cold and bitter heart.

Already Darkoth's army had absorbed seven of the ten northern tribes. Lodmar fell first and then Baedmar. The fighting was fierce when the Army of the Beast, as they were later to be named in the legends and sagas of the survivors, came to the shores of the Frozen Lake and engaged the clan of Nokkmar, for the Nokkmarian's were a mighty tribe, strong in heart and spirit. For nine days and nights the battle waged on, and even the women and children of Nokkmar took to arms and engaged the fell soldiers of death after a while; and they fought to the last man, for prophecy foretold that Nokkmar was not to be assimilated, but utterly annihilated.

Sethmar and Hoehnmar were the next to fall to the demon army, and then Rhinemar. Uttmar was the last of the clans north of the Frozen Lake to fall under the sword of the dragon. With the blood of those seven tribes, the Army of the Beast swelled in numbers and their strength was to be reckoned with, for they had become a force of nine hundred thousand, and still their lust for blood could not be appeased.

Darkoth realized that Grimthor the Strong had been slain, but the Bloodsword hailed from his tribe, the clan of Heidmar, and that warrior, he knew, was indeed a deadly adversary, yet where the Bloodsword was, he knew naught. The Volva had reported that Tulwryn had embarked on a mission north, a mission the dragon himself devised, which would bring the Bloodsword to his very doorstep where his evil magic was powerful and the balance of power could be caused to sway in his favor. He would have destroyed the wielder of the Bloodsword in one fell swoop, and taken the mighty relic as his own to wield mercilessly upon the people of Phantasodyssea, but such was not his fate. Vogelmir, under a Spell of Change weaved by the Volva, struck too soon and was himself slain in the attempt, and so foiled Darkoth's plan. Then, somehow, the three surviving warriors crossed paths with Halgi Mansbane, Grimthor's daughter, and she persuaded them to attempt a return to Heidmar, where the clan was amassing a great war machine to march on Rodmar for the slaying of her father. The warriors were themselves attacked by Gerdmorians on their trek home yet somehow escaped, although they were broken asunder and made their way out of the mountains on different paths.

A great frown crept across the dragon's aged face as he thought these grim thoughts, and foresaw the possibility of his own defeat. How could this be, he thought angrily to himself. How could a handful of mere humans put up such a keen resistance to his power? For true, he had slept his dark slumber too long. These savages had grown strong and fierce during his long sleep, for survival in the north was grim and uncertain and bred a hardiness uncommon in other lands. But even that was not enough to create such a resistance. There must be more, he grumbled darkly to himself, there must be more. The answer he knew could only be held in the Bloodsword, for prophecy foretold that wherever the Bloodsword was bore, so to with it went victory, and the powers of good and evil mattered naught, for the Bloodsword was beyond good and evil.

And Darkoth paced to and fro in his dimly lit throne room as shadows danced off the frozen crystal walls cast by burning tapers of human tallow. Tulwryn must be a man of men, he thought, for how else could he have mastered the Blade of Truth in such a short span of time. Legend had it that the Bloodsword, after its forging, would be as any other blade until it tasted blood for the first time. The first drink of human blood would awaken its true nature and so doing, the blade would create a magical bond with its owner. Even so, this bond could be broken if he who wields the blade were defeated early on, ere the bond be strengthened beyond breaking, for with each taste of blood the blade would grow in strength. But where was this slayer, Tulwryn, and how many lives had he already taken in a fortnight with the grim blade? The power of the blade was already clouding the dragon's mind and Tulwryn walk under a cloak of protection as old as the world itself.

The Volva had reported that her second Spell of Change had been successful and that Halgi Mansbane was indeed slain by the Bloodsword, but again, she had failed her ultimate task for the girl had been no virgin when she died and so the blade's power was weakened naught. After the slaying of Grimthor's daughter, Darkoth lost sight of Tulwryn. It was as if the Bloodsword had cast a cloak about him and veiled itself from the menacing eyes of the dragon.

In sheer anger the dragon roared.

"I shall utterly destroy this human they call Tulwryn Bloodsword, for no mere mortal shall defy me my office and destiny! And after the Bloodsword falls to my power, nothing shall stop me from crushing the whole of Phantasodyssea under my bloodstained talons!"

Suddenly there was a flash of light from behind the dragon and he whirled around in time to see a grim face materialize in the smoke that floated over the large brazier. Languidly, the dragon strode across the room and stopped within speaking distance of the magical item. In a voice that seemed to come from the bowels of hell, the face in the fumes spoke.

"Master, I am hither to do thy bidding. We have finally assimilated the last of the Uttmarians into our band and we now await new orders."

Darkoth smiled showing more fang than normal, and he waved a long taloned paw through the wisps of smoke as if to pat his puppet's head for a job well done.

"Good, very good," he said, "now turn the army to the east and march onward to Rodmar, for that clan will be the next to fall."

"As ye wish, my master," said the demon general, and then vanished from sight back into the darkness whence he came.

Darkoth grinned.

"'Tis almost complete," he said, under his rancid breath. "After Rodmar falls, then too shall Heidmar fall and mine destiny shall be made whole, for with the strength of the north behind me and with the power of the Bloodsword in my grasp none shall withstand my omnipotent rule!" The dragon then turned and strode proudly out of the throne room and onto his private balcony.

Darkoth paused and looked over the stone rail. He gazed from his lofty height down into the gorge that surrounded his fortified palace of ice and laughed. The terrible sound echoed off the cliffs and the animals and beasts of the forests shivered and were afraid; and even the land trembled in fear, for none could behold the laugh of a dragon and have naught the very marrow of their bones turn to ice. Turning his gaze from the shadows below to the darkly burning midnight sun high above, Darkoth stretched out his great leathern wings and leapt from the balcony. Silently, as a fell reminder of death, the great beast floated away into the night.

* * *

Tulwryn sighed a heavy sigh as he gazed at the modest cairn of stones that he had just erected over the body of Halgi Mansbane. His mind reeled in the recent events of his life and he wondered what evil cloud had settled over him with such a gripping stranglehold. Ever since that tragic day when his wife Durayn slayed his four young sons he had never known peace. Each day was worse than the previous, and his pain was silenced only when he drew blood and extracted his thirst for vengeance. But yet, the silence of his pain was short lived and his need to kill grew with each slaying. It seemed to him at times, that he was more savage than the barbarians he shared his life with, and that troubled him deeply. He knew that was not him, for he was a simple farmer forged into a deadly menace by some sad twist of dark fate. Perhaps he was simply at the mercy of dark gods who used him for their own ends. He knew naught, nor did he care. All that mattered was that he lived to slay, but the slaying of the daughter of Grimthor the Strong was not of his doing. He was the agent of sorcery and not even the power of the Bloodsword could have thwarted the death of Halgi Mansbane.

The air hung thick around Tulwryn, and melancholy consumed him, and the day was grey and overcast with low clouds, heavy with snow. A raven wheeled across the sky but cried naught, adding to the already somber mood. Sadly, Tulwryn looked at the shallow grave where Halgi slept. No tear creased his cheek, but he knew that with her he buried the last bit of his human love, the final speck of his humanity. Anger and rage welled up within his cold blue veins and he knew that she would be avenged.

"Much suffering will I extract in thy name," he mumbled to himself. "Rest mine love, for I will avenge thee unto mine dying day." Quietly, like a wraith, he turned and walked away from the grave to his stolen Gerdmorian horse, mounted, and then rode off east without looking back.

The day wore on as Tulwryn rode toward Rodmar and many thoughts crossed his troubled mind. First, he remembered the soft caresses of Halgi that night in the cave after the ambush. Then he thought of her words and her proposal of handfasting. Surely he could have become the new chieftain of Heidmar had he been bound to her in marriage, and a fierce leader he would have been, but now that dream had perished. It was not his dream anyway; he wanted not to lead men, but to slay them. And what would the clan of Heidmar think of him now, now with the blood of their own on his hands? Sorcery or no, he was the murderer of Halgi Mansbane, Grimthor's daughter, and that crime was punishable by death. Tulwryn thought of the deed and his heart sank, and he became ashamed. He would welcome death just to quiet the pain in his heart, this he knew. But he also knew that his death would not come soon, for that would be too easy and his life was anything but easy. No, his destiny would not be to perish for the slaying of Halgi, but to extract more blood from the frozen north ere he threw his life away.

Off in the distance a wolf bayed sadly, the wind whipped up around him, and Tulwryn turned his thoughts to contemplate the words of the shadow of the Bloodsword. He then divined the idea that he might not be the savior of the world, as the shadow had prophesied, but simply a mere pawn in a great and ancient saga of war. A battle between good and evil was afoot, this much he knew. It was a power struggle on a monumental scale but its purpose he knew naught.

Tulwryn reined his mount and brought the animal to a gentle trot. Glancing down at the crimson blade hanging lifelessly at his side he lowered his hand and touched the hilt of the sword. Instantly his mind was impregnated with images of carnage and war, and once again, the shadow of the Bloodsword spoke to him in a grim voice.

"Tulwryn, know that I am your power," spoke the shadow. "Did ye naught see Vogelmir's true form ere the others when you slayed the war wolf? I am the Sword of Truth, and ye shall know the Truth when ye wield me! When the Volva sat with the dwarf whilst he was forging the sword she was attempting to thwart the prophecy by the command of her master, the evil frost dragon Darkoth. But know this, the prophecy cannot be thwarted for the Truth is too powerful to be corrupted by evil, and ye are the tool that the Truth shall wield, as long as ye wields me."

Tulwryn fought hard to release the hilt from his grasp and to banish the vision, but he could not for he and the sword were fused as one. He struggled to drive out the visions and the words from his reeling mind, but all was in vain for the shadow of the Bloodsword proved too powerful.

"Tulwryn, 'tis your destiny to unite the warring clans of the north and march onward to engage Darkoth and his minions. Destroy the army of evil and thy destiny will unfold before you, and the world will kneel in your presence!"

With those final words, the shadow left him and Tulwryn was released from the visions. Slowly he removed his aching hand from the hilt of the sword and looked at it. His entire palm was burned a bright scarlet, yet there was no scarring or permanent damage. It was as if the sword had branded him with its sign; a mark of power was on him and his doom went before him like a banner. Gripping the reins in both hands, Tulwryn spurred his steed and rode hard into the shadows of Rodmar, and death rode with him.

Thus ends the Fifteenth Chapter of Book One

SIXTEEN

Preparing for War

The day came and went and still there was no sign of the brothers, nor did Halgi Mansbane return. Halgr, Grimthor's widow, was bitterly grieved and she wept silently in her tent, for her heart was heavy and she could no longer bear the losses she had incurred. Earlier that day she had given the order that Heidmar amass its army against Rodmar, and amidst much cheer and excitement, the troops were mustered. But she shared naught in their excitement for something in her heart told her that Rodmar was not guilty of the crime and that there was doom in the future for her clan.

It was the noon of the day ere the army of Heidmar began its march eastward to the realm of Rodmar with the grim hope of engaging them in war for the slaying of Grimthor, their chieftain. The midday sun burned brightly over the frozen wastes of the north and there was a midwinter thaw all about. Steel hoofed stallions sloshed through melting snow and wet shod troops marched on, still the mood was altered naught, for their blood was boiling for battle and vengeance.

Halgr Manslayer emerged from her tent as a force of fifty thousand strong Heidmarians rallied forth, all able and seasoned in the ways of warfare. There were men in tall helms riding atop dark warhorses, and women in gilded armor brandishing silver blades. Some walked, yelling shouts of war and victory, whilst others ran ahead of the army, spear in hand and frothing at the mouth seething for blood and carnage. A grim sight was the army Halgr had assembled; yet hungry for vengeance she was naught. Weak and frail she had become due to the pain of her losses and the stress of her position. She was not a leader, but a warrior, but this day she felt like neither. Today she was merely a woman, cold and alone and afraid.

Halgr mounted her steed and sat tall in the saddle, hiding her feelings as the army marched past. Time and again, she was saluted by the soldiers, and likewise, she nodded in recognition to their respect. After the last of the war machine marched past her, she gazed up at the sun setting low on the horizon far off to the west. Her mind reeled in melancholy thoughts and her heart pained to see the face of her daughter at least once ere she threw her life away. A raspy cough brought her back to the present and her attendant, sitting atop a golden Heidmarian mare, trotted close by.

"Shall we ride forth, m'lady, and take up the rear of the assembly," asked the squire, his young face glowing with anticipation of battle and glory.

"In the fashion of a true general?" There was a queasy uneasiness to her voice and her comment was posted more as a question than a statement.

"Aye," answered the squire, "as a true general!"

"Lead the way then," she commanded, "for ere the eve of the morrow we shall litter the ground with many corpses!"

"And may our might feed the ravens," answered the boy. The two spurred their mounts and rode off after the army, and Halgr Manslayer felt a cold hand grip her heart but she steeled herself as she rode on, unhindered by her fear.

* * *

It was late in the day when Tulwryn entered Rodmarian territory. Large sea birds soared high like grey clouds over a glassy sea and the scent of firewood drifted on the chill air. Tulwryn was still a ways off from the main encampment and so he dismounted and climbed upon a rock outcropping to survey the area ere he be taken by surprise by fierce Rodmarian sentries.

His eyes scanned the encampment on the horizon. Rodmar was a larger community than he had believed, and he wondered how so many could sustain themselves on so little this far north. Surey, Heidmar was a large clan, but they lived further south where the bounty was far greater. The area stretching before Tulwryn's dark eyes was that of a frozen desert and he knew naught the means of Rodmar's steel.

Huts of packed snow and hide tents dotted the frigid shores of the North Sea, and that foreboding body of frozen waves was set as an ominous backdrop on an already melancholy atmosphere. The grayish-white of the sky and shore melted into the grayish-white of the sea; the scene was surreal and dreamlike. Everywhere there were people; laughing warriors carried sword and spear and jacks of ale, women worked over hot cooking fires, and children played whilst the elderly looked on through clouded eyes. There was a peace that permeated the air over Rodmar that Tulwryn had never seen this far north and his heart wept for he knew that he brought grim tidings to this peaceful village and many would perish ere he depart.

Tulwryn drew a heavy sigh and climbed down from the rock. He realized that he would seem a lesser threat to the Rodmarians if he were on foot and so he decided to let his steed loose. Quietly, he untied the tether to his horse and smacked its buttocks with the flat of his blade causing the animal to gallop off into the tundra filled field behind him. Glancing about the area one last time he contemplated his odds. Even though he was not of Heidmarian blood, he understood quite well that the Rodmarians knew who he was, since he had engaged them more than once in Heidmar's many bloody raids and battles. There was a good chance that the Rodmarians would suspect foul play and slay him on sight, but he was counting on the Rodmarians to be smarter than that. The many seasons of war, he hoped, had taught them the battle strategies of the Heidmarians. Never in all their wars, had Heidmar used trickery to defeat a foe, and Tulwryn hoped that Rodmar knew this. Still, their rage at seeing an enemy, alone and on their land, could very well be enough to throw them into a blood frenzy. It was a chance that he had to take.

He had stepped from behind the bluish-grey mound of granite and walked no more than twenty paces when he found himself surrounded by ten fell warriors on horseback, all brandishing glittering blades of silver and long spears. Tulwryn looked up at the men and noticed that all but one had the facemasks of their great helms pulled down in the battle ready position. The warrior who left his visor up, Tulwryn quickly assumed, was the leader and so he addressed the man, warrior to warrior.

"I am . . . ,"

"We know who ye are," shouted the warrior. Fear mingled with hate in his voice, yet he showed it naught and he stood tall and proud in the saddle. "Ye are the Lion of Heidmar, the nameless warrior from the south whom Grimthor the Strong has taken to son over the blood of his clan. Many wars have ye fought, and much suffering follows in thy wake."

The leader was a man in his early thirties with thick loins and heavy thews, and Tulwryn could see that he was not new to war. Grim scars criss-crossed his face and forearms and under his leather jerkin could be seen the traces of corded rope-like muscle; over one shoulder, a heavy woolen cape was draped and from his saddle harness hung a mighty broadsword, its hilt worn, frayed, and stained from the blood of many battles.

"I come to slay naught but . . . ,"

"For true," the warrior interrupted, "but we can surely slay ye hither! Or perhaps we shall cut the blood eagle in thy back for the suffering thou hath extracted from our clan."

"Many men will die ere I am cut even once," spoke Tulwryn, defiantly. With the speed of a striking tiger, the Bloodsword hissed from its scabbard and Tulwryn cast the blade, point down, so that it stuck in the frozen ground. Ominously, the blade glowed a bright crimson and the warriors saw the sign and fear was in their hearts.

"So I see," said the warrior. "What shall we then do with thee?"

"Take me to the Rodmarian council and hear what I must

say, for much weight is carried in mine words, and to heed naught mine words will bring much suffering to thy people; more suffering than even I can extract, for there is a great evil afoot," answered Tulwryn as he re-sheathed the Bloodsword.

The warrior then commanded the others to sheath their weapons and thereby, in a peaceful manner, the ten escorted Tulwryn forward to the Rodmarian council hall. Much commotion rolled though the camp as the group made their way over the packed snow paths that wound amongst the huts and tents of Rodmar. Women ceased working at their fires to watch the ten and their prize stroll forth, children stopped their playing and ran, hiding behind huts and tents and adults to sneak a peek; and the elderly gazed through cataract clouded eyes straining to see the warrior from Heidmar that walked among them this day.

The air over Rodmar was electric and tension was as a tightly pulled bowstring. Dogs barked and a raven cawed and the cold wind from the North Sea whipped briskly over the camp; a shudder passed down more than one spine as Tulwryn passed, but none were bold enough to stare straight into his dark eyes. In a matter of moments, the group disappeared around a bend in the trail and life in the Rodmar camp returned to normal, at least for a little while.

Once inside the Rodmarian council hall Tulwryn was made to remove his weapons and he was stripped to the waist and searched. When the Rodmarian soldiers felt it safe enough, Tulwryn was given back his tunic and cloak and allowed to stand unguarded amidst the warriors until the council members filed into their places; but his weapons they kept.

Tulwryn watched as the council members entered the hall. There was twice the number as Heidmar, and they were older still; old warriors, male and female, all wearing chain maile jackets over which heavy woolen capes were draped. White hair tumbled down over many a shoulder yet their cobalt blue eyes blazed with a rage unremembered. Candles flickered and shadows danced off the log walls as a stout guard brought much wood and stoked the central fire hot and high.

There was a slight rumble alive in the crowd and Tulwryn knew the council to be talking amongst themselves about him and the purpose of his visit. He silently thought to himself the similarities betwixt Rodmar and his own clan and realized that these two peoples, nay, the entire population of the north, were at one time, perhaps far back in antiquity, one people, one clan. What prehistoric evil had befell upon them and dispersed them, set them fighting amongst themselves, and causing so much pain and suffering and death? He turned the question over and over in his mind, yet the answer was not to be his and so finally, he banished the thought and returned to the task at hand.

After a time, the hall became silent and a grey headed man with a clean shaven face stood and addressed the council in a strange tongue. Tulwryn understood naught the manner of talk being traded amongst the Rodmarians, but he realized it was of an evil nature and more than once felt that they were planning his death. He caught their sideways glances, twinkles of menace gleamed in their eyes and jagged yellow teeth shone through half smiles, some rattled their weapons in their scabbards and still others shouted obscenities in foreign tongues. Finally, all was silenced and the council leader turned to Tulwryn and spoke to him in his own language.

"So warrior from Heidmar, slayer of many of our people, we are now to ask ye what is the nature of this visit? Answer well knave, for to fail will surely bring ye death."

Tulwryn shrugged off the man's threats without a bother. He was used to threats, he was accustomed to danger, these things troubled him naught. For a moment he just stood there in silence, quietly looking into the eyes of all present. Some met his gaze head on, others did not. Finally, he cleared his throat and addressed the lot.

"Brave people of Rodmar, I come naught as an enemy but as a brother." A murmur of suspicion ran through the council at Tulwryn's words but he ignored them and continued.

"There is a dark menace brewing in the north. Many leagues past the Frozen Lake a great army has assembled and its plan is to crush the clans of the north. Already, 'tis my guess, some of the clans have fallen to this war machine. How many still remain whole, I know naught; 'tis my advice that ye send out ambassadors in all directions to inform the warring clans that we must now unite against a common foe."

"Why should we believe ye," snapped one old woman, haggled with age. Another sounded her evil reply and many more shouted for blood. The leader, after much work, was able to regain control of the council and addressed the group.

"But what if this man speaks the truth," spoke the leader. "What if there is an army heading our way? Should we not muster our warriors in defense?"

"Why should this Heidmarian dog warn us," asked one member. "He is a slayer of our people, not a savior. I believe him naught!"

"But he came alone and afoot. That 'tis naught the manner of Heidmar when they are out for blood and plunder," answered the leader.

Suddenly, a small warrior burst into the hall. Many heads were turned and Tulwryn noticed that the man was more a boy than a warrior; perhaps only a scout. He was out of breath and quite shaken. Tulwryn listened hard as the boy spoke through gasping breaths. He told of how he had been separated from his scouting party by a fell storm, more violent than any he and his party had ever encountered. They were scouting for richer hunting grounds northeast of the Frozen Lake and tracking a large herd of snow deer when the storm suddenly whipped up and blinded them. More than one comment of black sorcery was suggested but the boy continued without pausing or replying to the crowd.

He told them of how he had walked for days searching for his party but found them naught. What he did find was more terrifying than anything he could have ever imagined. West of the Frozen Lake, said the boy, was a large castle of ice greater than any citadel, real or legendary. From the castle, leading south, was a wide trail of packed snow made from the heavy feet of a great many warriors, beasts, and siege engines. He told the council of how he summoned the strength to pursue the army and learn of its intentions. What he discovered was beyond imagination. After a fortnight of tracking the army, the boy finally came to spy on the camp by climbing to a precipice high over where the company camped. His heart became heavy with fear for he was not ready for the sight he beheld. More warriors than he knew existed in the entire world gathered in one place filling the entire valley before him, horizon to horizon. Yet, these warriors were not of the human race, but of something else, something evil. They were twisted and grotesque, black and deadly, wearing maile armor as a man but not in the manner that a man wears his.

More murmurs tumbled over the council and many times fell glances were cast at Tulwryn, who remained silent throughout the commotion, whilst the scout continued with his story. The boy then told of how he remained on the army's trail for three more nights, and each night the scene worsened. There were demons afoot and floating in the air, and on the last night he witnessed a great evil, greater than in his worst nightmare. The evil he described was so grim that it sent shudders of fear down the spine of the most seasoned warrior, for when the army engaged its target it would not merely slay its foes, but would render them utterly. Many times did he witness the demons in combat where they would destroy a man's soul and thereby making him a slave and a servant of evil. The whole of this army was populated by the walking dead, for after the slain warrior was felled, a demon would sprinkle the corpse with powders and henceforth the body would shudder and return to life, yet not the life it had known prior but the life of something dark and evil.

"In the span of two moons," spoke the scout, "I witnessed the assimilation of seven tribes of our enemies into this evil army. Like a scared rabbit I ran, and ran straightaway for home to warn ye of this menace. But how we can save ourselves, I know naught. Its power is fell and we are outnumbered twenty to one."

After the scout finished with his tale the leader of the council quieted the group and turned to Tulwryn.

"How did ye know such things, knave, if ye are naught of this evil band?"

Tulwryn paused, then motioned to the man that held his sword.

"I am Tulwryn, keeper of the Bloodsword, blade of Truth. Many things I know, yet how I know them is my own business. Understand that I come as a friend and a brother. Muster thy strength, for need it ye will."

The warrior that held Tulwryn's sword was made to come forward. He held the scabbard tightly and felt a warmth emanate from within its leathery bonds and was filled with fear for he knew that something in the steel lived. He was commanded to return the sword to Tulwryn, but not ere the leader removed it from its scabbard. All gasped when the blade was held up high before them, for its surface glistened in the firelight like wet blood, yet the blade was dry to the touch.

"Truly," spoke the leader, eyeing the grim blade closely, "ye are naught the enemy that we were led to believe, but a prophet, for this blade is the Bloodsword. Much of its lore do we remember from tales told in our youth, yet we believed them to be merely myth and held them not as Truth. This is a day of doom, for much suffering is in our future. Go and return to thy people and inform them that Rodmar shall join ye in thy quest. We shall fight side by side against this evil and die unto the last man if that is our destiny."

"'Tis naught a day of doom," said Tulwryn, "but a day of rejoicing. For true there is much bloodshed to come, but on this day ye have ended the clan wars that stretch back fifteen hundred years. I am only saddened that three out of the ten clans are able to rejoice in the matter. 'Tis my hope that we shall be victorious against this evil and prosper another fifteen hundred years, united as one clan, strong in the ways of the north."

"My hope goes with ye, brother," answered the leader. Tulwryn grasped the warrior's arm in friendship and told him to send word to Gerdmor informing them of the alliance betwixt Rodmar and Heidmar, and plea for their aid as well. After much planning, the council dispersed and Tulwryn was allowed to leave. He was given a Rodmarian stallion as a token of kinship and bade them farewell as he rode off westward. The setting sun was impaling itself on the peaks of the distant mountains and the keeper of the Bloodsword was lost in its glare as Rodmar mustered its strength and readied itself for battle.

Thus ends the Sixteenth Chapter of Book One

SEVENTEEN

General Tulwryn

An eagle floated overhead and the northern sun beat down on Tulwryn's back. He welcomed the sudden warmth amidst the cold winter as he rode hard westward. It would be two day's ride ere he reach Heidmar, sooner than that, he realized, if Halgr had already mustered her troops and set them off on a forced march for Rodmar, as Halgi had warned. Whilst he was not above killing, Tulwryn often thought that his adopted family was a bit too quick to vengeance. In this case, he knew vengeance would prove their undoing, as it was a simple strategy of a common enemy to set its foes at each other's throats whilst it attacked their unprotected flanks. Death would come swiftly to both clans and Darkoth would assume his throne unopposed unless Tulwryn could reach Heidmar and inform Halgr of his alliance with Rodmar.

He slowed his Rodmarian mount to a soft trot and loosened his great cloak from about his neck. With a mighty heave, he snatched the garment from his shoulders and wound it about his arm, then shoved it deeply into his left saddlebag. Taking up his water skin, he took a long drink and then poured a small amount over his face and neck. Even though the air was brisk on the northern plains, Tulwryn had been riding hard for more than half a day and he was covered with sweat and grime. A thin film of sweat also covered his mount and he patted the animal behind its thick neck. He promised himself that at the next sign of fresh water he would rest and water the animal, and with that oath he spurred the beast forward to a hard gallop.

It was coming up on the noon of the next day, and Tulwryn's sinewy form shone under a glistening sheen of fresh sweat. Gooseflesh rippled over his olive hued skin on more than one occasion when the warm northern sun dipped its face behind grey clouds and the cold winter's wind brushed hard against him. The recent weeks of combat had been good to him and he felt strong and lean and well exercised. Although his armor had become rusted and soiled, his muscles, normally long and lithe, had thickened, and his byrnie had become so tight that its steel links appeared to have grown into his flesh. A grim sight indeed he was to behold, for he looked like something from a nightmare rather than a warrior of flesh and blood.

Finally, he came upon a stream that was about fives paces across and only shin deep. The water was moving fast and so it had remained unfrozen all winter long. By the tracks in the melting snow, Tulwryn could see that many animals used the stream as a source of fresh water, and so he kept his word and dismounted. Leading the horse by its tether, he walked the animal to the stream and allowed it to take its fill. He likewise took a long drink and then began to fill his half empty water skin. A rumble of hooves and footfalls off in the distance brought him around and he lowered the skin and peered through squinted eyes. He saw a great army approaching, still about three thousand paces off, but the numbers were so great that the ground shook with a terrible force. Scrambling quickly to mount his horse, Tulwryn spurred the animal hard in its flanks and in two great heaves of massive horseflesh, the beast bounded across the stream.

In a flash, the Rodmarian stallion crossed the plain and closed the distance betwixt them and the approaching army. The horse's muscles strained as it ran and Tulwryn's grit could be seen in his dark eyes. From a distance, the first line of Heidmarian pike men, with fear in their hearts at witnessing the fierceness of the oncoming rider, lowered their weapons. Suddenly, their fear was transformed into ecstatic joy when they saw that it was Tulwryn who rode at them.

Tulwryn rode past the pike men, and then on past the foot

soldiers. He reined his steed and cantered up to a regiment of cavalry. Many a questioning glance was cast his way as the warriors looked upon his steed and saw the brands of Rodmar on the animal's rump, but they remained quiet and spoke naught.

"Where is Halgr Manslayer," he shouted at the highest ranking warrior. "Much news do I carry and 'tis for her ears only. Quick man, waste no time!"

With a grunt and a groan, the mounted warrior pointed to the rear of the war train and then watched through puzzled eyes as Tulwryn quickly rode off and was lost to his sight amidst the crowd.

The roar of cheers was deafening as the Heidmarian army caught sight of Tulwryn as he rode swiftly past each company. Spears were lifted and swords were rattled in their scabbards, oaths of vengeance were screamed and many times the great horns of victory were sounded. Never before had Tulwryn seen the clan this set on blood and the sight turned his marrow to ice. Heidmar was the largest and strongest of all the northern clans, that much was certain. And surely, the Rodmarians were no match for the clan of Heidmar in mortal combat, this or any day, but it 'twas naught Rodmar that the army would battle this day. Tulwryn wondered how eager the warriors of Heidmar would be had they known their true foe. Even he, Tulwryn Bloodsword, knew naught the entire strength of the army of Darkoth, yet he was not about to underestimate the enemy, nor was he about to rush head long into the gaping jaws of death. Too many times had he seen men throw their lives away in battle, and he realized this day would be no different, yet it was his destiny to unite the clans and lead them to victory; and this day, he knew he could spare no fodder.

Upon reaching the rear of the war train, he reined his steed and cantered up along side of Halgr Manslayer. Her face was grim and she met his stern gaze straight on. Instantly, her head dropped and Tulwryn knew she understood. With soft words of comfort, as a son to his mother, Tulwryn did his best to console her, yet she could not be consoled for Halgi was her only daughter and a mother's loss is heavy indeed.

As they rode on, he told Halgr of his adventures and informed her that Halgi had been slain from a dark sorcery, yet he bit his tongue and told her naught of the details of that slaying. Then he went on and spoke of the dragon's army and of the dread evil that had amassed in the far north and had already crushed seven of the ten tribes.

"Rodmar," he said, "did naught to slay Grimthor, thou husband, but have agreed to unite with us in a quest to defeat the army of Darkoth. They have already sent word to Gerdmor to plea for their assistance as well, but so far, no word has come out of the mountains."

"These are strange times indeed," replied Halgr, glancing down at Tulwryn's Rodmarian stallion. "My husband and only daughter is slain, yet there is no target for mine wrath. What shall become of us when our enemies become our allies and demons become our foes? How can we battle dragons and devils and things that die naught?"

"First we must needs turn this war machine northward and rendezvous with Rodmar on the frozen plains. 'Tis my hope that Gerdmor comes to our aid as well, for alone we stand no chance, for we are already outnumbered at least twenty to one."

"Twenty to one." There was terror in Halgr's voice. The warriors of Heidmar were a fierce breed indeed, but never had they fought against such overwhelming odds, and her heart sank.

"Never mind the numbers, m'lady," answered Tulwryn, "for I carry the Bloodsword, and with it I shall slay the dragon ere a fortnight passes from us. Still, I must needs get close enough to wield the blade and to do so will cost many lives . . . ,"

"Many lives have already been spent," she interrupted. "How many more needs be thrown away on this doom?"

"As many as the gods deem necessary, I suppose. We are merely pawns fighting for survival and nothing more. May the gods be with us, and damn them to Odhinn's seven cold hells if they are naught!"

Halgr then went on to tell Tulwryn that neither Dillwyn nor Urgan nor any the brothers had returned hither from their mission and she shuddered to think the worst for them. Tulwryn once again advised her to turn the army from the east and march north to engage the dragon's forces. She acknowledged his advice and sent her esquire forward with the orders, and then appointed Tulwryn with the title of Master General. She also asked if he would accept the position of chieftain so that she could be released from the office to engage in personal combat as was befitting for a Heidmarian widow in mourning, but Tulwryn refused.

The sun was setting and the sky became as blood as the Heidmarian army slowly changed its course and rolled ever onward, due north, to the frozen slaying grounds just yonder of the mountains. Tulwryn spurred his stallion and left Halgr Manslayer to wallow in her own grief.

Thus ends the Seventeenth Chapter of Book One

EIGHTEEN

An Unexpected Gift

A thousand burning suns poked their needle sharp faces through the black firmament high over the land of the midnight sun. A large shadowy mass of writhing darkness blotted out the shimmering beauty of the aurora borealis as the army of Darkoth slowly marched east, toward Rodmar. The dragon, soaring high over the frozen plains on immense leathern wings greedily anticipated his victory over the weak mortals and laughingly gloated over his new realm.

"I am already king of Phantasodyssea," whispered the worm to himself as he floated silently over his army of evil. Then suddenly a great laugh rolled from his scaled reptilian lips and the land below trembled in fear.

"I am a king; the King! Nay, not a king am I, but a god; *the* God! All that must needs be done is merely to go through the motions, for the destiny is already mine. Many shall fall under my scepter! Thousands shall perish under my wrath! None shall be safe from my power and strength, and no place will be safe where any can hide from me. I shall cast down mountains and lift up seas, the oceans will boil and islands will be torn asunder. I shall rend the very fabric of time and space and all will bow before me and pay tribute unto me, the new God-King of Phantasodyssea!"

Far below the gloating dragon, his army of evil minions crept along at a steady pace across the frigid plains of tundra and scrub. Around the clock, the seething mass of death marched on, needing neither sleep nor food, for they were not an army bringing death, but an army of the dead. Cold animated corpses, many twisted and grotesque from their gruesome battle wounds, trudged over pack ice and frozen snow brandishing steel weapons in their cadaverous hands. Dead warriors from the clans of Lodmar and Baedmar marched onward under the dark enchantment of Darkoth's sorcery. Sethmar and Hoehnmar were there as well, and too were the mutilated soldiers from the clans of Rhinemar and Uttmar. Only Nokkmar's warriors remained unsoiled, for even a dead warrior cannot walk, aided by magic or no, without limbs or head, and the Nokkmarians fought to the last man and were cut to ribbons before a greater force of terrible evil.

The clan of Rodmar, Darkoth planned, would be the next to fall under his talon and be assimilated, then Heidmar and lastly Gerdmor in the mountains. No one was safe and all would be stamped out of their hiding places ere the winter turn to spring and the New Age begin.

Languidly, the massive beast drifted eastward on the night's cold wind, a faint stench trailing behind him, but the people of Rodmar slept naught but sharpened their blades and readied themselves for war.

* * *

There was a great commotion up ahead of the Heidmarian war train and Tulwryn, wearing the badge of the Master General of Heidmar, rode from the rear forward to personally inspect the disturbance. The day was cold and wet and a light drizzle had continued to fall for the past three days since Tulwryn joined the clan on their long march north. Gone was the bright northern sun with its false hope of an early spring and Tulwryn had once again retrieved his heavy woolen cloak from his saddlebag and wrapped the garment around his tanned shoulders.

Halgr and her esquire remained in the rear of the train, protected by a division of one hundred and fifty fierce Heidmarian warriors, personally hand picked for the job by Tulwryn himself.

He realized the importance of her position and knew quite well that without a living heir, should anything befall her, the entire clan of Heidmar would erupt in a civil power struggle to fill the coveted position of chieftain. Too much was riding on the outcome of this evil war and Tulwryn would not risk a petty squabble over her seemingly important royal office.

Yes, it was apparent, that even these barbarians realized the power that one wields when one leads men, whether by scepter or by sword. Tulwryn also knew that many of Heidmar's more ambitious warriors would immediately shuck their duties as soldier fighting under his command to assume the position of chieftain and grab the glory for themselves in the event that Halgr be slain. So, Tulwryn, unable to risk his forces being divided in the face of a superior foe, set the one hundred and fifty around his chieftain and turned his mind to more urgent matters.

Wearing his tall spiked helm and soiled byrnie, his dark cloak billowing in the wind, Tulwryn made his way to the forefront of the war train. His Rodmarian stallion whinnied and stamped the frozen ground and he reined the animal to calm it down and hold it under his stern control. The front line of pike men was yelling oaths at the warrior riding towards them, and Tulwryn had to squint hard to make out the figure for he defied imagination.

On the back of the largest snow beast that Tulwryn had ever seen approached a fell warrior wearing Gerdmorian armor. The man was in his mid forties, old for a barbarian solider, but the many scars he bore told the tale of his might and main. Clean shaven, with long golden locks and blazing cobalt eyes, the Gerdmorian could have passed for one of their own clan, save that he wore the armor of a rival clan and rode on the back of a monster. The Heidmarian steeds bucked and whinnied at the approach of the snow beast and so the warrior kept his distance.

"I seek the Keeper of the Bloodsword," yelled the Gerdmorian.

Tulwryn rode forward.

"I am he. Who are you and what business do ye have hither?"

"My name is Thorfinn the Merciless and I hail from Gerdmor. Our clan has aligned itself with Rodmar to fight against a grave evil amassing in the north. I was sent hither to rendezvous with Heidmar and inform ye of the alliance."

"Well met, Thorfinn! Seems ye has found us. Come, we ride north to battle. May the gods shine on us so that we may feed the ravens the bloody flesh of our foes!"

Thorfinn waved a thick hand in friendship and Tulwryn smiled a grim smile as he watched the warrior effortlessly turn his beast north and proceed with the rest of his train. Suddenly, there came a rush of excitement from the rear of the train and once again, Tulwryn spurred his mount and rode aft.

Galloping at a full run towards the rear of the war train, Tulwryn was greeted with a loud victory yell he knew only too well originated from the mighty lungs of his friend Dillwyn Anvilhand. Amazed beyond words, Tulwryn reined his horse hard and sat in his saddle gaping at the sight before him. Five enormous snow beasts galloped to catch up with the train, and he could see that it was indeed Dillwyn and Urgan, as well as the three brothers, Uther, Luther, and Gunnar, with their horses in tow, three Heidmarian warhorses and two beautiful Phaedronian steeds.

"Truly this is a remarkable day," laughed Tulwryn jubilantly. "The gods do indeed favor us, methinks! I thought ye were dead!"

"Hold up," cried Dillwyn, "we have been riding for a fortnight to catch up with ye. We are naught dead, but we are hungry and tired."

Eyeing the warriors, Tulwryn noticed their worn and tattered condition and ordered his esquire to fetch some grub from the quartermaster's wain, then he turned back to them and spoke:

"Why for thou come from the south? Where have ye been?"

"On a quest, Tulwryn," answered Gunnar. "We rode south to Covensted to . . . ,"

"Covensted! Are ye mad? There is naught in Covensted but witches!"

"Nay, master Tulwryn, we are naught mad, but we were made to accompany Urgan on his quest so as he could fulfill his destiny."

"Destiny?"

Urgan the Brave came forward on the back of his large snow beast and Tulwryn could see that the boy had aged many years in the short span of a fortnight. His skin was no longer pale but had been darkened by the black sun of Phaedron, and there was a grim menace in his eyes. Tulwryn knew well the evils of the southern world, where the innocence of the north is lost amongst dark jungles and wicked cities. His mind reeled with the thoughts of tangled destinies and forgotten legends.

"'Twas mine destiny to retrieve this shield for ye, m'lord," said Urgan, and he passed the Dragon Shield to Tulwryn. Never had Tulwryn seen such an exquisite piece of workmanship; everything down to the smallest detail had been carefully wrought. He accepted the shield with a nod of respect.

"'Tis the Dragon Shield, m'lord. It will protect ye from the hoary blasts of the worm when you meet him in combat."

"So ye know of the war," he asked.

"Aye, m'lord, we know. Omar came to me in a dream . . . ,"

"Dreams . . . and visions!" Tulwryn gritted his teeth as he interrupted Urgan's words. "Damn us to hell with these ancient prophecies! Come, eat your fill but rest in the saddle for we must needs make haste. We have a long march ahead of us and a longer battle still." And with those words, Tulwryn turned and rode to the front of the train, the Dragon Shield securely strapped to his thick left forearm and resting lightly on his thigh.

Later that eve, after much contemplation, Tulwryn awarded the five warriors badges of honor and bravery and bestowed upon each of them the office of general under his command, giving them each a force of ten thousand men.

Thus ends the Eighteenth Chapter of Book One

NINETEEN

Wrath of the Bloodsword

The days grew shorter as Tulwryn's army pushed further north into the wicked realm of Darkoth's evil horde. Many leagues had they already came and the warriors of Heidmar, four and fifty thousand strong, were worn and tired from the long journey. Tulwryn reined his steed left and rode upon Dillwyn, who was cantering near the middle of his column of men. The sky was darkening overhead and the silvery strands of the great northern lights were seen faintly off in the distance.

"This far north," said Tulwryn to the dwarf, "we shall fight the forces of darkness in darkness, bound by our wits with only the faint glimmer of the midnight sun to guide our blades and arrows. What thinks ye, mine friend?"

"Every warrior enjoys his strength until one destined day; sooner or later each man surrenders his soul to Odhinn's seven hells," answered Dillwyn, boldly in jest. "Perhaps that day will come sooner than naught."

"Perhaps, indeed, but a fell day it is when a warrior must abandon his soul on a dark battlefield."

"Do ye think we should have waited 'til the beast brought his forces further south? At least then we could have fought during the bright of the day."

"Nay," answered Tulwryn, "'tis better to do combat hither, far from the borders of the southern realms. The less the southerners know of this war, the better. Anyhow, we should be upon the rendezvous site soon. There we shall make camp and plan our strategy with Gerdmor and Rodmar. Betwixt the three of our clans we should fare better than alone, although I believe the losses will still be high and the outcome uncertain."

The dwarf nodded in understanding and Tulwryn rode off toward the front of the war train. Dillwyn watched as his friend galloped off and lost him in the crowd ahead, his mind a jumbled mass of anxiety and uncertainty.

From behind him, Dillwyn heard a familiar voice yelling his name, and he reined his mount hard and turned in his saddle.

"Master Dillwyn, master Dillwyn," cried a lad riding upon a small Heidmarian pony. The boy was clad in shining maile and a short sword, wide of blade, hung loosely at his hip. The old dwarf smiled a broad smile when he saw that the boy was none other than his adopted son, Ian the Eager.

"Ian," shouted Dillwyn, "ye have doubled in size since I saw ye last. What have ye been eating, whole sides of roast beast?"

The boy galloped up near the dwarf and pulled hard on the tether to slow his anxious steed. Excitement was on the lad's face and for a moment he could talk naught for ecstasy had overtaken him at the magnificent sight of his mighty foster father.

"I have missed ye, master Dillwyn," spoke the boy, his voice shaking with emotion. "But I knew ye would return, for ye are strong of thews and gritty indeed. Please, tell me of thy adventures when ye were afield."

For the remainder of the day, Dillwyn and the boy rode side by side, and the dwarf appeased the youngster with tales of adventure and intrigue. Every once in a while the dwarf would cease his storytelling to yell a command or two at his column of men and Ian's eyes would glow brightly as the pride in his heart swelled from seeing his father in action leading men of war.

Later that evening the war train came upon a valley lighted with the glow of many campfires. Tulwryn gave the command to halt and the parade ceased its northern journey for the present, and each troop mustered to give aid to the other and make camp. Tulwryn assembled his generals as well as the council and met with the Rodmarians and the Gerdmorians to assess the situation.

The meeting had historical proportions as well as strategic ones, and the air was alight with electricity. Each member was fully aware of the other, tension was tight as a bowstring yet all gave good council and the plans of battle were set.

Atli the Terrible, leader of the clan of Gerdmor, sent out scouts four days prior and upon their return the clans had the information they needed on the whereabouts of the dragon's army. Though it seemed the great beast's forces were amassed further north than any had expected, many leagues north and east of the great Frozen Lake, it was apparent by their location on the plain that they marched with the intent of striking at Rodmar first. Also, due to their vast numbers, it seemed they went without fear for they hid naught their numbers but marched boldly in the open.

Thrym the Bloodthirsty, a brave and terrible Rodmarian warrior, suggested the dragon's strategy may be a trick to lure the clans to battle on the open plains whereas an auxiliary force in hiding could fall down upon them as vultures picking the flesh of dead men. But Atli's scouts denied the possibility, as they reported witnessing no other forces in the area, yet Thrym argued that one should never underestimate their enemy, and he knew that any dragon, old beyond the count of mortals, would prove crafty indeed.

For more than three hours, the clans sat in council listening to the other and making plans for the coming battle. Tulwryn's five generals sat quiet, for the most part, listening to the debate and studying the battle lines. Time and again, plans were revised or done away with all together, then new plans drawn up. Finally, after some doing, all was satisfied, the meeting adjourned, and the warriors meandered back to their tents to rest themselves for the coming battle.

* * *

Early the next morn, the armies of Gerdmor, Heidmar, and Rodmar, broke camp and dispersed. Rodmar marched off in a northeasterly direction whilst Gerdmor went northwesterly, and Heidmar continued onward with its present course. The main strategy was simple, if Darkoth was bent on attacking each clan separate, and since Gerdmor's scouts assessed that Rodmar was the dragon's next target, then Rodmar was to be used as decoy. When the army of the dragon was in sight and about to attack, Gerdmor would descend on the foe mercilessly from the western flank whilst Heidmar hammer the enemy straight on. Rodmar would then defend itself and retaliate, counter-attacking on the eastern flank thereby sandwiching the dragon's army betwixt itself and Atli's warriors whilst Heidmar engaged the main body of the enemy man to man, due to its immense size over the other two clans.

A feeling of isolation rushed over Dillwyn's heart as the last few columns of Rodmar and Gerdmor pulled away from sight. Within moments, Heidmar was once again alone on the frozen plain. The dwarf glanced up and noticed what looked to be a large eagle wheeling across a dark sky. Suddenly, he felt the wet patter of cold snow on his face and he grumbled under his breath as his imagination told him of the uncomfortable days ahead. Slaying under a blizzard, he thought to himself, is no work for an adventurer nor a professional solider, and again he longed for the bright skies over the Golrin Prairie. Quickly he snatched his cloak from his pack and wrapped it around himself tightly then made his way to the equestrian wain to find his steed. Off in the distance, Tulwryn watched him like a hawk until he vanished from sight.

By noon, the blizzard was in full strength and visibility was nil. Rather than risk falling behind and arriving at the battle site too late to perform their required duties, Tulwryn gave the command to buckle down and quicken the pace. Men and beast alike strained hard but the order was followed to the letter and the army made good time considering the poor weather conditions.

For two days the storm raged and for two days the Heidmarian war train trudged onward, dedicated to their mission. On more than one occasion, Tulwryn summoned his five generals and held private council with them; not even Halgr Manslayer was allowed admission, which was fine with her for she was heavy of heart and her mind was amiss. What went on in those meetings none can say, although it is assumed that Tulwryn was disclosing alternative battle plans in the case that the original strategy failed, or possibly even informing his comrades on the intricate workings of the Bloodsword's power and the many hidden meanings of the ancient prophecies that they were all so intricately involved. Either case, Atli's scouts notwithstanding, no one, not even Tulwryn himself, was ready for what they encountered the day they arrived at their post and gazed down into the lower plain, seeing for the first time the vast army of Darkoth, the frost dragon.

Just as Tulwryn had feared, the fates were not on their side this day for the blizzard had hindered their march and they arrived at the scene of the battle hours late, the slaughter already underway. Tulwryn on his Rodmarian steed, and his generals perched on their massive snow beasts, gaped with shock and horror at the carnage afore them. The warriors were atop a tall hill, their war train a league or so behind them, hidden to conceal its huge size, and the rolling prairie stretched out before them like a great white carpet as visible as the naked eye could tell. Facing overwhelming odds and braving death to a man, the Rodmarians were dying by the score.

Tulwryn's eyes scanned the horizon, but nowhere could be seen the army of Gerdmor. Atli's warriors, Heidmar's Master General surmised, had been slowed by the same storm that ailed them and was likewise late in arriving. In the dark dusk of the midnight sun, Rodmar fought on with amazing bravery; their warriors buffeted by wave after wave of relentless attacks by the Dragon's seething minions of evil.

"Better late than never," laughed the dwarf in the face of death, and the others acknowledged his statement.

"No sign of the dragon on the battlefield, Master General," spoke Urgan. "Shall we ride forth and aid our comrades? I await thy command." Luther and Gunnar chimed in as well and Uther's snow beast roared with eager anticipation to do battle.

"Dillwyn, send forth a man to summon the war train," commanded Tulwryn. "There is no need for stealth now, speed is what we need!"

"Aye," was all the dwarf uttered ere he vanished like a wraith behind them, his snow beast galloping hard and tearing up the snow as they went. Turning to the others, Tulwryn simply shouted the command, "*contingency!*" and out of their sheaths came swords, sharp blades greedy for blood.

Focusing on a portion of the dragon's army, Uther and Gunnar's company rode hard and flanked the enemy whilst Luther and Urgan's company attacked the center in a steel wedge formation. Dillwyn's company was made to hold up until the entire war train was in attacking position. When the forces of Darkoth finally split in twain due to the sandwich attack of Uther and Gunnar's company, Tulwryn commanded Dillwyn's warriors to ride forth, and with Luther and Urgan's men, a portion of the dragon's army was separated from the mass.

A group of minions, twenty thousand strong, was herded into a wide area of the valley where Tulwryn stood before them, alone. With a terrible war cry, Tulwryn unleashed the fury of the Bloodsword. Unsheathing the grim weapon, he raised it high overhead then with one strong downward thrust, drove it a foot into the frozen ground. Standing rigid, both hands on the hilt, Tulwryn once again screamed his yell of death. At that moment, a great scarlet arc flashed from the blade of the Bloodsword and rained down crimson death on each of those twenty thousand fiends.

Time seemed to stand still for Tulwryn as the Sword of Truth lashed out, stealing life from its foes, and Tulwryn tasted their deaths intimately. He saw each man die a thousand times; he witnessed the dragon's dark magic and experienced them waking to the demon sleep after their first death, taking sword in hand to become Darkoth's minions. Then, as if time had no meaning, he saw them each die again, torn asunder by the might of the Bloodsword, screaming in unrepentant agony. Seconds later, the snow was charred black and none stood living in that valley but Tulwryn's men, dazed and confused, and in awe of his power.

"This man is a warrior born with the storm of vengeance in his blood," spoke Uther, shaking his head in disbelief.

"For true, the strength of the gods walks with Tulwryn for he smites his enemies with blasts from their celestial fire and leaves nothing but ashes in his deadly wake," said Gunnar, in amazement.

Tulwryn stood motionless, apparently drained of energy and extremely exhausted, then he teetered and fell. Dillwyn rode hard to the aid of his master, but the other generals were not given the luxury of rest, for as the twenty thousand fell, two hundred thousand more gave chase and entered the battle.

Urgan, surrounded by countless enemies, was knocked from his ride; his snow beast fell dead to a score of steel crossbow bolts. Springing up with the ferocity of a cornered tiger, sword in hand, he began to lash out at the evil warriors set on his murder.

Steel grated steel and sparks flew in the darkness as the hiss and rasp of combat echoed throughout the night. A frost giant, taller than Urgan and thicker of thews with blazing red eyes, attacked mercilessly. The Heidmarian youth parried but gave up no quarter. Hued in twain fell Urgan's foe; the creature's arms and head he hurled aside, but where the thing had stood, its legs sank down; Urgan was a fell warrior wielding death!

Entering the fray of battle, the aged Heidmarian war hero, Walter the Horrendous, lumbered forth on aged loins, brandishing a heavy war club. Many scars covered his war torn body yet his eyes were furious with the berserker rage of his people. Five demons descended upon him but the strength of the gods was in him and he slayed his foes henceforth. Yet, in a sally of combat thereafter, a deadly frost giant had sent him wheeling under heavy blows and Walter was separated from his weapon and he dropped the stick.

Close the giant loomed, his own blood drenched battle mace lifted high over his head and ready to deliver the final death blow. Yet, ere Walter the Horrendous was smitten, he, seething with anger, rolled upon his knees and smote the great beast in the governors with a mighty blow of his thick knotted fist. As the giant reeled from the attack and fell to his knees, Walter the Horrendous shot out his hand like a spear and with his large groping fingers, gouged out the monster's eyes. Screaming in pain, and blinded, the frost giant fought in vain, yet the old warrior of Heidmar mounted another assault and dispatched the beast quickly with a kick to the creature's throat. As the beast lay dead, Walter recovered his war club and bounded off, in search of another victim.

Gunnar, Uther, and Luther, likewise engaged the enemy, and for most of the night, the sounds of combat raged on. Dillwyn finally reached Tulwryn and dragged his friend's unconscious body from the fray.

Rubbing cold snow in Tulwryn's face to revive his friend, the dwarf noticed the marks. Both of Tulwryn's hands were burned a bright crimson with a deep patchwork that matched the hilt of the Bloodsword. Somehow, he knew, the energy that smote the twenty thousand had come from within Tulwryn and not from within the sword. Amazed at this revelation, but having naught the time to reflect on its meaning, he hoisted the body of his Master General upon his mount and took him to the rear of the war train to the medical wain. There he made an herbal tea and left Tulwryn in good care of the leeches so as he could return to the battle as soon as possible.

Dillwyn rode hard and arrived in time to see the entire Gerdmorian army emerge from over a small ridge. They were riding like the wind with fire in their eyes and death in their hearts. Regaining command of his company, Dillwyn gave orders to aid Luther's regiment in smiting a large portion of the enemy.

Turning in haste, and riding into the fray, the dwarf witnessed Gunnar fall lifeless from his mount, a dark shape attached like a parasite to his back. Gunnar screamed as the venom of the minion entered his being and seared every nerve and fiber in his body, then he twitched his last and was lost.

Atli the Terrible, Gerdmor's chieftain, wearing bright shining scale maile and atop a large snow beast, rode like hell itself was biting at his heels. His cloak billowed in the wind and the dim glare of the midnight sun shone off the visor of his war helm. With broadsword in hand, he entered the fray cutting a wide and bloody path ere he went.

From high up in the firmament, concealed by the dark sky, Darkoth floated. Silently, he surveyed the whole of the battle and witnessed the demise of the mortals as they died by the thousands. In a matter of hours, Heidmar's four and fifty thousand was reduced to less that three and twenty thousand, and Rodmar was all but annihilated, a mere fifteen thousand strong and many of them gravely wounded and exhausted. Only Gerdmor, arriving late, remained at full strength and so the dragon turned his focus on Atli's warriors and slayed them by the hundreds. And so came the night and eve of the first day of the last battle.

Thus ends the Nineteenth Chapter of Book One

TWENTY

Tulwryn and the Dragon

In time, Tulwryn regained consciousness. The leech, being advised by Dillwyn earlier, instructed the Master General to retire to his tent. Knowing the importance of his office and paying heed to good council, Tulwryn rose and left the wain, walking toward his tent.

As he strolled through the wains and tents of the war train, Tulwryn tried hard to remember the battle that had taxed him so. Unable to recall the grim scene, he decided to search out Halgr's tent with the hope that she witnessed his fall, and to possibly give him council on the whereabouts of his generals and the current standing of the war. Far off in the distance the sounds of combat could still be heard throughout the night and he knew men to be dying and so his heart went to them and he was in agony.

Behind the lines of battle, Halgr, Grimthor's widow and the newly crowned chieftain of the clan of Heidmar, laid in her tent, lamenting. Tulwryn entered through the flap, unannounced and saw Halgr lying naked on a bed of furs and warm blankets. Her shapely buttocks were sensuously illumed by the soft glow of many candles and for a moment, he felt his heart stir in his chest for she was the image of Halgi, only older.

"Are ye resting, m'lady," Tulwryn asked softly as he lifted a warm blanket of virgin wool from a chest and draped it over the naked figure of his chieftain.

"Nay, I sleep no longer," answered Halgr, sitting up on her bed and exposing her front to Tulwryn. The blanket fell away from her body and erotic shadows danced from her firm breasts and slender waist.

"All mine joy left me the eve Grimthor was taken from me; my soul was rent in twain the day Halgi died. Always I remain awake in mine torment and my mind has gone numb. Tulwryn, so cold is thy council. I only wish to see Heidmar once more in all its glory."

"Heidmar is done, m'lady. These are new times and the clans, however sparsely, are reunited."

Halgr sighed and collapsed back on the bed.

"So it is undone?"

"What would ye have me to do, m'lady?"

Halgr paused for a moment, thinking. Then she suddenly began to fondle herself, hoping to excite the love in Tulwryn's loins. Softly she spoke:

"Caress me, Tulwryn, and lay with me. Leave me naught on this cold bed alone, to die amongst these demons in a foreign land. Many nights I have spent in horror and loneliness with no one to know. Come, let me feel thy warmth."

"So soon after ye husband's murder? For certain, the spirit of Grimthor would rent mine very soul had I bed thee, his widow, so soon after his death. Nay, m'lady, I shall not betray mine father."

"Then ye denies me an heir," she said, ruefully.

"An heir?"

"Aye, m'lord," she answered. "Since ye refuse the office of chieftain, it be only fitting to provide me with an heir, even if thou are only Grimthor's adopted son, him being slain by sorcery less than two moons ago. Even so, thy mother I am naught, so there be no disgrace if we lie together this eve. It is in the custom of the north and Grimthor himself would approve if his heir sprung from your loins, for he loved ye deeply, more so than any of his own blood kin. This I knew."

And with these soft words, Tulwryn unbuckled his weapons belt and removed his maile shirt and trousers, and slid under her blankets and caressed the warm body of Grimthor's widow. A burning sensation he felt in his hands, but he concerned himself naught with his own comfort. The sound of dying men and animals faded far off into the distance and he lost himself in the loving embrace of Halgr Manslayer.

* * *

Tulwryn rose early the following morning, refreshed from his previous battle and apparently invigorated from an evening of lovemaking. It is amazing what a few hours in the arms of a beautiful woman can do for a warrior, and he made no attempt to cover up his nocturnal activities. He hurriedly dressed in his battle raiment and left Halgr's side for his place at the front. Many a head was turned upon seeing him exit her tent but no words were spoken.

All night the battle had raged on and the dead were piled in great heaps and strewn about yonder over the entire field of combat. Wolves were baying in the distance, attracted by the scent of blood and the helpless moaning of the dying. Tulwryn ordered that watch fires be set about the mounds, both, to illume the area and give much needed light as well as keeping the wild beasts at bay. 'Tis bad enough, thought the Heidmarian Master General, that a man be felled in dark combat against an evil foe; to have his noble flesh devoured by hungry wolves was an abomination that even he could not stomach.

The fires were set and Urgan came before Tulwryn and gave an account of the damage. Ere he was finished, Dillwyn arrived with his report as well. The two recounted the many details of the war after Tulwryn's fall. Gunnar was dead, as was Atli, Gerdmor's chieftain. Most of the Rodmarians were slain as well. The Heidmarian army retained only a fraction of its strength and Gerdmor was all but lost. The generals, aided by their steel constitution, simply stood and awaited orders from Tulwryn's parched lips. He stood quiet, then silently turned and walked away.

He was no more than ten paces from them when he turned

and called for his horse. Holding the reins of his steed, Tulwryn addressed the dwarf:

"Dillwyn, call back thy warriors, and order the others to do the same. Send word by means of a letter arrow unto the command of Gerdmor and Rodmar telling them to pull away. I shall ride alone into the gaping maw of hell as a defiant unto the hoary beast himself. When he sees the Sword and the Shield his pride shall overtake him and he will show himself. When I strike, ride forth and cut down all in thy path; if I fall, fight unto the last man. May the gods be with us!"

In a flash, he was amount his steed and riding like the wind into the very heart of the dragon's army. Ten thousand minions of evil parted like a great seething ocean of dread and allowed Tulwryn to enter into them. Screaming his legendary war yell, Tulwryn cried oaths and curses at the dragon and his minions. His blood was as ice and his marrow flowed naught in his veins for rage was his drug and he cared naught for life nor death but merely to slay ere he be slain.

Suddenly, the mass of evil closed around Tulwryn and entrapped him within their vast numbers. Uther, Luther, Dillwyn, and Urgan, watched in horror as their leader rode off to apparent suicide. They kept a keen eye upon his crimson shield and his dark cloak billowing in the wind. When he was lost in the haze, Urgan shouted the command and the whole of Heidmar roared forth to combat.

Steel sang off of steel and warriors continued to die by the handful. Urgan's blade bit deep through the flesh and bone of a creature that should not have been alive to fight, its flesh rent by a thousand cuts. Uther and Luther, commanding their sparse columns, hued many a head and arm and neck whilst Dillwyn's heavy hands caved in numerous skulls and left hundreds dead in his wake.

The mighty dwarf was in the heat of combat, smashing the face of a huge frost giant with his studded bronze gauntlets, knee deep in gore and entrails, when his being was torn asunder by the blood curdling shouts of a dying boy. As Dillwyn's heavy hand smote his foe for the last time ere the monster fell dead in its tracks, the dwarf looked around in time to see Ian, his son, cut down by a sword wielding dread minion of evil. The boy screamed his last as the creature's grim blade bit deep into his tiny body sheering maile and severing flesh and bone. In an instant, Ian lay dead on the ground, hued in twain at the waist by one mighty blow.

Dillwyn, running like a man possessed, unleashed his avenging wrath on Ian's killer and smote him dead with thunderous blows. Carnage raged like a wildfire all about the dwarf as he waded through the dead and dying to come upon the place where Ian fell. Softly he knelt down and caressed the lifeless body of his adopted son, tears pouring forth from aged eyes.

Far away, surrounded by thousands of the dragon's deadly warriors, Tulwryn fought with the frenzy of a madman. With every pass of the Bloodsword, ten creatures died in seething agony. Suddenly, the frothing army ceased its attack and parted. Standing before the Heidmarian Master General was a beast more ferocious than a living nightmare. Standing ten times the height of a man, the dragon sat up on its thick haunches and outstretched its massive wings. The creature's bulk was unfathomable.

"I shall be drinking fine wine from thy hollowed out skull ere this day is ended," spoke the dragon, and he flexed his great wings and took to the skies.

Tulwryn searched the dark firmament for the beast but the monster was lost in the darkness. Summoning strength from he knew not where, Tulwryn taunted the beast shouting curses thereat.

"Methinks naught, vile worm. Ere this day is ended, thou will breathe thy last when the Bloodsword bites deep into your wicked flesh."

From out of nowhere came a violent blast of fiery ice and Tulwryn was knocked off his feet, saved only by the strength of Mimir's Dragon Shield. Dazed and confused, Tulwryn staggered to his feet shaking stars from his ringing head. Quickly, he shoved the point of the Bloodsword into the ground, and with his right hand, he tore his great helm from off his head and his long black locks tumbled down upon his mailed shoulders. Throwing the dented and bloodstained headpiece to the ground, Tulwryn gripped the sword's hilt with both hands and cursed the dragon with all his might. In a flash, he felt the power surge through his being, but it did not drain him as it had done the day before, on the contrary, he was strengthened and his vigor was amplified a thousand fold. Instantly, a great arc of burning scarlet and crimson leapt from the Bloodsword's blade and searched out the soaring dragon. The celestial fire lanced deep into the underbelly of the worm and a canyon opened wide in his frozen flesh, spilling steaming entrails as he fell from the sky.

Dying, the great beast was hurtled from his lofty heights and landed amidst the field of battle with a momentous crash, crushing much of its own army and rending a deep canyon into the land. Slowly, and in much agony, the dragon pulled its head from the wounded ground and came eye to eye with his foe, the wielder of the Bloodsword.

"Go home, Tulwryn Bloodsword, wielder of the Sword of Truth," cursed Darkoth, hissing. "Go home, for ye are glad of your deed and now no man will see me again until the day hell gapes wide and my dark horde rides forth to the doom of the gods!" And with those words, the beast fell silent and died. Tulwryn gazed into the dead countenance of the dragon and was lost to his own thoughts for all about him was silence, yet the silence was deafening.

Urgan and Luther was knee deep in bodies and gore, cleaving heads and limbs alike when the dragon fell from the skies. Stained with the blood of their foes, muscles aching, all combat ceased as the creature breathed its last. In the span of one breath, the entire army of evil perished with their leader; as if it were his strength and power that sustained them, giving life to their dead corpses. The two Heidmarians stood amidst the carnage dumbfounded.

"Dillwyn," screamed a mighty voice from across the plain of battle. It was Tulwryn, striding proudly on powerful loins, his strength seemingly amplified by the life he just took. The Dragon

Shield on his left arm was battered but the sword he carried in his right was glowing a bright crimson, brighter than the dwarf had ever seen it before. For a moment, he looked hard at the blade, for it resembled naught the weapon he forged, and he knew its steel to be alive, a living thing with a mind and a spirit and a destiny.

"Hither, master Tulwryn," answered the dwarf, as he wound his way over the dead toward his friend. He breathed a deep sigh of relief and the crisp air bit his lungs deep, he grimaced, then gazed heavenward to behold the beauty of the aurora borealis sparkling high in the heavens. No longer was their wonder to be blotted out by the bulk of Darkoth's evil flying overhead, and now they shown in all their brilliant glory. It was a good day to be alive, he thought, and he continued, although with much effort, wading through the piles of death toward where Tulwryn stood.

"How many has perished," shouted Dillwyn.

"All of them methinks," answered Tulwryn, as he approached the dwarf, grabbing his big hand in friendship, "and many of us, as well, although some still might live. We needs tend to the wounded if we can. The gods were with us this day, even though victory was slow in coming. Hail Odhinn!"

"Never before have I witnessed such slaughter in such a short span of time."

"Nor I, my friend, nor I," replied Tulwryn, through gritted teeth, a dark grimace etched across his harsh face. "Where are the others?"

"Gunnar is lost, but last I saw Urgan and Luther still breathed. My foster son, Ian the Eager, fell earlier this day. I avenged his murder, but my heart is heavy at his loss. He was too young to war, but his spirit was strong and I could prevent it naught, for he dreamed of a warrior's death even at his young age."

"I grieve for your loss, brother," said Tulwryn. "What of Halgr; does she still live?"

"That I know naught, but I presume so. Last I saw her, she was being guarded by the men ye hand picked. To the best of mine knowledge, they all still live. A good choice of men ye have, my friend."

Tulwryn nodded with a smile and the two warriors began rounding up the survivors and wounded and seeing to it that the remaining warriors, strong and able, were roused to aid the infirmed. For the better part of a week, the surviving company patched their sick and buried their dead. In great mounds of rotting flesh, the survivors piled high the bodies of their foes and burned them to ashes. A great stench wafted across the frozen tundra as the flames consumed the evil that had once ensnared it. The massive corpse of the dragon itself was torn asunder and each piece, separated by many paces, was burned to ash separate of any other fire.

Finally, after all the gruesome work was finished, the remaining warriors assembled and began their long journey south. Urgan, Luther, Dillwyn and Tulwryn, once again riding great Heidmarian warhorses after releasing the snow beasts to their freedom, cantered along side their chieftain's wain where she laid inside, sleeping.

"So, Tulwryn," asked Urgan, "what now?"

Tulwryn paused ere he answered in haste, his mind reeling in deep contemplation. Suddenly a smile wormed its way across his scarred face and he answered.

"Urgan, my friend, methinks it time for me to return to mine home in the south." Unknown to the others, Dillwyn smiled to himself, overjoyed at the prospect of leaving the frozen north, since he knew, where Tulwryn travels so too does he go.

"What," cried Luther, "ye means to leave us? How can this be, for you are the greatest warrior the north has ever known. Ye must stay hither and sire many warriors so our clan can be made whole again."

"Nay," spoke Tulwryn, "I am naught of thy blood and mine seed needs be no part of your people. Keep my tale alive in the sagas if ye wish, but my destiny lies elsewhere. This much I know. Also understand this: Heidmar is no more. From this day onward, ye shall work diligently to build the strength of the north as a whole, for Gerdmor and Rodmar and Heidmar are made one. "

So mote it be," said Urgan, "Odhinn's decree is naught for we mortals to question. Go thither, master Tulwryn, and know that ye shall live on in our tales and legends for thou saved us from a great evil this day."

"A terrible evil has been destroyed in the entire world," replied Dillwyn, "naught just in the north, but over the whole of the land. I wonder if the sleeping southerners know how close they came to becoming dragon fodder?" The entire company exploded in laughter at the dwarf's question, yet Dillwyn was serious in his statement. Never, since the dawn of life on Phantasodyssea, had such a dangerous evil been spawned. Little known to them, it would not be the last. But for now, all was quiet and there would remain a great peace in the north for many years to come.

Tulwryn rode with the army for some leagues, laughing and boasting of the battle, but in time, when they were far enough south, and away from the darkness of the war, he turned to his friends and bid them fare well. The bright sun was burning high in the blue sky and the darkness of the midnight sun was many days behind them. A raven cawed loudly as it floated overhead and a brisk chill traversed down many a spine. Spurring his steed, Tulwryn turned west and galloped off into the distance, to future adventures in the south, but not to his home in Nuvia, and Dillwyn was close behind.

Halgr Manslayer was fast asleep in the chieftain's wain and buried under a great many furs and heavy blankets. She felt Tulwryn's seed stir within her womb as she dreamed of a New Age and a noble king, good and just. Tall and pale he was, with flowing hair the color of spun gold but with dark eyes that burned with the storm of vengeance.

Here ends Book One

BOOK II

Trail of Vengeance

Wales and cries of terror ripped through the night as the slaughter raged on. Zulanmalh and his family huddled low in a secret antechamber guarded by a legion of the most loyal of the king's Royal Guard. But even in the safety of their seclusion, they could not be protected from the horrific sounds of battle and mayhem that coursed through the streets of Phaedron.

Outside, the war ebbed and flowed like a red sea splashing blood and gore on the very steps of the palace. Lynch mobs, rebels, legionnaires, and vagrants vied for top position, yet anarchy ruled in the king's stead. Suddenly, a great blast rocked the main gate and portcullis of the city and a host of evil poured into Phaedron like a plague as fire fell from the sky consuming friend and foe alike.

On a huge black stallion rode Kimark Khan, warrior-wizard and sworn enemy of the House of Zula. He entered the city a conqueror, sword in hand and wet scalps dripping from his steed's bridle. His long and flowing dark cape billowed in the breeze of war revealing black gilded chainmaile underneath . . .

SYNOPSIS OF BOOK TWO

An ancient prophecy foretold that a stranger from the south, the *Bloodsword*, would unite the warring northern tribes against Darkoth, the evil Frost Dragon, and his minions. This Tulwryn did with great fervor. But the prophecy also foretold he would assume the throne of the House of Rexor, yet Tulwryn always said that prophecies were like destinies and they were made to be thwarted. Therefore, he left the grey frozen lands of the north and returned to the world of the south, yet he left his seed in the womb of Heidmar, and that destiny he did not care to usurp.

So, for many leagues did Tulwryn and the dwarf from Carthus ride. South did they come, crossing the Basalt River and finding their way to the Phaedron Wood, and with luck, they hoped to find employment in the great Citadel itself, for the south was much different than the north and a man's keep was often counted in gold coins rather than the strength of his thews. But the doom that had settled over Tulwryn long ago came back upon him and luck was not on their side.

Whilst traveling through the dark forests of the Phaedron Wood, the two had taken up company with a small band of L'hoehnian silk merchants. After only a fortnight of traveling with the cutthroats, they awoke one crisp morning to discover that they had been betrayed to a legion of the High Elder's guard. Their weapons had been taken by the outlaws, yet their stolen Phaedron ponies were left in camp to seal their fate. They had been taken prisoner for the crime of vagrancy and theft, for the horses they had been caught with bore the royal brand of the

High Elder, and Zulanmalh IV, the fourth Phaedron ruler from the house of Zula, was not a compassionate king.

Their trial was held and the sentence quickly set; they were to walk the final walk, the dreaded *Phaedron League of Death*, for the king saw in Tulwryn's dark eyes a great and indomitable strength, and he feared for his safety and the safety of his kingdom. But the High Elder had other worries besides these two unlikely heroes, for in Phaedron, there was new talk of the return of Kimark Khan, and that name the king feared even more.

And so, as Tulwryn and the dwarf sat in their dungeon cell and awaited their last days, far to the east, high atop the frozen peak of Malador, Kimark Khan brooded in his hall and plotted the plan that would allow him to extract his vengeance upon the king.

And here continues the heroic saga of Tulwryn Bloodsword, the Warrior of Phantasodyssea. Saddle up and embark with him on a fantastic odyssey as he battles his way across Phantasodyssea, a world filled with magic and heroic adventure; embark with him on a *Trail of Vengeance!*

ONE

Dungeons under Phaedron

It was a crisp morning, the music of birds hung in the air and there was a lightness of heart that danced over meadow and glen. Nowhere was the din of battle felt or remembered. The dragon was dead and the northern tribes united. Tulwryn breathed a sigh of relief. It was good to be done with the business of magic and prophecies, he thought to himself, yet the weight of the Bloodsword tugging at his side made his mind stir to darker times. He touched the hilt of the grim weapon and pushed the thought out of his mind. It had been many days since the last battle, and the shadow of the Bloodsword had been quiet. All the better, thought Tulwryn, to banish the spirit of the sword and forget the past altogether.

A raven cawed from the top of a tall ash, then stretched its wings and took to the sky. Tulwryn watched as the bird disappeared over the horizon, then slid off of his mount and walked to the edge of the river. It was late winter and most of the Basalt River remained frozen, but the past few days had been unusually warm and so there were a few patches of break water where the ice had thawed. Kneeling, Tulwryn bent over to get a drink from the cold, sweet water.

Snow crunched under his knees as his lips caressed the river's surface. The water was refreshing and his mind swam in ecstasy. After taking his fill, Tulwryn leaned back, but he was caught by his own reflection in the rippling waters. He saw the contours of his face; strong lines framed his chin and brow, yet he seemed years older. Had the last few winters with the northern barbarians aged him so, he wondered, or was it all the wars? Then a dark thought entered his mind, perhaps it was neither, perhaps it was the grim magic of the sword that was aging him.

Tulwryn tried to banish the thought from his mind when suddenly he noticed something in the water. He leaned closer to his reflection and sheer terror flooded his being, for in the creamy water of the river he witnessed his form changing into that of Durayn, his dead wife. Deeper into the reflection he was drawn, and once again, he relived the doom that had overshadowed his life. He saw his farm burning, and his four sons lying dead. His mind was reeling in the terror of his past and he fought hard to banish the scenes from his consciousness.

Time seemed to stand still, and in an instant, he was the center of the world. The sky was calm, yet dark and grey and wet, but a whisper of the wind told him that he was once again in Nuvia. Tulwryn glanced around, but he was alone. An overwhelming fear gripped his heart and he began to run. Like a hunted elk he ran, over hill and dale he ran, his heart pounding to the point of bursting. A large oak root sprung from the moist ground and tripped him as he ran, and he fell, a thousand lifetimes he fell, into a dark and foreboding nightmare.

When he finally stopped falling, he lay still for a few moments on the ground.

"Where am I," he asked himself, "and what is this terror by which I am imprisoned?" Slowly, he rose to his feet, yet his hands burned with fire. Glancing at his open palms, he saw them soaked with dark warm blood, and then he noticed the lifeless body of Durayn lying dead at his feet. Grieving, he knelt beside the corpse, wishing to undo the deed, but he could not. He looked into his wife's eyes, glazed with death, and suddenly her face became that of Halgi Mansbane, Grimthor's daughter.

Tulwryn screamed and grabbed for the sword that hung at his side, but it was not there. Spinning, he rose to his feet, hawk eyes scanning the area for his weapon. There was a shrill cry, and then laughter. He knew that laugh, he told himself. Yes, he knew that laugh. Then again, the body on the ground changed. The folds in the cloak billowed and the armor grew dark and grim. There was a creaking, the sound of bones long dead, mending. And then, huddled before him, was the sickening form of the Volva of Heidmar, the minion of the dragon and his dread enemy.

>From under the folds of her cloak came a skinless hand, its sharp finger bones reaching to slash his flesh, yet Tulwryn was bound as if by iron fetters and heavy chains and could not move.

"What kind of sorcery is this," he whispered silently to himself, "this witch has been dead for more than two moons yet she assaults me from beyond the grave! Surely this is madness."

Terror seized Tulwryn's flesh as he felt the razor sharpness of the Volva's talons pierce his skin, then suddenly everything went black.

"Wake up, Tulwryn, wake up."

Tulwryn, soaked through and through with the filth of his own perspiration, sat up on his small cot. Through squinted eyes, he gazed around the tiny cell. The putrid scent of a burning tallow candle floated on the stale air of the dungeon and barely illuminated the room. Dark stone walls, green with mold and wet with slime surrounded him. Through the dim amber glow of the candle, he could make out the friendly face of Dillwyn the dwarf peering back at him through the darkness of the cell.

"Another night spent in terror," asked the dwarf, as he fumbled with cloak and blanket trying to help Tulwryn to his feet.

"Aye," answered Tulwryn, as he took a ladle full of cool water from the dwarf and drank it down. There was a taste of iron ore in the water and it was not refreshing, but it was wet. He had had worse in past days, and so he did not complain. Taking a cloth from a pile of refuse in a corner of the cell, he dampened it with the stale water and wiped it across his burning brow.

"Mine soul is in torment, dear friend, and I cannot stop these nightmares. How this doom has settled on me, I know naught. But now ye have been drawn into this grim reality."

"Tulwryn, ye are mine dear friend," answered the dwarf, "and I do not hold ye responsible for this accursed situation."

"But 'twas I who was made to watch camp the night we were ransacked . . ."

Dillwyn raised a finger and silenced his friend in mid sentence.

"We were not ransacked. We were betrayed. And when we escape from this pit, we shall hunt those bandits down and have our revenge. But for now, we must maintain all of our wits or we will surely go mad."

For a fortnight, the two adventurers had been held captive in the lower dungeons under Phaedron, awaiting their execution. It was an unlikely predicament in which they found themselves. Most of the tale was but a grim memory in Tulwryn's mind, not much more than a hazy dream. He remembered that he and Dillwyn rode hard for many leagues. South they came, crossing the Basalt River and finding their way to the Phaedron Wood, and with luck, they hoped to find employment in the great Citadel itself, for the south was much different than the north and a man's keep was often counted in gold coins rather than the strength of his thews. But the doom that had settled over Tulwryn long ago came back upon him and luck was not on his side.

Whilst traveling through the dark forests of the Phaedron Wood, the two had taken up company with a small band of L'hoehnian silk merchants. At first, the companionship seemed an inviting thing since the two were able to trade in their northern attire for more fashionable southern wear, although Dillwyn kept his Carthusian chainmaile, bronze gauntlets, and gilded war helm carefully guarded.

Once suited in their new L'hoehnian silks and leathers, the two looked like they would be more at home amongst the tents and caravans of the Azazel Plain rather than having just spent the past three winters in the frozen north. However, after only a fortnight of traveling with the cutthroats, they awoke one crisp morning to discover that they had been betrayed to a legion of the High Elder's guard. Tulwryn had not known how this was possible, since it was he that had been chosen to stand at night watch. Perhaps it was some exotic drug or potion. Many a weary traveler have claimed more than once that the L'hoehnian's employed such poisons for their devious work at kidnapping beautiful young women from under the unsuspecting noses of their drugged husbands, only later to be sold as high priced slaves along with their illegal silk. Yet, how it happened was of no matter to Tulwryn; what did matter was the fact that their weapons had been taken by the outlaws, yet their stolen Phaedron ponies were left in camp to seal their fate. They were then taken prisoner for the crime of vagrancy and theft, for the horses they had been caught with bore the royal brand of the High Elder, and Zulanmalh IV, the fourth Phaedron ruler from the house of Zula, was not a compassionate king.

Their trial was held and the sentence quickly set; they were to walk the final walk, the dreaded *Phaedron League of Death*, for the king saw in Tulwryn's dark eyes a great and indomitable strength, and he feared for his own safety and the safety of his kingdom. But the High Elder had other worries besides these two unlikely heroes, for in Phaedron, there was new talk of the return of Kimark Khan, and that name the king feared even more.

And so, as Tulwryn and the dwarf sat in their dungeon cell and awaited their last days, far to the east, high atop the frozen peak of Malador, Kimark Khan brooded in his hall and plotted the plan that would allow him to extract his vengeance upon the king.

"Ye are right, my friend," said Tulwryn, "to dwell on the past is no matter. We shall deal with them L'hoehnian cutthroats when the time comes. But for now, we must needs figure a way out of this hole."

Suddenly, there came a slight knock at the heavy oaken door that sealed their cell, and a grim smile wormed its way across the dwarf's aged and lined face. "Aye, my friend," whispered Dillwyn, "a way out of this hole has already been found, and help has arrived."

There was the rasping sound of steel grating on iron and then the thud of a heavy bolt being dropped. Slowly, the aged wood of that ancient portal creaked as the door swung open. The outer corridor was dark and there was a faint mustiness lingering on stale air, much stronger than presently in their cell.

As the door opened, a foggy grayish mist entered the chamber. Every muscle in Tulwryn's body twitched with anticipation, yet across his brow was the confused look of caution mixed with amazement as the mist sent out long tendrils of wispy smoke and then, in a matter or moments, a small, darkly cloaked figure appeared before them in their chamber.

Looking at the dwarf, Tulwryn asked, "But how?" Again, the dwarf simply raised a stubby finger and silenced him.

"Ask naught, mine friend, just be grateful. I shall explain everything when we are free from these dungeons. Let us be off."

Tulwryn and the dwarf then followed the small creature out into the musty corridor where they turned east and hurried down the long, dark hall. Tulwryn noticed that four Phaedron guards lay dead on the ground just outside their cell door, and more confusion entered his tormented mind. How could a small being, such as their present guide, kill four trained Phaedron soldiers, and so swiftly and quietly? His head swam with images of magic and sorcery but he pushed the thoughts from his mind as he followed the two before him through the tunnels.

The lower dungeons under the mighty citadel, the city-state of Phaedron, were enormous and ran on for countless league after countless league. There were no window grates or portals of any kind to allow entrance of the light of day and Tulwryn knew neither if it were day or eve.

The long and twisting corridors were black as pitch, save for the soft illumination cast off by the few sconces that held the burning tallow tapers that lined the damp stone walls every few fathoms. Shadows danced across the halls and into the fugitive's minds as the candle's eerie glow guided their way. The reeking stench of the tallow was all but stifling and Tulwryn thought more than once that these burning tapers did not have the familiar scent of animal fat. Then he remembered, many years past, in Nuvia, his burning farm, and his dead sons; he knew then that these were no ordinary tallow tapers, but candles comprised of human fat, and he held his thoughts at bay, for the urge to lose the contents of his stomach were strong.

Tulwryn was a warrior, he had become out of necessity a professional killer and the thought of murder bothered him naught, but the idea of mutilating the dead for mere utility was something he could not fathom. He realized then what kind of man Zulanmalh IV was, and he vowed to himself at that moment, if ever he should escape this doom he shall return to destroy this king and extinguish his evil empire like he did to the dragon in the north so many moons ago.

Time ran on and on as the three crept through the dungeons. The drone of their footfalls were ate up by the dead air of the tunnels and an atmosphere of sorcery surrounded them. Tulwryn felt that the creature's magic was not only guiding them through the darkness of the maze, but cloaking them as well. He felt a strange prickling at the nape of his neck, and a thought ran through his brain: Where were all the Phaedron soldiers that normally stand guard at the various underground posts? He once again thought he was back in his own nightmare, doomed to creep on for eternity though the stifling underground blackness and trapped within his own mind. That thought, however, came to a crashing halt as a loud explosion rocked the entire corridor and a brilliant ball of white flame illuminated the entire area. For a moment, he was blinded by the intensity of the blast, his fully dilated pupils instantly shrank to pinpoints painfully and his ears were deafened.

"What the . . . ," screamed Tulwryn, unable to even hear himself. Dillwyn then grabbed his dazed friend's hand and hurried him to a dark alcove. All about them were dozens upon dozens of Phaedron soldiers, and in their midst Tulwryn witnessed their tiny guide transform itself into a seething and hideous dragon-like beast.

Soldiers assaulted the beast with rage and steel, yet the creature met each wave of assault with searing flame. From the mouth of the monster, billowed flames hot enough to melt iron, and the stench from the creature's innards were stifling. Warriors dropped like flies as they assaulted the beast, only to be instantly rendered into sizzling heaps of grey ash. Tulwryn felt his heart leap with the anticipation of battle, and his branded palms itched for blood. But, in a short eternity, came the voice of the Shadow of the Bloodsword:

"Not now, Tulwryn. Not here. There will be other battles for us, greater battles. For now, merely escape!" Never before had the Shadow of the sword spoken to him without the aid of the weapon itself, and Tulwryn was puzzled by the apparition.

During that intense battle, there was a moment of suspended time, where the dragon and the small creature were one. In that moment, even over the roar of battle, came a small voice, soft and tender:

"I cannot hold them off much longer; mine strength wanes. Quickly, ye must make haste if you are to survive. Run hither down yonder hall and turn south, then go north for twelve fathoms. Ye shall then come to a gate. Exit the dungeons through that gate and flee the city. If I am able, I shall rendezvous with ye at the appointed location. Wait only three hours. If I am not there in the allotted time, make haste and leave the area. For surely I am dead if I am not there. Quickly now, be gone at once!" Tulwryn blinked in disbelief as the small creature disappeared and once again, the frightening image of the dragon assumed its lethal assault.

Stumbling through the darkness, the din of battle behind them still ringing in their ears, Tulwryn and the dwarf made their exit. Down the long halls they ran, following the creature's directions to the letter. After a time, they came to the gate. For an endless eternity, the hero from Nuvia and the dwarf from Carthus stood motionless. The two, ragged and worn from weeks in their cell, were about to taste freedom once again, yet there was a sense of doom and apprehension in the air.

"Could this be a trap," asked Tulwryn.

"Nay, my friend. I know that sorcerer well. We are not betrayed."

"What kind of friends do you keep, Dillwyn? I have not known you to traffick in such affairs as magic and sorcery.

"A lot has befallen us since the days up north. There is much to learn, and much to tell. Quick, let us be through this gate and make our way to the rendezvous point. I will reveal everything once we are there."

Tulwryn looked down at his open palms. The scars blazed a bright red, brighter even than the day they were freshly branded by the Bloodsword. He did not like the idea of fleeing a fight, yet he knew that more battles lay in his future, so he fretted naught. Yes, he thought to himself, I am Tulwryn Bloodsword, and I shall return hither with a vengeance!

And with that thought, he followed his friend through the gate and into the light of day, where the blazing sun of the hot Phaedron Desert burned like a forge upon their tired minds.

Thus ends Chapter One of Book Two

TWO

The Devil's Anvil

"It appears that we were betrayed," shouted Tulwryn, in a fit of lusty anger. "I knew it! I am a warrior, not meant to cower and run like a timid lass at the first sign of trouble; we should have stayed and fought. Better to die in battle that be fried like a joint of mutton in this inferno!"

"Cease thy fury, Tulwryn," retorted the dwarf. "This is the last place the Phaedrons will search for us. Behold, the Phaedron League of Death, and the Phaedron Desert and Helheim Plateau beyond that, if we are lucky enough to make it that far. Anyway, how would ye suppose we have fought that battle back yonder in the tunnels? Presently we have naught weapons nor armor. 'Twould have been a slaughter. Even a warrior knows when to fight and when to run."

The Phaedron Desert, often called the Devil's Anvil, was the most forbidding place in all of Phantasodyssea; the Helheim Plateau stood as a virtual paradise in comparison. During the height of the day, surface temperatures soar high enough to melt lead, and at night, plummet low enough to freeze quicksilver! Only the strongest and most wily traveler can survive in such a hostile wilderness.

And with outstretched arms the dwarf smiled, for before them lay a grim and barren waste of red sand and parched clay. Images of sparkling diamonds glittered across the desert sands, yet those diamonds were not precious gems, but the bones of those long since dead. Nothing could be seen for leagues but the gleam of sunlight off the many shards of bones, bleached dazzling white by the intensity of the blazing Phaedron sun.

"And this is your great escape plan," Tulwryn sighed and threw his hands up in disgust.

"Come, dear friend, do not give up on me yet. Remember, I am keen on warm climates and my knowledge of desert lore far surpasses that of our frozen past up north. HA! If the north could not defeat us, why thinks ye that we shall perish hither?"

Dillwyn swiftly turned and strolled away westward on heavy loins before Tulwryn could answer. Sighing heavily, Tulwryn said nothing, but merely followed his companion into the heat of the desert.

The searing heat of the Phaedron Desert was legendary throughout the whole of Phantasodyssea, and for certain, the Phaedron League of Death was no walk in the park either. Tulwryn pondered about that especially grim form of execution that the Phaedrons so lustily employed, where the condemned were starved for a fortnight in the darkness of the dungeons beneath the city and then forced to exit the citadel through the very alabaster gate that they themselves had chosen to take on their escape route. Lesser fools would have stayed and fought, to the death if need be, but not them. No, thought Tulwryn, we are great fools, willing to test the very gods at their own dank games of peril. Many times they had cheated death, willing to throw their lives away at the drop of a hat only to find themselves alive, and scurrying on to the next adventure. When would their luck run out, he wondered. Now seems as good a time as any, and he glanced about himself, scanning the narrow corridor they were in, barely able to see the vast desert beyond.

Slowly the blazing sun inched its way across a clear and cloudless sky, and for a league, the two walked the corridor of death. The Phaedron League of Death was a massive man-made structure; on either side of them were walls sixteen fathoms in height, hand hewn from solid granite and topped with razor sharp iron spikes. The walls of the corridor were set a mere three fathoms apart, making the path a narrow focal point whereas to concentrate the intensity of the hot Phaedron sun onto any so unlucky enough to venture forth into its grim maw.

The bones of past victims that littered the corridor stood as proof enough that the elements of Phantasodyssea were more than a worthy adversary for even the stoutest warrior. Sweat poured forth from Tulwryn's brow like a waterfall, and in a matter of minutes, his entire body was thoroughly soaked and he felt the chills of dehydration, and the weakness of limb that follows. Still dressed in their prison rags, Tulwryn noticed through hazy eyes that Dillwyn carried no water or knapsack of food, and the thought troubled him.

"What provisions have you made for our sustenance," yelled Tulwryn to the dwarf.

Dillwyn, who was already a few fathoms ahead of his friend, stopped and turned around to look at the weakening warrior behind him. Looking through sweat soaked eyes, the dwarf began to laugh.

"Are ye hungry already, my friend?"

"Nay, but I see that you carry no waterskins or knapsack of food. How shall we survive this anvil of heat without water?"

"I have been instructed on the *how* and the *where* of this desert, my friend. First, we are to trudge on through this corridor. This we must do by sheer willpower alone. If we survive the League of Death, then provisions will await us at our first night's camp. But until then, we are on our own. Do not fret, we have seen worse days, have we not?"

A thousand adventures ran through Tulwryn's mind and he indeed remembered many grim days that they should never have survived. Why the gods were keeping them alive was anyone's guess. Probably for their twisted entertainment and nothing more, thought Tulwryn. He shrugged his shoulders, wiped the sweat from his face, and watched the dwarf as he once again turned and continued walking westward. Tulwryn simply followed. More thoughts of dark sorcery paraded through his mind at the folly of their entire escape and the unfolding plan that Dillwyn was leading him through, but speaking naught. High overhead, Tulwryn noticed black shapes soaring silently amidst the desert heat and wondered how long it would be ere his flesh filled the bellies of vultures.

Half a day had passed ere the two finally exited the League of Death. Tulwryn could hardly believe they were free from the corridor, and alive at that. However, when he seen the vastness of the entire Phaedron Desert laid out before him his heart was filled with doom and he was overcome with a sense of melancholy he had never experienced before.

"Is there no end to this hell," he screamed, his mind reeling in apparent madness.

"Over that yonder ridge is a sandstone outcropping, and a grotto. We shall camp there and be free from this heat for a while," answered the dwarf. "Now hurry on and tarry naught."

At once, Dillwyn turned and resumed his inhuman pace as Tulwryn stood in amazement at the dwarf's stamina and strength. Through the intensity of the blazing heat, vapors bent the rays of the sun and the entire world shimmered in Tulwryn's mind as he watched Dillwyn disappear over a distant hill many fathoms yonder. Summoning strength from he knew not where, Tulwryn trudged forth and followed the dwarf.

By the time Tulwryn arrived at the sandstone grotto Dillwyn had already pitched a makeshift camp and had changed into more suitable desert attire. The dwarf was seated beneath a small canvas tent, clothed in flowing linen robes of the whitest-white, a bejeweled dagger was stuffed in a sash of golden cloth that was bound about his waist. His sun-browned face and arms set a stark contrast to the robes he wore and on each finger was placed a silver ring encrusted with precious gems of ruby, sapphire, and pearl. Tulwryn took him for a seasoned desert rat rather than his close and trusted friend.

Staggering into camp, Tulwryn looked about the tent and then collapsed onto a soft red velvet cushion. Dillwyn handed him a large waterskin and a few choice mangos then reclined back on his own pile of cushions and resumed puffing on his long and gnarled pipe.

Tulwryn gulped down the water, colder and sweeter than

any he remembered, and then paused to gaze at his surroundings once more. Nothing made sense here. Under the small canvas tent was laid a king's ransom in the finest silks and hand loomed linen that he had ever seen. Cushions crafted in exotic hues and fabrics were piled high and strewn about the tent; plush woven rugs littered the ground underneath their charred and tired feet, and the air was cool and refreshing.

"What is all this," Tulwryn asked. "More sorcery?"

"Reality is what we make of it, old friend," replied the dwarf. "What ye see here is a gift from a friend." He took a few long drags of his pipe and blew a great smoke ring in the air.

"Do ye see this pipe," asked Dillwyn. Tulwryn nodded. "This too, was a gift from an old friend. At first, I believed it to be just an ordinary old pipe. But I later discovered that it held many secrets, as many as my old friend himself held."

"Whatever are you talking about? What old friend do you mean . . . one of the clansmen of Heidmar? I knew none of them to partake in smoke or secrets of magic. Please, tell me for I grow more confused by the second." Tulwryn fidgeted, finding himself unable to get comfortable in such surroundings, rolled to his stomach and propped himself up on one elbow. Taking a bite of the luscious mango, his dark eyes beamed at the dwarf and he listened to what his friend had to say, hoping to make some sense of the mystery in which he was trapped.

"I will tell ye everything, but first, get changed into these robes and find comfort under this tent. Once we are relaxed, I will reveal aught I know." The dwarf tossed a bundle of fine hand loomed linen robes to Tulwryn, yet the Nuvian warrior just gazed at him through confused eyes.

"Am I to don these, as ye have done? Ye look more like a desert dwelling noble than a dwarven warrior from Carthus! Where is thy armor? Surely, your magical friend could have outfitted us with armor and weapons rather than these robes and finery. We are warriors, not kings. We should be searching out that band of cutthroats and regaining our weapons rather than wasting time here under the comfort of this sorcerer's tent."

"In due time, in due time. But first, we must relax and regain our strength. We are lucky to be alive, Tulwryn. The Phaedron Desert is an unforgiving foe, and a stupid traveler survives naught. Get changed and we shall discuss more later." A large smoke ring emerged from the dwarf's pursed lips and he reclined back and closed his old and tired eyes as Tulwryn, robes in hand, disappeared from the tent.

The sun grew dim and night fell quickly on the desert. The two made no fire, but the large silver disk of the full moon cast enough light to illume the camp. A scent of jasmine and passionflower floated on the air and Tulwryn believed himself to be enchanted and in an intoxicated dream. The white robes he wore were an inviting change from the heavy iron chainmaile and stiff leather armor he was used to wearing, and much more comfortable than the rough burlap of his prison raiment. He felt their touch pleasurable on his skin, almost invigorating.

Languidly, Tulwryn returned to the tent where Dillwyn sat, sleeping on a heap of lavender silk brocade cushions and heavily embroidered rugs of plush fibers dyed a deep royal purple. The warrior from Nuvia, with the graceful poise of a jungle cat, approached the dwarf and silently sat across from him, but said nothing.

Sitting in serene silence and enjoying the comfort of the cool desert night, Tulwryn's mind drifted off to more peaceful days. Gone were the memories of war and battle, of blood and sorrow. Even the heavy burden he carried with him seemed lighter here. And the grim memory of the slaying of Halgi Mansbane was erased as well.

The dwarf stirred awake bringing Tulwryn back to the present.

"Aye, methinks ye will make for a fine desert lad, Tulwryn," spoke Dillwyn, eyeing the fine robes that his comrade wore. Smiling, he tossed the warrior a long dagger, not unlike the one he wore.

"I am here, relaxed and changed. Therefore, speak to me of all this madness," Tulwryn said, catching the dagger in his large hands. He looked at the exquisite weapon. The blade alone was a full cubit long, and the handle was carved from a single slab of ivory. There was a large emerald embedded in the pommel, and the silver scabbard was encrusted with emeralds as well. He unsheathed the blade and eyed the keen edge, then slammed the knife back into its sheath. "It seems real enough," he said, shoving the weapon into his sash.

Dillwyn reached once again for his pipe and tobacco pouch, and then sat up cross-legged.

"Do ye remember mine journey to Covensted with the Heidmarians?" Tulwryn nodded. "The wizard that we encountered there was the one who gave me this pipe; he was the Keeper of the Dragon Shield as well."

"These things are beginning to make some sense now," said Tulwryn, fingering the linen of his robe. "But what about our escape, and that shape changing creature?"

"Luckily, even though all our weapons were stolen by those L'hoehnian outlaws, my pipe was touched naught. Aye, the Phaedrons confiscated mine armor and replaced it with those course prison rags, yet I was able to stash the pipe and pouch for a later time. As I have already said, at first I assumed the pipe to be nothing more than a pipe, just a leisurely tool for relaxing enjoyment. Yet, one eve whilst ye slept in the dungeon, I lit the pipe and had a smoke. Now what amazed me at the time was the fact that I had smoked the pipe many times ere then, yet that night something strange and magical happened."

Tulwryn sat up and listened intensely, curiosity gripping his mind and pinching his nerves. The dwarf leaned closer, as to whisper in extreme confidence, and the atmosphere of the tent took on a somber mood.

"As I puffed on the pipe, a mood of lethargy enveloped me. I blew a large smoke ring and then it happened . . . I saw his face, the face of Mimir, the he-witch of Covensted!" Dillwyn paused, seeing that Tulwryn's face had become almost ashen with fear. He leaned back, and then continued.

"It is alright, old friend, Mimir is a dear and trusted ally, remember. His morals and ethics are legendary. Have ye ever heard of the legend of the Swine People?"

"Should I have," asked Tulwryn?

"Indeed, ye should have. 'Tis one of the most interesting of the old legends, and explains a great many things of ethics and magic."

"Enlighten me then, old man." Tulwryn pulled a few scarlet pillows closer and reclined back, awaiting the dwarf's tale.

"Alright, I shall. Once, ages ago, when the world was young, there sat an old wizard and a village chieftain. No one even remembers the village anymore, just this old yarn. During the meeting betwixt the wizard and the chieftain, some slaves stoked a fire pit nearby where the men were sitting, and then put on spits a large leg of pork. The old wizard looked at the roasting meat, his heart became heavy and he furrowed his brow. Looking at the chieftain he asked, 'Tell me sire, is thy village of good or evil men?'

"The chieftain, looking quite shaken and aghast answered readily, 'We are good and noble men; no where in my realm is evil permitted. Why?'

"There was a long silence ere the wizard spoke. 'Sire,' said the wizard, 'ye have summoned me here, with hopes to employ me, betting the life of thy village that mine spells can rid ye of the dragon that lives in yonder hills. Time and again, I have heard ye say that the dragon is evil. Now why is this so? Perhaps because he steals sheep and goats and sometimes even the lives of men; so, if the dragon is evil because he kills men, how can ye say that men are not evil, since they kill swine?'

"At this the chieftain was angered and let fly his fists in a rage towards the wizard, but a spell of protection was about the old man for he wore the Mantle of Covensted, a great cloak of invincibility, and the blows of the village chieftain fell shorthand and the wizard laughed at the foolish man.

"'I see,' said the wizard, 'that I am correct, and that ye and your village are evil as the dragon is evil. So, I will curse ye both to thy own plight!'

"And with that, and a word, the wizard laid a charm about the village; and every man of forty winters, and women too, were transformed into swine, and their flesh fed the whole of the village, but the village knew naught that the swine they ate was not swine at all, but human flesh. And the swine of the village then became as men, and women, but these new people did not eat of the dead meat knowing the terror they had once experienced, being swine. Also too, the wizard layed a charm about the dragon and so kept it at bay from entering the village from that day further. That old wizard was none other than mine dear old friend from Covensted, Mimir. And know this Tulwryn, if Mimir is that concerned about a nameless hog, how much more will he concern himself with his close and dear friends, such as I? Nay, fret naught, we are not betrayed by the magic of Covensted."

"Ye mean to tell me that this sorcerer that gave ye that pipe is eons old and is one and the same as the soothsayer in thy yarn. What ye make me for, a fool?"

"No, Tulwryn," spoke the dwarf, "a fool ye are naught, but aye, 'tis the same man, if he is even a man. There is more to know than can be seen under the stars of our world!" Dillwyn leaned back and smiled, weaving his stout fingers together behind his head.

"Still, this explains nothing of our escape and that dread creature that led us forth from the tunnels under Phaedron. Was that some grim sprite summoned by this ancient sorcerer?"

"Nay, that was no sprite, but Mimir himself, come to our aid. One eve as you slept on your cot, I puffed on my pipe and Mimir came to me as if in a dream. I told him of our plight and he fashioned a plan to spirit us away. Of course, all dealings with those of the dark arts has its price and he informed me of a charge we are to set forth on if our escape is made whole."

"A charge?" Tulwryn sighed heavily. "This is sounding worse by the second!"

"Everything has a price, Tulwryn. Do ye value your life naught, or does the idea of a quest set thy blood afire with excitement?"

A boyish grin of adventure wormed its way across Tulwryn's scarred face. Yes, his friend knew him better than he knew himself, and adventure was always on his mind, and in his heart.

"I can see the glint of excitement in your dark eyes," said the dwarf. "Get then, some rest for now, and sleep heavily throughout the morrow. From here onward, we shall trek at night where the heat of the day cannot harm us. We have a long journey ahead of us, for we must needs make our way across the desert, and then further across the Helheim plateau. Once off the plateau, we will enter the Foothills of Insanity, and then onward into the depths of the Sulphur Mountains. It will be there, in the bowels of those accursed hills, that we will rendezvous with Mimir himself, and he shall then disclose his charge to us in full. This is all I know, and I have kept mine promise to ye by telling ye this."

Tulwryn nodded.

"Aye, this news pleases me naught, but I suppose anything is better than wasting away in the dungeons under Phaedron."

"Mimir has friends in Phaedron, Tulwryn, and he has promised to return to us our armor and belongings. I doubt whether he can obtain for us our weapons of choice, but I am certain we shall not be empty handed when we leave his company. Please, rest now, for three days after the morrow we must needs cross the heart of the Devil's Anvil and we will need all of our strength for such a chore."

Again, Tulwryn nodded a grim nod, and then reclined back on his cushions, drifting off to a deep and noble sleep.

Thus ends Chapter Two of Book Three

THREE

Adivarapupeta

The two slept hard throughout the night and on through the heat of the next day, although they felt naught the heat under the safety of Mimir's magical tent. By the time Tulwryn woke from his slumber, the sun had already set and the moon was riding high in the sky, and the dwarf had already broken camp. Tulwryn shook dreams from his head and peered through hazy eyes. Everything was gone, save the tent. Nowhere were there any velvet cushions, or hand loomed linens. Gone were the many plush embroidered rugs and silk brocade tapestries as well. All that was left from the previous night was the tent itself, a large bowl of fruit, one half full waterskin, his bejeweled dagger and the white robes he wore. Even the fragrances of the jasmine and passionflower he remembered had vanished as if in a dream. The warrior still wore the fine white linen robe, and the blade Dillwyn gifted him was still stuck through his sash, but all else was gone.

With a start, Tulwryn jumped up and gazed about himself, then called out the dwarf's name. There was no answer. Angered beyond words, Tulwryn cursed the gods in his own Nuvian tongue and spat at the charred ground under his sandaled feet.

Suddenly, from behind him came a noise. He spun around quick as a flash of lightning, steel in hand, with muscles tensed for battle and teeth bared, only to see Dillwyn sitting atop a large Phaedron camel, and holding the reigns of another in tow.

Tulwryn was amazed at the sight before him. Even though Dillwyn was a dwarf, atop that noble steed he seemed like a giant. The dwarf's white robes billowed in the slight air of the desert eve, and a glint of moonlight sparkled off of the bejeweled dagger stuck in his golden sash.

"Why curse me, my friend," asked the dwarf. "Are you mad?"

"I thought . . ."

Dillwyn raised a hand and silenced him.

"Never mind. I need no explanations. Come, help me stow the tent and we can be off. We are wasting valuable moonlight." The dwarf slid from his saddle harness and began pulling up the tent stakes.

"Where is all the other gear," Tulwryn asked.

"What other gear," replied the dwarf, tugging at a tent line. "Are ye going to help me or naught?"

Tulwryn helped bring down the tent, and then finished his questioning.

"The other gear . . . the cushions, the rugs, the linen, and the tapestries. Where did ye stow all that?"

A great laugh boomed from the dwarf's rotund belly.

"Tulwryn, there was no such gear around us last eve. Just this simple canvas tent, the two daggers we now wear, and these robes, all stowed here in this grotto by a friend of Mimir. There is no magic afoot, as ye had assumed, just some simple trappings of a nomad desert wanderer, given to us for use by a friend; a small favor, I suppose."

Scratching his head, Tulwryn watched as the dwarf loaded the folded tent onto the back of his camel and then mounted up. He was about to ask about this mysterious friend, but bit his tongue. Enough of this magic, he thought to himself, let us be gone from this accursed place.

"Are ye going to saddle up or just stand there scratching your head," Dillwyn yelled from atop his mount. Then, in an instant, he spurred his beast and headed off westward, silhouetted by the brilliant silver of a large full moon.

For a fortnight, the two travelers and their camels trekked their way westward across the burning sands of the unforgiving Phaedron Desert at night. The stars twinkled like the forbidden gems of an unremembered treasure, and Tulwryn often pondered how long it would be ere he gaze upon the blue skies over Caiwryn again.

Thus far, the journey had proven uneventful, for none so bold as to brave the barren sands of the desert had crossed their path. And indeed, even if there had been travelers in the area, since the two traveled at night, they would be passed like wraiths in the darkness, being neither seen nor heard.

Tulwryn did notice that for the entire length of the journey across the desert, the moon's silver disk neither waxed nor waned, and he pondered what grim magic Dillwyn had employed from the arsenal of that ancient wizard the dwarf called Mimir. It mattered little to him though, since the moon's light was needed to illume their way. Also, there was no end in sight to the supply of fresh fruit and water that Dillwyn produced, seemingly conjured out of thin air, and Tulwryn knew better than to ask needless questions of magic and sorcery. Certainly there was magic afoot, even if his friend denied it, and so Tulwryn held his tongue and asked naught.

The dwarf had grown exceedingly quiet during the course of their present travels, and this troubled Tulwryn, since normally Dillwyn was a talkative lot. Much had changed along their travels, and the turnings of the seasons had brought many new circumstances to his life. Perhaps, thought Tulwryn, that dwarves began their life cursing magic and sorcery only to embrace it in their later years. This idea did not seem to flow with what he knew about dwarves, yet the dwarves of Carthus were a different breed from the others of Phantasodyssea, and Dillwyn was indeed a Carthusian dwarf. Much mystery surrounded their present journey, and he often felt himself yearning for the simple life with the northern barbarians of Heidmar. One day I shall return north, he promised himself, but he knew that day would be long in coming.

Riding atop his camel, Tulwryn unsheathed his dagger. Gazing at the weapon in the moonlight, he was amazed at the craftsmanship of the thing. Surely, the gems alone were worth a king's ransom, and that was not to mention the fine silver of the scabbard, or the ivory of the hilt. The blade too, was finely wrought and honed to a razor's edge. Many strange thoughts ran through Tulwryn's mind and he sheathed the blade and shoved it back into his sash. If worse comes to worse, he murmured to himself, we could always sell these blades for armor and real weapons.

And so, the two slept by day and traveled only at night, and in fourteen days they were safely across the desert. However, the Helheim Plateau proved no less a formidable adversary than the desert itself, and many times they were blown off course by violent wind storms that blinded their camels and all but blotted out the stars and moon.

On the fourth day into the plateau, and right before daybreak, the dwarf came to a halt and Tulwryn assumed him to be seeking a place to make camp. Tulwryn quickly scanned the area, the blue din of the rising sun casting an eerie glow across the flat of the land, yet he could tell there was no suitable cover whereas to pitch camp.

"What thinks ye," yelled Tulwryn to his friend, who was but a few fathoms ahead of him and afoot with his camel in tow. "This is no place to pitch camp. We will be burnt to a cinder at first light! Methinks ye are losing thy touch, old friend."

"Nay, I seek naught a campsite. Come hither at once, Tulwryn, do not waste time with idle speech!"

Tulwryn dismounted and hurried to the dwarf, and what he found was beyond his wildest expectations.

"Is she alive," he asked?

"Aye, but barely," Dillwyn said, kneeling over a tiny girl, naked and half buried in the sand.

Tulwryn noticed that the girl was no fair beauty, but darkened by the intensity of the brilliant Phaedron sun to an almost opaque ebony hue. Her long black mane was littered with debris, and her face was parched; yet, she had the features of nobility. The two quickly dug the girl from the sand, wrapped her in fine linen, and packed her onto Tulwryn's camel, then once again resumed their trail westward.

In a matter of moments, the dwarf had located a suitable campsite under an oasis of tall date palms and pomegranate trees that were nestled around a small watering hole. The two quickly pitched the canvas tent on the far side of the water hole, under the canopy of the trees. Dillwyn then tended to the camels whilst Tulwryn looked after the girl.

For an eternity, Tulwryn just sat there gazing at the unconscious girl, a thousand desires running through his mind. He remembered Durayn in Nuvia, and Halgi from Heidmar; this child was like neither of them, yet, at the same time she was both of them at once. He instantly pushed all thoughts of love and lust from his mind, for he knew his life was meant naught for such pleasures of the flesh. For him, sensual pleasures only ended with pain and sorrow, and he had enough of that to last a lifetime. Shouldering two burdens were more than enough; he needed naught a third.

Feeling the girl's dry forehead, he realized that she was blazing under a fever, probably due to being caught in the heat of the plateau during the height of the previous day. He therefore, picked her up and carried her to the watering hole, and with the hands of a lover, he gently bathed her from head to toe in the cool waters under the shadows of those tall date palms.

The sun blazed forth with the brilliance of a forge and sent unrelenting waves of heat down upon the flat of the Helheim Plateau, yet the travelers were safe under the canopy of the oasis. Tulwryn had carried the girl back to the tent and dressed her in the fine white robes they had wrapped her in when they found her earlier that day. He then laid her to rest on a pallet of palm leaves. Dillwyn soon arrived bearing an armload of fresh date palms, pomegranates, and freshly filled waterskins.

"The camels are watered and tethered yonder under the trees," said the dwarf. "How is she coming along? Ye think she will live?" He tossed Tulwryn a date and then sat on crossed legs at the far end of the tent eager to consume his own.

"She will live," he said, then devoured his date with a bite and motioned for the dwarf to throw him another. The two sat in silence for some time consuming their meager meal, saying naught but thinking much.

Finally, Dillwyn stirred and broke the silence. "What shall we do with her? 'Tis hard enough to keep the beasts and ourselves alive in this inferno, another mouth to feed may end us all."

Tulwryn was about to answer when a frail voice pined from under the white linen. The girl stirred awake, then sat up on one elbow and looked at the strangers through glazed eyes of liquid brown, yet there was no fear behind her dark lashes.

"Who are ye," she asked. Her voice was soft and frail, and she spoke in a broken Phaedronian tongue, yet her accent was thick and the dwarf could not place her heritage, but the sound of her words were familiar to Tulwryn, however vague. It was like something from a distant memory or dream had suddenly come alive and invaded his waking mind. It was all very confusing.

"We might like to know the same about thee, mine dear lass," replied the dwarf with a wily grin. Tulwryn just sat there, a skulking frown etched across his face and an intense look of consternation looming behind his dark eyes.

"My name is Adivarapupeta," answered the girl, smiling. "You can call me Adi. How did I manage to become here?"

"That is a bit of a mystery, lady Adi," replied Dillwyn. "Earlier this morn, my comrade and I discovered ye half buried in the sand of the plateau, and naked. How did ye come to such a formidable locale, and alone at that?"

"And ye bathed me, and clothed me, yet raped me naught? Are ye angels from the heavens sent to protect me?"

"We are neither angels nor devils," spoke Tulwryn, ruefully. "We are merely travelers."

"The Helheim Plateau is hardly a place for casual traveling," she said.

"Indeed, 'tis naught," answered the dwarf, "which brings me back to mine original question: What were ye doing to be caught so in this dire wilderness, and alone without a proper male escort?"

"I am of Baezutu, far to the south. Do ye know of my village?" Dillwyn shook his head in the negative, never having ventured further south than the vast Plain of Kem. Yet Tulwryn knew all to well that town in the southern reaches of the world, for it was in Baezutu that he would venture forth and sell his yearly take of mistletoe. But that was a long time ago and he did not want to relive those grim memories

"Our village," spoke Adi, "was assaulted one eve by a rogue band of L'hoehnian marauders and I was taken prisoner, most likely to be sold into slavery, along with many other women of my village."

Tulwryn's sun-darkened knuckles turned white as his clenched fists drove the blood from his fingers and rage welled up in his heart. He could not tolerate the idea of herding young maidens like cattle for mere profit, and the thought of them L'hoehnian curs brought back the memory of the theft of the Bloodsword, which infuriated him further. He wondered if it were the same band, or if there were more groups of these desert rats afoot.

"I was with the bandits for many moons, yet they kept us bound, gagged, and blindfolded, so I knew naught where they were taking us. For the longest time we traveled by day, but suddenly the climate changed from warm to a most unbearable heat and we began to travel at night. I realized that we must have been entering some kind of desert for the caravan to employ such a change in the mode of its travels.

"Then one day this grim thought entered my mind, and I feared that we were being taken to Knob to be sold as food to the hideous cannibals that reside there. So then, I decided to attempt an escape. Since I figured I was doomed already, after managing to free myself from my fetters one afternoon whilst the entire caravan was camped and asleep, I lifted a root of the Kiputu Cactus that I discovered the bandits kept in an unlocked chest. The L'hoehnians are so egotistical they cared naught to post a guard by the slave tent thinking that their fetters would hold us. Perhaps they held the others, but my wrists are so slender 'twas no task to wriggle free from the bonds that held my tiny arms.

"I then stole away from the camp, naked and afoot. I had

heard that the Kiputu Cactus lowers one's body temperature, and therefore hoped to use it to offset the heat of the desert; at best, I prayed the poison would render me unconscious so as I could die peacefully and without pain. I knew naught the intensity of the Helheim Plateau, but the fate of being eaten alive by those evil Knobites was a worse proposal, and so I braved the sands of Helheim. I wandered for many days, without food and water, chewing on the root of the cactus for sustenance. The drug put me in a stupor and I felt naught the heat of the sun burning my pale flesh black. Thinking myself dead, I laid down to die, and I assume that is where ye found me."

"Heart rendering indeed, lady Adi." Dillwyn sympathetically spoke the words although they made no sense at all, since the Helheim Plateau lies naught on the path betwixt Baezutu and Knob. Even still, he was not one to call a lady a liar unless given reason, so he bit his tongue, and then looked at Tulwryn. There was a gleam of compassion in Dillwyn's eyes that Tulwryn had not noticed before, and ere he could say anything the dwarf spoke again.

"I motion we keep the lass. I like her fighting spirit. Indeed, she may prove an asset and a worthy ally in the days to come."

Tulwryn smiled in agreement, and the girl smiled as well.

Thus ends Chapter Three of Book Two

FOUR

River of Doom

The following eve the three broke camp and left the oasis behind. Dillwyn and Tulwryn took turns on their camel, and afoot, so as to allow Adi a fresh mount, at least until she regained enough strength to walk on her own. A consistent diet of fresh fruit, continuously produced by Dillwyn as if almost by magic, and sweet water, brought Adi to full strength in record time. Soon she was shouldering her own weight, as her pride would not allow her to be treated like a convalescing invalid.

A day further on the trail and the travelers left the Helheim Plateau behind and entered the Foothills of Insanity. The foothills, so named for the mental condition of those hardy souls who perished naught in the Phaedron desert or Helheim Plateau, formed a natural break in the terrain. Once in the safety of the foothills, the three could resume their daylight travels, since the surrounding forests sheltered the land from the searing heat of the Phaedron sun.

After camping under the protective eaves of a thick stand of oak, Tulwryn rose early in the morn to catch a glimpse of the rising sun. It was the first time in many weeks that he was able to gaze at the powdery blue sky, and his heavy heart was lifted if even for a moment. In an instant, Adi appeared at his side, silent and on padded cat feet, for he heard her naught and she startled him.

"Damn ye wench," he growled, "why ye sneak up on me like that?" She grinned an innocent grin and he cursed himself under his breath for letting his guard down long enough to be approached.

For the past few days, Adi had taken a liking to the cold warrior from Nuvia. She found in him a security she had not witnessed in the men of Baezutu. Where they were coy, he was brazen; his bold mannerism and strong features gave him the impression that he was larger and stronger than he actually was, for Tulwryn was no giant of a man. He was indeed strong of thews, but no more than the average man of thirty-eight years. She moved closer to him, nudging her small dark head into his side. He apprehensively wrapped a knotted arm around her frail shoulders and she lovingly hugged him back.

A million thoughts ran through their minds and Tulwryn knew that to continue this charade was to invite trouble. Adi entertained no such thoughts, she only knew that in Tulwryn's arms she felt safe, safer in fact than she had ever felt in her whole life. Who was this man, she wondered, who was so bold as to venture forth into the searing wilderness of Phaedron without a caravan; such a man must truly be a formidable warrior, and what safer place in all of Phantasodyssea than in the care of such a man. She felt he carried a heavy burden, probably from a grim and bloody past, yet that troubled her naught, for she cared nothing for the past, only the future, and in her mind, Tulwryn was her future.

"How old are ye, lass," Tulwryn asked the girl. A look of puzzled confusion washed over her dark features. For the past few days, even though she had been attracted to him from the moment she first saw him, he seemed to show no interest other than that of a careful guardian. Now, for some strange reason he was making an effort at small talk. She smiled at the thought.

"In two moons I shall have seen thirty seasons change on the wheel of time."

"Thirty years old," exclaimed Tulwryn! "I took ye for a mere child of maybe sixteen."

She giggled.

"For true, I do appear younger than I am, for I am small of frame. But fear naught, my dear warrior, I am no weakling."

Tulwryn gazed at her intensely, and he could in fact see that she was not the frail and cowering type of woman he had come to associate with the southern reaches of Phantasodyssea. No, in fact, she reminded him of the steel of a northern warrior, albeit much smaller.

Suddenly, Dillwyn approached breaking the mood of the moment, and a large raven wheeled across the cloudless sky cawing loudly. The three watched the bird soar on thick black wings, dipping and swooning across the heavens. Tulwryn smiled, and then he saw a single black feather fall gently earthward in a clearing before them. Releasing Adi's shoulder, he strode on heavy loins to where the feather lay and picked it up.

"This should bring us luck," he exclaimed with a hint of joy in his voice. He looked skyward, but seeing naught the bird, stuck the feather in his tangled black locks and returned to his companions under the eaves of the forest.

"Why shall that feather bring us luck, mine friend? Is that black devil of the skies an omen in your part of the world," asked the dwarf.

Smiling, Tulwryn answered. "Aye, my friend, the raven is a very good omen indeed. Athrum, the patron god of mine people, often takes the form of a raven when he watches over his chosen."

"Does ye god grant wishes and answer thy prayers," asked the girl.

"Nay, Athrum is a grim deity, but even a grim and wrathful god is sometimes better than no god at all." The three laughed together at Tulwryn's twisted humor, although Adi hid her true feelings as her mind reeled in the haunting memories of dark tales of grim gods and wrathful demons from her distant childhood.

"Are ye all well rested," Dillwyn asked. The two nodded. "Good. Then let us be off. By mine reckoning, we should be free from these foothills in three days, and our rendezvous with Mimir in the Sulphur Mountains should be only one day past that."

"If he is still alive," added Tulwryn, grimly.

"Aye," echoed the dwarf, "if he is alive."

* * *

Indeed, the dwarf was correct and in three days, the travelers left the protection of the Foothills of Insanity and entered into the foreboding realm of the Sulphur Mountains. The day had begun uneventful but there was violence in its future for the sky was full of clouds heavy with rain. A grey front was pushing up from the south and off in the distance Dillwyn noticed a flash of lightning, but they were still too far off to hear the rumble of thunder.

"Looks like we may get a little wet," spoke Tulwryn to his friend, as the two tended their camels. The travelers had pitched a small camp the night before at the far end of a gorge where the overhanging willows shaded them from the intensity of the sun and a shallow brook provided them with ample supply of fresh water. The morning was still young and Adi lay fast asleep in the tent under a pile of fresh linen, dreaming about her brave warrior from Nuvia.

"Aye, we needs look for more secure shelter indeed," answered the dwarf, "for to stay here is to invite trouble. By the looks of that sky there is plenty rain on the way. If we are caught here when that brook overgrows its banks we will be swimming rather than riding, and that is a thought I do not like entertaining."

Changing the subject for a moment, Tulwryn turned to the topic of vengeance. He had been wanting to discuss the matter with the dwarf for some time, but chose to wait until they were alone and without earshot of the girl.

"Ye heard the girl; she had been a prisoner of them desert bandits. Ye think they are still in the area, and perhaps the same band we hunt?"

"Could be," answered the dwarf. "I have been thinking about that myself. Problem is, we have no weapons so to speak of, save these long daggers, and if caught by greater numbers, 'twould naught be us that would taste victory. Nay, we must needs be wise about such things."

"So what do ye propose, old friend?"

"Methinks we should meet up with Mimir first. The rendezvous point is up a few leagues yonder and he is sure to bring us provisions and weapons . . . ," ere Dillwyn could finish his sentence, he was interrupted by a crash of lightning and the heavy roll of thunder. The sound was deafening and Tulwryn recalled the explosions the old wizard threw around back in the tunnels under Phaedron.

"The storm is upon us faster than we realized," screamed Tulwryn, "quick, run for the camels, I shall get the tent!"

Tulwryn's thick loins carried him quickly over the muddy ground and back to the tent. Adi was already awake and dressed in her robes, being startled by the approaching storm. In a matter on moments, the two had brought the tent down and gathered their meager belongings. Dillwyn met them with the camels, their gear was stowed, and they were off and running. Tulwryn and the girl on one camel, the dwarf on the other, riding like the wind in an attempt to outrun the fury of the storm.

* * *

The sky grew black as the three rode out the storm. Rain was pouring from the heavens in great grey sheets and neither man nor beast could see much but a few fathoms ahead.

"'Tis the worse storm I have ever seen," screamed Tulwryn, his voice being drowned out by a crash of thunder. "We are surely the first men to be drowned without the convenience of a lake or river!"

"Methinks this is no natural storm, Tulwryn," answered the dwarf, a bit of rage in his gruff voice. "This seems to me to be the work of sorcery!"

"And what insane sorcerer would spend this much energy to soak a wilderness such as this?"

"That answer I know naught, but back in Phaedron there was talk of the return of some renegade wizard. Perhaps this is but a fraction of his work?"

"Methinks ye have trafficked too long in the company of

sorcerers, old friend. Your mind has become saturated with the talk of magic and the dark arts."

"Indeed," answered Dillwyn, "saturated yea, but with torrents of angry rain at the moment!"

A crash of lightning exploded and cut through the darkness like a knife. The entire gorge was flooding with deep runoff, but for a split second, the dwarf's keen eyes spied a cave high up on a ridge overlooking the southern wall of the gorge.

"Tulwryn," roared the dwarf, his outstretched arm pointing to his left, guiding the warrior's eyes through the storm and to the yonder cave. "Up on that ridge, a cave. If we can make it thither, we are saved!"

The two reined their soaked beasts hard and made for the cave. Tulwryn drove his sandaled heels deep into the flanks of his mount and the dwarf did the same; Adi buried her face in Tulwryn's soaked robes and held on for dear life. The animals heaved and strained, but they were stronger than the average beasts of burden. Being Phaedron camels, they were bred by the court of the High Elder for employment in the Royal Guard of the western reaches of the kingdom and they shunned naught any difficult task. How the dwarf came by them is anybody's guess, and the question crossed the transom of Tulwryn's mind more than once. It seemed to him that his old friend was often more resourceful than first meets the eye.

The beasts were across the southern end of the gorge in a flash, and laboring up the muddy ridge. In a matter of moments, the entire party was safe under the roof of the cave.

Dillwyn released the animals to the rear of the cavern, whilst Tulwryn and Adi disrobed from their wet attire. The dwarf stripped to his loinclout and sandals, but his modest pride kept him from going completely naked.

"Is there anything dry in yonder gear," asked Tulwryn, noticing the gooseflesh running along Adi's quivering skin. "This child will catch a death of cold, and we as well, if we are to remain naked in this cold cave for long."

"Methinks naught," replied Dillwyn. "We were soaked

through and through. Look around for dry tinder and we shall stoke a fire to dry out our belongings."

Time passed, and the storm raged on flooding the entire gorge almost to the height of the cave. Yet, inside all were safe and dry. A fire had been built, and their clothes thoroughly dried. The three sat around the fire in silence, bound in their soiled robes, and snacked on the last remaining pieces of fruit that the dwarf carried.

One by one, with bellies full, the three drifted off to sleep. The fire burned itself to coals as the travelers dreamed their dreams. Outside the cave, somewhere during the night, a raven cawed, yet none was around to hear, and the large bird lifted itself on massive wings and flew yonder off to the east, and Athrum smiled a grim smile.

Morning came, and with it the promise of a new day, fresh and clean. The black sky of the previous day had been magically transformed to the most brilliant blue, and the forest shimmered as the wet leaves of the trees glistened like shining diamonds in the gleam of the rising sun.

Adi slept late, still wrapped in her robes, yet Tulwryn and the dwarf rose early to scout the gorge and espy the damage of the storm. To their amazement, the gorge was now a river. Never had the men seen such a magnificent transformation of nature, and their hearts were heavy for their sanctuary had become their prison.

"We are trapped," roared Tulwryn, looking at the deep waters that were lapping at the mouth of their cave. "Had the storm lasted an hour longer we would have been flooded out and drowned."

"But it didn't, and we weren't," replied Dillwyn. "'Tis folly to stand here and stew over what we cannot change. We are alive. Let us make due with that and decipher a plan of action."

"A plan of action? Look man, the waters are deep. We need a boat, for even the camels cannot traverse such a river."

Dillwyn bit his lip and gazed hard into the muddy waters rushing past the mouth of the cave.

"Ye may be right, Tulwryn. A boat would be better than swimming. Have ye explored the cave? Perhaps there is another way out through the rear, a tunnel maybe."

The thought had occurred to Tulwryn, but the idea of crawling through damp caverns made him remember their escape from the dungeons under Phaedron, and that memory he did not care to recall. He shrugged his thick shoulders and sighed.

"Nay, I have naught explored the cave."

"Well, it is best we figure something, and quick. By my reckoning, I suppose that we are only a day from the rendezvous point with Mimir. He will wait no longer than a few hours, so it is much importance that we make the utmost haste." And with that, Dillwyn tuned and walked back into the depths of the cave. Tulwryn stood for a moment, looking at the deep waters of the newborn river, then disappeared into the darkness of the cave.

Thus ends Chapter Four of Book Two

FIVE

The Wizard of Covensted

Adi was already awake when the two men approached. She looked sheepishly at Tulwryn, a hundred lustful thoughts running through her mind, and smiled. He did not smile back. She shot a glance at the dwarf and knew by the look in his eye that trouble was afoot.

"What's wrong," she asked, rising from her sleeping pallet and wrapping her soiled robe tightly around her petite frame.

"The gorge has became flooded by last night's wrathful storm," answered Tulwryn. "For the moment, it would seem we are trapped. Dillwyn and I shall scout the rear of the cave to see if there is another way out."

The girl just stood there speechless as the two men strode past her and disappeared into the dusky gloom of the cave. For a time, she heard their heavy foot falls echoing throughout the cavern, and then, fading in the distance, they were silenced and she found herself alone.

A feeling of vulnerability suddenly crept over her and she decided to have a look about the cave as well. She looked about the campsite first. Finding a taper candle amongst Dillwyn's belongings, she lit it with flint and steel. The candle's soft glow illumined the cave, yet there was not much to speak of, just a few of the meager belongings that her two rescuers kept. There was a large empty waterskin and a small gunnysack of fresh fruit. She knew the sack belonged to the dwarf, but she knew naught how he kept it full of fresh fruit since she never seen him go to the forest to gather any.

There was also a small ditty bag containing a tiny amount of some course grained herb and a gnarled old smoking pipe. The scent of the herb made her nose wrinkle up. Oh, thought she, how the nasty habits of old men disgusted her. And her mind traveled back to the days when she was growing up in her town of Baezutu.

The town of Baezutu was located near the eastern border of The Wastes, many hundreds of leagues south of where she was now. It was peopled mostly by sand pirates and desert bandits, all of whom partook in the disgusting habits of smoke and drink, and even worse. Phaedron had maintained a garrison in Baezutu for many years, aiming to guarantee the smooth operation and safe passage of caravans traveling on the trade routes in that area, but due to internal corruption within its ranks, there were still many problems and dangers in the village and surrounding areas. She was glad to be free from the horrors of Baezutu, but her present situation was not much more promising, she thought. Sure, Tulwryn was a man among men, but did he really care for her? Her dark eyes burned with an unremembered lust, and she felt the pangs of desire welling between her thighs. But to be the wench of an adventurer was not an ideal life for one as small and frail as she, and deep in her heart, she knew that. She wanted to be strong, and true enough, she was stronger than most women of Baezutu, but still she was not a warrior. Perhaps, she thought, she could steel herself and learn to become one.

Adi replace the ditty where she found it and walked from the camp, heading off in the direction that the two men walked earlier, only to be startled by their return. Dillwyn glanced at the girl, but Tulwryn walked past her without saying a word.

"Well," she asked, "is there a way out of this cave?"

"Aye, there is a way out," said Dillwyn, "but 'tis too narrow a crevice for the camels; seems like we walk from now on."

"And what about the camels then," replied the girl, in a somewhat shaky but compassionate voice.

"I shall bring them up from the rear of the cave and show them the main entrance. They can either swim for it or stay here and starve; the choice is theirs. 'Twas naught mine plan to desert the beasts; seems like the gods are more cruel than I in these matters."

Adi may have been a strong and resilient girl for one so small, but her heart was breaking and she became ill at the prospect of abandoning healthy animals to a slow and cruel death.

"Is there nothing we can do," she pleaded.

"Camels are smart critters," Tulwryn retorted in a dread tone of uncertainty. "They shall fend well, and probably better than us, I would venture to say. Come, and let us be off. We are wasting valuable daylight."

The three quickly assembled their gear and headed south through the darkness of the cave.

* * *

It was the night of the first day after leaving the confines of their cave, and the three travelers trudged wearily along through the Sulphur Mountains afoot. There were no trails and the rocky terrain was hard on the feet as well as the mind. Sulphurous gasses belched hither and thither from cracks in the parched ground, and the hot steam that poured forth from the myriad geysers singed the eyes and the throat.

Tulwryn noticed that the moon had once again taken up its normal routine of waxing and waning and he breathed a sigh of relief that possibly the threat of sorcery was behind them. That idea suddenly came to an abrupt end when, after rounding a bend through a low pass, the three came upon a strange campsite that emitted an eerie glow of the most disturbing bluish-green hue.

The camp was pitched under a stand of tall dead wood, and was still a dozen fathoms or so in the distance, but Tulwryn could clearly make out that a cloaked figure sat near the strange fire.

"Might that be who I think," asked the warrior.

"Aye, Tulwryn, that is Mimir up yonder," answered the dwarf. "When ye look at him, ye look into the distant past, for he is as old as the world, or older even. Come and let the gods lead us where they may, for the charge of Mimir is no light undertaking and I fear there is much adventure in our future."

A chill ran down Adi's frail spine and she gripped Tulwryn's robe and buried her small round face in his shoulder. Tulwryn reassured the girl that everything would be all right; yet, deep in his heart he was as unsure as she.

The three approached the rendezvous point and Dillwyn called out in a low and husky voice to his darkly cloaked friend. As the travelers entered the campsite, the wizard stood up to greet them. He was much taller than Dillwyn remembered, and even Tulwryn was shocked at the man's overwhelming size.

"Welcome friends," came a grim voice from deep within the darkly hooded coif of the cloak. Tulwryn gazed into the blue flames of the campfire, then back at the giant wizard standing before him. He could see nothing that resembled a man, no face where his face should be, no hands where his hands should be. The thing standing before them seemed to be nothing more than an animated cloak, a wraith in the darkness.

"Have ye waited long, my friend," asked Dillwyn?

"Nay," said the wizard, "I arrived only moments ere ye approached. I thank ye for being prompt." There was a hollow sounding chuckle that rolled from the empty hood of the cloak, and Dillwyn smiled at Mimir's timeless humor.

"Please, sit with me," said the wizard, "for I have much to tell."

The four sat round the strange blue fire. Mimir, pulling up a sleeve of his cloaked robe, exposed his ancient flesh for the first time. From underneath the folds of his garment came a slender arm, creamy white as fresh milk, with skin as smooth as spun silk. Tulwryn glanced at the arm, and for a moment wondered if the so-called he-witch from Covensted was actually a female sorceress in disguise. From arm, to wrist, to hand, and even the long and slender fingers, everything seemed to say *woman*, rather than *man*. The mystery that was Mimir grew more intriguing with each passing moment, and Tulwryn found himself curious as to the nature of the being under the robes. He recalled the tiny creature in the tunnels beneath Phaedron, and how dangerous that apparently helpless creature actually was. A loud snap of Mimir's long fingers brought Tulwryn back to the present.

Lying on the sulphurous ground before them was a large oaken crate. Mimir waved his hands and the crate magically opened without a touch. The travelers peered into the depths of the crate and Dillwyn alone smiled at what he saw, for within that crate laid his Carthusian armor.

"I thought this may come in handy for ye, Dillwyn." And again, the wizard chuckled his grim laugh. "There are other things in this crate as well, such as raiment more suitable for mountainous travel than thy desert robes. And by what I can see of those robes, these trappings come at an opportune time. Also, find ye hither some well crafted weapons, but alas, I could naught secure the Bloodsword." And Mimir sighed, for with all his power and magic, the strength of the Bloodsword eluded him.

"What of my weapon," asked Tulwryn? "What has become of the Bloodsword?"

Adi sat motionless, not understanding the odd talk between these dark and strange men. She understood naught the workings of magic, nor trafficked in the handling of weapons. Yet, the name Bloodsword did send chills down her spine and fear was in her heart.

The wizard turned and looked at Tulwryn, and all was still for an eternity ere he spoke.

"What asks me of the Bloodsword? Why, ye are the Bloodsword, are ye naught? Look at thy hands and tell me that ye and the blade are not one."

Tulwryn's palms blazed with heat and he felt naked amongst his friends. Adi looked with horror upon Tulwryn's branded hands. Why had she not noticed the scars ere now, she wondered, and what did all of this mean?

Mimir looked at the three, then back at Tulwryn.

"If ye wish to regain thy blade, then ye must needs go to Bain, for the bandits that waylaid ye are there. But first, ye must execute my charge, for it is of the most urgent importance." He then glanced at the girl, paused, and address Dillwyn.

"I thought that there was just the two of ye, mine friend," asked Mimir. "Where did ye get this dark beauty?"

Whilst the dwarf was telling their tale, from the moment he and Tulwryn left Mimir in the tunnels under Phaedron to the present, the wizard produced three silver goblets and handed one to each of the travelers. The goblets were filled to the rim with a sparkling wine of the brightest gold, and its taste was clean and refreshing. Adi sipped her wine, but Tulwryn swigged his down in one gulp. To his amazement, as soon the goblet left his lips it was full again.

"Take heed, my friend," said Mimir, "that is no cheap wine, sip it like a gentleman, not a barbarian."

Although Tulwryn clearly knew that comment to be an insult, he took it as a compliment, considering the company he kept during the past three winters up north. And again, he emptied the contents of the goblet in one gulp. Then, wiping his mouth with the sleeve of his soiled robe in the most barbaric manner he could muster, Tulwryn glanced at the wizard and smiled a smirkish grin.

Mimir sighed, and then addressed the group. "Come closer, mine friends, for I have a dread tale to tell. And the successful outcome of my tale depends entirely on thee. Aye, indeed, these are dangerous times and the weight of my tale is heavy.

"Once, long ago, Phaedron was peaceful; it was not the vile den of villainy it is now. Nimrod the Just was a good and righteous king and ruled the land most pleasantly. For many turnings of the great wheel of time, Nimrod ruled, and the people of Phaedron loved him. But alas, as all things must one day come to an end, so did Nimrod meet his destiny at the end of a dagger.

"Nimrod's assassin was a man who once went by the name of Kaine Obel. He was a cruel and evil man, an eater of human flesh and a practitioner of dark rituals. After murdering Nimrod the Just, he usurped his crown and throne. Then Obel changed his name to Zulanmalh I, thus creating the Dynasty of the House of Zula.

"Gunrod the Just was Nimrod's only son and heir to the throne of Phaedron. But after his father, the High Elder, Nimrod the Just, was murdered, and the throne was assumed by his assassin, the evil cleric Kaine Obel, as I have already said, Gunrod fled Phaedron. Fearing for his life, Gunrod changed his name to Lord Jerrod Balor and fled Phaedron in a self-imposed exile. He later became an explorer and adventurer in his own right, and it was he that discovered the only pass through the Ymir Mountains. And even though he was not in the service of the High Elder, since he was originally of royal Phaedronian blood, his feat of discovering the pass through the Ymir Mountains was heralded as a great Phaedronian achievement. Ah, but that is another tale and has no bearing on the present saga.

"Anyhow, it was always Lord Jerrod Balor's intention to raise an army and regain his ancestral home, by force if need be, but the gods are often not that kind and thus was not his destiny; he died in exile, or so the story goes.

"Two moons after Kaine Obel assumed the position of High Elder of Phaedron, Kimark Khan, the infamous warrior-wizard that currently resides atop Mt. Malador, came into this tale. He originally hailed from Covensted, but centuries ago, after mastering the intricacies of magic, he left our quaint village of witches to seek his fortunes in the west. After coming upon the Phaedron citadel, he introduced himself to the king's court and was employed for some time as a seer for the High Elder. However, he soon fell out of favor with the king and had to flee for his life. He vowed to return one day to Phaedron, and extracting his vengeance, had promised to usurp the throne and take the crown for himself. And this brings us to the present, and the reasons why I have assembled ye hither.

"Most in Phaedron despise Kimark Khan, yet there are a few factions of rebels that constantly pray for his return. He is a vile and evil sorcerer, and I fear that if he assumes the throne of Phaedron then the whole of Phantasodyssea will feel his wrath.

"The current ruler of Phaedron, Zulanmalh IV, fourth High Elder of the house of Zula, is no better than his great grandfather. Some say he is even crueler that Kaine Obel ever thought of being. This I know naught. What I do know is this: Even though he is the High Elder of Phaedron, crowned king of the known world, there are many city-states lying beyond the reach of the Phaedron army that do not recognize his omnipotent authority, therefore it is possible that Kimark Khan's attempt to usurp his throne will be successful. This is an event that we must thwart! If the Khan assumes the throne of Phaedron then all life on Phantasodyssea is doomed."

Adi and the others stirred with this dread news, but knew naught how the three of them could thwart such unrelenting power. Dillwyn was about to speak, but Tulwryn spoke first.

"And how are we to foil the plan of a master sorcerer, may I ask?"

The old wizard paused for a moment, and then abruptly changed the subject.

"Ye ponder about me, do ye naught, Tulwryn? Ye ponder the reasons why I should send ye forth, ye who wield no magic, to confront him who is powerful in the dark arts. Ye ponder why I, who am old beyond the span of time and who commands such power as even the gods know nothing of, attack naught the Khan. And ye ponder also the beauty of mine face, and so ye shall have it, for behold, I am Mimir, and when ye looks into my face ye will see thy own soul!"

And with that, Mimir reached up with slender hands and removed the dark hood that had concealed his grim features. But alas, Tulwryn did not see what Dillwyn and Adi saw. For when the hood was removed, time stood still and he was staring at the beautiful face of Durayn, and he relived his nightmare again and again. In the blink of an eye, he endured an eternity of guilt and pain and shame, for the kinslaying weighed heavy on his soul.

"Ye are naught that man anymore, Tulwryn. Release thy guilt! Destroy the fetters that holds thee in bondage! Know yourself, for ye are now the Bloodsword, and nations will rise and fall at the wave of thy hand. This is your destiny, this is your doom."

In that instant, many of Tulwryn's questions were answered, and he felt a newly kindled strength burning in his breast. Mimir replaced the hood and time once again resumed.

"Here is my charge, dear friends," spoke the wizard, "ye must travel westward, and around yonder sea, the Sea of Fire! On the far side of the sea, ye shall find a village hidden in the high hills, and it is in this village that ye must seek out Cohado the Long. He is a banished priest, living in seclusion in the hidden village called Rhyan. He is called the *Keeper of Lies* because he discovered secret untruths that his priestly brotherhood, the Order of the Crystal Sphere, swore to keep hidden from the eyes of men. Angered that such evils could be kept under wraps, he threatened the security of the brotherhood by exposing the Order and its lies. Cohado was forced to flee for fear of death. He is still being sought by the brotherhood, which will stop at nothing to silence him forever. Cohado has long been the voice of Truth in Phantasodyssea and his magic is powerful indeed; he has always helped those in need, especially those pursued by evil. Seek him out and he will aid ye in thy quest. This is all I can say for now."

The blue of the morning was edging its way across the sky and Tulwryn knew that the four of them had been kept up all night, yet he felt not the least bit exhausted. Birds began to sing and one could hear the many forest animals waking from their slumber. The bluish-green flame was gone and not a coal could be seen in the fire pit. Suddenly, from behind them, came the sound of many horses, hooves thundering.

With the speed of a warrior, Mimir sprang from his seat.

"Quick, there are soldiers coming. Ye must needs make your escape." The wizard mumbled a few words in some archaic unknown tongue and in an instant three magical steeds appeared.

"Make haste," cried the wizard, "use these beasts to flee, but know that they cannot leave the Sulphur Mountains. Ye will have to find a way around the Sea of Fire without mine help. Be gone, and quickly now, for the enemy approaches!"

>From out of nowhere, a dozen Phaedron legionnaires appeared on warhorses, brandishing steel and hungry for blood.

Running at breakneck pace, Tulwryn grabbed up Adi and mounted one of Mimir's magical horses, tossing the girl onto her own steed. Dillwyn followed suit.

The three rode like the wind, yet Tulwryn paused to look back towards the camp, and Mimir. The wizard simply vanished into the air. He disappeared as a stone thrown into a lake, absorbed by the watery depths and concealed by the ripples on the water's surface. In a matter of moments, he was gone without a trace.

Tulwryn drove his booted heel deep into his mount's flank and then suddenly realized that he was wearing the clothes and weapons that Mimir had given them, although he remembered naught changing his raiment in the night. He glanced over his right shoulder at Adi and the dwarf, both riding hard on his heels, and saw that they too wore the mountain clothing that the old wizard had conjured.

There was much screaming from the Phaedrons, and the three could hear the thundering hooves of the warhorses gaining on them.

"What tenacity of Phaedron to make such a chase," Dillwyn screamed. "I cannot believe we are such a worthy prize that we should be tracked over a blistering desert, a scorching plateau, and into these dread mountains!"

"Perhaps Phaedron has learned of the ol'e wizard's plan," answered Tulwryn. "Ride on, old man! Now is not the time for dialogue. We will discuss our plans if we escape this ambush."

For more than an hour, the three were perused by the galloping legionnaires. Their horses, although magickally created, were beginning to show signs of physical fatigue. Over rocky ledge and sulphurous outcroppings the three rode, horses straining under saddle and spur, until coming at last to the end of the trail.

Tulwryn reined his steed hard and cried out to the others.

"Ho! Heed the cliff!"

When Adi and the dwarf arrived, they found Tulwryn afoot and standing on the edge of a steep cliff overlooking the Sea of Fire. The view from the rim was staggering, for as far as the eye could see was nothing but an endless ocean of molten lava and brimstone.

"Once again we are trapped," snorted the dwarf. "There is no place to go, and we cannot turn back for our pursuers are closing in."

"Have a little faith," retorted Tulwryn. "I thought ye believed in magic, Dillwyn. Behold, and watch Tulwryn Bloodsword work a little magic of his own."

The warrior from Nuvia then removed the raven feather from his hair and tossed it over the cliff. To his expectation, the heated air took the feather upward and outward over the sea.

"Ah, Athrum watches over us!"

He then hastily removed the canvas tent cloth from his horse and instructed Dillwyn to do the same. Tulwryn then quickly constructed a makeshift sail wing and fastened it to his belt. Grabbing Adi with his thick and muscular arms, he looked at her with stern affection. Ripping the silken skirt about her, just above the knee, Tulwryn fashioned a binding, and with that binding, he tied her to himself securely. They kissed a deep and passionate kiss, and then threw themselves off the cliff. For endless seconds they fell, plummeting at great speeds and for a moment, Tulwryn thought his plan would fail and that they would perish, either on the jagged rocks below or in the Sea of Fire itself.

The suddenly, the canvas sail wing opened with a start, and shook them both to a bone shattering halt. As the heated thermals filled the sail wing, it lifted the two high into the air and out over the Sea of Fire. The dwarf's sail opened in like manner, and so the three travelers escaped their deadly pursuers.

But now, a new danger existed, for even though the Phaedron soldiers were left standing on the cliff below and far out of reach, no end could be seen to the extent of the fiery ocean that lay beneath them. How long could they remain aloft on the rising thermals that emanated from below? How long would the makeshift sail wings hold up before their seams ripped out? How long before they were to set foot on land and finally be out of danger? Only time would tell.

Thus ends Chapter Five of Book Two

SIX

The Dark Mountain

Far to the east, high atop the frozen peak of Mt. Malador, Kimark Khan sat surveying the whole of Phantasodyssea and lusting over the ivory throne of Phaedron that one day he vowed would be his. Vengeance boiled in his cold, black heart, and his small, closely set eyes burned with rage.

His wrath transported him back generations, to the days when Kaine Obel usurped the throne of Phaedron for himself and took that bastard name of Zulanmalh. He remembered how the greedy patriarch, cruel beyond words, accepted him into his court and employed him as the head mage of Phaedron, the most cherished position in all of Phantasodyssea, at least as far as a sorcerer was concerned. Oh, how he remembered those lust filled days of that by-gone era; days filled with luxury, and wine, and song; of drugged naked women on sofas of red velvet and multi-colored Ningham silk brocade, and the alluring opiate of the L'hoehnian Kiputu. And the nights too, he remembered. Dark nights, cold and unfeeling, where he would sit for hours in grim silence communicating with the spirits of the damned, and casting black enchantments for his grim master.

Kimark Khan sighed a deep and regretful sigh through thin, tightly pursed lips and sunk down in his high backed ebony chair. His predator-like face, with its large hooked nose, small, dark, deep set eyes, and a large, single gold hoop piercing his left ear lent one to believe that he originally hailed from Kem rather than Covensted. But his pale complexion, shaven head, and the billowing silk robes of vermilion that concealed his magical chainmaile underneath told the real story. Kimark Khan was no mere puppet. It was no wonder that Zulanmalh removed him from the court of Phaedron over two hundred years ago.

There was rumor that the Dark One, as Kimark Khan was often called by other subjects of the High Elder's court, was plotting to murder the king in his sleep and take the kingdom for himself. Just remembering the past brought the wizard close to a fuming rage. How could they have known, he wondered silently to himself, how could they have known my true intentions? For over four generations of Phaedron rulers, he pondered this question, sitting up throughout the night and long into the morning hours, pushing his mind deep into his dark meditations, conversing with the demons of the nether reaches in hopes of discovering the traitor that thwarted his long past objective.

Indeed, he thought with a laugh, certainly this is folly. No one in all the world has mastered the ability of prolonging life such as I, he boasted. Even the very traitor that had foiled my plan so many years ago is surely dead by now and all my wrath is for naught. I shall henceforth put my efforts to a more positive aim, and to the ivory throne itself.

And so, once again the mighty warrior-wizard began to plot his evil plot for the overthrow of the seat of power in all of Phantasodyssea, the throne of the High Elder of Phaedron.

Kimark Khan stood and languidly walked to the balcony that emerged from the west end of his chamber. Opening the large crystal doors, he walked out onto the balcony and pushed open the stained glass windows of his oriel. He took a deep breath and inhaled the frigid mountain air, and then he gazed out over his bleak domain.

Mt. Malador, Phantasodyssea's tallest peak, its lofty head raised high over the canopy of the forest, was located in the northern reaches of the Enchanted Mountain Range and was completely surrounded by the Enchanted Forest. Legend had it that the mountain is so high, one can observe every corner of the world in a single glance and that is why it is believed that the warlock, Kimark Khan, made his home there. Yet, unbeknownst to legend and lore, are the other reasons the Dark Mage prefers that inhospitable wilderness to more civilized surroundings.

The vast Enchanted Forest was a magical expanse of flora and fauna containing many tens of millions of magical herbs, many of which the wizard himself used to control the passing of time and the lengthening of his longevity. Also, he cherished the solitude, as there are no roads or settlements to be found within the boarders of the forest, and even the Phaedron soldiers do not trespass there, for they fear the dread wrath of the Khan more than the cruel hatred of their own evil king.

But Kimark Khan did crave the civilized world, and hated it. He hated the fact that he was forced into exile at the threat of death. Him, with all his magic and power, his plan thwarted, and in a moment of despair, made to turn and run with his tail betwixt his legs like a cowering dog. And for two hundred turnings of the great wheel of the seasons, he fumed over his embarrassment; and vowed to unleash a vengeance upon the civilized world that would be legendary even by the cruel standards of Zulanmalh.

The wizard glanced out over the trees, westward. The setting sun was turning the forest to blood, and he foresaw the streets of Phaedron in that same hue. A pair of large Maladorian eagles soared on the cold thermals, spiraling two and fro in their poetic display of courtship, and Kimark Khan smiled.

Re-entering his chamber, he strolled across the fur strewn marble floor, out the north door, and down the long candle lit corridor that led to his magical sanctuary. Upon entering that room, he was greeted by a dozen deformed creatures, minions of evil that he no doubt had either summoned from one of the many cold hells of the outer plains or created himself by means of his dark sorcery. The creatures huddled close to the ground, submissively, paying obeisance to their dark master, a lasting testament to the evil covenant of blood by which he had bound them.

"Be gone ye vile beasts," screamed the dark mage in a wrath of fury, "be gone ere I burn every last one of you; I wish to be alone!"

In ecstatic fear, the little creatures began to scurry about, moaning and whining as if the separation from their master would bring them greater pain than the flames therewith he threatened them. One of the creatures, smaller than the others, bumped into a large, wrought silver candelabrum, overturning it and causing the candles thereon to spill hot wax onto a pile of ancient magical tomes thereby rendering them useless. As if to foresee its own doom, the creature squealed and scurried for the door of the chamber.

Seeing the damage, Kimark Khan flew into a frenzied rage. The creature was almost to the door, but the wizard's long legs carried him across the room in three paces. With a large, uncaring hand, the dark mage snatched up the little body by the scruff of its neck.

"Kayena vaca cittena pamadena mäyä katam," whimpered the creature, as it struggled to get free from the Khan's iron grasp. "Accayam khama me bhante bhuri-panna tathgata!"

"I have warned ye for the last time, Jerrub," roared the dark lord to the little minion that was writhing in his hand. "Out of all these little pests, ye are the most bothersome; always getting underfoot, always breaking something. And now, now, ye have destroyed centuries of work. Look, these tomes are worthless now! For this, thy punishment shall be most heinous!"

He cast the creature to the cold stone floor, and with hands waving frantically in the air, long slender fingers dancing, weaving an evil and painful spell, the Khan spoke the incantation of endless punishment: "Byadh mokkulh, byadh bizel-ahad, abe abe abe abhudalh!"

There was an evil gleam in the wizard's eye that defied description, for it was apparent that the creature's suffering brought him great enjoyment. Suddenly, the fabric of time and space was rent and a portal appeared in the thin air. A bluish fog limply floated into the chamber from this floating gateway and

Jerrub shrieked with fear at what he saw. Looking into the portal from Kimark Khan's magical sanctuary, he could see into another, more horrific dimension; a universe of eternal pain where neither form nor substance, flesh nor spirit, is free for even a moment of suffering.

First, there was a grating sound, like the grinding of a great winch, and then the sound of chains being drawn from afar. Then came the torment! Thousands upon thousands of rusted hooks came flying out of the portal at lightning speed straight at their target. With a scream, the tiny body was saturated with the iron claws, blood poured forth like a fountain of scarlet and stained the chamber floor as Jerrub fought in vain to free himself. The grinding of the winch began again, and slowly drug its struggling prisoner back into its gaping maw. In an instant Jerrub was gone, save for his screams, which echoed throughout the great halls and chambers that were carved like an immense maze in the bowels of Malador. Kimark Khan laughed a heinous laugh and clapped his pale hands thrice. At once, the portal vanished into thin air.

Spinning around, dark robes billowing in the breeze, the wizard surveyed his chamber. There was not a body anywhere; all the little creatures had taken heed to Jerrub's example and disappeared into hiding. All that was left, as a memory of Jerrub's existence was a bloodstain on the cold stone floor of the chamber, and a puddle of urine excreted out of fear and death. That was the cruelty of Kimark Khan; he was as quick to destroy, as he was to create.

Nonchalantly, and without a thought of remorse, the wizard languidly walked to the far corner of the room and stood before the great Scrystone. The stone, a black diamond as large as a man, hewn from the mines beneath Golrin and smuggled out of their guarded underground vaults by a crack unit of renegade Kemetian Mercenaries faithful to the dark Khan, was carved and polished into a single, unfaceted sphere.

The vile instrument was held suspended in the air by means of grim sorcery, and contained powers unremembered in all the world. From the seclusion of his chamber, Kimark Khan could employ the stone and thereby know the unknowable.

The Scrystone pulsated, a low hum droned from deep within its black bowels, and Kimark Khan gazed into its inky darkness. At first, only his own dismal reflection was visible, and then, the stone's hazy opaqueness began to clear and the wizard saw other, more useful things. Suddenly, he was drawn within the stone itself, and transported over vast time and space to find himself in the hall of a great king. Polished teakwood floors, immense pillars of ivory, huge, wrought iron sconces with dripping tallow candles, and the scent of burning human flesh instantly brought back memories he had not experienced for over two centuries, and his heart stirred. It was good to be back in the court of Phaedron, he thought, even if only as a fly on the wall, a spirit skulking in the shadows just outside of waking reality.

This was the power of the Scrystone, to enable its master not only to know the future by means of clairvoyance, but also to give him the ability to travel the plains in his dark ethereal form and invade the very walls of the citadel itself. With the power of the stone in his grasp, the whole of Phantasodyssea was at his mercy, for he could be everywhere at once, and in the blink of an eye!

The door at the far end of the hall creaked open and Kimark Khan's ethereal form drifted and swirled in an invisible cloud of hate to a shadowed corner of the room. A warm breeze entered the chamber, and then Zulanmalh IV, the High Elder. He was followed by an entourage of guards, soothsayers, and concubines, all of which whom were showering him with empty praises, for in Phantasodyssea, the High Elder was feared more than loved.

"How could they have escaped," screamed the king. "What folly is this when two vagrants can elude a complete regiment of my finest legionnaires?" This is a blasphemy unto my throne." Turning to his man-at-arms, the king glared daggers and began shouting orders. "The dungeons will flow red with blood for this outrage! Execute one hundred prisoners ere the hour is passed, I care naught of their offences!"

The soldier, a large and strapping youth of twenty-eight seasons, saluted the king and bowed.

"It shall be done, sire," he said, bowed again, and exited the hall. A handful of guards followed him.

Half naked concubines positioned themselves on cushions and pillows strewn about the hall. They went about anointing themselves with fragrant unguents and fumes, and exciting each other with loving, sensual hands. Many of the girls carried the scars of the king's rage, for they knew that when his wrath consumed him like this, they were his first target. Nothing gave him more pleasure than to flog a naked concubine, watching her ivory flesh turn bright scarlet under the weight of his whip. So, as a protective measure, the girls began to moan in a climactic bliss, apparently trying to arouse the king to more erotic emotions. However, nothing could have been further from the patriarch's angered mind.

"Who was in charge of the night watch," the king asked.

"I believe it was Gurdon Cudgel, sire," answered a burly knight in polished Phaedronian armor.

"Well, see to it at once that he is removed from his post," roared the king. "And toss his surly hide in with the hundred prisoners to be executed!"

"Sire," said the man, "Gurdon was murdered in the escape." There was tension in the air of the hall as the guard watched the king turn dark red as his anger came to a boil.

"Had he any family?"

"Aye, he had a wife and three young children; a boy and two girls."

"Good," the king said with a smile. He spun on a heel and walked to the Ivory Throne of Phaedron, where he then took his seat before his audience. "Round up the lot of them and add them to the hundred! The house of Gurdon Cudgel shall pay for his folly!"

A shadow glided across the hall and sent a chill up the king's cold spine. He glanced around the room but saw nothing. Waving the knight away, the king felt another chill rush his spine. The guard left the hall at once to do the High Elder's grim bidding and the king then motioned to another guard to bind up three of his concubines for a lashing. The girls screamed in fear and fell faint; for what they witnessed was worse than anything the High Elder could muster. In the far corner of the hall, apparently out of thin air, emerged a demon so dread that even the marrow of the cruel king of Phaedron turned to ice.

"Do ye remember me, oh dark king," said a hollow voice that seemed to reach out from beyond the grave. "Of course not, for ye were not yet birthed when I skulked these crimson halls. But in your veins runs the blood of the accursed, and for that blood, I shall have mine vengeance!"

Ere the king could scream, black hands struck out like daggers in the night slaying all the guards in the hall with a single swipe. Never before had the king witnessed such lethal power, and terror was upon him. He crumpled to the ground in a heap, begging for the mercy of the beast, but Kimark Khan heard him naught.

"Who are ye," asked the king, hiding beneath his royal gown. "Why have ye come into mine home and slayed mine servants? Am I to be slayed as well? Oh, mercy, my lord! Are ye a dark god or a grim demon? What transgression am I guilty of; have I not given ye sacrifice?"

"I am no dark god or demon, ye pitiful cur! I am Kimark Khan!"

At the mention of his name, two centuries of legends came pouring back into the terror filled mind of Zulanmalh IV. He remembered the curse set upon the House of Zula by the dread wizard himself after he was forced to flee for his life at the hands of his great grandfather's legions. Many a night he lay awake pondering about this very day, a day that was inevitable in coming.

"Please, lord," begged the king, "slay me naught, for the sins of Zulanmalh are not mine. I am not he, for we mere mortals have not the power of longevity as you. I beg of ye, slay me naught!"

"The fear of death is much more worse than death itself," spoke the shadow of the wizard. "Know this, ye ungrateful cur, I shall return, but not in the spirit as ye now see me. The next time we meet, ye shall look upon me in the flesh, and I shall rend thee to bits! I shall also take your kingdom as mine own, and shall slay all of your descendents in a most gruesome manner, for 'tis my desire to rid the world of your filth and the filth of your loins!"

And with that, the shadow roiled and swirled into a foggy mist, and in a matter of moments had vanished. And so Kimark Khan's dark spirit returned to Malador, leaving not a trace of his existence in that cold Phaedron court save for a roomful of dead soldiers, unconscious chamber girls, and a king, broken and frothing like a madman who soils his own bed at the first sight of a specter in the night.

Thus ends Chapter Six of Book Two

SEVEN

Death in the Forest

"Slay them all," yelled the tall man in the flowing L'hoehnian silk and linen robe. Dirt and grime stained his sun-browned face and his blade, an Azazel Barong, was wet with blood. The skies over Bain were dark with smoke and sulphur lingered in the air, mixed with the pungent scent of burning flesh. For hours, the man barked commands as the Woodlings of Bain died under the cruel wrath of L'hoehnian steel.

Why had the marauders come to Bain; the question was anyone's guess. But come they had, and they brought with them a deadly fury, long forgotten in the peaceful forest village.

Bain was a small village of Woodlings nestled in the heart of the Forest of Bain. The forest itself was extremely old and mystical, possibly one of the oldest in all of Phantasodyssea, and completely surrounded by the vast Golrin Prairie.

The Woodlings, small elf-like creatures with large pale yellow eyes and light brown skin, were an extremely friendly lot, although at times they proved to be quite mischievous, though never intending any real harm. Their village had no real export to speak of, and so many simply hired themselves out as trackers and guides for travelers and adventurers. They were rumored to be the best woodsmen in Phantasodyssea, but warriors they were naught, and this day they died by the score.

Screaming, a young Woodling slid off the pointed end of a Kemetian cutlass, his innards spilling onto the wet forest ground. The bandit turned, then slayed another. Carnage and chaos were everywhere; in the north end of the village, the intruders were burning the huts and murdering the women and children indiscriminately. Yet, on the western border, the small creatures were putting up some minute resistance.

A burly man, and tall, standing a head and a half higher than the rest of the intruders, was brandished a heavy war axe and boldly slaying the Woodlings left and right. So bold was this warrior, and confident in his ability to kill, that he entered the fray with no armor or shield; he simply went about hewing heads with his axe and roaring a grotesque L'hoehnian war cry, although it was clear to see that he was no L'hoehnian. But luck was not with him this day, for ere he slew four of the small creatures he was feathered with a dozen arrows, all barbed and dipped in the deadly poison that only the Woodlings are skilled at crafting. The big man fell to the ground, seething in agony as he was swarmed upon by the angered Woodlings, all brandishing stone knives and flint spears. And so, the battle ebbed and flowed, and the intruders did lose many men, but the Woodlings lost more.

Maztaque, the leader of the renegade band of L'hoehnian marauders, called his squire to fetch his mount. The youth disappeared south into a thick of scrub and vanished from sight.

"How many of these damnable creatures are in this forest." Maztaque yelled. Rog, a tall, swarthy warrior, extremely good with L'hoehnian steel was Maztaque's man-at-arms; he stood with his master amongst the confusion of battle.

"I know naught," answered Rog. "Perhaps we could slay all day and night for an eternity and still not empty this forest. What say ye our plans now?"

"I have heard that these creatures know the secrets of the prairie, and 'tis these secrets I am after. With knowledge of the prairie, the wealth of Golrin is ours! I will have that wealth, mine friend, by the blood of these small beasts, I will have that wealth!"

"Should we not then be taking prisoners and doing some questioning, rather than slaying the lot of them?"

Maztaque stood dumbfounded; his cruelty in battle won him a fell reputation throughout the whole of Phantasodyssea, and even as far south as the wastes there were bounty hunters seeking the fortune that Phaedron had placed on his head, yet he was not an intelligent man. Many men did follow him, but that was more due to his savage skill with a blade rather than his ability as a leader or strategist.

"I need none to question, old friend," said Maztaque, and he held up the crimson blade that he had stolen from the northerner many moons ago. Three feet of blood red steel shimmered in the warrior's hand and a chill ran up Rog's spine as he gazed upon that fell blade. "As long as I have this," he said, "I need question no man!"

"What say ye," asked Rog. "That is the sword ye stole from the foreigner. What power does it hold other than to slay? Is it a magical blade?"

"Indeed it is, though I have mastered it naught."

"How does ye know 'tis magical," questioned Rog.

"Aye, I know because the thing has spoken unto me. It has warned me to employ it naught, therefore I know the thing has power." There was a mad gleam in Maztaque's eye, and Rog was troubled.

"What; a blade that speaks! Are thou mad, or is it truly a thing of evil, forged by a sorcerer when the world was young?"

"I know naught where the thing gets its strength, but I am destined to find out," answered Maztaque. "I did not sell our companions to that ignorant Phaedron squad for mere steel; wielding this weapon is mine destiny, and with it I shall carve out an empire!"

"Maybe so," said Rog, "but 'twas a good thing them soldiers recognized ye naught, or we'd be sharing a cell with those two northerners rather than slaying these Woodlings here now. What thinks ye of them two?"

Maztaque shrugged. "I have thought about them, indeed; and quite a lot recently. Ever since I learned of the spirit of the blade, I have thought about the grim warrior who once carried it. I know naught of his destiny, or even how he came to own such a weapon. And he was grim indeed, yet I can tell that he was no wizard. But perhaps, he was in the employment of one."

The din of battle was fading all about the two warriors as they stood there contemplating the Bloodsword. Echoing screams of dying men, and Woodlings, were lingering on the wind, and the setting sun was casting shadows amongst the old trees of the forest.

In a blur, a tiny creature sprinted from under the fern scrub and leaped high into the air at Maztaque's throat, brandishing a small stone dagger. The seasoned warrior merely sidestepped the flying creature, and, with the flash of steel, rent the Woodling in twain. Landing in a heap of offal and guts, the small body baptized the cold ground with warm blood. With one smooth stroke, Maztaque wiped the blade of his L'hoehnian Kindjal with a swath of linen and returned it to the scabbard on his hip.

Turning back to Rog, he saw the terror in his friend's eyes, and remembered their battlefield conversation. Fear washed over Rog's stone-like face.

"Ye think that the northern barbarian was employed by . . . ,"

"Speak naught *that* name," Maztaque interrupted, "for to do so would be to bring the whole of Malador down upon us!"

* * *

A fortnight had passed since Kimark Khan's ethereal visit to Phaedron, and although the city's many residents knew nothing of the event, the High Elder spent his terror filled days and nights in preparation for the battle that was sure to come. For hours at a time, the king would skulk around his antechamber, refusing audience with even the most respectable of the city's nobles, in fear of the Dark One's inevitable attack.

As ordered, one hundred prisoners were executed, and along with them were the entire family of Gurdon Cudgel. Zulanmalh had all but forgotten his disfavor with the dungeon breakout until his counselor came forth with the royal paperwork acknowledging the grim punishment.

The king quickly looked over the papers, signed them, and returned them to his counselor.

"Methinks the guards will think twice ere they allow another prisoner to escape unscathed," said the man to his king, yet the words fell on deaf ears for Zulanmalh's thoughts were elsewhere. With a wave of his hand, the High Elder dismissed the man. He saluted, spun on his heels, and disappeared through the same ebon door that he entered through only moments before.

The king, gripped in a loathsome melancholy that was not his normal temperament, slowly rose from his desk in the antechamber and exited the room. Down long corridors he walked, corridors that even his loyal subjects and the royal courtesans did not know about, to his secret room of rituals.

Now, Zulanmalh was not a sorcerer, but he wasn't inept at calling on dark gods either. More often than not, he would spend his nights in silent prayer to the dark forces that existed just outside the boundaries of the human mind. Many times, these vile gods would command him to perform evil sacrifices unto them, and in humble supplication, these rites would be meticulously performed.

The High Elder entered the room, lit a few tall tapers, and removed his royal gown. The candles cast an eerie glow about the chamber and the king, naked and with head bowed in reverent humility to his dark gods, approached the alter that lay in the center of the room.

Falling to his knees before the black stone slab, the king petitioned his gods in a low tone.

"Father, mother, why have thou abandoned me? I am Zulanmalh, he who is to be feared, not he who fears! Why have ye not protected me from this dark sorcerer?"

The air in the chamber was still and the king's prayers fell on deaf ears, for his gods had abandoned him long ago, yet his faith in them was still strong and unshaken.

"Have I not given thee sacrifices," he cried out? "Have ye not tasted the blood of mine offerings?"

Tears of hopelessness poured forth from the dark eyes of the cruel king, for he was not used to being afraid, yet afraid he was, moreso than he had ever been in his entire life, and that angered him. Quickly he rose from his knees and walked across the room to where a silver gong hung. Taking the mallet, he struck the gong once. The tone rang loudly throughout the chamber, and in minutes, two large servants appeared before him. They were naked to the waist, their deep chest and large arms were corded with the thickly roped muscles of a thrall. Betwixt the men stood a small naked girl, not more than ten summers old, her bronzed skin and golden hair glowing in the faint light of the chamber.

"Place the virgin on the alter," said the king in a low tone, and the two slaves obeyed, dragging the fighting child to the blackened stone in the center of the room.

With stiff leather bonds, her wrists and ankles were tightly secured to the slab, yet her lithe body writhed like a snake on that cold dark stone. The king approached the alter and the thralls disappeared through the door behind him.

For a moment, the High Elder stood silently over the struggling child. He gazed into her cobalt blue eyes and fed off of her fear. With the loving hands of a father, he caressed her small, quivering breasts, and ran a warm finger up and down the length of her flat stomach.

"How old are ye, mine child," he asked.

"Next month, I shall be ten summers grown," the girl answered, trying hard to choke back the sobs as tears streamed down her bronzed face.

"Ah, the beauty of youth," said the king. "Fear naught, mine daughter, for ye will never have to bear the suffering of old age."

The child's fear turned to sheer terror when Zulanmalh's warm finger turned ice cold and she realized that it was not his finger, but the cold caress of steel on her writhing virgin flesh.

"Drink, mine lord and lady . . . drink of the blood of virgins and be refreshed," screamed the king, throwing his head back in ecstasy as he opened the child from navel to neck with one swipe of his ceremonial dagger. Warm blood gushed forth from the gaping wound, darkening the already black alter stone, and the girl's scream ripped though the silence of the chamber, and his troubled mind, then was stilled.

Trembling, Zulanmalh bowed before his grim sacrifice, yet his dark gods heard him naught.

Thus ends Chapter Seven of Book Two

EIGHT

Sky Pirates

The sweltering thermals kept the sail wings full and afloat. The three drifted on the hot air, high over the Sea of Fire, and the rising sun chased them across the warm western sky. Adi clung tightly to Tulwryn's waist, her tiny fingers clenched fast about him, as she buried her face into his thick chest. He could feel the girl trembling, yet he offered not a word of condolence.

Tulwryn had brought the cold of the north with him since leaving the barbarians of Heidmar, and his way with women was all but a distant chill. Sure, he was a man like any other, and his blood boiled with lust, on occasion. But his love died with Halgi, and Durayn, and he vowed to love never again.

Gazing out over that endless sea of brimstone, Tulwryn contemplated much. He thought of past battles and war, and of his friends left back in the north. He thought also of the old wizard's charge, and of Rhyan, and the strange sage they were to meet there. But what he thought about mostly was the lost Bloodsword, and how he would recover the blade. Again, anger welled up in his cold, blue veins just thinking about the sword in the hands of another. He clenched his fists and grinded his teeth; for some unknown reason he and the blade had been fused into one being. Perhaps it was the branding of his hands; perhaps he would never know. All he knew was that he must recover the sword; his life and destiny demanded it.

With feet dangling, and the boiling sea far below, Tulwryn tugged on the tethers that tied him and Adi to the sail wing. He scanned the interior of the canvas canopy for any sign of fatigue or seam separation. Thus far, all looked well and it seemed that luck was finally on their side. Adi was quiet, and her trembling had ceased; Dillwyn was quiet as well. The air around them was still, and empty of any bird, for nowhere in any direction could land be seen. Tulwryn lost track of time; how long had they been aloft, he pondered, hours or days? How much longer would they drift ere they find land or fall into the searing flames below? Maybe neither. Maybe they would drift forever and merely starve to death, still tied to the canvas wings from which they hung. A shudder came over Tulwryn as he pictured that macabre vision, three fleshless skeletons hanging from the hot skies, and drifting on the thermals over the Sea of Fire for an eternity. The thought entertained him naught. And his stomach rumbled for he was hungry.

The warm wind shifted, Dillwyn's wing came around port side, and Tulwryn noticed a stern look on the dwarf's ancient face.

"What ye thinking of, Dillwyn," Tulwryn shouted hardheartedly. "Thou face is but an expression of forlorn and melancholy." Adi stirred at Tulwryn's shout, apparently fallen asleep but now coming awake.

Pointing a thick forearm and gnarled finger southward, the dwarf answered back:

"Ye see off south?" Tulwryn nodded. "Far yonder, past this damnable sea, across the Golrin Prairie and beyond the reaches of the West Lake, forty leagues or better I would assume, lies mine home."

"Carthus?"

"Aye, Tulwryn," said the dwarf. "Carthus, indeed. The wheel of the seasons has turned many times since I have gazed upon mine people. Perhaps I am getting homesick and sentimental in my later years. That is all. Nothing more." Dillwyn sighed.

"There is nothing unmanly about missing kith and kin, dear friend. Perhaps we shall stop in Carthus on our way to Bain. It would be good to rest and refit our possibles prior to engaging those cutthroats in the old forest."

"This I would readily agree," shouted the dwarf, ecstatically. "And a jack full of cold Carthusian ale would be nice as well!"

"Aye, t'would indeed, mine friend, but don't get my tongue a wagging for cold drink yet. Only the gods know what our future brings, and still I see no land on the horizon." The two laughed a bit, trying to relieve the somberness of the moment. Again, the wind shifted, the thermals blew up, and the two wings rose higher in the warm air.

"The gods be damned, Tulwryn," Dillwyn roared as if smitten by the god of anger himself. "Seems the wind is kicking up again and now, if I am correct, we drift south!"

"South is not the way across this sea, nor does it lie in the direction of Rhyan. Perhaps the gods have other things in store for us than Mimir's charge?"

Suddenly, like a great crack of lightning, a blast of flame ripped through the sky. For a second the three were blinded by the intensity of the great spark, which licked up from the horizon far to their south. A second later, it was gone.

"What in hell's name do ye suppose that was," Dillwyn asked. "If I had to bet gold coin, I would say that blast came from deep within the borders of the Golrin Prairie. Only twice in mine life had I seen a flame hot enough to illume the entire sky from that distance."

"Aye," Tulwryn interrupted. "The sword beckons me; it calls my name."

The dwarf nodded. "I remember the blast that slayed the dragon," he said.

"Aye, the tongue of the shadow it was, that split the serpent's belly!"

"Ye suppose those bandits have discovered how to use the blade," asked Dillwyn.

Tulwryn paused for a moment, as if trying to decipher the situation. He looked down at the scars on his palms, and then gazed again back south in the direction of the blast.

"Nay, Dillwyn. 'Tis the bandits, that is certain; and thy wizard friend even told us they were nearing Bain; remember? But he who has the blade knows naught its purpose. The Bloodsword answers only to me, and I to it. No other shall ever wield its power, not even ye who forged it."

"Ye can have its power, Tulwryn. I have no need of that kind of strength!"

"Look," Adi shouted, interrupting the two, "land!"

And sure enough, far below the three floating travelers lay a queer land, strange to behold. Glowing red from the continuous blasts of searing flame from the Sea of Fire was a vast forest of towering Ironwood trees; their broad metallic leaves shimmering in the heat of the midday sun. On the western shore of that accursed ocean, just nigh a league in the distance, was a strange beachhead and cove. The many colors of its sands were absolutely spectacular to take a look at and the three were breathless at the dangerous beauty of the land. Inland, foothills and tall mountains could be seen towering in the distance, casting an eerie shadow of doom over the entire realm.

"Aye, lady Adi, land indeed, but westward," said Dillwyn, "yet, we drift on a southerly wind!"

"That we do," answered Tulwryn. "What ye suppose we do, Dillwyn? Are we to ride out our fate, or shall we try to steer these wings due west?"

"Steering on these thermals is tricky business, Tulwryn. I am a land dwarf, and have no business in the air! That guess, I leave up to ye. For mine self, I feel I shall let fate have her say."

"I hear tell that many armored creatures, such as dragons and gorkons, live within that vast and unbelievable forest," said Adi, interrupting again. "Most tales of such beasts prove deadly to people. Ye suppose we will encounter any in our travels?"

"Methinks ye are a black curse, lady Adi, for ye speak of dark things and look, they appear," yelled Dillwyn, pointing northward with a stubby finger.

Fumbling at the tethers and twisting their necks northward, the three spied a great beast floating on the air. The dragon, still many leagues thither, was immense even at such a great distance and Tulwryn wondered of the true size of such a monster.

"Look at how the great beast floats," Adi exclaimed. "How does such a large creature traverse the firmament thusly, moving naught a muscle that I can see?"

And for true, the dragon sailed through the skies north of them like a ship through water, pitching keel neither port nor starboard, and keeping straight away forward on toward its target. A cold chill of terror washed over Adi and she forgot the searing heat of the sea far below, and the dangers of the unpredictable thermals. Her sole fear now was focused on the approaching dragon and its grim intentions.

"Methinks the fell beast sees us," hollered Dillwyn. "See how it approaches!"

Tension mounted as the large creature soared closer. The three, hanging helpless from the roof of the world, held their breath in fear. Even Tulwryn and the dwarf, warriors through and through and not prone to fear, were frozen in terror over the searing flames of the Sea of Fire. A hundred hungry thoughts ran through their minds, and carried them to distant lands and bloody wars.

"This is it, I feel," roared Dillwyn. He raised a knotted fist to the approaching monster and yelled curses in his native Carthusian tongue. "Damn ye beast! So what if thou devours us three, but ye foiled our quest and because of that the whole of the world is doomed!"

"No, Dillwyn," screamed Tulwryn in ecstatic joy. "Look, 'tis naught a dragon, but a dragonship!"

The dwarf calmed himself down and ceased his curses long enough to focus on the approaching vessel. Adi gasped in awe. The ship was only a few hundred fathoms in the distance, yet its size was staggering. From bow to stern, a full league in length if not longer, the entire ship was made in the image of a great red dragon. Every detail had been meticulously wrought, down to even the smallest scale. The underbelly of the creature was a softer hue that the above, and the face of the dragon was carved in a most menacing grin. There was a strange hissing sound coming from the vessel that grew to an almost deafening pitch the closer it came.

"Are we saved or doomed," asked Adi, "for who sails the skies in such a ship?"

"Methinks they mean us no harm, but look, its size displaces the thermals beneath us. I fear if they move any closer to us our sail wings will collapse and we will perish in the sea regardless of their intentions!"

"Ye are right, Dillwyn! Quick, motion the ship away!"

The three began waving their hands frantically and shouting the ship away, but the vessel paid them no heed. Slowly the ship floated on the thermals, gliding effortlessly through the warm air. The sail wings fluttered in the breeze, their canopies straining to remain full under the displaced thermals. Suddenly, the ship turned port and swung in close, yet under the three. In an instant, they were hanging just mere fathoms over the great wooden deck of the dragonship, and then the canopies of their sail wings collapsed and they came crashing down onto the deck.

Landing in a heap of body parts, the two large, canvas sail wings floated down over the travelers, blotting out all light of the noonday sun. Tulwryn struggled to free himself from the tethers that bound him to Adi. However, when he tried to stand, he discovered his legs were useless, apparently numb from the many days dangling from beneath the canopy of the sail wing. Likewise, Adi and the dwarf were also struggling to stand, with no avail.

A firm hand gripped the large canvas cloth, and in one smooth motion, whipped it up and over the gunwale of the ship. Bright sunlight once again illumed the deck and the travelers found themselves surrounded by three score of grim warriors, all brandishing steel, and with a hurtful gleam in their eyes.

As the canvas sail wings went overboard, Tulwryn and the dwarf realized that now they were trapped aboard the strange vessel, for nowhere was there any means of escape, save death. For a moment, Tulwryn thought about unleashing his wrath with sword in hand, but that thought left him as quick as it had appeared. Even at his finest, he knew he could not best sixty warriors with mere steel; without the aid of the Bloodsword, he was helpless.

Frustration washed over him as he realized the full impact of the situation, and then he noticed something more, something strange and uncanny. None of the warriors that stood before him were breathing! Grim faces set with piercing eyes blazed in the glory of the sun. Sweat glistened off stone-like muscles, and jaws were set with teeth clenched and steel drawn, but none of the men breathed. And Tulwryn's frustration quickly turned to fear. Whilst he was not one to cower from a physical threat, he still had uncertainties about the world of mystery and magic; even with the Bloodsword in hand, he was unsure about the outcome of a battle with foes already dead, yet living. The odds of a victory over such evil with mere steel were fruitless, and he sighed, giving himself up for dead. The look on Adi and Dillwyn's face told him they felt the same.

However, in Phantasodyssea things are not always as they appear, and in seconds the situation changed. Like a sea being split down the middle, the warriors parted way, and before the three weary travelers, there stood a most interesting apparition. He was a man, tall and slender, wearing a saffron kurta and dhoti; barefoot, with a clean-shaven head save for a long braided topknot which emanated from his shining crown.

"Aha," laughed the man, in a deep-throated roar that seemed to defy his pious exterior, for he looked like a glowing saint yet sounded like a swarthy buccaneer. "Mimir told me ye were coming, but I knew naught ye would fall out of the steaming sky onto the deck of my ship!"

Tulwryn and the others sat in dazed confusion. How does this sky pirate know Mimir they wondered, unless . . . no, it couldn't be . . .

"I am Cohado the Long," he said with a grin, "and this is mine ship. I suspect thou art the three from yonder side of the sea?"

"Aye, we are," answered Dillwyn.

"Then come friends, stand and come with me to mine stateroom, for there is much to discuss." At once, Cohado snapped his fingers and all sixty warriors vanished into thin air; likewise, the numbness in Tulwryn and the others' legs instantly left and they were able to stand. A feeling of awe washed over the three at the magician's power, and they cautiously followed him to his cabin below the main deck.

Tulwryn and the others noticed the ship was completely void of servants or sailors, yet the immense vessel was spotlessly clean and cruised without sail or rigging.

"Is it just ye on this boat," asked Dillwyn? "Where is thy crew?"

"I have no need of crew, my friend," answered Cohado, "the *Fidelity* is run solely by mine thought power alone."

"But what of that group of swarthy pirates up on the main," asked Tulwryn?

"Illusion, my friend, mere illusion. Much can be accomplished through many hours of deep meditations."

"What say ye; you keep this great beast afloat with mental prowess alone? For surely thou art a great mage as Mimir has revealed," exclaimed the dwarf.

"Nay," answered the magician, "the ship's buoyancy is due to Levititium, a rare and magical mineral that the Rhyans discovered deep within the Sulphur Mountains long ago. The mineral has anti-magnetic properties and is used in Rhyan Windship engineering, and this, the Fidelity, is the flagship of the Rhyanian fleet."

The four traversed a long hall, with polished hardwood floors, and illumed by glowing crystal spheres that hung from the ceiling. Coming to a mahogany door at the end of the corridor, the group entered a large and stately chamber.

"Please," said Cohado, "relax and make yourselves at home." The room was aglow in sultry amber, and the scent of sandalwood drifted on the air; the three positioned themselves on a large comfortable couch, and the mage sat across from them on a small dais, strewn with plush cushions and silks. Cohado snapped his long, slender fingers and four crystal goblets appeared on the table before them.

"Here is a token of my hospitality, dear friends; something

to help calm thy tired nerves after such a stressful flight over the sea. 'Tis Rhyan sweet wine; smooth and refreshing. Please, drink thy fill."

Adi was the first to sip the sweet liquid. Her smile quickly taunted the others to do the same. The wine was cool and sweet, with a hint of almond. At once, the mood of uncertainty was lifted and the four were conversing like old friends.

"So, the Rhyans gave ye this ship," asked Dillwyn.

"Out of friendship, aye. They gave her to me, with the condition that I remain in Rhyan and teach them the Truth," he answered.

Cohado then paused, stood, and walked to the binnacle that graced the center of his chamber. He gazed at the ship's compass, made a few gestures with his hands, and returned to his seat. Tulwryn felt the body of the great vessel shift, and he realized that the mage's powers were far greater than he had let on, for it must take great concentration to operate a ship of this size on sheer willpower alone. The vessel's bow swung around westward, and Tulwryn and the others realized that they were headed for the mage's city at last.

"So, ye are a prisoner then," asked Tulwryn?

"Nay, I am no prisoner of Rhyan. I can leave at mine own desire, but that is something I desire naught. I have found sanctuary within the village, and its people are my new family."

"Please, master, tell me of thy people," Adi asked, her large dark eyes twinkling in the soft amber glow of the stateroom. Cohado was a celibate priest and a master magician, but his heart was soft and his love, transcendental. He looked at Adi as if she were a child, and to him she was for he was like Mimir; old beyond the count of time, yet he looked not a day older that Tulwryn himself.

Taking a sip from his own goblet, and then rearranging a pillow or two under his lean backside, he leaned back in an informal manner and began to tell a tale.

"Ah, Rhyan," spoke Cohado, "On the west side of the Sea of Fire, located atop a high ridge in the Crimson Forest, just on the southern most border of the Sulphur Mountains lies the mystical city of Rhyan, my city. No one in all of Phantasodyssea, save for Mimir or myself, has had contact with the native inhabitants of Rhyan in over seven centuries. Many people do not even believe the city exists anymore, which is good for us since it keeps unwanted visitors away."

"Are the people of Rhyan unfriendly," she asked.

"Nay, we are naught unfriendly, but we prefer our company in small dosages. Ye see, we are a spiritual people, and we spend our time in peaceful contemplation. Anyway, most people think Rhyan to be a fabricated work of folklore and not really factual. As legend goes, the Rhyans were a strong race of powerful wizards that understood the deep mysteries of the natural world. And indeed, this is no fiction, for the Rhyans are real, as ye will soon see.

"Long ago, they discovered, as I have already told ye, a mineral known as Levititium. This rare and magical gem has anti-magnetic properties and is used in Rhyan Windship engineering. The ships are utilized as a means of border defenses, yet they are cleverly constructed to resemble dragons thereby protecting the anonymity of the Rhyans themselves. The city and its people still exist to this present day, but they live obscure, reclusive lives, safely out of reach behind the wall of molten lava that is the Sea of Fire."

"If ye are so protected from the rest of the world," Tulwryn asked, "then why has Mimir charged us to seek ye out?"

Cohado shifted his gaze from Adi to the warrior. "Indeed," he said, "we are protected, but naught for long. Even as cruel as Zulanmalh is, he is a saint compared to the evil of Kimark Khan. It has been brought to our attention, through the use of our meditations, that the dark mage is planning to usurp the Ivory Throne. If this happens, then all of Phantasodyssea will be lost. It is our hope that ye can thwart his plan."

"Saving the world is a high charge indeed," answered Tulwryn.

"Ye saved it once, did ye naught." There was a gleam of playfulness in the priest's eye, and Adi wondered to what the mage was speaking. Who were these two unlikely heroes she had fell in with, she wondered silently to herself as she eyed the warrior and the dwarf with a look of complexity.

"Please," spoke Tulwryn, "enlighten us on this grim situation, and tell us what we must do. Dillwyn and I are warriors, this much is true. If there is adventure to be had, then I am all for it. Saving the world . . . well, perhaps we may save it accidentally through the course of our adventuring, but do not hold us responsible if we fail. We are merely humans and not ancient wizards."

"Ye are no mere human, dear friend," spoke the priest, with a somber tone in his voice. "Ye are the Bloodsword. Prophecy is prophecy, and thy destiny will unfold before ye, as well as the destiny of the world, for ye destiny and the destiny of Caiwryn is one!"

"Oh, not more talk of prophecies," sighed the warrior. "I was hoping to leave behind all that trouble when we left the north."

Cohado laughed. "Ye are in Phantasodyssea, friend; magic is a way of life here. Get used to it."

"Please," said Dillwyn, "tell us what ye know."

"Have ye ever heard of Chete," asked the wizard? The three shook their heads.

"All right then, let me tell ye the tale from the beginning, and in its entirety. Please, listen carefully. At the western-most border of the vast expanse known only as the Wastes, lies the small subterranean village of Chete. Surrounded by nameless mountains and burning desert sands, Chete was a peaceful place of contemplation. For centuries, mystics of all traditions came from afar to study in its many underground temples and monasteries, searching for the seeds of wisdom and enlightenment.

"But, before Chete, there was Vodmar; and Covensted ere that." Cohado paused and took another sip of his wine; the three seated across from him were held fast by his gaze and the intensity of the tale. Whilst Tulwryn and the dwarf had never heard of Chete or Vodmar, they had heard of Covensted, and that name they cared naught to hear again.

"It is believed," said Cohado, "that the old teachers of Chete were actually the very same priests that once occupied the Holy City of Vodmar in the Golrin Prairie, and indeed, I can assure thee that legend speaks the truth. These Vodmarian priests fled that Holy City from a fierce band of Knobite raiders, and they traveled south into the Wastes.

"After much wandering, they stumbled upon some underground caverns and decided that the place was suitable for a safe sanctuary whereby they could resume their metaphysical studies, hence Chete was built. And so, it was there, in the underground monasteries of Chete, that they discovered the secrets of immortality and ultimate knowledge. For many decades, Chete was dedicated to peace and compassion. But soon, things began to change.

"Coming from a distant and unknown land, were a group of priests that petitioned the mystics of Chete for entrance into their underground abbey. These priests seemed very holy and pious, and so were allowed to enter the monastery and study with the mystics. Even I, seasoned in the ways of magic, knew naught their dread goal, and warmly embraced them as brothers.

"Slowly, over time, a new brotherhood formed. The Order of the Crystal Sphere began like any other mystical lodge, and so many of us were oblivious to its true intentions. Somewhere, through the course of my meditations, I began to have my suspicions of the Order, and began a psychic investigation on many of its high-ranking members. My findings proved to be most shocking.

"Although these individuals were none of the original mystics that came to Chete from Vodmar, they were powerful indeed, and their intentions were fell. Once I discovered the ruse, I went to a few of my close friends within the Order to disclose to them, in complete security, my findings. However, what I did not know was that the evil had seeped in further than I had expected. Apparently, I was the only one who had not been poisoned by the dread evil of the Crystal Sphere. Why this was so, I knew naught.

"Anyhow, word flew fast through those grim caves and I was

named by the brotherhood, the *Keeper of Lies*, because of their evil secrets that I had uncovered. I was angered that such evils could be kept under wraps and thereby, I threatened the security of the brotherhood by promising to expose the Order and its lies to all the world. I swore to expose the lies that the brotherhood had kept hidden from the eyes of men for centuries. Needless to say, I was forced to flee Chete for fear of death, and so became a banished priest.

"Living in self-exile, I wandering Phantasodyssea until I came upon Rhyan and its wonderful inhabitants. To this day, I am still being sought by the brotherhood, which will stop at nothing to silence me forever. And so, I stay in Rhyan, living in seclusion."

"This is all very interesting," proclaimed Tulwryn, "but what does it have to do with the Phaedron throne and this Khan character?"

Dillwyn and Adi stirred a bit, seeing how Tulwryn's bluntness added a bit of uncertainty to the air of the room. Cohado calmed them all with a wave of his hand, and once again stood and walked to the ship's compass to make another adjustment in her course. The vessel reeled and swayed, completely submissive under his mental reins. Languidly, he walked back to his platform and returned to his seat.

"It has much to do with Kimark Khan, dear warrior," spoke the wizard. "For the Khan 'twas the Order's high priest and the supreme ruler of the brotherhood!"

"So, what was this evil that ye uncovered then?"

"'Tis Kimark Khan's plan to usurp the throne of Phaedron and rule the whole of Phantasodyssea. Ye see, he has been gaining knowledge and strength for eons. First, he studied in Covensted. 'Twas there he first learned of magical lore and enchantments. His great intelligence allowed him to learn rather quickly, and so he advanced past many of the witches of that town. He then left Covensted and wandered a bit, we know naught where. When he settled in Chete he was already strong beyond all compare. Even if Mimir and myself were to join our magics we would be no match for his power!"

"And we are supposed to best him," cried Tulwryn. "What ye take us for, fools?"

Suddenly Cohado looked off into the distance, as if almost in a trance. His mind seemed to wander to some far and distant land, or across some dusty old tome. In a low pitched drone, he spoke:

"During the dark times, his wrath had become great and entire nations rose and fell at the wave of his hand, and so it seemed that he was of the land and the land was of him, for their two destinies had merged and become one."

The three had no idea what the old mage was talking about, and sat in utter confusion.

"Have ye never heard these words ere now," Cohado asked. The three sat silent. "'Tis a quote from an ancient and holy book: *The Selah*. It is the book of prophecy. And in that book, the greatest of all prophecies is that of the Bloodsword. The dark times began with the stirrings of the dragon, Darkoth." Cohado paused and gazed at Tulwryn, and smiled. "Ye smote him effortlessly, indeed. But with each passing moon, the days will get darker and the evil that threatens Phantasodyssea will grow. Let us put our heads together and discover a way to end this threat once and for all."

All was quiet in the stateroom for some time, the mood somber, almost meditative. Amber beams danced off the cherry wood walls and the scent of sandalwood grew even stronger. An eternity passed in seconds and seconds seemed to last forever, then suddenly Cohado stood and walked to the door.

"Come, friends, the ship now docks. Come and see mine wonderful city." And with that, he led them from the cabin and into a world of magic and mystery.

Thus ends Chapter Eight of Book Two

NINE

A City in the Clouds

Rhyan was a beautiful city, almost majestic in appearance, yet extremely simple and serene. The four stood on the high bridge overlooking the bow of the ship. From their vantage point, they could see great stretches of the Crimson Forest laid out beneath them, and a high ridge poking through the dense canopy of tall Ironwood trees; and perched on that high ridge stood Rhyan, regal and bold.

The ship swayed in the warm breezes, yet beckoned to every mental command of Cohado the Long. She sailed proudly, with head held high, for she was the mightiest of all the windships in Phantasodyssea, the crowning glory of Rhyan technology, and its flagship. The dragon's scales glistened and sparkled in the late afternoon sun as the beast drifted into her main slip on the dock. Tulwryn and the others could see countless people, all dressed exactly like Cohado, in long saffron robes, barefoot, and with their odd headpieces, running to an fro on the dock in great anticipation of Cohado's return.

The ship came to a halt and the tall mage escorted the three to the main deck, and from there, down onto the dock itself. There was a large mass of people that awaited them, and the three were quite amazed at their reception.

At first, there was much commotion, and so, Cohado raised his hands and the bustling crowd quieted. "Dear friends, mine people of Rhyan," Cohado said, speaking loudly, with a hint of authority, "behold, I bring ye the salvation of our world!"

With those words, the crowd erupted into a violent frenzy of cheers. Tulwryn and the others looked at each other and then turned to the mage.

"What is all this, Cohado," asked Dillwyn. "I do not know how mine comrades feel, but I for one do not like being made a spectacle."

"Calm thyself, friends, ye are naught a spectacle, but an answer to our prayers. Come, let us celebrate."

"'Tis normal to celebrate ere the victory," asked Tulwryn?

"Ye must know, we Rhyanians are an optimistic lot, indeed."

"There is nothing wrong with being optimistic, as long as that optimism leads ye naught to stupidity."

"Very well said," answered the mage. "But anyhow, come now, thy people await you." And with no further ado, Cohado thrust his head high like a general returning from a successful campaign, and marched down the gangway into the seething hoard that awaited on the Sky Wharf.

"I am liking this less and less as the day draws on," said Tulwryn.

"Aye," answered the dwarf, nodding in agreement. The three then followed the wizard into the cheering crowd.

It seemed that the entire city had descended onto the windship dock that afternoon, for never in Tulwryn's life had he seen so many people congested together in one place. He had heard about large metropolises such as this, but coming from a small farming community, he had never witnesses such numbers first hand, except in battle. His country upbringing demanded that he be courteous and polite to the people he met. But such numbers made him feel uneasy and his sword hand fidgeted unceasingly with the hilt of his weapon hanging loosely at his side.

The four strolled down the gilded walkways of Rhyan, shaking hands with many of the villagers. Young boys came running, hoping to steal a glance at the mighty warriors that prophecy claimed would save their land; others begged to be told tales of past adventures and heroic deeds. Some of the youths, perhaps in their late teens or early twenties, hoping to one day become great warriors themselves, asked for admittance into the ranks of Tulwryn's army, only to leave with their hope shattered when he told them that he had no army in which they could serve. On more than one occasion, Cohado himself had to intervene saying:

"Dear boys, go home and study thy scriptures, and practice thy meditations; for a prince of Rhyan is no warrior, but a priest. Our way is naught the way of war, but the way of peace. This is Tulwryn Bloodsword; he is a warrior supreme and is an army unto himself. Hope naught to follow in his footsteps, as a warrior, but live by the principles that he fights to uphold! And thank the gods that he has agreed to aid us in our plight."

Likewise, many youthful maidens, primed for handfasting, came forward to see the grim warrior of the north. And once again, Cohado's work was bitter, for he ran them off by the score. Perhaps it was the danger of Tulwryn's occupation, or the lure of forbidden love, maybe even the grand idea of becoming a warrior's wife and setting off for a life of grand adventure, one can never know what folly ideas infiltrate the minds of young girls, hungry for lust and love. And it did trouble Cohado that even here in Rhyan, a city cloistered from the rest of the world, that lustful ideas could propagate even amongst the most pious of virgins, and he realized that the evil that was overshadowing Phantasodyssea was even more powerful than he had originally assumed.

"Why ye run off these fair lasses," asked Tulwryn, with a frown. After the death of Durayn and Halgi, he was not seeking love, but he was still a man and he had his needs. "If ye are sending me off to mine doom, would it naught be good for me to partake in a night of love ere I meet my fate with no one to know?"

"Ye have other things to think about, warrior," Cohado answered, "we must make plans, and ye all must rest ere ye set forth on the quest."

"Work, work, work," Tulwryn sighed. "Ye Rhyans are naught a very hospitable lot. Ye wish me to risk mine neck, yet will naught allow me the pick of thy wenches. Perhaps your city would naught need hire mercenaries such as I if ye had thy own warriors. Allow thy maidens to breed with a warrior and warriors ye shall have! 'Tis makes no sense to me at all why I would even accept this proposal."

An angry look boiled in Cohado's eyes, and Tulwryn was amazed for he knew naught that the holy mage could be pushed to wrath.

"First, know this warrior; the maidens of Rhyan are naught mere wenches, as ye say. They do naught frequent beer halls nor do they associate with ruffians. Our girls are the jewels of Caiwryn, and we protect them most definitely. And second, ye help us because ye are the Bloodsword and that is thy destiny, for even ye cannot turn back the hands of Fate! Would it be better to have rotted in that Phaedron cell? 'Twas I who freed thee, me and Mimir; and ye owe us for that!"

"Naught much of a rescue," Tulwryn mumbled under his breath.

"And anyway," said Cohado, pointing to Adi, "I thought this beautiful maiden was your woman. Why insult her with thy adulterous comments?" Adi flashed her dark eyes to Tulwryn and smiled; he simply sighed and followed the magician into the cottage that they were approaching.

The house was small, yet cozy, with thickly woven rugs covering a finely crafted hard wood floor and a central hearth made of stone. There was an iron cauldron hanging over the fire pit and split log benches strewn around the main room. Cohado stooped to light a few candles, then pulled up a stool and asked the three to have a seat wherever they wished.

"The sun will be setting soon," said the mage, "we must make our plans this eve for time is running out. We can sup after we discuss our plans, and then we will retire for the night."

And so, under the light of flickering candles, the four made their plans to recover the Bloodsword and save the world. By the time dinner was ready, it had been decided that Tulwryn, accompanied by a regiment of Cohado's warriors, those mystical illusions that he was so fond of creating, would head for the

River Adronn, whereby the group would follow the river southeast to the Golrin Prairie and then east toward Bain. The warriors, Cohado assured, would follow every command given by Tulwryn, thereby aiding him in his quest to secure the Bloodsword.

Dillwyn and Adi were to join Cohado and his mystical crew aboard the Fidelity and sail east toward The Enchanted Forest. There, at the base of Malador, the three would await Tulwryn's return. A rendezvous site was agreed upon, and from that base camp, they were to launch an all out assault on the khan.

Cohado and a mystical servant set a table fit for a king, and the four sat to sup with the mage of Rhyan. The food was delicious, the wine excellent, yet the talk became sour and melancholy.

"So, Dillwyn," said Tulwryn, "it seems like ye will naught see thy home for yet a few more moons. Perhaps I will still pass through the village. Might there be anyone there I can give a message?"

"I really have no family there, not much to speak of anyway. Most of my blood kin is dead, and I am the last in the line of the Anvilhands."

"Please then, dear friend," asked Tulwryn, "tell me of Carthus and thy people." Cohado raised an eyebrow at the mention of Dillwyn's namesake, for he realized him to be of dwarven stock, but had no idea he hailed from Carthus, or the house of the Anvilhand, whose legendary heroics were very well known throughout the whole of the world. Adi pulled up a chair as well, since she was always keen to hear a tale told well. The idea of leaving Tulwryn and sailing east with Dillwyn and the wizard pined her soul, but she knew it for the best. She prayed to her gods that she be united with her warrior in the end, yet she knew naught the price of that prayer.

"Carthus is a medium sized town located in the northwest reaches of the Golrin Prairie, just south of the Sea of Fire, and a stone's throw from the Lower Crimson Forest. My people, the Carthusian dwarves, are the only dwarves in Phantasodyssea that reside above ground, and our architecture is most grand. Ye will be amazed, Tulwryn, at the grandeur of the city." The dwarf paused for a moment and shot a glance at Cohado. "No offence to ye or your city, master." The mage simply smiled and gestured him to continue his tale.

"Mine people are a mighty race of dwarves, and we pride ourselves on being fine engineers and mighty warriors. 'Tis no secret that long ago, ere Carthus was established, the Dragon's Needle began to rumble, and so the mystics of Golrin employed my people to build a firewall dam at the southern rim of a lone valley north of our village. Even though we did naught believe in the story that the mystics told, that the Dragon's Needle would erupt and spew so much fire and brimstone that the whole of the Golrin Prairie would be flooded, we nevertheless took the job and built the dam.

"We were paid in Golrin coin, and with the finances from the job, Carthus was able to expand into the thriving city it is today. Needless to say, those ancient mystics were correct, for one day the Dragon's Needle did erupt and flood the entire Valley! The Sea of Fire that we drifted over is proof of that event. Yet, the eruption did not happen for about six hundred and eighty years after the great dam was built. And now, almost seven centuries after being built, and with practically no maintenance or upkeep to speak of, the dam still holds. This has put my city, and people, on the map. Carthus is heralded as the foremost place of learning for those interested in engineering and architecture. And at last count, the lava flow from the Dragon's Needle continues to fill the Sea of Fire even to this day!"

"Ye are a walking source of lore, Dillwyn," said Tulwryn, "and ye never cease to amaze me with your knowledge."

"Methinks that my people will greet ye with open arms, for they are naught like other dwarves; my people love adventure and heroics, and I am sure that without Cohado here to fight off wanna-be warriors, thy ranks will swell beyond counting. I foresee ye entering Malador with a mighty host indeed!" And with that, he emptied his wine glass, wishing all along it were a jack of cold Carthusian ale instead.

"The night grows, dear friends," said Cohado. "Let us take our leave and retire for the night. Dillwyn, ye can have the cottage across the way; Tulwryn and his lady may have this one." The old wizard smiled at the warrior, and winked at Adi ere he left. "I am off to mine own place of rest, the Temple of Rhyan, for a priest never sleeps lying down but rather rests seated in deep thought and holy meditation. Good night."

The wizard left the cottage and the others conversed for a while longer ere Dillwyn said his goodnights. As the door creaked behind the dwarf, Adi nudged closer to Tulwryn.

"So, 'tis just us," she said, with a lustful gleam in her eye, and a smile.

"Aye, m'lady," Tulwryn answered. "I suppose 'tis naught a noble thing to ignore what the gods have decreed." And so, that night, high up on a ridge overlooking the vast Crimson Forest, in the Holy City of Rhyan, a mighty warrior surrendered his heart to love.

The morning came sooner than Tulwryn had wished, for the night was well spent in the arms of Adi, and she was pleasing to him. The two rose, dressed, and broke their fast together around a bowl of warm porridge and dark coffee. After eating, they washed up and left the cottage to assemble with Dillwyn and Cohado down at the docks of the Rhyan skywharf.

The morning sun was casting a bright gleam over the city, and its people were bustling down the walkways toward the windshipyards. Tulwryn and Adi strolled past many meticulously manicured lawns and beautifully painted homes. The entire atmosphere of Rhyan was stunning, thought Adi, but at what cost. Even though the city was beautiful beyond compare, she noticed an air of sobriety, as if Rhyan was a city without love. Indeed, she remembered the night before, and how Cohado had frowned on Tulwryn's comments towards their maidens. Was sex and love forbidden in this place, she wondered; and if so, what good was it to save such a city, whose values went against everything she knew in her heart to be wholesome and pure. Sure, rough animal sex, without affection or love, was indeed worthless and vile; but not true love. True love, like the love she and Tulwryn shared late into the eve, that was indeed a good thing and she knew naught any reason why such an act should be banned. She squeezed the warrior's hand and he cast her an affectionate smile.

"How long ere ye rendezvous with us in Malador," she asked.

"I know naught," he replied.

"Will ye miss me?"

"Ye will just have to wait and see, I suppose," he said with a grin, and then threw a thick arm around her slender shoulder.

Together the two roused Dillwyn from his slumber, and they meandered through the streets of Rhyan, talking with the villagers on their way to the docks, and the slip that held the Fidelity.

Cohado, with two hundred of his mystic warriors, met the three adventurers on the Rhyan skywharf, a fantastic structure that jutted out over the edge of a high ridge. From the main deck of the wharf, one could see for endless leagues in all directions. Tulwryn and the others noticed numerous windships, all superbly wrought in the images of dragons, sailing the skies over Rhyan. There was tension in the air and Tulwryn felt it. It was as if the entire city was mustering for battle, or perhaps a mass evacuation; but that knowledge was not to be his, for his destiny lied naught with the Rhyans, but with those that occupied the plains far below.

The tall mage approached the three and took Tulwryn's hand in friendship.

"Peace be with you, brother," he said. "This day is to be recorded in the Rhyan histories as a great day indeed, for this is the day that the Bloodsword embarked on the quest of quests, and it if from our great city that this quest begins."

Tulwryn nodded, not caring to discuss heroics with the man before him. He cared little for poetics, and it seemed to him that Cohado was more a poet than a wizard, at least for the moment, and to him both were equally useless. He glanced at Dillwyn, and by the somber look in the dwarf's eyes, he understood that he felt the same.

"Well then, I have crafted you one hundred of my best fighting men to accompany you on your journey," Cohado said. "The other hundred will sail with your two friends and me on the Fidelity. I fear that thy journey is the more perilous one, and I pray the gods and good fortune go with ye. Depart now, whilst the sun is high."

The wizard then turned to address Tulwryn's troops, and he did so in a strange and archaic tongue. Tulwryn and the others watched as Cohado barked commands to the warriors and they fell in a double line, single file yet side by side, before the northern warrior. "The soldiers are at your disposal now," Cohado told the warrior from Nuvia. "Command them and they will serve ye well. Farewell barbarian, and Godspeed; until we meet again under the shadow of Malador, be off!"

Tulwryn said his good-byes to Adi and the dwarf and then walked back to the front of his assembly. He glanced a quick glance at his motley crew, warriors that were neither alive nor dead; yet undead all the same, conjured from sorcery. He never imagined in all his life that he would lead such a group, nor did he realize that he would crave the company of others as he found himself now craving. These grim warriors neither ate, nor drank, neither slept nor made merry. They were created for one fell purpose and that purpose was to serve him, and to kill.

A single tear creased Adi's sun-browned cheek as she watched Tulwryn walk away, then she herself turned and walked away as well. Tulwryn mounted a great magical steed that Cohado had conjured, and then watched as Dillwyn and Adi followed the wizard up the gangplank and boarded the great windship. From his position on the skywharf, he gazed eastward, into an uncertain future and wondered what destiny had in store for him and the others. The sun rose high over Rhyan that day, yet his heart was heavy to watch his two companions sail off into the distance.

With a deafening hiss, the great engines of the Fidelity began to churn, and slowly the great ship glided out of her slip and into the warm air over Rhyan. She then reeled starboard and came about, passing the skywharf. Those there assembled, the people of Rhyan, civilians and nobles alike, gave a cheer as she sailed away into the glare of the rising sun.

Ere the great ship was even out of sight, Tulwryn gave a yell and commanded his men to follow. He was to lead them through the forest, to the River Adronn, and beyond. The warriors mustered themselves in their double rows and followed suit behind their grim master.

Wearing the magical gear that Mimir had given him on the far side of the Sea of Fire, and seated atop his steed, Tulwryn appeared as a fell warrior indeed. His leather armor, dyed coal black, shone like polished obsidian in the glare of the sun; and his tall helm, wrought in dark steel, possessed deeply carved magical symbols of strength and protection. From his hip hung a great broadsword, and two more fighting blades were shoved through his sash as well. A large, round oaken shield hung from his steed's saddle horn.

With a tug on the reins and a kick to the flank, Tulwryn's beast cantered forward down the lane leading away from the skywharf. Through the city they went, the barbarian general and his ethereal army; and the people of Rhyan cheered as the warriors passed, just as they cheered when he entered their city the night before, and just as they cheered as the Fidelity sailed away only moments ago.

For some strange reason, he knew not why, Tulwryn felt an emptiness, almost as if he knew these people were doomed. He could not place the feeling or the reason why he felt it, just that he did, and that was all. He looked upon the people of Rhyan for the last time, as a man looks upon the face of one condemned just ere the executioner's axe falls, and he knew he would never see their smiling faces again.

It did not take long to travel through the city, for Rhyan was small despite its numbers. The army took the southern trails that led away from the city, and followed them through the forest. The terrain was not as harsh as Tulwryn had imagined. The going was rocky, yet there was no undergrowth to slow the pace. He was the only one on horseback, and so at times, he dismounted and walked with the men to give the beast a rest, although he realized that the creature was conjured from Cohado's sorcery and needed no rest as does a creature of flesh.

The River Adronn was the only river in Phantasodyssea that flowed north, therefore it would prove useless to take watercraft and sail the river. Nay, the army would not traverse the waters of Adronn, they would simply follow its shoreline south to the Golrin Prairie.

And for many days, Tulwryn's fighters trudged over the charred land of the Crimson Forest, saying naught a word but heeding his every command. The nights were long for Tulwryn, for these warriors spoke as little as the breathed, and they breathed naught a breath. And therefore, he would sit 'round the campfire in silent contemplation, alone, save for his own grim thoughts and the burden he carried.

It was four days since he left Rhyan ere he came upon the shimmering waters of Adronn, and there on its banks he broke his force into quarters and posted four watches around the camp, one in each direction; and in each watch there stood a score and five sleepless warriors guarding his stead. The fire was quickly built, not because he needed warmth, for he did naught since the forest was heated by the brimstone sea wherefrom it got its name. Nor did he need the fire for cooking, for Cohado lent him a pouch of magical foodstuff, which needed neither cooking nor preserving. Perhaps he built the fire for mere companionship. A friend indeed that fire became and it served him well that night, and even in the nights ahead, for save for himself and the breathing flames of the campfire, naught else breathed in the Crimson Forest, or at least that is what he had come to believe.

Tulwryn sat there, gazing into the licking flames of his lonely campfire, and on occasion, he would glance up at the brilliant stars twinkling high up in the heavens. The nights in the forest were dark and the sky was the blackest he had ever seen; the stars shone like sparkling gems on a black velvet throw. But still, even amongst all the natural beauty that the land unfolded before him, Tulwryn's heart was heavy for he began to miss Adi, and Dillwyn, his friend.

Suddenly, his eyes returning from the stars above back to the fire itself, Tulwryn found himself not alone and he was startled, for across from him sat an elderly gentleman in a forest green cloak and smoking a long pipe. The man was completely bald, save for a long strand of braided gray hair, which gently fell from under his hood, down onto his right shoulder.

Tulwryn stood with a start, tossing his cape up over his right shoulder, his sword leaping from its scabbard in one smooth motion.

"Who are you," he said, angrily. "And how did ye breech my forces to approach me thus at my fire?"

The old man chuckled.

"Calm down, my dear boy, calm down. There is more here than meets the eye, Tulwryn. Are you naught lonely for some companionship? Well then, sit and we shall converse."

"Who are ye, and how do ye know my name?"

"Who does naught know the mighty warrior from Nuvia? The man who slayed his woman as well as the dragon, up north?"

Tulwryn sat dumbfounded. Surely, there was more in Caiwryn than meets the eye, he thought. On more than one occasion, he had been warned by many people about the strangeness of the land in which he dwelt. Mimir, Cohado, and others had told him the land was magical and indifferent to the forces he deemed natural. Yet, he always found himself to be amazed when such forces materialized.

"I am Daithi Mac Bhurrais," said the old man, "but most just call me the Green Wanderer, for none know whence I hail."

"And where is that, may I ask?" Sweat beaded down Tulwryn's brow, and he wiped his face. The old man seemed to display no threatening gesture, yet Tulwryn could not help but feel vulnerable in his presence. This man, old and feeble, was able to somehow circumnavigate his defenses and slip past his men. This, Tulwryn knew, could only be done with powerful magic and so he realized that he was in the company of a great mystic.

At first, he believed the man to be lying. Could this be Kimark Khan, he wondered? Tulwryn knew naught the image of the great

Khan, and with the tales told by Cohado and Mimir, he believed it possible that the evil sage could take any form of his choosing. What better way to thwart the rebellion than to slay me now ere the battle even begins, Tulwryn thought silently to himself, and me without the Bloodsword!

But the old man read his troubled thoughts and put his mind to ease.

"Nay, dear boy, the one ye seek I am naught. But I have news that may serve ye well in thy quest."

Tulwryn sighed in relief, yet was unable to totally relax.

"All right," said he, "speak, and give the tales ye have brought, but waste naught my time with useless yarns, old man." There was still an air of uncertainty 'round the camp, yet the old one dismissed Tulwryn's arrogance and inhospitality as a simple mortal flaw.

"I have come from the prairie yonder, east of the forest. I have been where ye are to go. I have seen many grim days, and there was much suffering. I fear there is will be even more to come."

"What say ye, of the prairie," asked Tulwryn. "Speak naught in riddles, old man."

"On the Golrin Prairie, there was a band of L'hoehn bandits wielding a grim weapon; I believe ye know the weapon of which I speak."

"I do," answered Tulwryn. "'Tis the Bloodsword that I seek."

"Well, know this, you will find the weapon naught on the prairie, but in Phaedron. The bandits have been consuming everything in their path, like a parasitic disease, they leech off the land and wealth of others. For many moons they went unopposed, the power of their grim weapon unstoppable. But they knew naught how to wield such a weapon! And then something happened, something strange and terrible. The band met some fair resistance on the southern boundaries of the Golrin Prairie and a bloody skirmish erupted. Not much is known about the resistance; perhaps it was a group of Knobites, but the leader of the bandits, the one who had been brandishing the weapon, attempted again to use the grim sword but was struck down by a great blast from the heavens!"

"Aye," interrupted Tulwryn, "I seen that blast!"

"So ye did, so ye did. Well, in the chaos that resulted, the bandits were driven apart and fled in the four directions like chaff in the wind. It is known to me that a man, the second in charge of the marauders, has secured the sword and is attempting to take it to Phaedron, where he will sell it to the High Elder for a fortune in coin."

"This is naught pleasant news ye bring to mine ears, old man," Tulwryn snorted. "My plans were to . . ."

"I know thy plans," said the old man, "and plans must change from time to time. Forget your friends in Malador for the moment. Ye must forsake Carthus as well; but go ye to Bain as had planned. There ye can rest and converse with some of the surviving Woodlings. They will give ye good counsel. From Bain, ye can cut north over the trade route and sneak into the Phaedron Wood to ambush the man that has stolen the sword. Slay him if ye must, but surely recover the weapon ere he enters the citadel! For if Zulanmalh received the Bloodsword, then all is lost."

For a time, Tulwryn sat motionless, gazing into the coals of the fire pit, trying to decipher his next move. Like a strategic game of chess, he had to be clever, not rash. When he returned to the present, the old one was gone; he had vanished as silently as he had appeared, and again, this troubled the warrior from Nuvia.

All that night, Tulwryn slept naught, but kept a watchful eye and ear to the wind. Yet, in the morning he found himself to be awake and well rested. Thoughts of sorcery danced through his skull but he dismissed them and mustered his men.

The sun rose high and hot that morning as the fighters marched eastward, Tulwryn astride his large mount and the others in their double row behind him. Onward they marched, following the waters of Adronn out of the forest and down into the valley that merged with the prairie below.

Thus ends Chapter Nine of Book Two

TEN

The Gorkon

Two days had passed since the Fidelity had left the skywharf at Rhyan; the air was warm and the day was clear. It was a day like any other, pleasant and serene, and there seemed to be no threat in its future, but Cohado, priest of Rhyan, knew different.

Cohado the Long had put the ship on a northerly course, which would cut across the northwestern corner of the Sulphur Mountains near the Dragon's Needle in a day and a half. The wizard knew the dangers of cruising over the mountains unescorted by smaller, more maneuverable sky craft, but time was not on his side and he was determined to arrive at Malador in record time. With the brooding threat of Kimark Khan's evil looming over the whole of the land, Cohado deemed it a necessity to sail through the Gorkon infested skies over the Sulphur Mountains. He knew the risks, and had taken every precaution thereof. Since it would take all of his mental strength to maintain control of the ship, his magic would be useless for defense, so he mustered his mystic warriors. On either side of the Fidelity, he had stationed a score and five of his best archers, and they stood there poised and at the ready, with poison arrows notched in their bows and eyes keen on the horizon.

Adi, not satisfied with the mage's orders to remain in her stateroom during the journey, snuck out of her chamber and down the long hall of the lower deck. Silently, on tender bare feet, she passed through the shadows in the bowels of the great ship.

The belly of the beast was dark, save for a glowing crystal sconce every so often, and that merely added to more confusion than aiding in sight. More than once, she stumbled and stubbed her precious toes on the hard wood walls of the ship. Cursing under her breath, she wished that she had been allowed to go with Tulwryn rather than become Cohado's prisoner on his floating craft. However, deep down inside she knew the decision was made in her best interest since Tulwryn would inevitably see battle and battle was exactly what Cohado was trying to avoid.

Sure, thought she, the wizard claimed there were monsters in the skies over the mountains, and these creatures proved to be dangerous over the years, but with his skill and magic, could he naught outwit them? She didn't recall that he traveled with escort when he had rescued them from drifting over the Sea of Fire. Even so, there was no guarantee of the ship's safety; she could be in as much danger onboard the Fidelity as with Tulwryn, and in a fight, she believed her best chances of survival would be in the company of the warrior rather than with an ancient dwarf and a Rhyan priest. So, tossing caution to the wind, she donned a lacy Rhyan sari and headed for the upper deck where she could breathe the warm air and darken her skin in the soothing rays of the sun.

Within moments, Adi found herself on the forward deck near the bow. She had forsaken the clothes of a ruffian that Mimir had given them, for the more lady-like attire of the Rhyans. She found the soft fabric of her sari to be absolutely sinful, and the colorful print, dyed in the most exotic hues of peach and saffron, stunning. Knowing that Dillwyn and the others were working midship, she felt fairly safe from prying eyes, and decided to sun bathe.

The view from the bow of the ship was breathtaking, and the air was warm, fresh, and clean. The sky was the deepest hue of blue that she had ever seen and its serene beauty mesmerized her. Untying her garment, Adi let the sari fall to a puddle about her feet, and she danced naked on the bow of the ship. Her long black hair tumbled down over sun-browned shoulders, and her lithe body swayed to the heartbeat of the craft. She was a tiny thing, with silky brown skin the color of dark mahogany; her shapely feminine form, more girlish and innocent than a woman of thirty, shimmered in the light of the midday sun.

After exhausting herself with the erotic play of a Baezutuian dancing girl, of which she had been bred, Adi spread her sari on the warm deck of the Fidelity and laid down to bask in the sun. Closing her eyes, she drifted off into a lustful slumber and relived the passion filled night that she spent with Tulwryn in Rhyan. The hissing of the ship's engines had bled down to a soft drone, almost hypnotic in rhythm, and in no time, she was fast asleep.

Suddenly, a shadow in the shape of a man appeared and hovered over the naked elegance of the sleeping woman.

"Better not let Cohado see ye in this manner, m'lady," said Dillwyn, in a scruffy voice and trying to restrain a laugh. "Ye just might give him a heart attack, since I am sure his priestly eyes t'would melt in his head after seeing such a beauty in the flesh, for certain, there has been no goddess in all the world that rivals ye."

Adi rose with a start, her heart was bounding in her throat and her tiny brown breasts were rising and falling with the quickening of her breath. Nervously, her fingers fumbled over the cloth to cover herself with the discarded sari.

"Is it proper to sneak up on a lady bathing in the sun," she retorted, rather angrily.

"Is it ladylike to sunbathe on the bow of a ship primed for war," questioned the dwarf, in reply. "What were ye thinking of, m'lady? Did Cohado remind ye to remain below in thy stateroom?"

"Aye, that he did. But I refuse to remain a prisoner onboard this ship."

"Ye are naught a prisoner, lady Adi," said Dillwyn, "but a treasure of precious cargo. Indeed, there would be hell to pay if ye were harmed in any way, ere we reunite with Tulwryn. Methinks he cares for ye quite, and so Cohado and I shall do our best to protect ye. But prancing around in the nude aboard the bow of this ship whilst make our job near impossible. Now get dressed and return below. 'Tis for thy own safety."

The dwarf was about to turn around so Adi could dress without being discomforted by his prying eyes, when all of a sudden there came a crash from beneath the ship. The force of the impact was so traumatic that Dillwyn was knocked off his feet.

"What was that," cried Adi?

"I know naught," replied the dwarf. "Quick, hasten to thy quarters at once. I am off to the bridge!" And he rose in a flash and ran fast for the gangplank that led away to the upper bridge leaving Adi, naked on the bow.

All about her, she heard the cries of men, primed and ready for battle; she stood, fumbled with her sari some more, and then was knocked off her feet by a second impact. Fearing the worse, she dropped the dress, rose, and sprinted for the corridor that led to the lower decks.

Like the wind, Adi ran, her naked form bounding through the lower halls of the ship like a nimble fawn from a pouncing tiger. The ship's warning siren blew its deafening roar and the frightened girl knew that danger was afoot. A third impact and the ship reeled under the blow. Adi lost her footing and was thrown against the hard mahogany wall of the corridor. Dazed and bruised, she lifted herself and continued the long run toward her chamber.

In the confusion that followed, she was unsure of what was happening. Was the ship under attack, or caught in some dread thermal displacement over the mountain range? All about, there were bustling warriors, running from the lower decks and passing her in the halls. Yet, not one of the mystic fighters even turned to take a second glance at the dark beauty that blurred past them, for they were dead to the world and had only one fell purpose, and that was to serve their master, Cohado the Long.

Finally, Adi came to the door of her stateroom. She fumbled with the lock, open the heavy wooden door and entered the chamber, diving across the room and onto the bed. The entire ship was pitching keel to and fro and she knew naught witch way was up. And so, like a scared child not accustomed to wars and battles, she wrapped her lithe body in the soft linen quilt that graced her bed and huddled low in a corner of the room. There, in the shadows of her mind, she closed her eyes hard and prayed her mantra:

"Tulwryn, my Tulwryn," she whispered under her breath, "ye are my life and my hope. Ye rescued me once from death; I pray thee, rescue me now." But Tulwryn heard her naught and her prayer fell on deaf ears; and so she drew her knees up to her chest and buried her face therein.

Battle raged on the upper decks like an enraged sea on angry shores. Dillwyn raced up the stairs that led to the main bridge, but still knew naught the enemy that besieged them. He entered the room, and there stood Cohado, tall and grim with saffron robes flowing in the breeze, his long arms waving violently and chanting in some unknown tongue.

"What gives," cried the dwarf.

Cohado gave the intruder a fell glance and screamed at the top of his lungs.

"A gorkon attacks us; the largest I have ever seen! Now be gone, for my work here is most difficult without ye interfering!"

"Why cannot thee slay this gnarly beast with thine own magic," Dillwyn asked.

"The warriors must kill the beast, for mine purpose is to captain this ship. I am attempting to climb altitude over the beast, yet he is a crafty serpent indeed, and stays under the keel and out of range of our arrows! I cannot fly the craft and battle at the same time. Make haste, and assist the men; ye can do nothing hither!"

Dillwyn turned and ran from the bridge, down the gangplank, and onto the main deck of the Fidelity. His Carthusian battle armor blazed in the light of the sun as he roared commands to the warriors leaning over the gunwales trying to get a clean shot at the creature that was harassing them. More often than not, a hero fell overboard and was lost in the fray.

He knew naught what a gorkon was, save for mere tales told around campfires ages ago; some form of odd dragon he assumed, but more akin to a serpent, without having arms and legs and claws. Stationing himself on a high post, betwixt the fighting men and the bridge, Dillwyn knew that Cohado could see him from his captain's chair, and so he was able to maintain visual communication with the mage as well as with the warriors.

The ship bucked under the mental power of the wizard, and slowly the craft continued to rise into the thin air over the Sulphur Mountains. Time and again, the great beast blasted the Fidelity with its fuming breath, and the dwarf wondered if the ship would fly apart under the fury of the attack. But hold together she did, and the men continued to loose their poison arrows blindly over her sides at the hidden foe beneath.

"Turn port and climb for the heavens," yelled Dillwyn to the wizard, "I have an idea!" Cohado acknowledged the dwarf with a slight hand gesture and continued his chanting. The ship obeyed the wizard and turned into port, into the glare of the sun.

Dillwyn raised a knotted arm and made a sly gesture of his own toward the window of the bridge and the wizard smiled, for he understood the wiley mind of the dwarf. And the Fidelity climbed higher into the heavens.

"Hold tight men and brace yourselves fast, for we are pitching keel to get a good look at the beast once and for all," Dillwyn screamed, over the din of battle.

The archers, two score and six hot for battle, braced themselves, for suddenly the entire ship went inverted. For a moment, all sunlight was blocked out by the hull of the ship and the men had their first look at the creature. Hovering in the shadow of the ship was a fell beast, the likes of which Dillwyn had never laid eyes on before. It was huge, easily twice the length of the Fidelity, and sickly covered with a thick layer of iridescent greenish slime. The thing had enormous wings that kept it aloft, but was without any limbs at all; the face was a grotesque array of whiskers and saber-like fangs.

In the confusion, Dillwyn realized that his plan had worked and that the beast had lost the ship in the glare of the sun. Quick, thought he, time was naught on their side and the archers must act fast, for the men could not hold fast forever nor could Cohado maintain this position for long. Sooner or later, the beast would change directions and sight the ship again, so lethal speed was of the essence.

"Hold tight, men," yelled Dillwyn! "Now! Loose those arrows and be done with it!"

In a blaze of fury, poison arrows were loosed and the gorkon was feathered from head to tail. The beast reeled in pain as Cohado's magically conjured poison surged though its being. Writhing back and forth, the great serpent coiled about itself in disgusting convulsions, and steam poured forth from its great green nostrils as it attempted one last blast at its unseen target.

Realizing that the beast was attempting to spit its deadly flames again, and this time at an unprotected deck, Dillwyn motioned to the bridge in haste. Cohado summoned his strength, and instantly the ship rolled back to upright and continued to climb high into the sky.

There came a roar underneath the craft, and a huge ball of fire was seen coursing through the heavens north of them. Indeed the fell beast did get off one last shot ere it fell from the sky, dead of Cohado's magical poison.

Dillwyn rallied the men and did a head count. There seemed that a few were missing, apparently lost overboard during the maneuver, but most remained at their post and alert.

"Maintain watch, men," cried the dwarf. "There could be more of them beasts! I am going to the bridge."

When Dillwyn entered the bridge, Cohado lay exhausted in his captain's chair. Sweat beaded on his pale brow yet his eyes glowed with firm determination.

"It will take more than a flying lizard to undo Cohado the Long," said he, "yet that one came close."

"Nice work," said Dillwyn, smiling. "Have ye ever tried that move ere now?"

"No, and I wasn't even certain it would work!"

"Why not," asked the dwarf?

"This is a large craft, indeed. It may be the flagship of Rhyan, but it is no dogfighter. She is prone to certain weaknesses due to her size. And as for keeping her afloat, well, I had to magically counter balance the Levititium, for once we went inverted, the anti-gravitational forces emitted from the engines were doing all they could to cast us to the ground! It took all my strength just to keep her above the beast." The dwarf gave a deep belly laugh and patted the wizard on his wet bald head.

"Ye did well, old man. Indeed, ye did well. So what now, are we out of danger or is there more of them beasts around?"

"I have made adjustments to our course, and we sail north by northeast. We are still in danger, but that danger will end soon, for once we are past the Sulphur Mountains the gorkons will attack us no more." He sat up and patted the sweat from his face with the sleeve of his kurta. "Go yonder and send a few men over the gunwales with rappelling gear to check the damage. We can mend the hull once we are in friendlier skies. Please, leave me now, for I must rest."

"Aye," said the dwarf, and he left the bridge to carry out the wizard's commands.

On the main deck of the Fidelity, the warriors were still standing at the ready, faithful to serve to the last man. Dillwyn passed Cohado's orders to the commanders of the crew and disappeared below deck as men laid aside their bows and donned rappelling gear. Overboard they went, brave men dangling like spiders on silken threads, ready to assess the battle damage and make the preparations for the needed repairs.

Once below the main, Dillwyn hastened to Adi's quarters. He had no idea if she had made it safely back to her chamber, and with that daring maneuver of turning the ship completely on end, he wondered how she fared.

Upon entering her chamber, his heart almost came to a complete stop, for one entire wall was gone and he was left standing, looking out of the gaping maw at the world below. Apparently, one of the gorkon's fiery blasts had made a direct hit and ripped a hole in the ship's hull. Terror seized him as he thought the worse, and then he heard Adi's tender voice calling from yonder.

At first, the dwarf thought it to be his mind that was playing him for a fool, and then he remembered the girl's strength. She was stout for such a small creature, and he hoped for the best.

"Adi," he called out. "Where art thou?"

"I am hither, and hanging by a thread. Please help." Her voice was a whimper of despair, yet there was still a bit of hope heard in the tone.

Dillwyn glanced quickly about the room, but it was bare. Everything was gone; the bed, her chests, everything, apparently sucked out of the craft when the wall of her stateroom gave way under the fury of the blast.

Suddenly, Dillwyn spied the woven quilt that she had wrapped herself in when she entered the room ere the main fray began. It had been lodged betwixt a few shattered and charred boards. Quickly, the dwarf snatched up the thick blanket and inched his way to the large gaping hole at the far side of the room. For the first time since entering the room he saw her, still naked and hanging under the hull of the ship, her tiny fingers, lacerated and bleeding, straining to maintain her iron grip.

"Hold tight Adi," he hollered. "Grab the cloth when I drop it down to ye and I shall hoist ye up!"

"I cannot move or I will fall unto mine death"

"Nay," he bellowed back, "say naught such things! Just grab the quilt and I will do the rest!" He tied a stout knot in both ends of the blanket and, grabbing the close knot, dropped the other out the hole and dangled it in front of the frightened girl.

"Grab it now," he screamed! With a shred of hope still left in her, she released her iron grip on the hull of the Fidelity and grabbed at the knotted quilt. For an instant, she felt her stomach lurch as she became weightless in the air under the ship. Adi realized that she was falling and clenched tight to the blanket. With a jerk, the quilt stretched to its breaking point, yet held fast; a second later she was back on the floor of the stateroom with the shadow of the burly dwarf looming over her.

"Methinks that ye are more trouble than thou art worth," he said gruffly.

Lying in a heap at his feet, Adi buried her face in her dark hands and began to whimper like a frightened doe. Dillwyn tossed the quilt over the girl and walked across the room.

"Get dressed," he said, "then have Cohado mend them hands. I will arrange for ye to be assigned another room."

She lay crying as he left the chamber, her pride more injured than her body. Adivarapupeta was a resilient woman, small yet strong, but for an instant, she felt weak and helpless and that frustrated her. And so, for a time she lay naked, save for a bloody quilt draped over her by an old dwarf, and wept.

Thus ends Chapter Ten of Book Two

ELEVEN

Eastward though Golrin

A fortnight had passed since the attack of the gorkon; the crew had all but repaired the battle damage and Cohado had long past regained his strength. Clear skies were seen on the eastern horizon as the mighty ship sailed north by northeast, and out over the Western North Sea. The warriors still maintained their posts but the atmosphere aboard the craft was relaxed. Dillwyn stood near the port gunwale gazing over the rail and down at the world far below, as an evening sun crept nigh across the firmament readying the world for night.

"What thinks ye," came a tiny voice from behind. Dillwyn turned with a start, and spied Adi, in woolen breeches and tunic, standing behind him. She handed him a heavy bearskin. "Cohado thought ye might need this."

"Thank ye," he answered, as he took the garment. For a moment, he held the skin and, running his thick hands through the glossy fur, his mind traveled to Heidmar and back in a blink of an eye.

"Come hither," said he. "Ye see that smidgen of land over yonder? That is the Northern Territories." She strained to see; yet far off in the distance, many leagues below and through the broken clouds, she faintly saw the contour of a possible shoreline.

For many days, the daytime temperature had been steadily dropping and so, she assumed that their course was due north, but it was not until Dillwyn's revelation, that her assumptions had been proven. Adi looked over the rail at the frozen sea below and then again at the coastline far off in the distance. A feeling of despair washed over her and she huddled close to the dwarf for added warmth.

"That land looks bleak," she said.

"Aye, bleak it is," answered the dwarf. "Ye see that far ridge off in the distance?" She nodded. "Those are actually tall mountains; it all looks mighty different from up here. Anyhow, north of them mountains is the territory of Heidmar. Tulwryn and I camped for three winters with that clan and enjoyed many a bloody battle . . . good times and warm friends indeed. Many are still down there, I suppose."

"It sounds as if ye miss them."

"Perhaps," he said, with a wily grin, "I wonder what they would think of ol'e Dillwyn now, if they could see me riding on a dragonship and cruising over their huts." The two laughed a bit, enjoying each other's company and the relaxing atmosphere.

"Have ye spoken to Cohado," she asked. "He seems to have become quite reclusive in the days since the attack. What thinks ye of his somber mood?"

"Aye, methinks wizards and priests are a strange lot indeed," Dillwyn said. "Perhaps the journey taxes his strength, for not only does he fly this ship, but his magic also sustains the crew. His job is a most difficult one, indeed."

"And he sleeps naught."

"That is true. I entered his stateroom once, a few nights back, and found him seated on that platform of his, eyes closed but more alert than any man I have ever seen. He is a strange one, that is certain."

* * *

The horse rose with a start, ripping the reins from Tulwryn's hands, and galloped off into the distance never to be seen from again.

Such was life and death on the Golrin Prairie. For even after death, nothing is left to rot under the Golrin sun; vultures first pick the bones of the dead clean and then hyenas scavenge the bones themselves, leaving naught a scrap for even ants or worms. In a matter of hours, after a creature has fallen to its doom, there is never even a trace that it had ever lived at all.

The storm raged on for some hours, but in time, the fury of the gods ceased and the clouds parted. The dry grasslands of the prairie drank up the waters of the storm and the warm sun dried what little dampness remained. The air was humid for a time and many buzzing insects sprang from nowhere to feast on the many puddles of water that had formed after the rain. Yet, these puddles disappeared as quickly as they were formed, for the high prairie was dry and thirsty.

Tulwryn, now without a steed, walked with his fighters yet talked naught for they were a grim lot and conversed little. Since the waters of the River Adronn were not fit to drink, Tulwryn had not been able to refill his waterskins whilst in the forest. He remembered Dillwyn mentioning a lake on the prairie, north of Carthus, whilst floating aloft over the Sea of Fire and so decided to make for it. Mustering his fighters, and commanding them to keep a keen eye out for bandits and Golrin armed forces, he attempted to head northeast and cut straight across the prairie in hopes that he would find the lake ere his water supply completely run dry.

The sun rose and dropped many times as the fighters trekked across the grasslands of Golrin. Buzzards circled the group, yet Tulwryn's resilient men trudged on heeding naught the scavengers; dead men may feed vultures, but those undead, animated by sorcery and not by spirit, feed neither the bellies of beasts nor empty graves.

Four days past the storm, Tulwryn noticed smoke on the horizon north of their location, and realized that a small group of men lay betwixt them and their water hole. Perhaps they were a regiment of Kemetian mercenaries he thought, for 'twas no secret that a maze of underground mines and vaults criss-crossed the prairie of Golrin, and these great storehouses, where the Magistrate of Golrin hoarded his precious black diamonds, red gold, and liquid steel, were jealously guarded. Anyone found wandering the prairie and not confined to the main trade route was seen as a threat to the wealth of Golrin and normally apprehended. Of course, a force as large as Tulwryn's company was in no danger of being bested, but was sure to instill suspicion all the same. He realized that if he and his fighters were spotted word might be sent to Golrin for military reinforcements. The possibility of drawing Phaedron into the skirmish was great indeed, since a regiment of Phaedronian legionnaires patrolled the main trade route east of Golrin itself. Being assaulted by a larger Phaedronian force did not settle well with Tulwryn, nor did fighting a needless battle with Golrin, since he had no affair with them. His sole purpose was to recover the Bloodsword and rendezvous with the others under Malador, yet he needed a fresh supply of water ere he continue on his quest, and that water lay on the far side of the encamped men.

At once, he commanded his men to halt and circle up. Kneeling in the center of a great circle of warriors, Tulwryn used his dagger to draw battle lines on the dried ground. First, he would send out three scouts with orders to spy out those encamped in the distance, make positive identification of their numbers, armor, and weapons, and learn, if possible, their intentions. This would be done under the cover of darkness, and there was to be no killing unless in the utmost need.

The remainder of the troops would be split into thirds, one group traveling with Tulwryn, whilst the other two flanking his, both east and west. The plan was simple: All four groups would silently descend on the unsuspecting men. If the scouts returned with news of the slightest hostility, Tulwryn's fighters would attack center whilst the flanking two groups would swarm in on both sides cleaving a large wound in the opposing force. The slaying would be quick and violent and no survivors would be left to warn Golrin, Phaedron, or anyone else of Tulwryn's presence on the prairie. If, by chance, the group of men posed no threat, then the four groups would simply circumnavigate the encampment, and reunite on the far side and continue on to the lake.

An hour after sunset the scouts vanished into the darkness of the night. There was no moon this eve, yet Cohado's undead warriors were hindered little, for whether in the bright of day or the black of night, their senses were as alert as the most fearsome of predators. Tulwryn and the others sat quiet, and without a fire, waiting patiently for the three to return.

Time drifted, and Tulwryn's mind with it; he remembered more peaceful days, long ago, and wondered how he came to be that which he had become. So many years, thought he, had separated who he used to be from who he presently was. Where the Tulwryn of old was, he knew naught. Perhaps dead, he thought, for the past swallows up everything. But where was he going, and what did the gods have in store for him? These were questions with no answers. He remembered the words of Mimir, and Cohado, and even the prophetic ramblings of the Volva, long dead. He grew weary of magic and sorcery, and prophecies. Why was he not allowed to forget his past and shake off the doom that had overshadowed his life? Only time would tell, he assumed. And with that, he drifted off into a slight slumber.

He had barely closed his eyes when the scouts returned. Luckily, they had not been spotted, and even more interesting was the fact that the encamped group was not Kemetian mercenaries at all, but a small group of L'hoehnians; stragglers apparently cut off from the rest of their group after Maztaque's fateful episode with the Bloodsword.

Knowing the nature of fighting men, and the fact that his group had been on the trail for more than a month without wetting their swords, he realized the importance of this opportunity. For certain, he thought, the gods have given me this fodder whereas to feed my men's fighting spirits ere the great battle with Malador begins.

Kneeling once again in the midst of his troops, he whispered his plans under a moonless sky. There was fire in the eyes of his fighters that night and for a moment compassion welled up within him, for he knew there was no hope for those who camped yonder. One scout informed him that the men camped on the shores of a large lake, possibly the one they sought. Smiling, Tulwryn spoke thus:

"Tonight we rest, for tomorrow we will wet our blades and feed the vultures of Golrin." There was no hearty cheer that eve, nor were there any anxious comments of victory or boasts of heroic battles. All Tulwryn saw were one hundred pairs of eyes blazing red for the lust of the kill.

Thus ends Chapter Eleven of Book Two

TWELVE

Massacre on the Prairie

When morning came to the prairie of Golrin, the L'hoehnians found that their numbers had swelled to a man, for standing amidst their bedrolls and pallets was none other than Tulwryn the warrior. The sun cast an eerie glow over the land and death was in the air. The barbarian, brandishing neither sword nor shield, stood amongst the bandits with teeth clenched and eyes ablaze.

"Look men, 'tis that damnable barbarian that cursed us with his sword," yelled one man, as he rose from his blankets. The others were roused from their slumber and a raven wheeled across the morning sky, cawing as if death itself was on its tail.

"'Twas naught I that forced thy master to steal mine weapon, dog," roared Tulwryn in reply. "I have no grievance with ye, but I do seek your lord. Where is that bastard Maztaque?" Tulwryn, already knowing that Maztaque was dead, was merely feigning ignorance with the hopes of stirring the small band to fight as well as enraging his own men, who watched from only a few fathoms thither.

"Let us hamstring him and leave him for the vultures," screamed another.

"Step forward, he who seeks death first! Tulwryn Bloodsword is no easy prey for curs and swine with no stomach for bloodletting." The barbarian of Heidmar laughed a haughty laugh. He remembered the berserker battle rage of the north but never witnessed it from southern warriors, let alone common thieves and bandits. He knew that standing alone in their midst and posing no threat would excite them to murder, and he was rather enjoying himself, for he, like his men, was hungry for blood.

"Come brothers," said one gold toothed man, wearing a soiled turban and white desert robe, "let's skin this dog and sell his bones to Phaedron. Perhaps we can get more gold from his bones than Rog can get from that accursed sword! Look, the fool comes into our camp carrying naught a blade." The man drew steel and approached Tulwryn, but the warrior of Heidmar held fast and made no attempt to protect himself.

"Rog, says ye," Tulwryn asked. "A man named Rog has mine blade?"

"Aye," said another, circling the stranger, and eyeing the gold toothed man, sword in hand. "Rog took that blade after the gods struck down Maztaque for wielding it! Damn ye, cursed us with that blade . . . and curse Rog as well; he is a thief among thieves! How dare him to steal the blade for himself. I pray that the gods strike him down as well."

"And what of Rog? Where has he gone with mine sword?"

"To Phaedron methinks; to sell the grim weapon to some evil sorcerer I would assume, for no mere mortal would carry such a blade. Who are you, the bastard son of the devil himself?"

"Tell him naught of our matters," hollered a fat man from behind the others, "he needs naught know our business." The man wallowed out from behind the others brandishing a large Kemetian war axe and wearing nothing save a blue loincloth. He was huge and browned from the sun, but spoke in a strange tongue that Tulwryn had never heard.

Another man, rail skinny and naked to the waist, answered the fat man.

"What dose it matter if we tell him," he said. "He will be dead in a minute anyway." The group slowly surrounded Tulwryn and pressed in close for the kill.

"Enough talk of murder," roared Tulwryn. "I have learned what I came to learn, now I will litter the prairie with thy filthy hides!"

That morning on the Golrin Prairie, fourteen men circled

one man, yet that one man was a man among men. Tulwryn Bloodsword stood tall and gave his war cry, a shout that would become legendary even ere his passing into legend. In the seconds that followed, not even the bandits understood what happened, for suddenly they themselves were surrounded by a hundred grim warriors in battle armor and bare steel. Heads were cleaved to the chin, and bodies hewn in twain at the waist. Tulwryn himself slew the fat man, opening his great belly with a dagger he had concealed in his sash and spilling his steaming innards on the dew-covered ground. The fight ended as fast as it had begun, and all that was left was an echo of pain that rolled across the flat of the land as the last L'hoehnian died under Rhyanian steel.

"Search their gear," ordered Tulwryn. "If the Bloodsword is hither, bring it to me. I care naught for gold coin, but if there be water or meat, bring me that as well. Let us camp hither this day; we can resume our travels on the morrow."

Tulwryn's warriors searched the tents of the marauders but found nigh, only a half filled wineskin and an old joint that seemed to be mutton was brought before the barbarian from Heidmar. The wine was sour and the meat rancid, then Tulwryn remembered the wizard's tale of the swine people, and his stomach lurched for even he was nigh to feast on human flesh.

The day was long, but night soon came, and with it came thoughts of war and bloodshed. Tulwryn realized that his memories of Nuvia were slowly fading, drifting off to some ethereal realm and being replaced by thoughts of murder. This, in itself, was no worry of his; he was glad to be rid of the dreams. The guilt of the kinslaying weighed heavy on his soul, even though Durayn so deserved her end for killing his four sons. But the murder of one's wife, no matter how deserving she may be, was a burden hard to carry. Perhaps, thought he, the gods were lifting his doom. He chuckled under his breath. The gods were never so kind, for if they removed one curse they usually imposed another. And so, Tulwryn banished the thoughts of Nuvia but embraced the ponderings of the Bloodsword.

Where the blade was, he knew naught. All he knew was that Maztaque was dead and the sword taken by another. This angered him to no end, for Maztaque's face was burned into his brain, for he was the leader of the bandits and the one who stole the Bloodsword. With Maztaque dead, Tulwryn's wrath would now fall on another. What am I to do, he thought to himself; chase this accursed blade to the ends of the world? Where shall this trail of vengeance lead me, but to the very gates of hell!

And indeed, the trail he was on was a trail of vengeance, and his anger boiled in his veins.

"If Maztaque were naught alive to suffer mine vengeance for the theft of the blade," he vowed silently to himself, "then he who carries the sword will suffer my wrath in his stead, whomever that man shall be!"

Tulwryn slept naught that night but gazed into the blackness of his own soul and his mind wandered over the land like a wraith seeking death. His men, likewise, did not sleep, nor did they eat, nor did they breathe. Cohado's mystic warriors kept silent vigil with the grim barbarian of the north and naught a sound came from that camp, save but the rasping of whetstones on steel. A few hungry eyes burned in the darkness and more than once the short chuckle of a hyena was heard off in the far distance.

Morning came sooner than expected, and Tulwryn's men had already filled many waterskins at the lake and were breaking camp when the Woodling arrived. He was a slight creature, wearing course tree bark armor and carrying a flint knife and bronze short sword. By the looks of him, he had seen battle, for his armor was chipped and worn, and there were sword cuts on his shoulders, but other than this, he seemed to be in good health. The little fellow stood only waist high next to Tulwryn, but the fire in his eyes told the barbarian he was much older than himself.

Two large fighters brought the Woodling before Tulwryn. He dismissed the guards, as the creature seemed to pose no threat, although the words of an old man in the Crimson Forest rang through his mind:

"Things are naught what they seem in Phantasodyssea; be on your guard." And so, he loosed his sword and settled back to parley.

"My name is Beck," said the Woodling. "I am a forest runner of the Woodlings of Bain. My village was ransacked a few nights ere last by bandits and my people scattered to the wind."

"What is that to me," asked Tulwryn.

"I am told that ye are the Bloodsword."

Tulwryn sat up, his brow furrowed and his eyes glared. "What says ye that name," he asked, his large hand caressing the hilt of his sword.

"Relax, sire," said Beck. "I come in peace. Whilst the bandits slew my people, I overheard one man speak to another. They spoke of a grim weapon, a sword made by the gods—or of evil sorcery. They knew naught which. That was a day before those very gods smote the one man, and then the blade was carried off north by the other."

"And so ye saw this man?"

"Aye, with mine own eyes, sire!"

"Whither did this thief go," asked Tulwryn, leaning back and reaching for the wineskin.

"Methinks the man will go to Phaedron. Why, I know naught. Perhaps he beckons to either sell the blade or attack the city himself; for he seemed quite mad."

"Say ye that he travels alone?"

"Aye, alone, save only the blade," answered Beck. "Could he attack the city, sire, or is he truly mad?"

"Mad he may be, indeed," answered Tulwryn, "and attack the city he could, had he possessed the knowledge of the sword, for that blade *is* strength and none that stands against it will live to see another sunrise. But methinks he will attempt to sell it to the High Elder, for that evil king is in league with sorcerers and they would pay handsome for such a grim weapon." Tulwryn handed the Woodling the wineskin with a smile. "Take this, mine little friend. Ye have earned it, and I give it to thee in friendship."

Beck's eyes grew large and a bright smile ran from ear to ear.

"Well, damn mine black soul," he said. "Those sand pirates steal not only good steel but good drink as well! This is Woodling ale, distilled in Bain from the P'tu mushroom. Best drink in all the world, if ye ask me!" Tulwryn's eye popped wide as he watched the creature drink the skin dry.

"So ye are the Bloodsword," he asked again. Tulwryn simply nodded without a word. "Well then, sire, may I quest with ye? I am a good scout and might serve you well. Anyhow, all mine kin is slain and I am anxious for an adventure."

"How old are ye, Beck?"

The Woodling smiled. "At the end of this season these eyes will have seen three hundred and twenty-four summers."

"Well I suppose anyone with that much experience is bound to be helpful."

Thus ends Chapter Twelve of Book Two

THIRTEEN

A Wizard's Map

Thus far, the journey had been uneventful after the gorkon's attack. The skies over the Western North Sea were clear and the sailing was pleasant. Cohado seemed to be in better spirits and most of the ships damage had been repaired by experienced hands.

Once over the Northern Territories, temperatures dropped drastically. The air was cold and bitter, the nights almost unbearable. The wizard informed the crew that conditions would get worse until passing over the continent, whereas they would then set down in the waters of the North Sea itself and sail for a safe haven in a secluded cove that he had discovered in his youth, long ago. Most of the crew passed their days and nights working in the lower decks or resting in their quarters when not on guard duty. And even though Cohado promised no more aerial attacks from unsuspected creatures, he still maintained a score of archers on the main at all times.

Late one evening, Dillwyn retired to his quarters to relax with his pipe. The day had been frightfully hard since he was required to maintain command of the ship whilst Cohado rested. He was a warrior, and not one to lead men, this he knew. The responsibilities of command he favored naught. Where one man wished for power and subjects, Dillwyn merely dreamed of battles. He had no visions of grandeur, no quest for a golden throne. Let other men be bothered by such nonsense, he always said, for me, all I care is to slay my enemies and the enemies of my friends. And at the end of a long and hard day, he would enjoy the camaraderie of good friends, strong wine, and loose women. But aboard the Fidelity, he had nothing but his pipe, and that would have to do.

After retiring to his cabin, he removed his maile and armor and slipped into a warm woolen nightshirt and breeches. He then wrapped himself in his bearskin and grabbed his pipe and tobacco pouch from the top of his chest of drawers and settled down into a large, high backed rocking chair. For a few moments, he just sat at gazed at the pipe. It was old and gnarled, but maintained its dignity and class. Anyone else would have discarded the thing eons ago as rubbish, or traded it in for another, newer pipe. But Dillwyn knew the advantage of an old, well broken-in piece. The bowl was properly caked, and the briar was thoroughly dry from many years of use. But there was something more, something fascinating. His old pipe was not only a gift from a friend, but a tool of magic as well. Just the thought of magic made his skin prickle up and his nape go to bristle. He was a warrior, thought he, and should not be trafficking in the likes of sorcery. But things change. Tulwryn's life had changed, and so it looked, his life too, would change.

"Perhaps 'tis for the best," the old dwarf said to himself, looking at his aged arms and hands. They were still corded with iron muscle, but they were also criss-crossed with scars and battle wounds; his fingers, broken countless times, were knotted and bent. He sighed.

"Aye, maybe I should just settle down in some hut and become a mystic. I probably wouldn't be the first dwarf to do such a thing. The glory of battle is for the younger people; us old timers need to learn to let youth go. Ah, nothing lasts forever."

Leaning back in his chair, he lit the old pipe, took a long draw and relaxed. His mind drifted along with the ship, rocking and swaying high in the sky over the mountains of the north. He thought about the people many leagues beneath him, toiling on the frozen wastes of that forbearing land. Did they know he was even up here, coasting through the heavens on some magical ship? How many times, he wondered, had Cohado soared the skies over Heidmar when he and Tulwryn were slaying their enemies on the frozen tundra below?

Soft amber light filtered into the chamber from the sconce held crystal that was mounted on the far wall and cast the entire room in an eldritch haze.

"Thoughts," said he, quietly to himself. "Too many unnecessary thoughts." And he closed his eyes to rest.

Taking another draw, he relaxed and blew a great smoke ring. The ring fluttered a bit then disappeared as normal smoke usually does. A few moments later, not thinking about anything in particular, Dillwyn blew another ring of smoke and this one likewise vanished. Yet, the third smoke ring that exited his ancient lips hung thickly in the air, and within that ring, the old dwarf spied a face, ancient beyond the span of time.

"Well met, old friend," said the face in the ring. The old dwarf smiled.

"Well met, Mimir," he answered.

"I see that ye have taking a liking to fine leaf."

"Aye, indeed," Dillwyn replied. "This tobacco is fine weed indeed; relaxing and pleasurable. Of course, t'would be nice to share a bowl with ye around a warm fire, rather than cruise through the heavens in this freezing crate. Anyhow, what brings ye hither, old friend?"

"News of Tulwryn."

"Tulwryn, says ye," the dwarf said with a start, and quickly sat up. "What news?"

"As often happens in life, things are subject to change," answered the wizard. "I have come to tell ye of Tulwryn's predicament. He does not have the Bloodsword yet, and it seems that he will not make the rendezvous with ye under Malador."

"But what . . . why?"

"His company came upon a group of L'hoehnians in the Golrin Prairie. They were the same ones that stole the blade and betrayed ye to the Phaedrons, but the leader had been slain and the sword taken by his second in command ere Tulwryn caught up with the bunch. Tulwryn and his men slew the lot of them, but naught ere he discovered the renegade's plan to sell the blade in Phaedron. This was confirmed by a Woodling who survived the L'hoehnian assault on Bain."

"What says ye? Tulwryn is going to Phaedron to recover the sword."

"Aye," answered Mimir. "He plans to ambush the rogue and recover the Bloodsword ere he enters the city. Inform Cohado of this turn of events and waste no time in Malador. Perhaps thy troops can rendezvous with Tulwryn's men near Phaedron and from there thwart Kimark Khan's plan."

"It shall be done!"

Mimir's face faded away and the smoke ring with it. The old dwarf sat for a time contemplating the conversation, and then tamped out the ash in the bowl. Rising from his chair, he donned his boots, wrapped the bearskin around him tightly and left the room, heading for Cohado's quarters. All that was left in the dwarf's quarters was a creaking rocking chair, a gnarled old pipe, and the scent of cherry almond lingering in the air.

* * *

The night was black as coal when Dillwyn left his quarters. He walked the long, dimly lit corridor to Cohado's cabin contemplating the tale he was to share with the wizard. Cohado knew Dillwyn to be a friend of Mimir, but he knew naught of the magical pipe that the he-witch from Covensted gifted him. For a bit, he was worried that Cohado might try to steal the piece by way of magic. But then he dismissed the notion, since a wizard of his ability needed no such trifle to summon entities from beyond the world to do his bidding.

He arrived at Cohado's door, knocked thrice and waited. The old wizard yelled and the dwarf entered unassisted since the door was unlocked. The entire room was scented with sandalwood and lavender, and there was a hint of lilac in the air as well. Thick rugs adorned the maple floor and rich tapestries hung from the oaken walls. Dillwyn paused and noticed the changes in the room since he and Adi had been there the first time. Truly, thought he, this Cohado was an eccentric fellow for he would stop at nothing to surround himself with extravagances, whether real or illusion.

The wizard was standing over a large oaken table in the far corner of the room and mulling over some parchment scrolls. A small candle lantern was casting dim light over the dark corner of the cabin and Dillwyn approached cautiously. While he wasn't put off by men of steel, wizards on the other hand, kept him on guard. He had heard tales of common folk being turned to stone for gazing haphazardly on the dreadful scrolls of wizard's incantations and so shielded his eyes carefully.

"What brings ye hither," asked the wizard, not taking his eyes off the parchment that lay before him.

"I have news of Tulwryn," said the dwarf. "He will not make the rendezvous in Malador."

Lifting his ashen face from his work, Cohado's dark eyes rested on Dillwyn's aged face, and a feeling of uneasiness washed over the dwarf.

"And why is this," asked Cohado?

"He is still questing for his blade."

"So, the outlaws have eluded him?"

"Aye," answered Dillwyn. "He and his men slue many of the bandits, but still he possesses naught the sword. Word has it that the blade is bound for Phaedron, and so Tulwryn pursues thither."

"This plot thickens," yelled the wizard, and he slammed his lean fist into the oak of the table. "I am too old for this. Damn that Mimir, I told him that he should ride out this quest, naught I." Cohado stood, sighed, grabbed the scrolls from the table then walked to his platform and took a seat.

"Come Dillwyn; talk with me."

The dwarf walked across the room and seated himself on the large brocade couch in front of the wizard. Cohado, seated on his platform, folded his legs effortlessly into a tight knot and then handed the parchment scrolls to the dwarf. Dillwyn hesitantly took them.

"Go on, they are safe. Merely maps, 'tis all," spoke the wizard.

Looking at the ancient maps, stiff and yellowed with age, Dillwyn studied them for some time ere he spoke.

"What be these strange lands," he asked.

"What ye have in your hands is the map of the world," answered Cohado. "'Tis older than every living being in Phantasodyssea, and most of the kingdoms as well."

"And how did ye come about such a treasure," queried the dwarf, still groping over the old scroll.

"I drew the map myself," said Cohado. "Well, Mimir and I, that is. For eons passed, we two wizards have criss-crossed the world countless times, and each time, we recorded our travels and the routes we have taken. The world changes little over the years. For many centuries, we traveled together, as Tulwryn and ye do presently."

"Presently, Tulwryn and I have gone separate," snapped Dillwyn, correcting the wizard and reminding him of their present situation.

"Aye," answered Cohado, as if almost drifting off into a trance, "ye two are separated, indeed. In time, Mimir and myself also went our separate ways, but for the sake of the world, we kept in touch. He settled in the east, in Covensted, and I settled in Rhyan, watching the west of the world. With eye pitched keenly on the horizon, we sat and waited for the doom we knew would come. Our agreement was simple: I protect the western reaches and Mimir, the eastern. 'Twas he that drew out the part of the map that we must needs use now. I seek a safe haven in a secret cove due north of the Fords of Doom." He paused for a moment, deeply inhaling the fumes of the incense. Dillwyn felt a pang of nausea hit the pit of his stomach at the words of the wizard. Fords of Doom, thought he, sounded not like a place that he wanted to visit.

"But if Tulwryn is naught for the Malador rendezvous, then why are we to set down east of the mountains," he asked, fidgeting a little in his seat as a nervous child. Dillwyn might have been well into his nineties, but next to Cohado, he was still a mere youth and he knew it.

"There is no place else to set down this craft but the sea. There are no skywharfs in all of the world but the one we left in Rhyan, and to attempt to tether this craft to a mountain peak would be suicide. Either the elements would destroy the ship, or the dark Khan would, for to sail any closer to his domain that is necessary is to invite his curiosity."

"So, he knows naught of thy windship?"

"Nay, only the people of Rhyan know of this technology. No one in Phantasodyssea, save Mimir, ye, and your friends, know of the fleet of Rhyan. 'Tis why we cloak the ships in the likeness of dragons, for none would care to venture too close to such beasts. Our secret is secure indeed, but Kimark Khan is not so squeamish. He knows that dragons soar the western skies but none have ever been seen this far east. If he spied our ship, it would certainly stir his curiosity, and that would fail us, and our mission. To conquer the Khan we need ultimate surprise."

"And so, ye are telling me that we shall remain on course, even though Tulwryn will not make the rendezvous," Dillwyn asked.

"Aye, 'tis what I say. We shall proceed as originally planned."

"I am not liking the sound of this," Dillwyn protested. He glanced at the map and with a gnarled and bent forefinger, he measured the distance from the Fords of Doom on the eastern coast, over the Enchanted Forest, through the Zinjan Ice Fields, and finally around the base of Malador, deep in the Enchanted Mountains. The journey was long and it twisted and turned, treacherously snaking its way over many leagues through enemy lands. Even with a crack unit of mountain dwarves, the going would be rough, but with sky buccaneers, an ancient wizard, and a girl, Dillwyn thought the task all but impossible. "If we fail . . ."

Cohado lifted an ashen hand and silenced him ere he finished his thought.

"We must not fail," said the old wizard, "for to fail, then all is lost. At least for me that is not an option."

The old dwarf nodded.

"By the way, Dillwyn," spoke Cohado, "may I ask how ye came about this news of Tulwryn?"

Sweat beaded on the dwarf's brow. He looked deep into the wizard's eternal eyes, was about to speak and then hesitated.

"Oh, the pipe," Cohado said with a smile. "I always wondered who would inherit that old pipe. Seems Mimir has chosen an heir after all. Well, I must admit, he could have done much worse."

Dillwyn sat speechless for a time, then Cohado dismissed him, and he left the room. Walking back to his quarters, Dillwyn detoured and decided to have a walk on the main, his mind swimming with awe and confusion. The crisp air would do him good and would clear his head as well since the fumes in the wizard's chambers had all but clogged his senses. The wizard was keeping something back, thought Dillwyn. He felt it in his old dwarven bones. Cohado wanted to confide in me, he thought to himself, but for some reason, at the moment of the telling, he decided against it and stilled his lips. He shook his head and tallied naught below deck.

Once on the main, he traversed the stern decks, and then went forward to the bow. All the archers were still at their posts, neither sleeping nor talking amongst themselves. Even after all these days with this crew, Dillwyn was not used to such silence. Yes, fighting men were always serious when on duty, but the grim fire in the eyes of Cohado's mystic buccaneers was stifling even to Dillwyn. Even fighting men should have some leisure time to make merry, thought he. But these were not ordinary fighting men, they were not even men at all, but mystical creatures conjured in the likeness of men from the nether reaches of time and space and employed for one fell purpose: to destroy Kimark Khan.

"So I am to be a wizard's heir," Dillwyn said, whispering the words quietly to himself. He would have never believed it, not in a million years, yet in his heart he knew Cohado spoke the truth.

Dillwyn leaned on the railing of the main and glanced off into the distance, first to the east and then to the west. The ship was floating high in the heavens over the eastern shores of Phantasodyssea. Soon she would break land over the North Sea and there the wizard would set her down in the ocean's icy waters to make for Cohado's secret cove. The dwarf breathed deeply the cool air. The black of the night sky was thinning and the blue haze of the morning grew at the promise of a new day. Dillwyn gazed into south, toward Malador, and off in the distance he noticed clouds on the horizon. He foresaw the coming of a storm, a storm that would paint the whole of the land a ruddy scarlet of suffering.

Thus ends Chapter Thirteen of Book Two

FOURTEEN

The Crystal Sphere

The sun rose high in the heavens over the Golrin Prairie, yet the air was sweet and the grassland pleasant. As far as the eye could see, there wasn't a cloud in the sky and the promise of an easy day was on them. Tulwryn knew now why Dillwyn craved this part of the world so much. The thought took him to Dillwyn and Adi, and he wondered how his friends were faring aboard the Rhyan wizard's floating ship.

Earlier that day, just before braking camp, Tulwryn separated the men into groups for the march to Phaedron. The bandits' belongings were searched the night before, as were their tents, and it was found that fourteen Azazel camels had been tethered to stakes hammered in the ground behind one of the larger tents. Tulwryn rode astride one of the beasts and designated thirteen of his commanders to ride the others. One camel he offered to Beck, but the Woodling refused the ride explaining his people were used to running and therefore riding atop a strange beast would simply not do. Tulwryn wondered about this strange custom but nonetheless shrugged his shoulders and resumed to delegating his authority to the troops.

He knew the trek to Phaedron would pose few problems since his men needed neither food, water, nor sleep, nor did he feel vulnerable to Phaedronian legionnaires, for he traveled with a great host. Even so, he knew naught how many days ahead of his band Rog and the Bloodsword was, and he wondered the best plan of action to intercept the rogue ere he enter the city.

Time and again, Tulwryn turned the scenario over and over in his mind. How could he have lost the blade in the first place? How was it that this lowly bandit came to possess his grim weapon? How was it that he was chosen to carry the Bloodsword only to lose it? Will he even be able to regain it, and if so, will he be able to use it to thwart the dark Khan's plan? Too many questions, not enough answers; it didn't matter anyway, he thought to himself. For some strange reason, the gods picked him, yet he was only a mere pawn and nothing more. Sure, there were prophecies and wizards, battles betwixt good and evil, wealthy kings and poor peasants, yet what did all that have to do with him. Ever since the doom came and shadowed his life, it had seemed that the entire world had been turned on its ear. Nothing made sense anymore.

And gazing at the rising sun, Tulwryn spurred his camel and rode in the forward ranks of his great war host leading his men eastward, to Phaedron. Unbeknownst to him, atop the mountain of Malador, a great Crystal Sphere pulsated with unrelenting power and Kimark Khan grew stronger by the second.

* * *

There were whispers circulating through the great many halls of the royal palace of Phaedron that the king was mad. These rumors filtered their way from salon to salon and even unto the very streets of that great city-state. Noble and peasant alike worried as the fate of their lives hung in the balance, teetering on the very sanity of their ruler, apparently shaken by some strange incident at the royal court.

In the weeks since Kimark Khan's relentless ethereal attack, Zulanmalh had grown careless and desperate. He began by rearranging his royal schedule every other day, changing his itinerary so as no one, other than his closest advisors, would have access to whereabouts.

Zulanmalh, taking precautions to protect his many wives and sons, his kingdom, and his throne from the evil wizard of

Malador, increased the numbers of royal guards patrolling the palace grounds, as well as doubled the strength of his entire ground forces inside the city's great wall. There was also talk around the city that the High Elder had been secretly employing vast armies of newly hired wizards and spending his nights in audience with evil priests caught up in dark rites to appease his many grim gods. The daughters of Phaedron were not safe and more than once, late in the eve, did a scream shatter the night as another virgin was slaughtered atop the king's black alter.

The king, after a particularly stressful evening in audience with his priests and gods, sat on the Ivory Throne in his audience chamber with heavy lidded eyes, half asleep. The large doors slowly creaked open and a small man in purple brocade robes entered and approached the throne. Dropping to one knee with head bowed and eyes lowered to the floor, the man spoke: "Sire, 'tis I, Bolo Chun, your majesty's advisor and servant, come with a message of high importance."

"Rise and speak," said the king, with a voice more closely related to a death rattle of some dying invalid than a noble sovereign lord.

The advisor stood, still not looking the High Elder in the eye, and fidgeted nervously for a second ere he spoke. The tension in the court was pulled as tight as a Knobite bowstring as the king anticipated the heavy news that Bolo Chun was about to reveal.

"Sire," said the advisor, "there is a man at the city gates that wishes an audience with ye."

Suddenly, Zulanmalh's face paled in the light of the royal court, his bloodshot eyes, stricken with terror.

"Who is this stranger," asked the king in a shaky voice.

"I know naught, my liege, yet he claims he is a friend of Phaedron and has news of vital importance. Shall I admit him, sire?"

For a moment, the king was lost in thought, wondering if this could be another of Kimark Khan's traps. Nay, thought he, the Khan is too bold for such tactics. He would rather storm the city and take the throne by force. This visitor must be who he says he is, perhaps even a gift from the gods come to protect me and mine from the dark Khan's evil threats. Still, caution must be exercised.

"Aye, Bolo, admit this man but double his escort. I want him surrounded by ten of our strongest warriors just in case this is some ruse. Dismissed."

The king sunk back down into the thick cushions of the Ivory Throne as Bolo Chun exited the hall. Long minutes passed ere the king's advisor returned, but when he did, he was accompanied by ten Phaedron legionnaires and one swarthy looking rogue.

Zulanmalh straightened his back and took deep breath trying to make himself look more majestic, after all, the role of the king was merely play-acting and his family had done the job well for over two hundred years. With his eyes beaming on the man, the king tried to measure him up, but this proved not an easy task, for the rogue was a rough looking sort and quite elusive to say the least.

Wearing his soiled L'hoehnian silks over rusted maile, Rog approached the throne and knelt before the High Elder of Phaedron with head bowed. The king glanced at the man kneeling before him, then to his advisor.

"Here is the man that requested audience with ye, sire," said Bolo Chun. "He came only with this. He claims that it is a gift for thee, your majesty." Bolo approached the throne and presented the king with a long roll of elegantly crafted purple silk brocade.

Taking the gift, the king said: "This is mighty heavy for silk."

"'Tis not silk, your majesty," said the kneeling man to the king, "but a mighty weapon."

With a puzzled look and trembling hands, the High Elder unwrapped the silk from the weapon. A look of terror first washed over the king's face, then quickly turned to ecstasy.

"Is this what I think it is," Zulanmalh asked?

"Aye, sire," answered Rog. "That is the Bloodsword. 'Tis a grim . . ."

The king silenced the rogue with a hand, and then sat in quiet for some time simply fondling the blade that lay across his knees, dreams of grandeur swimming through his twisted mind. As the king embraced the flat of the blade, concentric rings rippled like wet water through a crimson pool, yet when he glanced at his fingers, it was dry, as was the sword. Finally, the king looked up at Rog and asked: "How did you come by such a formidable weapon?"

"Sire, I am Rog, first commander and man-at-arms for the L'hoehnian nation. I was serving under captain Maztaque when we encountered this immense force west of your city deep within the prairie of Golrin. This weapon was taken from one of the rogues of that band that my regiment engaged."

"Hmmmm. Very interesting," said the king, with a look of suspicion gleaming in his eye. "And where is this band of yours, this L'hoehnian regiment?"

"We were slayed, my liege," answered Rog. "None escaped but me."

"None escaped but you, and ye with this fabulous blade. Interesting, indeed."

An air of tension hung thickly throughout the royal court; Bolo Chun sat on pins and needles and the ten well-armed Phaedron legionnaires stood at the ready to do the king's bidding. Slowly the king stood and addressed the hall.

"So, the gods have return to me what has been mine all along," said Zulanmalh, a look of arrogance shining on his grim countenance. "Perhaps I can use the Bloodsword to safeguard my kingdom and my throne."

"No, sire," Rog interrupted, but not before he realized his fatal mistake. The High Elder's dark eyes cast an angry glance down at the man before him.

"No? Why say ye this?"

"Sire, forgive me, but I came to give this weapon to ye not to be used against thine enemies, but so thine enemies could not use it against thee. It is a fell blade indeed. Mine commander, captain Maztaque, was quickly slain by this weapon after he himself tried to use it."

"Slain; how so?" There was a puzzled look on Zulanmalh's face coupled with frustration. He sat back on his throne and listened to the Rog's tale.

"I am not quite sure, sire. One minute Captain Maztaque was there, sword in hand, and then the next minute he was gone, reduced to a smoldering pile of ash. He was smitten by a great flash, a celestial flame! It seemed to originate from the blade itself. It is at great cost to mine life that I dared bring it to thee. Please accept it from me, as a friend of Phaedron." Showing humble obeisances unto the High Elder that was not normally in his nature, Rog lowered his eyes.

There was a long pause as Zulanmalh turned the story over and over in his mind. Finally, he stood to address the man.

"My son," he said, "ye are indeed a friend of mine people, and more than that, for ye are a long lost son of Phaedron. A gift deserves a gift! Come, mine son, approach the throne and receive thy reward."

Rog rose from his position and slowly approached the king. Zulanmalh placed the Bloodsword on the ground next to the Ivory Throne then stood. With outstretched arms, he took the L'hoehnian into his arms as a son and embraced him deeply. Immaculate Phaedron brocade mixed with soiled L'hoehnian silk and the two men stood there, arm in arm.

Suddenly, a flash of steel caught the eye of Bolo Chun and he lurched to his feet, but it was too late. Taking a step back, red blood smeared over his immaculate robes, the king smiled as Rog fell dead before the Ivory Throne.

Bolo Chun froze in his tracks and Zulanmalh laughed.

"Get this cur from my sight," he ordered. "The L'hoehnian nation! Did you hear that bunch of rubbish? There is no L'hoehnian nation, only a bunch of sand pirates living on the Azazel Plain. A thorn in mine side they are, to say the least. Are ye alright, Bolo?"

"I thought . . ."

"Me? Ye thought he killed me?" The king laughed

uncontrollably. "When will you realize that it will take more than a roving bandit to slay Zulanmalh IV?"

Thralls were summoned to remove the body and the king retired to his antechamber to change his soiled robes, Bolo Chun followed.

"So, you do not believe his story," asked the advisor.

"Partly, yes and no. He probably acquired the blade out west, but not from some large force hostile to Phaedron. If the truth were known, he probably stole the blade himself. L'hoehnians are known to be thieves and cutthroats, but moreso they are liars. Even so, I have heard of the tale of the Bloodsword. Grim indeed is that yarn. If this is that accursed blade, perhaps part of his story is true. Methinks it best to destroy the blade, since if it fell in the hands of the dark Khan, then for sure all would be lost."

The advisor nodded in agreement.

"See to it personally, Bolo, that this weapon is destroyed. I care not how. Also, have a detachment of legionnaires sent to Golrin. If there is a rebel force operating on the prairie then I want to know about it. You are free to take your leave."

"As ye wish, sire," Bolo replied. Taking the Bloodsword, he bowed before his king and left the chamber.

* * *

Snow laden clouds hung heavy over the waters of the North Sea and the sun was low on the horizon, far to the west. A glimmer of red shown through the grey clouds as the huge dragon descended from the frozen sky to the icy waters below.

Cohado, the wizard of Rhyan, chanted archaic words in his stateroom and the great beast was magically transformed into the image of a large and noble merchant galleon. The ship rocked as its hull came in contact with the icy water.

Looking at Dillwyn, Cohado spoke: "Muster the men and set sail for yonder harbor." He handed the dwarf a map with coordinates of where the secret cove was located. "Once the ship is harbored, we can then go ashore and begin our trek through the Enchanted Forest. The Zinjan Ice Fields will be the roughest portion of the journey and the most dangerous. After that, we will cross into the thick of the Enchanted Mountains and on to the foot of Malador."

"Aye," answered the dwarf, spinning on his heels to leave the room. Adi was already on the main when Dillwyn appeared. The deck was alive with the hustle and bustle of activity as the buccaneers hoisted the sails and worked the ship's rigging. The two were amazed at Cohado's magic, for suddenly the ship appeared as a mighty triple-masted galleon, sturdy and true.

"This is remarkable," cried Adi, over the noise and commotion of the crew. "I was hither during the transformation. It all changed right before mine very eyes!"

"Get below to thine quarters, Adi," Dillwyn roared. "Fetch your warmest raiment, for we go ashore as soon as we are harbored."

The girl nodded and disappeared amidst the crowd. The dwarf turned to the buccaneers and began barking orders like a true sea dog. Ere the sun had set, the ship was cruising fast for the Fords of Doom and Cohado's secret cove.

All was dark when the Fidelity approached the harbor. Not even a sliver of the moon's thin crescent shone through the heavy clouds that eve. The sails were full, and the men stood at the ready. Cohado, alone on the bridge, chanted commands and waved his long fingers in the air and the Fidelity obeyed.

Gliding on a sea of glass, the hull of Cohado's ship cut silently through the water, turning a sharp starboard into a tiny crescent of a cove, heavily concealed by a thick forest of pine and spruce. Dillwyn was afore on the main as the ship pulled into the natural harbor and was amazed at the seclusion of the place. Not even on a clear day and in complete sunlight could a ship moored hither be seen by passing vessels. Incredible, he thought to himself.

It didn't take long to weigh anchor and muster the men into formation for their long journey to Malador. Dillwyn was amazed to discover that Cohado was not leaving a detachment behind to guard the ship. Cohado explained that the cove was secure, and he further went on to say that he could spare no men, for if their mission failed, no one would be returning to the ship anyway. A sour feeling rose in the dwarf's stomach at the thought of failure, then he steeled himself and went to find Adi.

The going was rougher than had been expected, but even so, the journey through the forest and ice fields went relatively uneventful. On the eve of the fifth day after leaving the ship, the group came to settle in the shadow of Malador, and a fell moon rose high in the heavens.

Cohado ordered the group to stop so that they could pitch a camp and use the time to spy on the dark Khan for a few days. Time flew as fast as a soaring eagle for the band, for on the night of the second day at their secret camp, whilst the group hid in the shadows of Malador, one of Cohado's scouts returned with dark news. Earlier that eve, the warrior said, he saw a vast army, evidently raised by magical means by the dark Khan himself, leave the mountains and march west, apparently to Phaedron.

Immediately, Cohado ordered the warriors to strike camp, which they did in haste and with great zeal. The group mustered into formation and followed in pursuit. Dillwyn, using keen senses from he knew not where, smelled blood on the horizon.

Thus ends Chapter Fourteen of Book Two

FIFTEEN

A Friend in the Shadows

"Tulwryn, Tulwryn." The voice was almost as if in a dream, yet the warrior from Nuvia knew the source. It was the shadow of the Bloodsword, that much he knew, and a chill ran down his spine. Thus far, the shadow had only given him bad news and there was no reason why the present should be any different.

Tulwryn walked along the wastes of the prairie, it's tall grass waving in the breeze like some green ocean. The sky was a hazy grey, which was peculiar to say the least. There were no bird or animal life present and even the chirping of insects were nil. It was then that he realized he was not in Phantasodyssea any more. The shadow had summoned him to that ethereal dream world, an eldritch realm betwixt reality and insanity. He had been here before; he was no stranger here.

"I am hither. Speak," spoke Tulwryn, in a stern voice. The wind whipped up briskly for a moment, then died out all together. A hazy mist swirled before the warrior, then parted. The shadow, an ethereal double image of Tulwryn himself, stepped forth from the fog and approached him.

"Greetings friend," said the shadow. "I have news for thee."

Tulwryn noticed that the shadow appeared more lifelike than it had in the past. It almost seemed corporeal, even though somewhat translucent. He wondered silently about this sudden change in the thing's appearance, yet pushed his fears aside.

"The news I bring ye is fell indeed, yet hear it you must." The shadow's voice was light and airy, but still held stern authority.

"Speak, I said. I have not time for your childish riddles. I must regain the sword and complete this wizard's charge. Get on with it!"

"Thy quest is for naught, for the one ye seek has already made the city and been granted an audience with the High Elder."

"What says you," cried Tulwryn. "Ye bring me grim news indeed." The two turned and walked a ways, pausing under a great leafy elm. Tulwryn, grieved beyond words, sat beneath the boughs of that great tree and fell into a deep melancholy.

"The Bloodsword is now in the High Elder's possession," spoke Tulwryn, angered at his failure. "How can this be? How can I get the sword back to stop Kimark Khan? Athrum blast mine fool soul!"

"Rest assured that the blade resides with the king for the time being, but all is not lost. Remember, as I have always said, you *are* the Bloodsword, Tulwryn, not that mere blade. It is *you* who has the power. The blade is merely a tool, although a powerful one."

"I feel I have no power without the sword."

"In time that will change," answered the shadow.

"Well then, what must I do? Council me, mine friend."

There was a long pause, and then the shadow began his retelling of *The Selah*, and the *Order of the Crystal Sphere*. Cohado had already told the tale to him before, back when the warrior and his friends were in Rhyan. But much had happened since then, and so the shadow reminded him of his true purpose, and the only weakness that Kimark Khan possessed.

"The Crystal Sphere was not just some fraternal Order of evil priests," spoke the shadow, "but is the ultimate source of Kimark Khan's power. The Bloodsword itself will not kill the wizard; nothing can kill him unless the stone is destroyed first!"

"Stone," asked Tulwryn, puzzled. "Where is this Crystal Sphere and how must I destroy it?"

"The Crystal Sphere is a huge black diamond, stolen from the mines beneath Golrin by the dark Khan ages ago. It is that very diamond, the Scrystone, which resides in a secret chamber in Malador where Kimark Khan performs his evil magics. Tulwryn, the stone must be destroyed to defeat the wizard."

"This is very well and good, but how can a diamond be destroyed? I am no wizard or gemsmith. How am I to destroy a tool of magic? Flesh and blood villains I can fight, but sorcery?"

The shadow laughed a grim laugh. "You will find a way."

Suddenly, the shadow faded from view and Tulwryn found himself seated around a small campfire. The night was black and a thin crescent of the moon was riding low on the horizon. Nothing stirred but the chirping of crickets in the scrub.

* * *

The heavy alabaster gate swung closed and two hundred and fifty stood atop the burning sands of the Phaedron League of Death. A rasping of iron on steel told the condemned that the gate was barred from the inside and there was nowhere to go but west, down that long corridor of blazing inferno heat from which only death would deliver their suffering.

With Rog dead and the Bloodsword in the king's hands, Zulanmalh once again began to feel powerful and returned to the cruelty for which he was legendary. After a short deliberation with his closest advisors and generals, he resumed his daily schedule of executions and torture.

A fortnight after slaying the rouge in his court, and by his own hand, the High Elder came and stood before his subjects on the royal balcony overlooking the city square. The day was overcast and a chill of death was in the air, for there were rumors circulating of rebellion and unrest. The city's residents had had enough of Zulanmalh's tyranny and they demanded a change. Many cried out for justice, denouncing the evil two hundred year reign of the House of Zula and cries for blood where echoing throughout the streets of Phaedron.

Stepping out on the balcony, the High Elder, with an entourage of his highest ranking generals, advisors, and beautiful courtesans, spread his arms wide and addressed the people of Phaedron:

"Mine people, the noble people of Phaedron, I stand before thee as thy friend, thy father, and thy king. It has been brought to my attention that our great city's security has been put in jeopardy. There is talk of tyranny, and of rebellion, and this I cannot tolerate!" The king's voice rose to a frenzied pitch and the people below cowered in the shadow of his wrath.

"I will not tolerate such ideals," screamed the king, "therefore, I am forced to publicly announce the new laws and punishments that me and my court advisors have decreed this day. These new laws are for the benefit of Phaedron and are designed to destroy all thoughts and ideals contrary to the crown!"

A rumble murmured throughout the crowd below the balcony, and a grim silence followed. High overhead a raven cawed loudly; the High Elder continued his speech:

"By means of torture and death, either under the knives of my royal abattoirs or by means of the League of Death, will I punish anyone remotely affiliated with any rebel faction beginning from this day forth. Know that I will not bend from this law, and anyone, be they noble or commoner, will fall to their death under my judgment if they but oppose my will and my throne!"

"Ye cannot kill us all," came a roar from the seething crowd. "We will stand against you and your evil regime!" Zulanmalh was aghast at this outburst. Where at first he felt cowardice and fear from the masses below, now he saw rage and fury.

In a matter of hours, the people of Phaedron began a frenzied revolt and the city was thrown into chaotic anarchy. Five hundred thousand Phaedrons, hungry for royal blood, mobbed their way through the city's streets and came before the doors of the royal palace, chanting the name of Kimark Khan.

Fearing for his life, the High Elder dispatched his soldiers to the streets of the city in groves. The high walls of Phaedron, built centuries ago to keep out barbaric invasion, now worked in reverse, containing the populace and making escape impossible.

The legionnaires began their fell duty and hundreds were slaughtered daily in the streets turning Phaedron into a massive charnel ground.

* * *

Four days after the internal siege of Phaedron had begun, the mighty army of Kimark Khan, four and eight hundred thousand strong, approached the walled citadel. The dark Khan rode to the forefront of his war train to lead the assault.

From high atop the wall, no guards could be seen, nor were there any manning the portcullis at the main gate. Strange, thought the wizard, for what insanity is this, for a king to leave the front door of his kingdom unguarded?

Then suddenly, something graced the dark Khan's ears, for he heard his own name coming from inside the walls of Phaedron. Amazing, it seemed, for it was as if thousands upon thousands of people were chanting his name.

"What is this," he spoke quietly to himself, "that my return is welcomed by the masses of the city. What fools! For I will crush them all under my wrath."

Instantly, the low drone of the chanting was drowned out by screams of terror and the sounds of battle.

"HA!" Kimark Khan laughed loudly. "The city is besieged from within and a revolt is in progress!"

Laughing a grim laugh, Kimark Khan proceeded to cast an evil sorcery to cause plagues and added suffering unto the people of Phaedron. Fire fell from the sky and hundreds died in the celestial mêlée. With a word, the main gate was blasted and the dark Khan's army entered the city. War and carnage flowed thick that day and the streets of Phaedron became as blood!

A mighty blade hung loosely at the dark Khan's hip and from the bridle of his great war horse hung the wet scalp of Bolo Chun.

Thus ends Chapter Fifteen of Book Two

SIXTEEN

Return of the Khan

Wales and cries of terror ripped through the night as the slaughter raged on. Zulanmalh and his family huddled low in a secret antechamber guarded by a legion of the most loyal of the king's Royal Guard. But even in the safety of their seclusion, they could not be protected from the horrific sounds of battle and mayhem that coursed through the streets of Phaedron.

Outside, the war ebbed and flowed like a red sea splashing blood and gore on the very steps of the palace. Lynch mobs, rebels, legionnaires, and vagrants vied for top position, yet anarchy ruled in the king's stead. Suddenly, a great blast rocked the main gate and portcullis of the city and a host of evil poured into Phaedron like a plague as fire fell from the sky consuming friend and foe alike.

On a huge black stallion rode Kimark Khan, warrior-wizard and sworn enemy of the House of Zula. He entered the city a conqueror, sword in hand and wet scalps dripping from his steed's bridle. His long and flowing dark cape billowed in the breeze of war revealing black gilded chainmaile underneath.

"Let the sky be darkened and may the sun be swallowed by the demon of night until I sit on the Ivory Throne," cursed the dark Khan from the mighty back of his mount. Just then, the bright sun over Phaedron blinked and sputtered, then was gone, throwing the city into utter darkness and chaos. Fire continued to rain down on the masses, and the streets became as brimstone mixed with blood. The dark Khan rode on, and death rode with him as he slew friend and foe alike. Even those factions that had been, for so long, praying for his return, felt the wrath of his steel and iron.

"General Graf," yelled the dark wizard, "take a column of your men and seal off the main gate after the army has fully entered. Make certain than none leave the city alive! Give orders to General Ulu and Commander Shedalasom that they are to secure the city by whichever means they deem necessary. My regiment and I shall storm the palace. Understood?"

The general looked at his master and nodded, death blazing in his cold dead eyes.

"Good," said Kimark Khan, and reining his beast he yelled to his troops: "To me, men!" And with that command, the dark Khan spurred his steed and his men to a frothing madness, and the party galloped off through the carnage towards the palace of Phaedron with death in their hearts and blood on their sword blades.

* * *

Zulanmalh IV sat fidgeting, worrying about the results of the battle that raged beyond the palace walls. He had given the Bloodsword to his chief advisor, Bolo Chun with orders to destroy the weapon, but now he was regretting that decision, for the power and fearlessness that he felt when he held the sword had vanished like a dream, and once again, he felt helpless and afraid.

Yun Chuu, second advisor to the king under Bolo Chun, entered the antechamber where the High Elder and his immediate family hid. Bowing deeply, the fat man addressed the king in a grave tone.

"Sire, I think it best if we evacuate the palace immediately."

"Evacuate," repeated the king. "Does the battle go that bad for us?"

"I am afraid so, your majesty. Not more that an hour ago, the front gate was breeched by a great blast, fire is raining from the heavens, and a large host of warriors has entered the city by force. They slaughter not only our own soldiers, but the civilians as well."

"So the day of reckoning is upon me," Zulanmalh whispered silently to himself. Nervously, the king fiddled with a strand of thread dangling from his royal gown, then steeling himself for the worse, stood and addressed Yun Chuu.

"So, it seems that Kimark Khan has returned to extract his vengeance. Aye, make haste and ready the royal entourage for immediate evacuation. Dismissed."

The man was about to turn and leave the room when the king called after him.

"Yun Chuu."

Pausing, Yun turned back toward his king.

"Yes, your majesty?"

"What is the status of Bolo Chun? I have not seen him for days. Do you know of his whereabouts and the errand I sent him on?"

A stern look of peril wormed its way across the yellow face of Yun Chuu, and sweat beaded upon his brow. He quickly approached the High Elder and dropped to one knee.

"Sire," said the man in a whisper, "Fearing the worst, Bolo Chun gave the Bloodsword to your top commander, General Puc, with the orders to take the blade far from Phaedron and have it destroyed. I believe it was Master Chun's wishes for the general to travel west and toss it into the Sea of Fire."

"Very good idea," said the king, smiling.

"But sire, I fear the plan may have went awry, for none has seen the general or Master Chun in many days."

Just then, the doors of the king's antechamber slammed open and two score of darkly clad warriors stormed into the room, followed by none other than Kimark Khan himself. Terror was written in the eyes of Zulanmalh, for hanging at the hip of the dark warlord was the Bloodsword.

"And so, we meet again," bellowed Kimark Khan, laughing. "Thy reign is ended, and so is the House of Zula! I have come to take what is mine, but first I will have you grovel at my feet!"

The king's family, surrounded by the dark Khan's men, sat in horrified silence at the nightmare unfolding before them. Yun Chuu, faithful unto death, stepped in front of the king.

"Ye must kill me first, ere mine king perish by thy grimy hands, ye foul cur!"

"Oh what brave and foolish servants ye have, Zulanmalh!" The Khan's long dagger quickly hissed from its scabbard and, traveling faster than the eye could follow, skewered the man standing before the High Elder.

Yun Chuu dropped to his knees before his king, blood gushing from the wound in his fat belly and bubbling from his gaping mouth.

"Please remember this sacrifice, my lord," he gasped, dying. A bloodcurdling inhuman laugh was the last thing he heard ere he lay down and died.

Wiping the blade clean on the dead man's raiment but sheathing it naught, Kimark Khan glanced about the chamber.

"Any more brave and noble heroes?"

All stood silent and as still as stone statuary. The dark Khan, arrogant beyond belief due to the strength in the blade he bore, not the naked dagger held in his hand, but the sheathed Bloodsword dangling at his waist, strutted about the room taunting his captives. Finally, he sheathed the dagger then drew forth the grim blade of the Bloodsword.

"Ye would have a servant destroy such a fine weapon," Kimark Khan asked? A puzzled look came over Zulanmalh, for these strange twists of fate he understood naught. Indeed, it was apparent that the dark wizard had somehow thwarted his plan, stole the Bloodsword ere his men could destroy it, and probably slayed those he stole it from, but how he achieved all of this was a mystery. Even so, it mattered naught, for he and his reign was undone. This much he knew was certain.

"Aye, dog, I know about thy plan to cast this fine blade into the Sea of Fire! What ignorance, indeed; your general Puc and that fat slobbering servant of yours, Bolo Chun, begged me for mercy ere they told me of thy plan. But did I give them mercy?

Nay, mercy is not in mine blood to give, and so I ripped the flesh from their heads with my very hand whilst they still lived!" And with that, the dark Khan sheathed the sword with one hand and with the other, tossed the two scalps onto the marble floor at the feet of the High Elder.

Zulanmalh's eyes glanced down at the dried dead skin lying before him, a hundred fears coursing through his veins. He then paused, and then, looking into the eyes of his usurper, the king's spirit was broken and he fell to his knees like a dog that had been beaten once too often.

"Are ye to beg for my mercy as well," asked the dark Khan, most arrogantly.

"I ask for nothing but for the lives of my family. Please spare at least the children, for they are not a part of this war."

"You are more of a fool than I had originally believed," laughed the wizard. "Do you not know anything about politics?"

And drawing a slender finger horizontally across his own throat, the warriors of Kimark Khan immediately launched themselves into a blooded frenzy, and with flashing blades of crimson steel went about slashing the necks of everyone in the room, adult and children alike. Screams and yelps of pain echoes throughout the halls of the palace as the entire House of Zula was slain in one fell stroke of Maladorian steel.

And so it was, that he was forsaken by all of his sorcerers, and all of his dark gods, and in his hour of need, Zulanmalh was abandoned, for the last head to fall that day was the High Elders' himself after he witnessed the gruesome execution of his entire family. After cleaning the Bloodsword on the soiled raiment of the king, Kimark Khan sheathed the grim weapon, and then stepped to where Zulanmalh's head had fallen. Looking down at the face of the dead king, he grinned. Slowly, the dark Khan knelt and removed the crown from the severed head of Zulanmalh IV, and with trembling hands that had waited two centuries for this day, placed the jeweled crown of Phaedron on his own head, and ascended the throne, with the blood of the dead king still dripping from the whiskers of his blue-black beard.

* * *

A week had passed since Beck joined Tulwryn's men and the band was already three days east of Golrin itself. Whilst they were still within the boundaries of the prairie, Tulwryn thought it best to bypass the Phaedron trade route and stay to the deep grasslands in lieu of attracting unwanted attention.

Tulwryn reined his camel in a southeasterly direction, which did not faze the warriors in the least, but Beck, being a nature savvy tracker lifted an eyebrow and eagerly jogged up along side of Tulwryn's steed.

"What is up," asked the Woodling to his leader.

Tulwryn, looking down at the small man running along side his mount, tugged the reins and brought the beast to a slow walk. Raising a hand to the others behind him, his men fell in line and did the same.

Bringing his attention back to Beck, he asked: "Why so do ye ask?"

"I thought we were bound for Phaedron," answered the Woodling, "yet, you steer us southeast, away from the city."

Tulwryn grinned. Indeed, this little fellow was a master tracker. One could not deny that, yet he was not in the habit of having his every move questioned, nor did he like to waste time explaining his plans in great detail. Anyhow, he could see that Beck was fast becoming an important asset to the group so he decided to inform him of the change of plans.

"Beck, mine friend," said the warrior to the Woodling, "there has been a change of plans, for the spirit of the sword has informed me that the Bloodsword has already fallen into the king's hands."

A look of terror splashed across Beck's dark face. "So what now? Why southeast?"

"Do ye know of Mt. Malador," asked Tulwryn.

"Only in tales, for I have never been east of the River Phaedron," Beck answered. "I hear tell that Malador is a grim place, surrounded by vast forests and legions of evil creatures of the most hideous kind controlled by a mad wizard. Why?"

"That is where we are bound," replied the warrior.

"And I hope there is a reason for this madness?"

"Indeed, there is. The spirit of the sword tells me that there is an artifact hidden deep within the bowels of that mountain that will sway the events of the coming war in our favor whereas we can destroy the evil that threatens to ensnare us."

"What are we to do, become moles and burrow into the very rock of the mountain?"

"Nay," answered Tulwryn, "there are many tunnels and passageways that criss-cross the innards of Malador. They were cut there eons ago by the mad wizard you have just mentioned. It is that very wizard that I was charged to destroy."

Beck's eyes rolled back and Tulwryn could see the little fellow's bones turn to water.

"Fear naught," the warrior said, "all will be achieved, even at the cost of some lives. You said you wanted adventure, did you not. Well, I aim to please. How many days ride do ye think it will take to reach the mountain?"

"I know not, for as I have already said, I have never been that far east. Have thee a map?"

Tulwryn tossed him a small scrap of parchment onto which was scribbled a rough sketch of the realm. The Woodling looked the map over and tossed it back up to Tulwryn.

"Perhaps a fortnight, maybe only one week if we double our pace," he said.

"Very well," answered Tulwryn, "then we double our pace." And thus said, he drove his heels deep into the flanks of his camel. The beast lurched forward at a fast gallop and the others in the band did likewise. Shaking his head, the Woodling picked up his pace for the long jog east.

* * *

The journey to Malador took many days but not near as long as Beck had anticipated. The Woodling had no idea the constitution of Tulwryn's men, and was amazed at their stamina.

Of course, he, Tulwryn, and the camels, needed food and water, but he never once seen the soldiers eat, drink, or sleep.

The passage across Phantasodyssea had been a hard one, not just for the many leagues trekked, but because Tulwryn ordered complete stealth as well. Crossing a continent with one hundred armed warriors, fourteen camels, and one Woodling, was not an easy chore; doing so stealthily was all but impossible.

Whilst the Golrin Prairie was fairly easy to navigate, being sparsely populated, once the group crossed the River Phaedron into the Plain of Kem things got worse. All throughout the plain were roving bands of brigands and marauders, hungry for loot and blood. More than once, Tulwryn's men were attacked by suicidal thieves and bandits bent on plunder. Even whilst fording the Obsidian River, a dozen blood hungry rogues swarmed the group, only to be cut to ribbons by Rhyanian steel. The black waters of the Obsidian flowed red with Kemite blood that fell afternoon.

Two days journey and the men were across the plain and had entered Darkwood, just north of Nuvia. Many times did Tulwryn's head turn south, pondering the ghosts and memories of his past, and his four sons that lie in shallow graves in a high pasture near that small farm town. No tears creased his cheek, for his heart was hardened, and his mind on the task at hand.

It was a difficult decision to make, but make it he did. After fording the River Agu, Tulwryn gave the command for the group to turn northeast and, cutting a diagonal across the heart of the Eastern Steppes of the Azazel Plain, made his way straight for the Enchanted Forest and Malador beyond.

The sun blazed hot over the desert steppes, yet Tulwryn's warriors slowed not their pace. Often, he thought he glimpsed a tent or caravan far off along the northwestern horizon and he remembered the L'hoehnian bandits that stole the Bloodsword. Gritting his teeth, he spurred his mount on, fighting hard his desire to ride forth and extract his vengeance for that theft. Yet, he knew that in time, he would regain the blade and so, he held his wrath in check and continued northeast to complete the wizard's charge.

The sun was setting low on the western horizon as the group descended from the northern reaches of the plain and crossed into the Enchanted Forest. Beck had related to Tulwryn that he had been impressed as to the speed that they crossed the desert. Two days journey, without stopping for food or water, and the desert was behind them. Of course, he and Tulwryn were parched, but the warriors and the camels trudged on unscathed.

Only after crossing the Basalt River, did Tulwryn raise his hand and bring the party to a halt. He ordered the men to pitch camp, and then posted sentries in the four cardinal directions five hundred paces from the camp's parameter. Whilst the warriors braved the wilds of the Maladorian wilderness, their keen eyes scanning the scrub and brush for hostile attack, Tulwryn and the Woodling of Bain relaxed around a small and humble fire with food and drink. They both knew that this would most likely be their last luxury until the final battle was fought, therefore they ate their meal in silence saying nary a word.

Thus ends Chapter Sixteen of Book Two

SEVENTEEN

Rendezvous

To make haste to the mountain of Malador, Tulwryn forced his men to march on throughout the night. He had released the camels at the border of the Azazel Plain since the animals would pose no benefit to forest and mountain travel, and decided that the rest of the journey should be on foot.

Trekking though the Enchanted Forest seemed to be no problem, however, Tulwryn pondered about the quiet serenity of the area. All his life he had heard that this particular forest was alive with fell beasts and evil creatures, both physical and of the spirit, that lie in wait to rend a man's flesh as well as his soul. Yet, all was quiet and nothing dangerous was seen.

Overhead, the forest's canopy was thick, but in places, there were enough openings to allow ample moonlight to filter down to the cold forest floor. Moonbeams flowed like a gentle stream of bluish-purple over a darker background of black. Occasionally, a firefly flickered in the still air and then was lost to sight as quick as it had arrived. Other than that, the entire forest seemed void of insect life.

Tulwryn's keen ears suddenly picked up a sound, not far off in the distance. The moon had disappeared behind the clouds and for a moment, the entire area was cloaked in darkness. Raising his left hand in a knotty fist, he silently called the men to halt, his nostrils flaring to pick up the scent of something unseen.

Beck inched his way up from the rear of the line to fall in with Tulwryn.

"What is it," asked the Woodling, crouching down on all fours by his leader.

"Ye tell me," whispered Tulwryn. "You're the tracker. I feel we are being watched, but by what I cannot say."

All of a sudden, five score of eyes appeared off in the darkness, blazing red with the lust of murder. Tulwryn and the Woodling saw the red eyes, yet did not move.

"It looks like I am out of my league," whispered the tracker. "In all my days, I have never seen eyes as such. But one thing is certain, I feel we are surrounded."

The warrior smiled, and exhaled a sigh of relief. "Perhaps ye have not, but I have. These are not the eyes of beasts, but warriors!" Tulwryn stood and yelled off in the distance, ripping the sheet of silence in half.

"Ho, Warriors! 'Tis I, Tulwryn!"

Just then, the forest erupted in a bold frenzy of handshakes and back patting as Tulwryn's group made rendezvous with Cohado and his warriors. Dillwyn was there, as was Adi. She batted her dark eyes at Tulwryn, and his heart leapt. Smiling back at her through the hazy light of the pale moon, he saw the look of lust on her face as well. The reunion was warm, but brief, and in no time, Tulwryn and his men were led back to Cohado's secret camp.

With sentries posted all about, Tulwryn, Cohado, Dillwyn, Adi, and Beck, found themselves seated around a small fire that the wizard had ignited by magical means. Tulwryn introduced Beck to the group and recalled his adventures in the west and the incident that had brought the Woodling into his employment. Likewise, Cohado briefed the warrior on their windship journey, the Gorkon attack, and then began to recap the details of their discoveries whilst in the forest itself.

"Kimark Khan has left Malador," said the wizard.

"That probably accounts for the quiet then," replied Tulwryn. "If he has left the forest, perhaps his magical guardians have gone with him as well. I noticed that the forest is void of all but the most benign life."

"Aye, probably so, Tulwryn," said Cohado. "He seems to have organized a sizable army for the taking of Phaedron. Our scouts saw him leave many days ago and I am sure he is probably in the city by now."

A smile creased Tulwryn's face. "Perhaps, this is the opportunity that we have been needing," he said. "Do ye suppose he left any guard in place at the mountain?"

"By the looks of things, no. His army was enormous. There may be magical beasts guarding the place, but methinks he took all his warriors with him to Phaedron."

Tulwryn then went on to tell the wizard and the others about the shadow's revelation, and the Scrystone. The night wore on as the five sat and discussed plans. The objective was fairly simple: They would proceed to the dark Khan's secret abode and thereby destroy the stone. Cohado had advised that a group of three scouts be dispatched to Phaedron to learn about the news there, and Dillwyn was chosen to lead the reconnaissance. Of course, it was usually the simplest plans that succeed and it seemed that there was not any way to make their plan any simpler. But still, Tulwryn had his doubts.

As the fire turned to coals in the early morning hours, the five decided to turn into their blankets and sleep throughout the day. The following night they were to engage their plan and assault Malador. Dillwyn disappeared into the shadows of the forest, as did Beck. Cohado merely sat, legs folded before the dying embers of the campfire, alert eyes hidden beneath heavy lids. Tulwryn and Adi had different plans. It had been many weeks since the two felt the warmth of their love, and so they fell in together, arm in arm, under the eaves of the Enchanted Forest.

The next day came and went, and the evening was upon them quicker than anticipated. Tulwryn was present when Cohado gave Dillwyn a small pouch of *Spelldust* with simple instructions:

"When ye learn some important news," said the wizard to the dwarf, "take some of the dust herein and sprinkle it in the air whilst ye says this enchantment."

Cohado mumbled a phrase that Tulwryn could not hear but the dwarf smiled acknowledging his understanding.

"The dust will become a carrier pigeon and will fly back to me to informing me of your news." Cohado rested a firm hand on Dillwyn's broad shoulder and Tulwryn couldn't help but notice the strange transformation he was seeing in his friend.

Dillwyn, dressed in the black robes of a Covensted he-witch rather than in his usual Carthusian battle armor, broke camp with the three scouts dispatched to Phaedron. Tulwryn was sad to see him go after such a brief reunion, but realized the urgency of the mission. Enough time for reunions when the task was finished, he thought silently to himself, and smiled as the four vanished through the underbrush of the forest.

The rest of the united troops broke camp an hour later and continued on their trek to Malador. High in the canopy of the forest, a single raven eyed the warrior and his band, and an old god smiled.

* * *

In Phaedron, the dark Khan's army sustained themselves on a daily diet of violence and death. Likewise, Kimark Khan, the new High Elder of that besieged city, had the severed head of Zulanmalh IV, as well as the heads of all that dead king's wives and children, set atop tall pikes lining Phaedron's main road as a sign of his omnipotent authority.

There were a few rebel factions sympathetic to the dark Khan, but most residents of the city realized that they had received the worse of two evils. The new king, once seated in full power upon Phaedron's Ivory Throne, brought the rebellion to a close, yet the blood did not cease to flow. Even though the fighting in the cobbled streets of the city had long since ended, daily executions and torture were the mainstay of Phaedronian court entertainment.

In the city's grim shadows, Dillwyn and his three companions lurked, espying the situation in Phaedron. By means of his newfound wizardry, Dillwyn released his magical pigeon. The bird rose quickly on thickly muscled wings, circled the walled citadel thrice, and then, gaining altitude, soared eastward to Malador.

* * *

The evening was fast becoming night, and the group was about to break camp to begin their travels back to Malador when a fat carrier pigeon fluttered down through the forest canopy to land upon Cohado's lean shoulder. The stout bird rubbed its chubby head affectionately on the wizard's neck and softly cooed its fell message in Cohado's ear. The wizard's face suddenly went pallid and with an outstretched hand, he braced himself against the trunk of a tall pine.

"It seems that events are not unfolding in our favor," he said to Tulwryn and the others that stood near him. The warrior exchanged glances with Adi and the Woodling, and then his eyes fell back on the wizard.

"My little friend here," spoke Cohado, gently stroking the neck of the cooing bird still resting on his shoulder, "informs me that not only has Kimark Khan entered Phaedron, but he has also killed Zulanmalh, and taken the crown for himself. But worse yet, he has gained possession of the Bloodsword!"

"Athrum blast mine soul," cried Tulwryn, through gritted teeth. "This is my fault!" Adi reached out to console the warrior, but he pulled away from her embraces.

"Nay, Tulwryn," said the wizard, "ye cannot blame yourself. Often times, these things happen. Such is the twists of fate as willed by the gods. We can only expend the effort to do our best. Come; let us tally no longer hither, for we must needs get to Malador and destroy the Scrystone."

It didn't take long for the soldiers to strike camp, and within the hour the group was trekking through the dense underbrush of the Enchanted Forest, northeast toward the mountaintop abode of Kimark Khan.

Apparently, the wizard had been correct in his assumptions, for it seemed, in his arrogance, the dark Khan had not left any safeguards in place to secure his domain atop the mountain.

"For certain," spoke Cohado, "the dark Khan had no intentions of returning hither."

"Perhaps his bold arrogance will be his own downfall," answered Tulwryn.

But just in case, Tulwryn ordered sentries to guard their movements whilst the wizard searched out a means to gain access to the tunnels under Malador. By method of his Rhyan magics, Cohado located a hidden entrance in the mountain on its southern foot. Cautiously, he and the others entered. Exploring the vast tunnels and chambers under Malador proved to be no easy task, and Tulwryn divided the troopers into groups of five and sent them down various tunnels with orders to return if the chamber holding the great Crystal Sphere was discovered. Beck went with one group, whilst Cohado, Adi, and himself went with another.

Time dragged on, and hours seemed as days ere one of the soldiers returned with the news that a chamber was located that contained a great stone.

"As tall as a man, it was," spoke the soldier, "and from within its inky form a great light pulsated." Cohado smiled.

"That has to be the stone we seek!" He was about to rush off in the direction the man indicated, but Tulwryn grabbed his arm.

"Wait," said Tulwryn. Then, turning back to the soldier, he asked: "Have ye or any of the others came across any resistance in the tunnels?"

"Nay," answered the man. "Methinks the labyrinth is deserted, yet there are many tunnels and chambers not yet explored."

Motioning to the wizard and the others, Tulwryn advised the use of caution. He knew they were too close to completing their mission and did not wish to fail by heedlessly blundering into a regiment of the dark Khan's troopers. The others nodded their understanding, and then the group proceeded toward the chamber of the Scrystone, stealthily on padded cat feet.

By the time the party arrived at the chamber, Tulwryn's nerves were pulled as tight as a Knobite bowstring. The group entered the room silently, with bare steel in hand. Cohado was the first to enter the chamber, followed by Tulwryn and the others.

The room was large to say the least, with a high ceiling and a richly polished floor; in the center of the chamber, stood the great Scrystone. The large crystal floated in the air, evidently supported by sorcery. Other than the large sphere of that accursed black diamond, eerily pulsating with unfathomable eldritch power, the entire room was bare. Cohado thought this odd, as it was plain to see that the chamber was indeed the dark Khan's magical sanctuary. Nowhere were there any books or other magical paraphernalia that was common amongst even the most novice of magic users. Indeed, thought he, the dark Khan never intended to return hither, thinking that his source of power, the Crystal Sphere, was safe from the prying eyes of his enemies.

Cohado quickly turned to look at Tulwryn. The warrior did not like the strange gleam in the old man's eye and he swallowed hard for he knew that look, he had seen it before.

"Tulwryn," said the wizard. "This stone is more than a stone, it is a portal. Come hither."

Apprehensively, the warrior approached the Rhyan wizard.

"I have a plan," said Cohado the Long to the Lion of Heidmar. "Ye must gaze deeply into the stone. Lose yourself in its opaqueness and you will be transported through time and space, to Phaedron, and into the very court of the king! Be on your guard, though, for ye will emerge in your etheric form and still vulnerable to the dark Khan's magics. Once you are through, I will destroy the stone from this side of reality. You will know when the stone has been destroyed because you will materialize back into your true corporeal form. Once the stone is destroyed, Kimark Khan will be defenseless. Strike quickly, warrior, ere this mission was for naught!"

"I like naught thy sorcery, wizard," scowled Tulwryn, "but to end this damn charge . . ." His words trailed off as his thoughts drifted on the wind. Glancing over his shoulder, he looked at

Adi and smiled. "Once again, we are parted, my lady. Until we meet again."

"Remember, whilst in thy etheric form ye are helpless to Kimark Khan's sorcery. Therefore, use everything to thy advantage! There might be some slight disorientation during the transportation through the portal, as well as when ye materialize back into your physical form. Attack quickly, but not in haste. May the gods be with thee!"

Tulwryn strode on thick loins to stand before the Crystal Sphere. He stood there for a moment, body tensed and heart pounding in his throat, for he knew not what to expect. The others about the room gasped at what they saw, for in an instant, the air around Tulwryn shimmered and became translucent, then became as liquid. A second later, he was gone.

Tulwryn was not gone more than a few minutes when Beck and a score of mystic warriors poured into the room. Cohado was standing in front of the Scrystone chanting incantations with hands waving violently in the air whilst Adi watched the door.

"Is that thing destroyed yet," asked the Woodling, gasping hard to catch his breath. Adi noticed that he was bleeding profusely from a dozen cuts on his arms and shoulders, and the short sword he carried in his dark hand was wet with blood. She then looked at the other warriors and they likewise had battle wounds.

"Cohado is in the process of destroying it now," she answered. "You're hurt?"

"Make haste then," Beck said, ignoring her comments of his well-being. "There is treachery afoot! All our warriors are dead; we are all that is left."

"But how?"

"We were ambushed in one of the lower tunnels by grim warriors. Our troops were out numbered three to one!"

"So the dark Khan did leave guards hither to protect his domain." It was more than a statement than a question. Hearing heavy footsteps in the corridor yonder she turned to look out the door, drawing her dagger in the process.

"More than guards," answered Beck, "there is a whole garrison hidden in the tunnels and chambers below. I do not think we were followed hither, but I cannot know for certain."

"Ye were followed, for listen, they approach!"

The following seconds flew by in a bloody haze as sixty fell warriors stormed the chamber. Steel rang on steel and the grunting and moaning of men locked in mortal combat echoed throughout the halls of Malador. The remaining numbers of Cohado's mystic warriors threw themselves into the fray, and Beck engaged the intruders as well. Adi, after cutting one warrior down with a dagger slash to the neck, ran to the wizard screaming wildly to hurry his work ere they all perish.

Cohado flashed her an angry glance.

"Do not rush my wizardry, lady Adi!" He risked no further words and returned to his task at hand.

Adi turned back toward the fray just in time to see Beck cut down by a heavy blow of one of the intruding warriors. The Woodling's tiny body, already battered beyond all recognition, but still fighting with a seething battle lust, was severed in twain by a single slash of Maladorian steel. Intense agony emerged from Beck's mouth in one long and painful scream ere he died.

Carnage and mayhem swirled all around the chamber of the Crystal Sphere. Kimark Khan's dread warriors did all they could to slay their way through the wall of Cohado's mystic warriors, fighting hard to get at the wizard himself ere he destroy the stone.

Cohado's voice rose to a fevered pitch and the stone glowed and pulsated as never before. Adi noticed, out of the corner of her eye, one of the dark Khan's warriors raise a dagger in the air. Seconds seemed like hours, yet she seen the release. Flying at blazing speed, the launched blade rocketed toward the wizard chanting before the Scrystone. Without heeding her own safety, Adi dove in front of the flying blade.

Suddenly, from deep within the stone came a rumbling noise. It was as if a thousand storms had been unleashed within the very bowels of the sphere itself. There was then the sound of breaking glass, and finally, an intense explosion rocked the entire mountain with a blast of celestial glory equivalent to a thousand radiant suns. A blinding light seared the chamber and Cohado was knocked across the room by the force.

Shaking stars from his head, the wizard slowly stood. Lifeless bodies littered the chamber and then Cohado noticed the girl, lying silently on the ground where the Scrystone once hovered. Rushing to her aid, the wizard knelt beside the fallen child.

"Adi," he said, rubbing her tender face. "Child, speak to me."

Through glazed eyes, Adi looked up at him. Tears filled his eyes, for he then saw the dagger, still protruding from the gaping wound in her heaving breast. Blood spilled freely on the floor, her still beating heart straining hard to pump her life's blood from her body.

"Is it done," she asked, coughing, blood bubbling from her mouth and nose.

"Speak not mine child," answered Cohado. "Reserve thy energy."

"Why," she answered. "These wounds will not heal. Better to die saving you, than have your death kill Tulwryn."

"Aye, the stone is destroyed. Kimark Khan is undone."

"Good," Adi said with a smile. "Then my warrior is back in his physical form." She paused, her head swimming with blurred visions from the lack of blood. Struggling hard to breath, Adi reached for Cohado with trembling hands.

"Tell him I wait . . . please, tell him I wait on the other side . . . for him." Then her face became as ash and as her final breath escaped blooded lips; Adi closed her eyes and died.

"Curse the damn gods," Cohado said, spitting the words from his priestly lips. "Why must ye take this child?"

In the silence of that dank chamber, deep within the bowels of Malador, Cohado, the high priest of Rhyan, sat holding a warrior's woman, and wept.

Thus ends Chapter Seventeen of Book Two

EIGHTEEN

The Ivory Throne

Tulwryn's mind reeled and nausea swept over him in a rush. One minute he was standing before the Crystal Sphere and the next minute he was surrounded by a legion of fell warriors and standing before the Ivory Throne of Phaedron.

Since his consciousness was encased in his etheric form, the warriors did not notice him. And so, he slid back against the rear wall of the court, concealing himself in the shadows as best he could. There, amongst the tapestries and flickering candles, Tulwryn attempted to wait out the transformation, hoping that the nausea would leave him so as he could orient himself with his new surroundings and slay the man he came to kill.

But once again, the gods seemed to hear him naught and his prayers fell on deaf ears, for even though the Khan's royal guards did not notice the warrior in their midst, the dark Khan certainly did. Rising from the cushions of his Ivory Throne, Kimark Khan roared at the mystic intruder.

"How dare ye breech mine sanctum," screamed the warrior-wizard, spittle frothed from his wet lips staining his blue-black beard as his menacing his eyes frantically searched the room. The dark Khan, sensing the shade rather than seeing him, resorted to using his grim sorcery to spy out the intruder.

"I know ye are hither, rogue," he said. "I can smell thee. Show yourself at once, and I will promise you a quick and painless death. Toy with me any longer though, and thou will suffer unnamable horrors of endless punishment!"

Remembering what Cohado said about his vulnerability, Tulwryn tried to steel himself against revealing his location ere he regain his corporeal form. However, the dark Khan's tauntings roused his wrath, and he was eager to lock blades with the dog and cut him down.

All of a sudden, and in a fit of rage, Kimark Khan drew steel and dove from the royal dais down to the marble floor of the court. As the Bloodsword hissed from its scabbard rage and fury grew in Tulwryn's heart as he spied the man who dared wield his blade.

Tulwryn could restrain himself no longer, and in an instant, he was rushing toward the dark Khan with fire in his eyes. The warrior-wizard saw the shade of Tulwryn the warrior bounding toward him and instantly realized his dilemma. He re-sheathed the Bloodsword, and then spun on his heels toward the attacking ghost.

"A steel blade might not kill a demon," laughed the Khan, "but mine sorcery certainly will. Prepare to meet thy doom, ye son of a lice infected dog, as I chant the incantation of endless punishment!"

The new king of Phaedron raised his hands and began chanting in some strange and foreign tongue, attempting to dissolve Tulwryn's shade by means of magic and send his soul into eternal torment.

"Byadh mokkulh, byadh bizel-ahad, abe abe abe abhudalh!" But something was amiss, for rather than dissolve, Tulwryn's shade suddenly materialized into his true physical form. Fear clung to the bones of Kimark Khan as he watched the shrieking warrior descend upon him and a blinding rage.

The warrior, still running toward the king, stumbled and fell. A rush of nausea swept over him, but was gone in an instant. Looking up from the marble floor, Tulwryn gazed into the mad eyes of Kimark Khan; unbelief saturated the king. And then suddenly, the two men were alone in the courtroom.

"What sorcery is this," cried the warrior-wizard, "where my entire legion of warriors and guards are made to vanish before mine sight."

Raising himself on his powerful loins, and stretching his arms to test their strength and flexibility, Tulwryn laughed.

"It seem that thy power is gone, ye worthless thief. Cohado must have been successful in destroying thy precious Scrystone."

"Cohado? The Keeper of Lies, still alive after all these centuries?" Rage and fury welled up in the dark Khan's heart at the mention of Cohado's name. "Very well then, I will slay him after I cut ye down. I see that ye have regained thy true form. Shall we now test our steel then?"

Without a thought, Tulwryn bared his dagger, a thousand shards of light reflect off the large emerald encrusted in the weapon's hilt as the Bloodsword leapt from the scabbard of Kimark Khan. The two warriors circle each other like hungry lions, each looking for a weakness in the other.

Tulwryn, armed with only his bejeweled dagger, a common weapon of regular steel . . .

"What," he thought quickly to himself, "regular steel vs. the Bloodsword?" In that instant, the dark Khan attacked with blinding speed, thrusting the crimson blade in a frontal assault. Tulwryn dodged the blade and parried with his own. Slash, parry, chop . . . Stab, block, slash . . . broadsword against dagger, two men locked in the heat of mortal combat where the fate of the world rides on the blade of the victor.

The warrior from Nuvia spun on his heel and then dropped to one knee. Faster than the eye could follow, his dagger leaped out and back like the tongue of a serpent and a thin red line emerged across the left thigh of Kimark Khan.

"Damn ye rogue," cried the Khan. "Thou hast cut me!"

"It won't be the last time mine blade tastes your filthy blood," answered Tulwryn. "Come and get some more, you cur!"

Charging like a wounded tiger, the dark Khan attacked. He feigned an overhead slash with the Bloodsword and Tulwryn ducked, only to be knocked to the hard marble floor by a heavy blow from Kimark Khan's large knotted fist.

Shaking stars from his hair, Tulwryn rolled and rose to one knee ere the Khan could deliver the fatal overhead stab. The

Bloodsword stuck marble and crimson sparks showered the hero from Nuvia. Rolling in front of his attacker, Tulwryn bolted up to a standing position as Kimark Khan swung his blade wild for a follow up, second attack. The Bloodsword bit only air as Tulwryn stepped inside the dark Khan's guard. Grabbing the man's sword wrist with his free hand, Tulwryn spun Kimark Khan around and delivered a powerful knee strike to his exposed stomach. The warrior-wizard reeled back and fell, gasping for breath.

Diving on his grounded adversary, Tulwryn grappled Kimark Khan and the two fought hard for top honors in this battle to the death. The two warriors, locked in each other's unforgiving embrace, struggled to their knees. Grappling, sword and dagger inches away from the other's vitals, the two manage to struggle to their feet. Suddenly, the emerald on Tulwryn's dagger hilt began to blaze and yet, Tulwryn felt the power coming from within him rather than the weapon. A blinding flash of light knocked the two apart and they fell, sprawling across the court. Bounding to his feet, the dark Khan, in a fit of bloodlust and fury, raised the Bloodsword and attacked. "Die for once, ye son of a maggot," screamed Kimark Khan!

Tulwryn, still on his knees, and somewhat drained, raised his dagger in defense to Kimark Khan's assault. Again, the emerald on Tulwryn's dagger hilt blazed hot as the green flame lashed out at its victim. The blast smote the hand of the dark Khan causing him to drop his blade. At once, Tulwryn threw his dagger at Kimark Khan and dove for the Bloodsword. The dark Khan dodged the thrown blade, and then jumped on the warrior from Nuvia attempting to wrestle the crimson sword from his foe's iron grip.

In a heap of limbs, the two combatants began a primitive ritual, trading heavy blows whilst still on their knees. In the blink of an eye, a blinding flame jetted out from the blade of the Bloodsword and engulfed the entire chamber in a massive celestial fire.

Instantly, the physical body of Kimark Khan was burned to

ash, but from the scorching inferno came a voice that ripped though eternity:

"I shall return . . . one day, I shall return and I shall wreak my vengeance upon you and all your descendants as I have done this day to those of the House of Zula . . . Tulwryn Bloodsword, know this, that ye are cursed from this day forward, for I shall return!"

Crawling on hands and knees, Tulwryn took up the Bloodsword and hurried out of the burning palace, unscathed. Once through the main door of the courtroom and out into the hall, Tulwryn rose to his feet and jogged down the corridor that led out of the crumbling building.

Thinking of the final words of the dark Khan, Tulwryn chuckled silently to himself.

"Ha," he said, "I am already cursed, for the weight of the Bloodsword is upon me as well as the dark burden I carry in my heart. I fear not your feeble curses, wizard. I bested you this day; I will best ye again!"

And looking down at that grim blade, Tulwryn's heart was lifted for a charge well met. He turned and walked out of the palace of Phaedron into the light of day, and witnessed the city in ruins.

* * *

A raven wheeled across the skies over Phaedron as a single warrior strode through the cobbled streets of that ruined city. Doubtless, there were some survivors of the siege, but Tulwryn saw them not. Down a deserted alley, the warrior glanced, only to see stumbling before him, the robed figure of a battle weary dwarf.

"Well met, Tulwryn," cried the dwarf.

The warrior spun on his toes and lifted his blade. Dillwyn approached the armed man and then laughed as he lowered his hood.

"I am surprised to see thee, mine friend. After that blast rocked the city, all the fighting ceased. I suppose the Khan is dead?"

"Aye," answered Tulwryn, "as dead as an immortal wizard can be I guess. Anyhow, I thought you were supposed to be spying. It looks as if you were engaged in the actual battle instead."

"For true. When the fighting started, I could not restrain myself. Once I espied a fallen warrior, and seen his fine blade lying in the sun, I rushed in and swooped up the weapon. It was blood and carnage ever since."

"Ha! I knew ye to be a warrior and naught a wizard," laughed Tulwryn, "'Tis strange indeed to see thee out of thine armor."

The two walked on, talking about the battle and about one another's adventurers. For hours, it seemed, they walked through the empty streets of Phaedron, witnessing the damage done by the evil of greed and power. After a time, the two made their way to the main gate of the city and without looking back, they left Phaedron behind.

It was the better part of a week ere Cohado arrived at Tulwryn and the dwarf's camp. The warrior feared the worse, for neither Adi not the Woodling accompanied the wizard. Instead, there was a tall, thin man in their place. The stranger wore neither the robes of a cleric or the armor of a warrior, but rather, the simple raiment of a farmer. His face was handsome, with dark eyes and olive hued skin; long tawny locks tumbled unkempt over sun-browned shoulders.

"Well met," Cohado called out as he and the stranger entered the warrior's camp. "Friends, allow me to introduce Ja'Que the Blessed, a descendent of Lord Jerrod Baylor and the rightful heir to the throne of Phaedron. Ja'Que here, vows to rebuild the city to its former glory and bring peace to the whole of Phantasodyssea."

Dillwyn glanced at the man and then at Tulwryn. "So the others . . ."

"Dead," answered Cohado in a most grieving tone. "She offered herself, and took a dagger blade that was meant for me. She did it to save you, Tulwryn. She knew that had I died ere the stone was destroyed you'd have been vulnerable to the dark Khan's magics. If it's any consolation, she says that she waits for thee."

Tulwryn did not answer, but just sat there, saturated in his own pain. Ja'Que, trying to break the somber mood of the moment, thrust out his hand in friendship to the warrior and the dwarf. Tulwryn took the man's hand and couldn't help noticing the strong grip. Certainly, this was not the hand of a nobleman, but a common laborer. Strange, indeed, he thought to himself, the twists that fate often take.

"Here, master Tulwryn," said the new king of Phaedron, "I want thee to have this." And he thrust a pouch of Phaedronian gold into the warrior's large hand. He offered the same to Dillwyn, but the dwarf refused the reward saying that where he was headed, money was not needed.

And so it was, that the evil House of Zula had been destroyed ending their dark two hundred year reign of tyranny, and the Ivory Throne of Phaedron returned to the bloodline of Phaedron's true and righteous kings. Cohado, the strange and mystical priest of Rhyan, headed east, back to the Fidelity, docked in a distant cove near the Fords of Doom, and Dillwyn the dwarf, still wearing the black robes of a Covensted adept, traveled afoot east to that village, and to a dear friend's cottage. And Tulwryn Bloodsword, seated on the back of a large Phaedronian warhorse, with that grim crimson blade once again hanging loosely at his hip and a pouch full of royal gold strung about his neck, rode south for another adventure . . . alone.

Here ends Book Two

BOOK III

The Flesh Merchant

Blethno lominpye mortu
Lythno lominpye panyanu

Birth guarantees death
Life guarantees suffering

All about him, fronds of ferns and flowers nodded their heads in an ominous breeze. The silence was deafening, the fragrance bewitching. Suddenly, there came a crashing from above as if some great flapping beast was descending upon him. His heart jumped up to his throat, but ere he could even sit up, a strong and sinewy net enveloped him. In an instant, he was surrounded by five burly men in heavy leather jerkins and beige pantaloons, all bearing war clubs. Tulwryn struggled to get to his feet, but his fight was in vain. A tall rogue swung his heavy cudgel and Tulwryn knew nothing more; and fell silent on the damp ground of Darkwood.

SYNOPSIS OF BOOK THREE

It had been over five years since Tulwryn Bloodsword defeated the dark Khan and restored peace to the citadel of Phaedron, and in that time he had traveled far and wide, first south, and then west again, searching for the clues that would free him from his dark burden. But no clues came and he continued to carry the weight of the kinslaying on his blackened soul. Only the act of killing his foes would ease the pain of his anguish, yet even now, soon after the grim battle on the parched land of the Golrin Prairie had ended, the weight of his burden was once again on him, and he grieved.

Tulwryn was a man of forty-three years, and in that time, he had seen many things, both horrible and miraculous. He trafficked naught in dark sorcery, but lived by the strength of his sword arm and the will in his heart. This alone gave him the power to endure the curse that the gods had laid upon him.

But yet, his curse would prove his salvation, for he and the Bloodsword were one, and in this fact, Tulwryn, the grim warrior of Heidmar, had caught the eye of Octavia, the princess of Neturu. But the princess herself had caught the eye of Yalad Munstur, an evil flesh merchant and trader of virgins. Yalad had struck a vile deal with Chief Talbod, the king of the Forbidden Island, to kidnap the princess and deliver her for a ransom more valuable than gold or jewels, for Yalad craved the power of sorcery over all else.

And so, once again, Tulwryn was called upon by the powers of the land to use his might and main, and the strength of the Bloodsword, to intervene where even the gods cannot go, for the fate of Phantasodyssea was bound to the princess Octavia and Tulwryn was her only hope.

And here continues the heroic saga of Tulwryn Bloodsword. Embark with him on a fantastic odyssey as he battles his way across parched desert and over the high seas in pursuit of Yalad Munster, the *Flesh Merchant*.

ONE

Blades over Golrin

Blood dripped from the sword in Tulwryn's wet hand and all about him lay countless dead. The whole of the Golrin Prairie had become a graveyard; bodies littered the ground for as far as the eye could see.

Tulwryn stood amidst the dead, and dying, under the relentless heat of the blazing sun, apparently the sole survivor of a long and exhausting battle. Weary with fatigue, the warrior waded through the crimson corpses that stained the parched prairie a deep ruddy scarlet. A sea of red gore engulfed him, and a thousand shards of sparkling sunlight gleamed like burning razors reflecting off the maile and broken blades of the fallen.

It had been over five years since he had defeated the dark Khan and restored peace to the citadel of Phaedron, and in that time he had traveled far and wide, first south, and then west again, searching for the clues that would free him from his dark burden. But no clues came and he continued to carry the weight of the kinslaying on his blackened soul. Only the act of killing his foes would ease the pain of his anguish, yet even now, soon after the battle had ended, the weight of his burden was once again on him, and he grieved.

Tulwryn was a man of forty-three years, and in that time, he had seen many things, both horrible and miraculous. He trafficked naught in dark sorcery, but lived by the strength of his sword arm and the will in his heart. This alone gave him the power to endure the curse that the gods had laid upon him.

And what of the gods, he often thought to himself? Many priests and sorcerers and wizards had their theories, but how many possessed the truth? Certainly there were those who claimed to have come face to face with their deities. But just as certain, these same charlatans did so under the influence of heavy intoxicants and bitter narcotics. What truths can be found in such practices? If the truths of reality were so easily grasped, then every drunkard would be a priest, every drug addict, a wizard. Tulwryn laughed to himself. Yes, he knew there were forces at work beyond the veil of human site, but likewise, he knew than no matter how those forces were defined by the human tongue, those grim definitions would always fall short of the real truth.

Anyhow, wizardry and magic and even the gods did not concern Tulwryn. All he cared about was quieting the roaring misery of the burden that he carried. And so, he wandered endlessly over the face of the world, living by the strength the gods had bequeathed him.

Tulwryn had squandered much of the gold that Ja'Que the Blessed had given him for defeating Kimark Khan, dead five summers past. Two moons prior, he had come up from the south and entered the wealthy city of Golrin in hopes to sell his sword arm to the highest bidder and regain his status in the world. But five years plays hard on a man's reputation and none remembered the warrior that saved Phaedron, so he was forced to leave the city, penniless and in shame.

Aimlessly, he wandered the prairie until he came across two great hosts engaged in battle. There, he reckoned to carve out a place for himself and thus, he entered the fray, naked, save for a long loinclout of soiled white homespun linen and rawhide sandals. In his right hand, he carried his only weapon, a grim blade of crimson steel a yard long, and straight: *the Bloodsword.*

Utilizing his battlefield experience, he immediately summed up the strengths and weaknesses of the two hosts, and determined which side he would assist, if any. He cared naught about the political reasons of their war, for he was not a crusader. Tulwryn fought for his own cause, and for the lust of battle that would silence his pain, even for a moment. Yet, there was something that always beckoned to his sense of right. Perhaps it was his Nuvian upbringing. Or possibly, it was the Prophecy of the Bloodsword itself. Most likely, none will ever know, least of all Tulwryn.

In a blink of an eye, he made his decision and threw caution to the wind barreling headlong into the seething mass of armored men. His bare chest and naked arms, browned by years of wandering under the hot southern sun of Phantasodyssea, startled the maile clad warriors, for never had they witnessed such blinding ferocity and rage, nor had they ever seen a naked man spewing death as easily as did Tulwryn.

Armored men fell before the weight and fury of his sword, and he walked unscathed through the grinding mill of sword, axe blade, and arrow. Even the pikemen fell to the naked warrior with the scarlet blade. His long black hair billowed in the breeze and his dark eyes shone with the grim gleam of death, gritting his teeth, he slew until there were none left to slay.

Yet, that was then. And now the battle was over, so he walked amongst the dead seeking for anything usable. A good pair of boots, perhaps a cotton tunic, or even a small pouch of coppers would have been gleefully accepted. But Tulwryn saw quickly that to find any of these things would have been a miracle. For looking at the fallen warriors, Tulwryn's heart became heavy. Something was wrong here. These were no majestic armies, but two paltry bands of desert rats fighting over the same scrap of worthless wilderness. He noticed that the warriors of both hosts were clad in old and rusted maile; even their steel blades were pitted with specks of brown rust. There would be nothing worth keeping this day, and Tulwryn's mind reeled as to why these men eagerly threw their lives away for apparently nothing.

Suddenly, from the corner of Tulwryn's eye a faint movement startled him and he spun around, sword in hand, still dripping to its hilt with chunky crimson gore. Less than fifty paces away he espied a man approaching him afoot. His black skin, bright yellow hair, and glowing red eyes, told Tulwryn that he was no Golrin rebel but a lone Knobite warrior come to loot the dead of the battlefield.

"Hold there," yelled Tulwryn, his mighty baritone voice carried across the plain like the ferocious roar of a lion. But he could see that the Knobite was not impressed or afraid. "Stand back, dog, or I'll feed the black belly a yard of mine steel.

Perhaps the cannibal did not understand Tulwryn's warning, for he spoke the Golrin tongue with a rough Nuvian accent. The cannibal merely hissed, baring a mouthful of razor sharp teeth.

Tulwryn had heard of these men-beasts before; a race of humans, more akin to animals than man, who lived a fairly nomadic lifestyle in the southern reaches of the vast Golrin prairie. Their cannibalistic tendencies were vile; their warriors ceremonially filed their teeth into sharp points, for eating the bodies of the dead or for weapons in battle, none knew for certain. Yet, fierce they were, and a plague of the southern prairie.

With blinding speed, the Knobite hurdled corpses and sprinted toward Tulwryn, hissing a terrible rage and frothing at the mouth. The man-beast was completely naked, yet carried a lone slender shaft of maple, as tall as a man and topped with a flint blade, nineteen inches in length, of polished obsidian.

Tulwryn, screaming his famous war cry, charged the fighter with an intensity the Knobite had never before seen. When the black warrior was almost on him, Tulwryn stopped on a dime, and dropped to one knee. Spinning to the left, the Bloodsword licked out like the tongue of an angry serpent, but the cannibal was faster, and his tall lithe body easily dodged the crimson blade by a hair's breadth.

Now the two foes circled each other like a pair of hungry wolves fighting over a single scrap of tainted meat. The eyes of both men were fraught with battle madness, and in that instant Tulwryn knew that his soul had merged with the wilds of the land; he had finally become a raw savage in the truest definition of the word. Between him and this cannibal, there was no difference.

The Knobite lunged with the blade of his spear and Tulwryn

ducked, but a breath later, he was knocked to the ground by the butt end of the Knobite's spearshaft, swung like a club by the skillful black warrior. Tulwryn went down to one knee, the Bloodsword still vertical before him, in the guard position. A second later, the spear was fast again flying toward his face, the Knobite screaming in a death frenzied rage. Tulwryn curled himself into a ball, then by the strength of his mighty loins, rocketed himself into the air. The cannibal's flint blade caught him in the shoulder and opened a deep gash, but Tulwryn's momentum was carrying him up hard and the spear's blow did not stop his aerial assault. The beast-man bared his razor fangs for a savage bite, but with one smooth motion, Tulwryn's right fist, still clutching the crimson sword, slammed into the Knobite's jaw shattering teeth and bone. Tulwryn followed through with the strike, then in a flash, reversed the blade with a powerful backhand. The Bloodsword sheered effortlessly through flesh, bone, and organs, rending the body of the Knobite warrior in twain.

His bronze chest heaving from the intensity of the fight, and splattered with blood and offal from head to foot, Tulwryn glanced down at the dead man at his feet, and wondered what madness spawned such a race that they would fill their bellies with the raw flesh of other men. In disgust, he turned and walked away from the battlefield, disregarding the gaping wound in his left shoulder.

The hot southern sun was inching its way across the colorless sky over the prairie, and Tulwryn realized that it would be night soon. He did not fancy the idea that he would be caught at night in the unforgiving wilderness of Golrin, especially since he had no way of knowing if there were more Knobite's around. Certainly, the warrior was not acting alone, he thought. Indeed, Knobites usually hunted in packs of a dozen or more, and as soon as the one he slayed came up missing, the others would relentlessly search out the killer of their brethren.

Still, this was not what was puzzling Tulwryn. Why had he slayed with steel alone, he pondered? Not in five years had the

Shadow of the Bloodsword spoken to him, nor had he been able to evoke its celestial fire in battle. It seemed that the power of the Bloodsword had waned, or even left him, yet his scarred hands still bore the scarlet brand of the blade.

Glancing down at his open palms, his mind swam in confusion. Pushing the grim thoughts of the Bloodsword away, Tulwryn continued his trek south, looking for a suitable shelter whereby he could elude the Knobites for the night. Better to survive the night, he thought, and then face them all on the morrow. Dying in the bright of the day, like a warrior, whereas he could look his foes in the eye troubled him naught; but being poached at night like a cowering beast in hiding did.

Off in the distance, a lone wolf bayed as the sun set on the western horizon and the large silver disk of the moon appeared in the eastern sky. Yet, it sounded more like the laughing of hyenas or the insidious chuckle of jackals than the howls of wolves, and Tulwryn once again wondered what fell tricks the gods were playing on him.

Thus ends Chapter One of Book Three

TWO

The Princess of Neturu

The whole of the Golrin Prairie was a flat green table with light greenish-yellow grasses that swayed in the soft breezes of the day. Few trees dotted the land and those that did were stunted and twisted. Off in the distance, a small black dot of a man trekked southward in hopes of eluding a score of Knobite cannibals hungry for vengeance, and more. Suddenly a slender hand delicately dipped into the Great Pool of Neturu and the vision of the man on the prairie faded under the azure concentric rings trailing the lithe fingers of that delicate hand.

Just then, a man, tall and handsome, strode out through the large bronze doors and exited the Neturuian Temple of the Cat. Past the two large marble lions, the man walked, and silently approached the young girl sitting beside the cool waters of the pool. From his girdle hung a short sword, its scabbard gilded like the robe he wore, yet its ebon hilt was encrusted with a scarab of lapis lazuli. In his right hand, he gripped an ivory walking staff topped with a large blue sapphire that sparkled like living flame.

"What art thou doing, sister," asked the man as he drew near the young girl sitting by the pool. He was elegant, with strong limbs and a heavy chest yet light of waist. The man wore a short toga of fine golden silk, gilded knee-high sandals of silk and leather, and there were bright yellow poppies laced through his dark tresses, which hung limply down over his wide olive hued shoulders. The girl, favoring the man's sturdy features, looked up at him though tear-stained eyes. She also wore the golden toga of the royal class of Neturu, but in her dark hair were woven pink poppies and she was barefoot, save for the sparkling rubies and emeralds that graced her dainty golden toe rings.

"I am watching my savior," she sobbed, and then turned her beautiful face back toward the pool. The man approached her and gazed into the depth of the water watching the tragedy unfold. The man on the prairie was being followed by a band of savage cannibals, and they were closing the distance at an alarming rate.

"Dost thou truly think he is the one, Octavia," asked Branjadom.

"Yes, I do. The prophecies foretell . . ." she was saying, but was abruptly interrupted by her brothers prompt words.

"But look," he said, in an arrogant and vile tone, "he runs from the savages! Even now, prophesy or no, he carries the blade of death but does not call on its power to defeat his enemies. Perhaps he has lost the power. How long have you been watching him, five turnings of the great wheel of the seasons? And in all that time has he evoked the power? No! Perhaps the prophecies are wrong. It wouldn't be the first time, ye know."

Octavia turned and glared at her brother, a look of frustrated anger welling up in her royal veins. It was true, for the past five years she had sat there, by the Great Pool of Neturu and gazed upon the life of Tulwryn. She had watched him go from being the savior of Phaedron after defeating the vile warrior-wizard Kimark Khan, to becoming a penniless adventurer, squandering his wealth and reputation on wine and women, but yet she never lost hope in the fact that he was the one. Indeed, her heart sank at the idea that one of such noble and honorable status could recede to such lowliness, but she knew of his grim burden and hoped that one day the gods would put things aright and set Tulwryn on the path to his destiny once again.

"Brother," said she, "Tulwryn is a great warrior. He fears naught man, beast, nor gods, and if he is running from those savages then I for one believe there is good reason."

"Ha! Look at your mighty warrior now," laughed Branjadom, pointing with his sapphire tipped staff. "The Knobites surround him with a crude and barbaric tactic. A great warrior would never have allowed himself in such a sad state."

"Why must you always criticize Tulwryn," she screamed. "Art thou jealous of his prowess in battle, my dear brother?"

"What, me jealous of that drunken barbarian? Dear sister, I am a Neturuian. Every race in Phantasodyssea deems us gods, and this is so, at least as mortals are concerned. So why do you suggest that I am jealous of such a man as that Nuvian rogue?"

Octavia looked at him intensely, her dark eyes penetrating his very soul, and Branjadom stirred because he knew that she realized his jealousy. And jealous he was, not of the man Tulwryn, but because he knew his sister truly loved the warrior and this troubled him profoundly. Never in the history of the world had a Neturuian wedded any outside their godlike race, and to even contemplate such an act was a blasphemy to their existence. But the Neturuian royal knew deep in his heart that Octavia wanted Tulwryn as her own, to bring him into the royal house, and make him a god. This Branjadom could not allow.

"Octavia," he whispered, "There are other men more suitable for thine love. Please reconsider your true motives; it is just a young girl's lust that stirs in thy breast, not true love."

"How do you know what stirs in mine heart, brother," the girl scowled in foaming rage. She sprang up and wheeled at him in the blink of an eye, a short straight dagger clenched tight in her petite hand. But in a heartbeat, the man's massive hand had flashed out and held the girl's frail wrist in an iron grip.

"You wouldst slay thy own brother," he asked, "over that Nuvian dog? What has gotten into you?"

Squirming in vain to get free, the girl writhed like a helpless insect caught in the claws of a mantis. Branjadom squeezed harder on the slender wrist and Octavia moaned under the pain. "Release me, damn you."

In an instant, the dagger dropped from the girl's numb grasp and the man dashed his captive to the cold stone ground. She looked up at him through her tangled black locks; hate seething through her body like a storm.

"Remember this, Octavia," Branjadom said, "if we are to be worshipped as gods in this world, then we must act like gods. No Neturuian has ever mated, let alone wedded, with an outsider. Put this nonsense out of your mind or you will destroy everything that our ancestors have worked so hard to accomplish. We have what we have because of the guise we live by. Destroy that guise and you destroy Neturu. I will not let you do that, by Bast!"

"Do you not understand," she begged, "Tulwryn is the chosen one. I did not choose him, the gods chose him! Yes, I am attracted to him. Perhaps I even love him. But in truth, we are not gods, just a superior race, strong and intelligent. If, by some act of fate, I am able to wed with this man whom the gods have chosen for greatness, it will not destroy Neturu, but elevate us to the status of real gods. Canst thou naught see this?"

Branjadom knelt before his enraged sister and stroked her hair with a gentle hand. In soft words he spoke: "Octavia, mother and father are gone and you and I are all that is left of the ruling class of Neturu. Our people deserve better than this drunken cur. You may be the royal princess of Neturu, but you are very young, and still it will be many years ere you are of the marrying age. Perhaps this Tulwryn will be slain ere you can wed him. He doesn't even know you exist. What thinks you that he will choose you anyway? And moreover, it seems that every woman that loves him falls to a grim end. Is that what you wish for yourself and your people?"

She sat quiet and did not answer. Shaking his head, the man stood up and walked away. Octavia waited until he was gone, then she brushed the tangled black mane from her eyes, straightened her toga, and crawled back to the pool's edge. For many hours, she sat there gazing into the deep azure waters watching her warrior, her savior.

Thus ends Chapter Two of Book Three

THREE

Cannibals in the West

All through the night, Tulwryn sat listening to the howls of wolves, knowing full well that the fearful sounds he heard were not wolves, nor hyenas, nor jackals, but the grim communications of the band of Knobite cannibals that were following him. For most of the night, he trekked south, but after fatigue gripped his mind and body, he was forced to cease his run and make for a shelter. This, he chose, was a hollowed out trunk of a small prairie elm. Wriggling his strong frame into the narrow gap, he pulled his knees up to his chest and with his chin propped upon his knees, he nodded off to a restless sleep; his left hand still clenching the scabbard of the Bloodsword.

Slowly, and without fear, Tulwryn's tired mind drifted off to a grey and misty dream world, full of amazing and wonderful things. He was at once in a great marble hall and surrounded by a myriad of beautiful dancing girls. There was a soft piping music wafting through the air, as well as exotic scents such as the fragrances of burning incense like sandalwood, and lotus, and asafetida. The girls, naked save for their thin gossamer gowns of peach and vermilion, and their equally flimsy veils of purples and oranges and yellows, added to the musical piping as they danced, their soft bare feet stamping out a lustful tune that stirred Tulwryn's heart.

One lithe beauty, a voluptuous redhead with a heaving bosom, thin waist, and wide hips, danced close to him on soft cat feet. The twinkle of her peridot and amethyst encrusted toe rings played havoc on his mind and he reached for her, but she was faster and eluded him. With a long slender finger she beckoned him, and he rose from his mahogany dais and followed her into the midst of the others. Tulwryn, clothed in the royal pomp of a prince, was tossed to and fro on a sea of passion as the dancing beauties pressed against his iron muscles. Time and time again, he reached for a girl, but alas, his trembling hands never touched flesh. Frustrated, he dove with all of his might only to fall on the cold marble floor of that large hall.

Quickly, as a jungle cat, he was once again on his feet. Sounds of laughter boomed in his ears and he could see the girls giggling at his drunkenness. Steaming with lust, he grabbed at the gown of a brunette, and then a blonde, and then the redhead again, but time and again, his groping fingers gained nothing. Suddenly, a horrific change overshadowed him and his blood became as ice in his veins. The girls, once beautiful and alluring, became as one, and their countenance resembled that of his wife Durayn, long since dead.

In a fit of rage and panic Tulwryn woke from his slumber, and exited one nightmare only to enter another. Still seated within the confines of the elm, the muscles of his thighs and calves ached from the many leagues he had ran, as well as from the cramped conditions of his makeshift shelter. Outside, beyond the safety of his shelter, he heard nothing.

Through squinted eyes, Tulwryn gazed out from the narrow crevice whence he had crawled to his sanctuary, into coal blackness. The night was darker than he had ever remembered, and he had no idea of how many more hours he would have to remain in hiding ere the sun rise and he return to his task at hand, trekking south and evading the cannibals that tracked him still. For certain, thought he, that he would face many warriors this day. Slay some, he would, but in the end, he too would fall. This he knew. A shudder of appalling hideousness ran up his spine at the thought of his flesh being digested in the bowels of the surviving Knobites. He tried hard to shake the visions from his wracked brain.

Time seemed to stand still in the darkness that surrounded him and he passed the hours by wandering through his memories. First, Tulwryn released the scabbard of the Bloodsword and grabbed at his mighty hand axe. A thousand thoughts ran through his brain about the man who gifted him the weapon. What was Dillwyn Anvilhand doing at this time, wondered Tulwryn, surely not holed up in some hollow tree trunk hiding from seething cannibals. He chuckled softly to himself at the irony of the situation.

Dillwyn always fared better than most, Tulwryn realized, but the idea of him leaving the adventurer life for a placid hovel in Covensted confused him. Destinies are a strange lot, and never in a million years would he have thought his mighty friend from Carthus would forsake warring and looting for the life of a soothsayer. A sigh escaped his thin parched lips for he missed the dwarf's company.

His mind then went on to other things. He remembered past adventures with the northern barbarians, like the heroic War of the Dragon, and even lesser fights like the Battle of Gerdmor Gorge. He recalled slaying the Great War Wolf, which in essence was really the traitor Vogelmir the Bold, ensorcelled by the evil witch of Heidmar. Tulwryn's heart then sank low, for he pained for Halgi, and Durayn, and his four sons.

How long he sat there thinking, none can say. But an eternity of thoughts and adventures ran past him in an unbroken stream of crimson fury. Suddenly, as if stirring from a dream, Tulwryn noticed the blue of morning creeping in around him and decided the time as good as any to crawl from his shelter and renew his trek southward.

Like a newborn babe, Tulwryn emerged from the womb of that dead elm on numb and aching legs. His loins burned from the many hours he had sat in the cramped shelter. Rolling onto his back, he painfully stretched his sore legs and willed life back into them. In a matter of moments, his Nuvian constitution surging through him with even greater will to survive; he roused himself from the prairie floor and began his run south.

He hadn't gone more than two score of paces when he saw the first Knobite, off to his left and brandishing a long spear. Tulwryn quickened his pace, knowing that the warrior was not alone in his hunting, but before another breath was taken, he saw the others.

The day was hot and the sky was a searing white over the pale green of the prairie table. Tulwryn, desperate as a cornered badger, turned his course from south to west and ran like the wind. In a matter of time, the blood mad cannibals would be on him, yet he knew he would sell his life at a heavy cost and many would parish on the flat of Golrin ere they taste his flesh.

Why he turned west, he knew naught, instinct perhaps, or just dumb luck. The reason mattered little, what mattered was that he put as much space betwixt his pursuers as possible ere the fight began. He had all but lost confidence in the ability of the sword to strike down a multitude of enemies, yet his burning palms told him different. Still, he could keep his pace for many hours, turning to engage a fighter here and there in single combat, hoping to avoid being surrounded and swarmed to death in a frenzy of mad lust.

For an hour he ran, with the howls of lust and vengeance hounding at his heels. Farther west he ran, his mighty bronze chest heaved and his heart was to the point of bursting. Suddenly, the worse happened and his doom became reality. Once again, Tulwryn felt abandoned by his gods and he cursed a grim oath, for all about him in a great circle were a score of hungry Knobite cannibals.

Surrounded, and with no possible hope of escape, Tulwryn stopped and unsheathed the Bloodsword. Some of the grim warriors stood silent, knowing they had trapped their prey. Others dropped to all fours and began howling in triumph over their victory.

"What are ye dogs waiting for," yelled the angry Nuvian with the crimson blade. "Come and taste mine steel." He held the sword aloft and the Knobites shook their heads in wonder at a blade that seemed wet with blood even though the battle was not yet fought.

In an instant, the cannibals charged. Twenty black bodies hurled themselves in a blind rush of red fury at the lone man in their center. Tulwryn chose the largest of the men and attacked him first. With a mighty blow, the Knobite was rendered headless, a sprawling corpse spurting a trail of red on the green prairie. With a quick backhand, the Bloodsword tore through another's midsection, and a spray of scarlet droplets soared through the air as another cannibal fell to Tulwryn's angry wrath.

Tulwryn's wounded shoulder, slightly healed from his first battle with the lone Knobite only a day earlier, once again began to bleed after a strike from an assailant opened the wound anew. Pain shot through his body, but Tulwryn maintained his focus and ignored the throbbing shoulder. Many of the warriors, excited to see their prey bleeding freshly, renewed their bloodlust and hardened their attack.

With a howl of lust and fury, Tulwryn fought like a man with nothing to lose. The minutes seemed like hours and one by one, the Knobites fell under the weight of his sword. In a mad desperate rush, the last two warriors swarmed down on the Nuvian with an intensity unremembered in bygone days of battle. The man on the right charged hard, his spear held high toward Tulwryn's head; the man on his left aimed low. Tulwryn, with the reaction of a panther and not taking the time to think, dropped to one knee and then bounded hard toward the man coming to his right. Like a human bullet, the steel body of the Nuvian slammed into the Knobite knocking him off his feet. Tulwryn went down in a ball of elbows and knees, then sprang up to his feet and turned to the other cannibal.

The Knobite's eyes were white orbs of fear as he witnessed the impossible, for flying toward him at unbelievable speed was a heavy hand axe. Before the man could duck out of the way, the short blade of the axe bit deep into his face, splitting his head to his teeth.

Wiping the grime of battle from his brow, Tulwryn languidly strode to the Knobite warrior, still lying unconscious on the ground. With a howl of triumph, he raised the crimson blade and drove the man through. The body shuddered under the pressure of the steel, and then fell silent.

Tulwryn tore the Bloodsword from the dead body and once again glanced at the gore stained blade asking silently why the spirit of the sword had not aided him in his fight. For five years, the story was the same: Steel felled his enemies, but the command of the sword's power, and the ability to evoke its celestial flame, was not to be his. He sighed.

"To hell with this damned prophecy," he cursed. Just then, he caught a glimpse of a great form soaring high overhead and had a strange and unnerving feeling that he was being watched from afar by grim wizardly eyes.

The beast wheeled and turned in the white sky, and the hair on Tulwryn's nape bristled as he saw the thing. The creature was not a bird, but a monster of huge proportions, with the body of a cat and the leathern wings of a dragon. He raised his sword and released a great yell of defiance. The thing, paying him no heed simply disappeared in the glare of the noonday sun.

Laughing at his apparent easy victory, he shrugged his shoulders and walked to the dead Knobite with a cleaved head. He retrieved his hand axe, shoved it into his belt, and started again his long walk south.

Thus ends Chapter Three of Book Three

FOUR

The Silver Saber

In a shadow haunted corner of the Silver Saber, Kemet's most notorious tavern, home to countless bloodthirsty pirates and cutthroats, sat half a dozen desperate men. They were crammed like sardines in a curtained booth where the odor of salty fish, stale beer, and unclean bodies permeated the rank air of the establishment. The six dirty faces seemed not to notice the horrid conditions as they sat around the oak table, arguing their next job of plunder.

A small oil lamp cast its amber glow from the center of the table, and soft shadows danced off hard faces, reflecting shards of light that bounced from silver earrings, golden teeth, and eyes ablaze with greedy hate.

"And how are we supposed to pull this off," asked a robust pirate, his breadth twice that of a normal man. He was Ulrich Mancrusher, a Kemetian outlaw that was wanted in half a dozen cities throughout Phantasodyssea as well as for crimes committed on the high seas. His blue-black beard was long and unkempt, and a patch was covering his left eye, from under which a long pale scar wound its way, serpent-like, across his darkly lined face.

The man across from Ulrich answered in a low and uncaring tone.

"I care not how ye snatch the lass," said Yalad Munstur, "just as long as she is intact and unharmed at the time of deposit. Mokksbod is almost upon us, and if my plan is to succeed, then we need to act fast. Chief Talbod has already given word that we will have his protection if we pay him tribute on this holiday. I tell ye this, with the chief's protection, then all the plunder on the high sea will be forever in our grasp and we can retire as rich men! But we need this gift of flesh if this is to be ours."

Dietrich Oarsbreaker, another Kemetian outlaw and a rough contemporary of Ulrich Mancrusher, if not as large as his companion, as equally deadly, fidgeted with a large copper coin whilst eyeing the others. His gaze bounced from man to man, finally stopping on Yalad ere he spoke.

"So, say this again," he said, lowering a tankard of stale beer from his lips. "Ye wish us to travel the width of this accursed continent, sneak into the City of the Gods, and steal away the princess of Neturu. Only to then return to this filthy seaport, and then brave the waters of the Ocean of No Return; as well as the reefs of death that protect the Forbidden Island, and finally to deposit the girl on the eve of Mokksbod to that fat king of nothingness; and all for what, his supposed promise of free plunder on the high sea. If ye ask me, it doesn't seem like a very intelligent plan. How is this chief supposed to protect us? I see no fleet guarding his Island. For Jang's sake, the Forbidden Island is a penal colony, not a kingdom!"

There was a murmur of agreement that went around the table, but Yalad quickly put down the mutiny with a word.

"Wealth untold," he said, "will be ours if we are to pull this off, for the princess is a goddess of extreme power. Once in the grimy hands of the chief, he will have his witch doctors cast spells on her and she will do all that he commands. After this, the seas will be ripe for us to pick clean!"

Ulrich, chewing a piece of hard cheese and washing it down with a tankard full of beer, gave a hearty laugh.

"Yalad, ye take us for fools. We are swarthy buccaneers, not land pirates, although some of us have seen employment inland on many of the land's rivers. Nor are we slavers and flesh merchants, that is thy trade not ours; and all this to steal a goddess? Are we so desperate to risk damnation of our very souls? By Jang, god of sea rogues, I'll have none of it."

"You'll do this," answered the flesh merchant, "or die in your sleep!" His eyes were ablaze with hateful intensity, and the others felt their hair prickle on their scalps. Smiles suddenly went sullen with Yalad's threat and more than one hand gripped a cutlass hilt.

"You'll not threaten the lot of us," cried Dietrich, angry to the point of murder.

"I threaten ye naught," laughed Yalad, "but 'tis a promise. Chief Talbod will have this wench, for reasons of his own, and I will see to it that his wish is carried out! And for this, I have my own reasons too. But know this, you bunch of pathetic sea wrack, the chief's witch doctor has been given certain items, from each of your possessions, and from these items, he can extract much hurt. It is in thy best interest to comply with my will. Ye will be heavily paid upon completion of the task."

"What is this treachery!"

"'Tis the cost of doing business in Kemet," answered Yalad, with a grin. "As I have said before, I care not how the task is done, only that it is done ere Mokksbod, and for that, ye have but a fortnight." And with those words, the flesh merchant straightened his sea coat and sword belt, rose from the table and exited the booth through the soiled oily curtain. Behind him, he could hear the grumbling sounds of dead men, arguing over a job they could not pass up.

"So what now," asked Dietrich to his companions.

"Well," said Ulrich, "I suppose the old thief has us where he wants us. Curse the day we accepted his offer, and to think that we haven't seen even a copper for our trouble."

"Death is what we'll be paid, I am certain of that," said one pirate, not to anyone in particular, but simply voicing his opinion aloud.

"I know nothing of this City of the Gods, nor of Neturuian royalty. I always thought it to be myth anyway," said Ulrich. "But of the Forbidden Island, I know plenty." The eyes of the others grew wide with curiosity as the burly man leaned forward on his thick elbows and began his tale of that grim rock located many leagues east of the shores of Kemet. It was late in the night, and the dregs of Kemet's seedy red light district were finally beginning to give way. The tavern seemed quieter than usual, or was it the doom in the pirates voice when he spoke of that forbidden island that quieted the atmosphere of the booth.

"Over five thousand years ago," spoke Ulrich Mancrusher, "the people of Kem split violently in a bloody civil war. Those that came south established the city of Kemet. With them, they brought slaves, Kemites who were taken as prisoners in the war. After these slaves outlived their usefulness they were banished to the then un-named, Forbidden Island. In time, Kemet declared sole ownership of that nasty piece of rock in the southern corner of the Ocean of No Return; for the past four thousand years it has been a place of exile; a prison colony. Most Kemetians believe that one condemned to exile on the island is guaranteed a certain and heinous death. But on the contrary, the island is a virtual paradise. Actually, the internal area of the island is the paradise, yet the beaches of its coasts are extremely hellish. The Kemetians have never ventured inland, and so they assume the entire island is similar to that of its coasts. Anyhow, the island is inhabited by the decedents of long banished prisoners. They have developed a primitive tribal society and are quite self sufficient in their existence. The current chief is that Talbod of which the flesh merchant spoke. I have heard many dread tales of his cruelty. Mokksbod is the annual holiday that celebrates the chief. I can only guess what heinous evil the princess will endure if we go through with this vile plan."

"Why does this devil of a chief want that Neturuian princess," asked one of the pirates.

"'Tis my belief," answered Ulrich, "that he wishes the control of this goddess for more than meets the eye. Rather than merely control the seas around the island and Kemet, I feel that he will use the wench to liberate himself from the island. If this is the case, once he is afoot on the mainland, no one will know peace, for his treachery and evil are legendary!"

"And so, we are to go through with this?"

"What choice do we have," said Dietrich. "Ye heard Yalad. Chief Talbod has bound us with sorcery. It is our souls if we fail this job!"

"But to loose this vile devil on the main," answered the other, hotly, "would that not damn us even the more?"

Ulrich sat back on his wooden stool, his mighty weight making the aged wood groan, and laughed.

"Men, we were damned the day we decided on the life of a sea rogue. What difference does it make now? Forget this talk of damned souls and let's live the life we chose. It's our life for the life of some petty royal lass. Why should we care of good or evil anyhow? We have work to do. We must assemble a band of land rogues and ride for the western reaches of this accursed land. All that, and less than a fortnight to do it in."

The others did not like the sound of doom in his voice, but more than the gods, they feared Ulrich Mancrusher. He flashed his motley crew a grim glance and commanded Dietrich to settle up with the barkeep. "Meet here in the morning, for tomorrow eve we ride west!"

And with that, the large pirate stood and disappeared through the curtain into the darkness of the evening.

Thus ends Chapter Four of Book Three

FIVE

The Gods of Neturu

Buzzards littered the white sky over the vast Golrin Prairie like a black cloud of dots, soaring high on the hot thermals, eyes ablaze for carrion. Far below the soaring menace, a deathly breeze gently drifted across the flat of the land, but this breeze did not bring comfort. Sandwiched between the Helheim Plateau and the Phaedron Desert on its northern border and the Wastes to its south, the Golrin Prairie was hot and dry most of the year, with sparse water, blazing sun, and blanching winds trying all but the hardiest souls. The bones of many heedless wanderers littered the entire plain.

Off in the distance, a lone figure trudged on, though it was plain to see he was burdened by fatigue, thirst, and starvation. For many leagues, Tulwryn had searched, in vain, for sustenance, but no oasis or wells were found; nothing stained the prairie but bleak grasses and stunted trees.

A creeping pain worked its way into his mind, and he realized that his shoulder wound was beginning to fester. Soon, he knew, he would be overcome with fever if he were unable to locate a watering hole and obtain the proper medicinal herbs by which to heal himself of the only injury he received during his battle with the cannibals. To fail would mean to fall unconscious and become prey for the vultures, hyenas, and other carrion eaters of the prairie, and this raw truth pained him more than the throbbing wound itself.

Tulwryn knew he was many leagues south of Knob, probably somewhere in the southwestern corner of the Golrin Prairie, but he had no way of knowing for certain. He had never been to this section of Phantasodyssea before, and with his mind swimming with hallucinations from the heat and his festering shoulder; he realized that he could no longer trust his instincts.

There were no trade routes or settlements of any kind in this corner of the world, and the entire landscape was a bleak nightmare of rolling prairie and shimmering grasses. Even the few trees that dotted the horizon were nothing more than twisted and deformed shrubs. There was rumor that a pristine river wound its way through the southern reaches of the land, but of this river, he knew nothing. The Xu River, as far as Tulwryn was concerned, was a myth.

So, for league after painful league, Tulwryn walked, stumbled, and crawled, hoping and praying for a final ounce of endurance. Struggling hard to wring out one last bit of strength from his wracked form, he unsheathed the Bloodsword and slammed the blade, point first, into the hard ground. He paused a moment, scanned the white sky through bloodshot eyes, and then gripped the hilt of his weapon with both hands. With a ferocious cry, he called out to a score of gods, both cursing and praying for the strength than would not be his.

The black clouds of circling buzzards loomed closer, and Tulwryn's heart sank. What prophecy is this, he thought, that he should win countless battles and wars, only to become a meal for carrion birds? The irony of the situation played on his brain and he wondered why his gods, and even the Shadow of the sword itself, had forsaken him.

Slowly, he released the hilt of his weapon and, looking down at his open palms, he began to laugh uncontrollably. The brands were still there, but they blazed not as they once had. Sinking to his knees, in final desperation he uttered a single, unintelligible word, and fell unconscious before the impaled prairie, the Bloodsword his apparent grave marker.

* * *

Tulwryn woke with the sweet taste of the Kiputu cactus on his lips and a thousand luscious dreams floating through his head. Through sleep filled eyes, he glanced around and thought himself to be in some great palace for he was lying on a large bed strewn with luxuriant silks and furs. The chamber where he lay was furnished with exotic tapestries and thick plush rugs and carpets. There was a commode and basin atop a small mahogany table next to his bed, which were crafted of fine porcelain and accented in gold leaf. To the north of the bed, there was an open window, and beyond that, a wide balcony where lush green plants and fragrant yellow flowers could be seen nodding their heads dreamily in the breeze. The entire room smelled of poppies; the scene, something out of a distant opium dream.

After a few moments, Tulwryn noticed that his gaping shoulder wound had been tended to, and was healing nicely. He was dressed in a fine tunic of red silk, beige breeches of course linen, and his hair had been washed and scented with exotic oils. Sitting up, the warrior from Nuvia tried to remember his last memory in hopes of discerning how he came to such a fantastic place. In true, he wondered, had he died on the prairie, and if so, was this paradise?

Slowly, he rose and left the comfort of the bed, gliding across the jade green marble floor toward the window. He paused at the basin to douse his face with fresh clean water that sparkled like liquid diamonds, and then continued out through the large window and onto the balcony.

The balcony was large and sparsely furnished, but the teakwood railing was carved in exquisite talent, although Tulwryn noticed that the feline form was the predominating focus for most of the art. He leaned on the rail and looked out over the whole of a wide courtyard. From his vantage point, he could tell that he was in a tower of some large structure, and at least four stories in the air. Far below, the yard was well groomed, and the shrubbery was trimmed to perfection. There was a tall wall surrounding the entire court, for the yard contained seven majestic lions, roaming free and unhindered. A sudden twinge of fear washed over Tulwryn as he thought the worst: was he in fact a prisoner in this paradise? Only time would tell.

A sound from within the room behind him caused him to wheel like a cat, and in an instant, he was back in his chamber. He was greeted by a tall, richly dressed woman, standing next to a very tall man. Both people seemed more akin to gods than royalty, yet he knew them to be at least mortal, if not human.

"Who art thou, and why am I here," were his first questions. "And where is mine sword? Am I a prisoner here?"

"Are prisoners usually treated so well, Tulwryn," spoke the man, with a grin. "Please, rest assured, thou art no prisoner. Art thou wounds healing nicely?"

Tulwryn realized that there was no pain in his shoulder, and he moved his arm with surprising ease in its full range of motion. He then glanced back to the man, and the woman beside him. "How is it that ye know my name?"

"You will find that hither in Neturu, we know a great many things."

Neturu? Tulwryn recalled that name, is was the mythical City of the Gods. But certainly, it was just a myth, yet here he stood, in Neturu, and before two of its citizens. But were they gods? Both, the man and the woman, were taller and leaner than he, and both were beautiful beyond belief, and yet, he felt that they were still merely mortal and certainly not mystical deities.

"Again I ask, who art thou?"

Branjadom smiled. He then looked to his female servant and beckoned her to fetch some wine. Turning back to Tulwryn, he motioned for him to follow him to an outer alcove just beyond the door of the chamber where the two of them could sit and talk while sipping sweet Neturuian wine.

Once seated, the servant poured sparkling golden wine into

two emerald goblets and then vanished down a long corridor. Branjadom lifted his goblet to his lips, drank freely, and then gazed deeply into the warrior's dark eyes.

"Tulwryn, my name is Branjadom of Neturu. I am the prince of the city, and the heir to the throne. Actually, I already sit atop the throne of Neturu, since my father is dead."

"So gods die," interrupted Tulwryn, replacing his goblet back on the table after taking a long drink of the sweet nectar.

"Yes, we can die. We are mortal, as art thou. But our life span is much, much longer. Longer even than dwarves, in fact. But that is not why you are here."

Tulwryn nodded to the prince, and sat back in his chair; evidently relaxed by the heady wine he was drinking. The prince continued.

"For the past five summers, my sister Octavia had been watching you by means of her skill."

"Sorcery?"

"You may call it that, but no, it is not sorcery; at least not in the common sense of the word. She believes in you Tulwryn, and in the prophecy. I am sorry to say that I do not hold much to my sister's beliefs, but I see no other place to turn, and that is why I sent for you. Personally, I find your behavior rather barbaric. All the drinking and wenching and looting are, in my opinion, unbecoming of one whose destiny is interlaced with that of the land. But alas, you are my only hope."

There was a tension in the air that Tulwryn could sense, and he could tell that the prince was about to eat his pride. At what cost, he knew not, but his experience told him that something horrible had happened, perhaps in Neturu, or maybe elsewhere in Caiwryn. He took another sip of his wine, and waited for Branjadom to continue.

"Tulwryn, my sister has been kidnapped. A fortnight ago, she was abducted from this very palace by a host of desperate men. They vanished into the shadows of the night and have not been seen from again. Octavia was the only one who had the ability to use the Great Pool of Neturu, whereby the whole of the land could be observed, so even I, with all my powers, cannot locate her whereabouts." The prince paused, shame written across his handsome face in helpless frustration.

"And why me," Tulwryn asked. "I have no power of vision. And besides that, methinks this whole prophecy business is lunacy. I am worthless and used up. The spirit of the sword speaks not to me any more, and I cannot even evoke the blade's celestial fire. How can I aid thee in thy quest?"

"I know naught how ye can aid me," said the prince, "but aid me thou must; Octavia's life depends on you! Tulwryn, I rescued you from certain death on the Golrin Prairie and nursed your wounds myself. My sister is gone at the hands of vile men. You must help me, you must!"

The two sat there for some time, thoughts of grandeur swimming though Tulwryn's head. Perhaps this was the break he had been waiting for, thought he; perhaps this is how the gods plan to put him back on top of his destiny. With a hearty smile, he drained his goblet in one great gulp and slammed it down on the table.

"Very well," he said, "who am I to look a gift horse in the mouth? Outfit me with armor, a fine horse, water and food, and my sword, then tell me all you know, and I will set off on this quest ere the sun sets this eve."

Branjadom, with a satisfied look at this news, clapped his hands thrice and the female servant appeared with more wine. The two men sat for some time discussing the matter, all the while Tulwryn's mind was racing toward the rewards he would reap if he were successful in rescuing the princess of Neturu, a living goddess.

Thus ends Chapter Five of Book Three

SIX

An Unexpected Visit

Just ere sunset, Tulwryn rode out of Neturu on a fine steed. He was wearing a gilded Neturuian cuirass and helm, the royal blazon of Bast deeply embroidered in cloth-of-gold on his velvet surcoat, over which was wrapped a great purple cloak. From his hip hung the heavy Bloodsword, and tied to the left flank of his horse was a mighty shield of round, mirror polished steel. Likewise, his mount also wore steel plate armor over its head, chest, and flanks. Heavy leather saddlebags were hung from the rear of his war saddle which were loaded with fine cheeses, sweetmeats, and hard bread; two waterskins hung from his saddle horn and a small flagon of fine Neturuian wine was tethered to his sword belt. For the first time in many years, Tulwryn felt proud again, almost akin to being royalty himself, and he smiled a grim smile as he rode out of the city.

The dark mantle of the eve was creeping in upon him as he spurred the beast forward. Behind him, the setting sun was turning the western forest to blood, yet before his eyes, dark clouds loomed with evil menace. Far in the distance, a flash of lightning slashed its way across the darkening sky, yet the storm was still too far away for any thunderclap to be audibly heard.

There were no crowds of riotous citizens to see him off, no roars from the mouths of excited youths, nor were there sweet glances from beautiful maidens as he made his way from the city. No one was to be seen, and so, Tulwryn exited the city alone, a grim feeling of despair looming over his heart that made the burden of the kinslaying pale by comparison.

His mind was awash with thoughts, yet he knew not where to begin his search for the princess. In a land as large as Phantasodyssea, he knew full well that the bandits could be anywhere, especially since they had already been on the trail a fortnight.

Then an idea came to him. Since he had no vision, nor controlled the workings of magic or sorcery, he was as lost in his quest as any blind adventurer. But on the contrary, wizards could see into the future, as well as into the hearts and minds of men, and so, with a tug of his reins and a swift spur to his ride's flanks, he turned his beast northeastward, and on toward Covensted. It was there, in that accursed town of black witches, that he hoped to find his old friend Dillwyn the dwarf, and possibly the answers to his many questions. As he rode on into the night, a gentle rain began to fall.

* * *

It wasn't long ere the gentle rain grew into torrents of wrathful fury, and buckets of water poured down upon him and his steed in great grey sheets. He spurred the beast on through the storm, his heavy cloak wrapped tightly around him, but soon the gale and the opaque darkness of the night demanded that he seek out a shelter whereas to weather the storm until it passed.

Thunder ripped through the dark night with a deafening roar and a blast of lightning illumed the vale in which he rode, even for a split second. In that desperate second, Tulwryn espied a small structure off in the distance. About a hundred and fifty paces yonder, under the eaves of a great gnarled oak, stood a hut of seemingly antique vintage. He urged his steed through the cold rain and made for the small shelter as quickly as possible.

Cautiously, he cantered up to the hut. In a loud tone, he roared out to any possible inhabitants, but from the structure, no reply came. The hut was tiny, and made crudely; large stones packed tightly together over which sod and mud had been liberally applied as some sort of primitive mortar. The roof, barely much taller that Tulwryn himself, was nothing more than simple thatchings, woven together as a course carpet of twigs and dried leaves.

Dismounting and drawing his dagger, Tulwryn entered through the hut's door to peer inside. Without windows, the interior of the structure was darker than even the night. Quickly sheathing the dagger, he reached into his tinder pouch and produced a small flint, steel, and some charred cloth. With this, he struck a light, which illumed the interior of the hut. To his amazement, the hut was comprised of a single room of about ten feet square and completely void of any furnishings. The place looked as if it had been lost, forgotten in time.

Tulwryn quickly summed up his options and decided the hut would make a perfect shelter for the night. He left the structure and gathered his horse's reins in his bronze and scarred hands. Patting the beast gently on the head, he guided the animal into the interior of the hut and bade it lie down on the smoothly packed earth. After some time, he had shed his own armor and removed that of his horse as well. Groping in the darkness, he fondled through his saddlebags, produced some cheese, and sat down beside the animal for a sparse meal ere drifting off to sleep.

It was there, somewhere in the night of his dreams that an old visitor returned to him. A dark and pallid shadow it was, grim and unfeeling. Tulwryn stirred, and faced the intruder with his dagger drawn, but as soon as his eyes focused on the being, he relaxed his stance and re-sheathed the knife.

"Why come now," asked he, as he drew up his cloak and sat himself beside the sleeping horse. The shadow drifted closer but said nothing. An air of tension hung thickly in the gloom, and even though there was no fire or light of any kind, the interior of the hut was illumed by a dusky green glow of preternatural intensity.

"Come now," said Tulwryn in haste, "ye didn't come all this

way, and remain silent for five summers, to merely torment me. Please, grim friend, tell me the nature of thy visit."

Finally, in a pall and low tone that resembled the dirge of funeral bells rather than human speech, the Shadow of the Bloodsword spoke: "Greetings, brother."

"Ye can dispense with the pleasantries," replied Tulwryn, rather agitated. "Please, get on with it and state your business."

"Still rushing through life, I see," recalled the shadow. "When wilt thou learn? Often times, I am amazed as to why the gods picked you for their champion." There was a bit of sarcasm in the thing's ghoulish voice and perhaps a slight jest as well. The shadow knew, as did Tulwryn, that often the gods did things of their own nature and none but them ever knew the whole meaning of their lunacy.

"So, ye are on another quest," spoke the shadow, "and this time the trail lies on the path of royalty. Interesting, indeed. Are you up for the challenge?"

"I will do what must be done, if I can."

"I see. Very well, I have nothing to tell you at this time. Continue on to Covensted and locate thy friend. He has become a very powerful wizard in his own right, since he has not wasted the past five summers wenching and drinking away his wealth as thou hast done. I am certain that he will be of much use to you."

"What," cried Tulwryn, "you came all this way and have no message for me? What good are ye then? And why canst naught I evoke the blade's celestial fire? Am I the man of the prophecy or naught?" He fidgeted with his cloak, as if to conceal his uncomfortableness of the situation, his heart heavy with anxiety.

"Tulwryn, I am hither so that ye will not lose heart." The shadow spoke softly, almost as a father to a son, with much compassion and patience. "As I have always told you, thou art the Bloodsword. You are me, and I am you. The blade is but a simple tool and nothing more. Your greatness is beyond your comprehension, but in time, you shall come to know everything in its complete fullness. Just be patient and all will unfold as it was intended." As suddenly as the shadow appeared, it vanished, and with it, so too disappeared the green glow that lit the room.

Tulwryn sat in the inky darkness, his mind swimming in confusion with serpents of madness coiled about his writhing brain. For certain, the shadow had been still for many years, and now, with this chance meeting, no more questions were answered. It seemed that every time the shadow came, it brought with it more confusion than naught. Perhaps the past five years were a quiet sanctuary, in which the shadow hid itself in his inner soul and offered neither counsel nor strength. Tulwryn shrugged his shoulders. It did not matter. The only thing that mattered to him was rescuing the princess and reaping the reward of that task. If there were a prophecy to fulfill then it would come later. And, without resuming sleep, Tulwryn sat there beside his sleeping mount, awaiting the dawn of a new day.

Thus ends Chapter Six of Book Three

SEVEN

The Wandering Mercenary

Morning came, and with it awoke a freshness Tulwryn had not experienced. The Forest of Neturu was a truly remarkable place. It was an immeasurable expanse of land carpeted in thick foliage, high green canopy, and heavy undergrowth, more akin to a jungle than a forest. The forest was located at the southwestern point of the Golrin Prairie and it completely surrounded the Endless Mountains and the city of Neturu. Due to the many thousands of thorny, briar-like undergrowths and the countless strange and dangerous creatures that reside therein, many adventurers have avoided the forest at all costs since the dawn of time. No known maps of the area are known to exist and for the most part, it is considered impassable. To be sure, the wrath of the Neturuians was also feared by most, and although this godlike race had treated Tulwryn with kindness, he did not want to think of what his destiny might have been had he turned down the prince's request to rescue his royal sister.

So, without further ado, Tulwryn re-armored himself and his steed and continued on his eastward trek towards Covensted. About an hour after breaking camp and leaving the hut behind, he exited the Forest of Neturu. This point on the compass was just north of Chete and was the junction of where the Forest of Neturu, the Golrin Prairie, and the Wastes came together at a single spot. At this junction, the Xu River also wound its way eastward from its origin at the Great Pool of Neturu only to empty itself in the Gulf of Baezutu, many leagues yonder, beyond the searing dunes of the Wastes.

Before him, and to his left, lay the wide expanse of the Golrin Prairie. A shudder crept up his spine knowing that if not for the Neturuian prince, this desolate land would now be harboring his bleaching bones. And to his right, as far as the eye could see, were the endless sands of the Wastes. He realized that the best plan of action would be to keep to the northern bank of the river, although five leagues thither and the prairie would give way to the encroaching sands, thereby leading him through the very heart of an unforgiving wilderness. The river would guarantee life, and clinging to that tiny ribbon of water was his only hope of surviving the searing heat of the desert. He knew a sudden sandstorm or thundergale could potentially blow him off course and away from the river, thus sealing his doom. Shrugging that grim thought, Tulwryn reined his steed through the tall shimmering grasses of the prairie and left the Forest of the Gods behind.

He turned slightly south and followed the north bank of the Xu River, due east, and just ere the noon of the day, he left the grasses of Golrin and headed off through the Wastes. To make good time, Tulwryn ate and drank in the saddle, stopping only long enough to water and feed his horse. Every third day he would stop and pitch a small camp, whereas his trusty mount could enjoy a much needed rest.

The Wastes were a large expanse of barren lands more than twice as large as the Plain of Kem. Most inhospitable, only but the most hardy desert dwellers live here, and these being a curt and bloodthirsty lot. Contrary to popular belief, there is a wide array of edible, non-poisonous flora and fauna to be found in this inhospitable region.

By mid-afternoon of the fifth day, the scorching heat of the desert was beginning to tax both man and beast and so Tulwryn began to seek shelter, but none was to be found and so he trudged on, risking life and limb. He knew that if his steed died, then he too would perish, for no man could hope to traverse such a hell and live. Sure, thought he, that years prior he and Dillwyn

Anvilhand had successfully traveled afoot the entire breadth of the Phaedron Desert and the Helheim Plateau. But the Wastes covered at least twice that much area, if not more. His only hope was to keep close to the river.

The journey was slow in going, and at times, his mind would drift to the task at hand. He would often wonder how the princess was faring in her captivity, and what kind of frustrated wrath Branjadom was brewing back in Neturu. He knew he had been on the trail just shy of a week, but the kidnappers were many weeks ahead of him. Neither he nor Branjadom had any idea where the bandits were bound, or what reasons they had for their theft of the princess. Thus far, no ransom had been asked. The whole escapade was a complete shadow haunted mystery.

On the eve of the thirteenth day after leaving Neturu, the Golrin Prairie once again loomed into view, and with it, off in the far distance, was the Phaedron Trade Route, linking Baezutu to the dead town of Bain. Looking northward, Tulwryn imagined that he saw the shadow haunted towers of Vodmar looming on the horizon, but realized the ruins of that accursed city lay well beyond the curve of the land and far out of view.

A league or so past the Phaedron Trade Route, Tulwryn found himself at the junction where the Xu River and the River Phaedron come together. The day was bright and sunny, and thus far, his entire journey had been rather boring and uneventful. There had been a few straggling caravans pass him on the trail, and more than one offer for his fine steed passed the ruddy lips of caravan drivers, apparently grown tired of traveling atop bouncing camels. The last offer, twenty Phaedron gold Rands, Tulwryn quickly accepted, and once his possibles were removed from the saddle, he patted the fine beast's head for the last time and turned northward afoot.

At the junction of the two rivers, Tulwryn used a bit of his gold to book passage on a Phaedron River barge. The craft was a sturdy flat-bottomed vessel, slow and cumbersome, but capable of handling a heavy payload. The cruise proved to consist of a large shipment of Mok-Torian Bluewood, and was heavily guarded by a stout regiment of Phaedron troops, traveling incognito as savvy river dogs. Tulwryn recognized a few of the curs from his bygone days in the citadel city, but keeping to himself, none so much as paid him any heed. He was merely looked upon as a traveling noble, and thereby, not seen as a threat. He did wonder what reason Phaedron had with Bluewood, which was used exclusively in shipbuilding. Since Phaedron was land locked and had no navy, he could not understand their interest in the stuff. He nonchalantly shrugged his shoulders, for Phaedronian imperial ideals concerned him naught.

Making his way to his berth, he unloaded his belongings and then wandered out on the bow to soak up the sights of the river's leisurely cruise. He propped an elbow up on the fore rail and lazily gazed out into the distance, the roll of the bow putting him into a somewhat hazy lethargy.

The craft lazily floated upstream on the mighty River Phaedron, traveling past the Azure Wood off on the east bank and the Golrin Prairie to the west. Further north, the Plain of Kem came into view on the eastern bank of the river. The Plain of Kem gets its name from the town it surrounds, the vile bowery town of Kem, home to many cutthroats and river scum. The plain is mainly a large expanse of open savannah and sage fields. In the spring, the whole area comes alive with the cornucopia of colorful wildflowers, and is truly an amazing, although deadly, sight, since the plain is home to many large herbivores and some predators as well, including the two-legged variety.

From his vantage point on the barge's bow, Tulwryn could not see the seedy river town of Kem, for it was located on the far side of the Obsidian River, many leagues to the east. But still, the looming threat of Kemite river pirates in the area subconsciously caused his hand to remain close to the hilt of the Bloodsword. It had been some time since he had engaged in any swordplay and secretly he hoped to espy a pirate craft with bold buccaneers up river. But alas, his crimson dreams of bloody steel would have to wait, for the river was still and serene this cruise.

A day and a half after boarding the barge, Tulwryn

disembarked from the craft at the junction of the River Agu, whereas he once again resumed his eastward travels, now afoot, following the northern bank of the river all the way through Darkwood to Covensted.

Thus ends Chapter Seven of Book Three

EIGHT

The Malevolence

The silver sliver of a sharp crescent moon was visible through the dark billowing clouds over the calm southern sea, yet Octavia saw it naught, for she was bound, gagged, and blindfolded, deep within the bowels of the hold aboard the *Malevolence*. The beautiful Neturuian princess knew nothing except the pain in her lithe limbs and the horrid stench of the slave ship on which she was held captive. The heavy hulled ship glided effortlessly though the dark waters of the Gulf of Misery, propelled by the world's easterly winds filling her black sails, and the gentle tossing to and fro of the vessel's motion though the frothing waves put Octavia in a tormented state of lethargy.

High above the hold, on the forecastle deck, stood two large and imposing figures; both men, desperate pirates by trade, were dressed in dirty captain's long coats, over which hung salt saturated cloaks. Ulrich Mancrusher, the captain of the *Malevolence*, leaned over the port rail gazing out over the black waters of the Gulf of Misery, lost to his own grim thoughts. His blue-black beard was damp with ocean spray, as was the patch over his left empty eye.

"How do ye think we'll fare on this accursed voyage," asked the other man, his first mate, Dietrich Oarsbreaker. For more than twenty-five years, these two sea dogs had plied their bloody trade together and painted the oceans of the world red with the blood of their prey, but both men knew they couldn't endure the pace much longer, especially after falling in with likes of Yalad Munstur, the flesh merchant.

The deck creaked under Ulrich's weight, stout and rotund he was, but as savvy as a jungle cat in combat. Many years had seasoned him to fighting atop the swaying decks of ships, and his balance and poise baffled those that witnessed his prowess during fits of rage with cold steel in his hand and battle wrath on his mind. He turned and looked at Dietrich through his one good eye with a piercing glance. The leaner man swallowed hard and sweat beads formed on his pale brow. Even though he and his captain were good friends and had been so for many years, the larger man was as unpredictable as a thundergale in August, and he knew Ulrich treaded a fine tightrope on this cruise.

"Not well, I am certain," replied Ulrich. "You know as well as I, that Yalad is a cutthroat like the worst of them. He would stab us in the guts as look at us. And I for one do not like trading in flesh. Gems and gold is one thing, but thieving a princess from her own palace and delivering her into the hands of a savage, well, that is not to my liking. If not for the accursed sorcery Yalad has hung over our heads I 'twould have slit his throat that night in the Silver Saber."

"Aye, methinks ye are right, ol'e friend," answered Dietrich. "This whole job reeks of foul stench. Even this ol'e barge we bartered for stinks of death."

"Well, you can't purchase a pleasure craft on buccaneer wages, and this rickety old slaver was all we could afford. She's seaworthy, I'd say, but not much else." In the dim light of the moon, Dietrich could see the face of his captain turn ruddy as he thought about their situation. The pale scar that emerged from under the eye patch and wound its way, serpentine-like, across his face stood out in bold relief from the dark features of the burly pirate and Dietrich knew not to press the issue.

"How much longer 'til we reach Kemet," asked Dietrich?

"A few days, give or take; no way of knowing on this old tug; this dog has seen better days."

Ulrich was right. The *Malevolence*, whilst a sturdy ship in her prime, was now old and worn. A large, triple masted galleon she was, and with fifty large cannon to boot, but after four long decades of use, the last eight years of which she had been utilized as a slave ship, had taken its toll on her. The hull was worm eaten and encrusted with tons of barnacles, the black canvas sails were old and worn, and the rigging was dilapidated. This, both men knew, would be her final voyage.

"Why don't you go below and get some rest? I'm heading up to the poop to relieve the helmsman." And without waiting for an answer, Dietrich turned and walked away, leaving his captain standing at the rail of the quarterdeck once again lost to his own grim thoughts.

But Dietrich had grim thoughts of his own. As he strode through the ship toward the high poor astern, his mind relived the adventure of stealing a princess. He had been a pirate for more than half his life, but never had his pilfering on the high seas brought so much risk as this present job.

The entire escapade was a nightmare of logistics. First, he and Ulrich had to employ a sturdy band of land rogues, and on what Yalad had paid them, that task alone had proved almost impossible. After assembling the band and leaving Kemet, the marauders hastily traveled across the entire continent of Phantasodyssea toward the fabled city of Neturu, the City of the Gods. Crossing the Wastes almost killed them, and in the Forest of Neturu, three of their group had fallen prey to savage lions. The actual theft of the girl had proved surprisingly simple and went off without a hitch, since Ulrich had some knowledge of drugs and utilized this wisdom in performing the actual capture. Exiting the palace went slightly awry after the group made a wrong turn and wandered into a regiment of castle guards. Fighting like a man possessed, Ulrich slayed four of the would-be bodyguards, whilst the others made off with the princess and left the palace through the darkness of the night. They then followed the southern bank of the Xu River, and once again cut their way across the Wastes all the way to the Azure Wood. Riding hard to the point of killing their mounts, the bandits turned south after entering the wood and headed for Mok-Tor. It was there, in that seaport town that they purchased the *Malevolent* and set sail for Kemet.

Dietrich wondered if Yalad Munstur would be true to his word. In Kemet, Yalad promised, he had made provisions for the *Malevolent's* crew to transfer its precious cargo to a fast, low keeled sloop whereby they could carry the princess to the Forbidden Island and into the evil clutches of Chief Talbod. The whole business stank to high heaven, but as Ulrich had already pointed out, sorcery had bound them; it was the princess or their souls, and even sea rogues had souls. A shudder went up his spine as he ascended the poop, relieved the helmsman, and looked out forward over the length of the ship. Treachery was a part of every pirate's life, he knew, and only time would tell when the treachery of the flesh merchant would finally catch up with him.

Far below, in the reeking hold of the *Malevolent,* a once beautiful princess silently cried herself to sleep, caught in her own nightmare. With the rhythmic swaying of the ship, Octavia, princess of Neturu, faded off to sleep, her body aching from the fetters that held her, her mind a mass of tormented horror.

Thus ends Chapter Eight of Book Three

NINE

The Flesh Merchant

By sunset, the Plain of Kem was far behind them. The river, slower now than in most spots along its long and winding path, broadened out wide on its watery shoulders as if to embrace the doom that it was about to enter. Up just ahead, the sinister boughs of the tall trees of Darkwood loomed out over the waters of the River Phaedron spreading their twisted limbs in a menacing posture, waiting to grasp any unsuspecting sailor who wanders too close to them.

Tulwryn, experienced by years of adventuring, knew better than to take this forest for granted. When he informed the barge's captain that he was bound for Covensted and would jump ship at the junction where the River Agu flows east from the River Phaedron, the sailor shuddered with superstition.

"I'll not dock near those accursed brambles," scowled the captain.

"No need to," advised Tulwryn, "I can swim as good as any man, and I'm in need of a good bath anyhow."

The barge captain leaned heavily on the sweep and the large vessel swung wide to starboard, giving the short shoreline where Darkwood kissed the river's edge a wide berth. With a splash, Tulwryn was overboard and swimming like a madman for the shore. Normally, the River Phaedron is fairly safe to swim, even considering its treacherous undertow and fast current, for it does not harbor dangerous aquatics. But this close to the inlet of the River Agu, one can never be sure if that river's monsters, vast schools of flesh eating fish, might haphazardly find their way into the open waters of Phaedron's mighty river. So, with all his steel might, Tulwryn battled the waves of the river and swam straight for the eastern shore, and under the grim eaves of Darkwood.

Tulwryn was just climbing up out of the water as he paused and looked back at the barge he had just left. It was already upstream a half a league or so, and disappearing around the bend that would take it through the watery pass of the Ymir Mountains and beyond.

Shaking the water from his hair, as well as from his sword and scabbard, Tulwryn situated himself as best he could and trudged onward, alone. Off to his left, lay the silty banks of the River Agu. The river was actually a shallow, salt-water stream that emptied into the Ocean of No Return on the east bank of the Seething Swamp many leagues to the east. Legend had it that the river was laden with gemstones of unlimited magical value, and more than once Tulwryn glanced deeply into its dark waters hoping to espy a glitter of wealth waiting to be plucked by his pilfering hand. But alas, no sparkling gems were seen and so the warrior from Nuvia trekked eastward, on toward Covensted.

Many years had passed since he had trudged through this portion of Darkwood, and often he found himself reminiscing about the old days. It had also been many years since Tulwryn graced the streets of Covensted with his presence, when he would visit the small village to sell his yearly harvest of mistletoe to the dark sorcerers that call that town home. He silently wondered what changes had taken place in that eccentric village, as changes do inevitably occur in time; and he also pondered on the fate of his friend, Dillwyn the dwarf. How such a battle hardened rogue could abandon the thrill of combat to settle down with placid wizards, he would never know or understand. He shrugged the notion aside and continued on.

The sweltering humidity of the forest did not aid in drying his possibles from his short dip in the river and after an hour or so he was mightily uncomfortable. His leather breeches began to tighten and chaff his inner thighs. Luckily for him that he was able to sell his steed and armor back on the plains, for the heavy platemaile of the Neturuians would have drowned him in the water, and rusted maile serves no purpose anyhow.

Up ahead the forest opened to a small clearing, and Tulwryn decided to pitch a small camp, get rested, and dry out his belongings. First, he built a small fire in the center of the clearing, over which he constructed a makeshift rack where he hung his clothes. Then he stripped naked and reclined on a bed of club moss under a large oak, resting whilst the clothes dried.

All about him, fronds of ferns and flowers nodded their heads in an ominous breeze. The silence was deafening, the fragrance bewitching. Suddenly, there came a crashing from above as if some great flapping beast was descending upon him. His heart jumped up to his throat, but ere he could even sit up, a strong and sinewy net enveloped him. In an instant, he was surrounded by five burly men in heavy leather jerkins and beige pantaloons, all bearing war clubs. Tulwryn struggled to get to his feet, but his fight was in vain. A tall rogue swung his heavy cudgel and Tulwryn knew nothing more; and fell silent on the damp ground of Darkwood.

Tulwryn had no way of knowing how long he was unconscious. All he knew was that he was still naked, with a throbbing head from the blow he suffered at the hands of his assailants, and that he was in some sort of bamboo cage atop a great lumbering beast. The first thought that came to him was that he had been captured by a caravan of slavers, but this idea puzzled him for he never heard of slavers operating this far north, and especially this deep in Darkwood. Most sane people avoided the forest as if it was a living thing, but then again, how sane could men be that betrayed their own race and preyed on other men for mere profit?

There were others in the litter with him, although most still were quiet and unconscious. He crawled to one side of the cage and peered out. The cage was indeed atop a creature Tulwryn knew to be a Phaedron elephant, a wooly beast of mammoth proportions. Its great head swayed back and forth, and the long white tusks that protruded a yard or more from its mouth and trunk shone like gleaming blades in the glistening blue haze of the early morning. Behind his beast, Tulwryn could see at least three others, but the low hanging eaves of Darkwood obscured any more from view.

Below him, probably walking or on horses, he heard men talking. The voices were low and muffled, but he could make out some conversation since they spoke in the civilized tongue native to eastern Phantasodyssea. Whilst the pronunciation was slightly different from his Nuvian language, he could still understand enough words to get a grasp of his current situation.

"Art thou certain that those sea rogues acquired the princess in Neturu," asked a rough voiced man, whom Tulwryn could not see.

"Aye," answered the other. "The group should be half way to Kemet by now." The second man, Tulwryn could see, although the haze of the morning's first rays played havoc on his beaten mind. This man looked middle aged, and was dressed in flamboyant clothes unlike the others of the party. He wore a tall hat with a wide brim and a fluffy ostrich plume graced the hat's narrow snakeskin band.

"I hope you are correct, Captain Munstur," replied the other. "The expense of operating two crews is stifling."

"Do not worry about the finances. After we haul the princess to the Forbidden Island, our worries are over. Chief Talbod has promised us wealth untold. And this trip to the south will put more gold in your purse than you've seen in years. The Baezutuians pay good coin for arena studs such as these we've rounded up. Once we drop this shipment off, we'll turn southeast and rendezvous with Ulrich and Dietrich in Kemet. I already have a sloop waiting at dock for our arrival. We are rich men!"

A sick feeling welled up in Tulwryn's stomach and he slumped back along the edge of rough bamboo staves making up the wall of his prison. He had heard enough. In all of his days, he never imagined that he would fall prey to Yalad Munstur and his bloodthirsty slave crew. The man was a cancer upon the land and many grim tales were told about his abominations. The man trafficked in flesh, operating many slave crews across the width and breadth of the land. He captured and sold men, women, and even children, for slaves, or worse. Some stories tell how he would even sell his human cargo to the Knobite cannibals, like two-legged cattle, bound and gagged for slaughter.

An insatiable rage welled up in Tulwryn's veins, and a need to unleash his berserker wrath and break free from his cage set his head to throbbing. But alas, the lacquered bamboo staves were as strong as iron and even if he could break free, the noise would bring his captor's attention, and since he was naked and unarmed, as well as outnumbered, he knew the situation was hopeless. Gone were the days when he could evoke the Bloodsword's celestial flame and lay waste to entire legions. Now he was nothing more than a rat in a trap.

One good thing had come out of his situation though. Now he knew not only his fate, but the fate of Octavia as well. He had heard the flesh merchant say she was aboard a ship bound for Kemet, and then the Forbidden Island. Whilst he had no idea of knowing what devilry Chief Talbod had in store for her, he knew it couldn't be good. And as for his own manflesh, he was bound for the arenas of Baezutu. Of course, there could be worse destinations for a slave, and perhaps, a situation would arise where he could escape his tormentors and bolt to freedom, or even be granted his freedom by a rich slave buyer. This last thought made Tulwryn laugh, for no sane man would buy a slave only to set him free. Sure, he had heard of some gladiators winning their freedom, but that was usually after many years of active combat in the arena, and time was something he had very little of.

Finally, behind him, there was a rustling and one of the prisoners stood. The man loomed up, a head and a half taller than Tulwryn. He was naked and his skin was the hue of pale marble; a mighty chest of thick slabs of muscle stood out like rough hewn granite and heavily corded arms hung limply to his side. The prisoner shook his blonde mane and stroked his bushy beard with a wide hand, strongly knotted with muscled fingers and knuckles.

"Where in hell am I," asked the giant, shaking stars from his brain.

"Looks like we are mates aboard a slaver's caravan bound for Baezutu," answered Tulwryn, thrusting out a hand in friendship. He knew a man as large as that who stood before him would prove to be a dangerous enemy. Equally well known, he realized that the rogue would also be a valuable and strong ally, and so he hastily went to work to gain the man's trust and friendship.

"Baezutu?" The man looked at Tulwryn through glassy eyes, his forehead a mass of dried and clotted blood over a roadmap of lacerations and superficial wounds. "Why are they taking us there?"

"'Tis my guess that we are to be sold to the arena," Tulwryn said, shrugging his shoulders.

"I thought gladiatorial games were outlawed throughout the whole of the land."

"They are, yet the games flourish on the underground market in a score of seedy towns and villages. The games are illegal yet they prove to be incredibly lucrative for both pitboss and gambler alike. Anyhow, perhaps if we put our heads together we can make a break if the situation presents itself. I am Tulwryn Bloodsword, of . . ." Tulwryn was about to introduce himself to the stranger, but at the mention of his name, the burly giant interrupted.

"Tulwryn Bloodsword, of Heidmar," asked the giant, apparently shocked at this news.

"Aye, in the flesh."

"Well, skin me alive and boil my guts in whale blubber! I am Thegn Odinson, of the Gerdmorians. You are quite a legend up north, especially how you survived the Battle of Gerdmor Gorge and then went on to slay that accursed ice dragon single handedly. How ye come by this fate?"

"Wrong place at the wrong time, I suppose," answered Tulwryn, his pride and ego stoked for the first time in years. "Perhaps the gods are teaching me a lesson, but albeit for me to be a quick learner."

The two men laughed as though they were visiting in a warm and cozy tavern, considering the grave circumstances of their situation. Thegn told Tulwryn of his adventures and the warrior likewise repaid the favor. For three days, the two passed the time talking thus and reliving old times whilst the caravan trudged southward toward the Baezutuian arena. The other prisoners in the cage mostly slept and kept to themselves, for fear and madness was etched across their grim faces. Fodder for the games, thought Tulwryn of these broken fools, but these men were not on Tulwryn's mind. What occupied his waking hours, even through all the long and boisterous conversations with the mighty Gerdmorian was escaping his captors and rescuing Octavia. At least he knew where she was bound for, and he needed no wizard for that information. As it seemed, he would not be going to Covensted on this trip.

Thus ends Chapter Nine of Book Three

TEN

Execution on the High Seas

The old ship rocked to and fro, and the boards of her hull groaned in agony as the waves pounded her old sides. High above in the dark heavens, a quarter moon showed its yellow face through grey storm clouds. And no track could be found in the greenish-black waters behind her, for no ship followed the slaver; and the pirates were overcome with a grim joy, albeit they were grown tired of the peril of the journey thus far. And for many days the sails had been full to the point of bursting as the winds kept up their relentless effort to drive the ship eastward.

Below deck, deep in the hold of the *Malevolence* Octavia tossed about on her straw pallet. Nightmares danced through her brain and the pain of her confinement was with her, yet she was proud and showed no fear. More than once, a burly sea rogue would come to her with gruel and water and a loaf of hard bread and cheese and beg her to eat, yet the princess defied them all and vowed herself to starvation rather than be allowed to wallow in the freakish agony of thralldom.

Time and again, she wondered the motives of the buccaneers, and why rape had not yet been attempted. Her skin crawled with the thought of herself being ravished by the stinking rogues and she begged Bast for a quick and painless death rather than die in degradation at the hands of the pirates.

High on the quarterdeck, two figures huddled under worn cloaks as the falling rain mixed with salted sea spray and smote them hard on their lean faces. "What think you of this storm," asked Dietrich Oarsbreaker to his grim friend, a note of uncertainty in his voice.

"Methinks it is the work of sorcery," answered Ulrich Mancrusher. The big man rearranged his cloak and sea coat, pulling his hood down over his face, then continued. "For more than half my life I have sailed these waters, and whilst the name of this gulf is truly given, I have never seen the likes of a storm such as this. For the better part of a fortnight the winds have blown with wrath yet the waters are calm and we cut away cleanly through the night as a sparrow flies through the air."

"True, indeed, these thoughts have crossed my mind as well, old friend. Perhaps Yalad has bidden us with Chief Talbod's magic already?"

"Speak naught those names," whispered Ulrich, "for to do so will more likely bring doom than good tidings. We are not out of this mess yet."

Dietrich nodded, and for some moments the two stood in silence contemplating the doom that had befallen them, and fearing what the future would bring, they thought deeply about their journey and their mission. Suddenly, a fell mood passed over the ship like a dark shadow, and the nape of both rogues bristled with dreary gloom.

The ship was half way across the Gulf of Misery when the winds died down and the *Malevolence* came to a halt, but adrift. Angered, Ulrich demanded that the male slaves be chained to the oars and travel once again was underway. The creak and thud of the oars in their locks was drowned out only by the sound of the heavy leather lash creasing the backs of the slaves, and by the moans of their agony. But still, the oars moved and the ship once again coursed through the black waters of the gulf.

In time, Ulrich's mind was drawn back to the precious cargo in the hold and he beckoned his mate to attend to the princess. Taking his leave, Dietrich left the poop and journeyed below deck to see to the girl's needs.

Deep in the hold the light was dim and only small lanterns were kept burning for fear of razing the ship at sea. The lean buccaneer strode through the halls and cabins of the underdeck and made his way to the cell that contained Octavia, princess of Neturu. But as he opened the small oaken portal and stepped within, his skin crawled and he became wrathful for he was angered at the sight that befell him.

"What goes on here," roared Dietrich Oarsbreaker at the top of his lungs. The timbers of the ship shook as if soaked with fear, and his heavy cutlass flew from its scabbard.

As it has come to be known in the tale, Dietrich had caught a grimy pirate named Burke in the act of attacking the princess. Yet he caught the rogue ere any damage had been done to the lass. For certain, she was frightened and battered, but her womanhood was intact and untouched. With a stout backhand, Dietrich smote the man on his noggin with the flat of his cutlass and followed the blow with a heavy punch using the steel of his sword's basket hilt. Burke fell unconscious, a stream of blood gushing from his nose and mouth.

In an instant, Dietrich was on the princess and seeing to her hurt, but she was unharmed, although slightly roughed up. Sobbing, she fell from his grasp back to her straw pallet and the pirate let her lay where she fell ere he left the cabin, dragging the smitten rogue behind him.

It was the afternoon of the following day when Burke awoke from his beating. Gone were the tempest winds and the storm clouds, and the day was bright and sunny. But there was a shadow of doom, which lay about the decks, and Burke feared the worse, for he knew Ulrich Mancrusher to be a hard man and a fell captain.

Through bloodstained eyes, the condemned glared at his comrades, who had been mustered on the main to witness his punishment. A score of hard men they were, and yet pity and fear was awash in them.

"To all here mustered," bellowed a stout voice ringing true from the poop high above, "witness this punishment, and know that ye yourself will be held accountable for your actions! Whilst it pains me to condemn one of my own men, it angers me to wrath even more so when I am crossed. So be it!"

There was a slight murmur in the men as two burly rogues brought Burke forth from below deck to stand amidst his peers and await his sentence, which he knew was always death on the ships that Ulrich Mancrusher commanded. He was hog-tied hand and foot by a heavy rope of hemp and walking was difficult. Instantly, Ulrich clapped his hands and Burke's guards began to untie him. Many thoughts ran through Burke's tormented mind, for he knew Ulrich Mancrusher was a captain that always extracted death from his men at a moment's notice. Yet, why he was being untied was anyone's guess. After he was untied, Ulrich nodded to the guards. Burke was rubbing his bloody wrists, when two more buccaneers came forward and knocked him to the ground. Then the other rogues began to retie Burke, but not in the fashion that he had previously been hog-tied. This time, they took him and tied his arm to one long rope, his feet to another. A sudden blast of fear swept over Burke, for now he knew his hideous fate.

A shudder of disgust washed over the men, as they were about to witness the harshest punishment in all of piracy. Many of the rogues had heard of Ulrich's savagery, but few men had ever witnessed firsthand the keelhauling of one of their own.

"Before I commence with this punishment and have this scoundrel keelhauled, does the accused have any last wish or statement?"

Burke looked up at the grim figure standing above him high on the poop through glazed eyes, but said nothing. He knew his crime, nothing needed said and no explanation would save his soul now. He accepted his fate as does all buccaneers, with a strong sense of unmovable pride.

With a motion of his large hand, Ulrich's command was heeded and Burke was dragged to the bow of the ship and thrown overboard. The four pirates, two holding the rope that was fastened to Burke's hands, the other two holding the rope that secured his feet, then proceed to drag him along the keel of the Malevolence. The pirates pulled and tugged, dragging the body of their comrade under the hull of the ship. Ulrich had chosen the executioners well, for they knew that if they dragged to slowly

Burke would drown and if they pulled the ropes too quickly he would be beat along the bottom of the ship and be cut to ribbons by all of the barnacles that were stuck to the ship's hull. These four men knew their craft well. The sickening sounds of the pirate's body slamming against the ship's hull thudded through the *Malevolence* and many of the rogues lost their stomach and their strength, for Burke was a friend to many.

In time, Burke's bloody and unconscious body was pulled from the waters and left to dangle in the salt air for a few moments. Even though there were no signs of life left in him, Ulrich's wrath was not ended and he roared out once again.

"Know this, ye sea dogs, any man that crosses me shall reap his reward!" And with that, he had Burke's throat cut from ear to ear, then he slashed the rope with his cutlass and the men watched as the body of their comrade fall back into the grim waters of the Gulf of Misery.

Thus ends Chapter Ten of Book Three

ELEVEN

The Arena of Baezutu

And in time, Tulwryn and the others were brought before the flesh merchants in the Baezutu slave market. The morning was grey and overcast, yet the fire of defiance was in Tulwryn's heart and his eyes were set with quiet fury. A large thrall was ordered to unlock the cage that kept Tulwryn and the others, and Thegn glanced at the other with crimson thoughts dancing through his head; and Tulwryn smiled.

There were large crowds gathering round the slave market, as word had spread quickly that much of the manflesh of this month's haul was destined for the arena, and curiosity was much on the minds of the eager public. The first of the slaves to step from the cage was Thegn Odinson, and he was greeted with howls of lust and fury, for the people of Baezutu saw in him a great warrior, thick of thews and heavy of chest.

After the Northman, there were others, smaller and less stout, and therefore the excited crowd died down and became silent, for these men were not men, but fodder for the games. And in them, the crowd saw dead men standing and nothing more.

Then a dark cloud of doom settled over the slave market, and the slavers grew restless, as did the crowd, for as the last man stepped from the cage a sense of awe permeated the marketplace and fear became a tangible thing.

Tulwryn stepped from the darkness of the cage and entered into the hazy light of the day; his eyes burned black as he looked at his captors, and those of the crowd. Whilst he was not as large as the Northman, the atmosphere around him reeked of violence and the people of Baezutu knew that death walked with him like a beloved friend. After a moment, the silence of the crowd erupted into shouts of frothing lust and they knew they looked upon their champion, if even for a moment.

The slaves were then bound with heavy iron fetters and led to the block. Whilst many of the slaves crumbled under the weight of their chains, Tulwryn and Thegn stood as granite, defiant and bold in the face of their captors. All about the block were scores of buyers, eager to purchase the wares of the flesh merchants. But most of the people there were not merely slave buyers, but pit bosses. These men were not interested in purchasing slaves for mundane thralldom, but rather, they wanted savage fighters whereas they could pit them against each other in the arena and gain much profit, even though the slaves themselves gained death.

Many of the weaker manflesh fell under the lash, and death quickly took them for life had seeped from them the day freedom was denied. But in Tulwryn and the Northman the bosses seen a great strength, and they were pleased at that strength, if even they feared it.

It was late in the afternoon when the two were sold. The man who purchased them looked more akin to a toad than a boss of gladiators; short and fat he was, with a greasy baldhead and bulging eyes that seemed to protrude from his round ruddy face. His dress was as odd as his stature, for he did not wear the garb native to Baezutu but rather some other, more oddly crafted raiment. Dark and filthy was his clothes, and they reeked of the stench of the sea.

As the man approached his two newly acquired pieces of living property, he waved a greasy hand before them and spoke thus:

"I am Lothar Dun'egain, last Heir of the House of Hudlthem. I have purchased ye and your lives are bound to me, for ye will fight and ye will die at my behest, in the arena of Baezutu. Dost thou understand?"

Whilst the Northman nodded, Tulwryn stood as still as stone

and showed no emotion. Lothar at once grew agitated at this defiance and raised his whip to bring it down hard against the warrior's heavy bronzed chest. The lash smote hard across Tulwryn's flesh and a thin ribbon of blood appeared where the whip bit into his skin. But still, the warrior did not move.

Lothar took a step back, then paused. "What is thy name, man?"

The warrior from Nuvia, bane of the North, and Son of Heidmar, then spoke thus:

"I am he who defies you. And I am he who shall steal thy life, as ye have stolen mine. That is all ye need know."

For a moment, there was an air of tension between the master and his slave, and then Lothar laughed.

"Fine, very fine! I see that finally I have acquired quality manflesh, and in you I see great strength and boldness of heart. thou shalt do well to please me in the arena, if thy actions are as bold as your words. Fight well, and ye shall be rewarded; fight poorly, and ye shall die. From this day forward I shall call thee Amwe, which means *the Defiant One* in my native tongue, since ye keep from me thy true name."

"Etnu Caiwryn, blethno lominpye mortu; lythno lominpye panyanu," spoke Tulwryn, in his rough native Nuvian tongue. Seeing the man understood him naught, the barbarian from Heidmar repeated himself in the common language, "In Phantasodyssea, birth guarantees death; life guarantees suffering."

Lothar shrugged his shoulders, apparently unmoved by the barbaric philosophy of his new slave. He simply turned and clapped his hands and his henchmen came and escorted the two warriors from him and took them to a holding cell where they were fed foods of course grain and rice, and watered down wine. They were also clothed in heavy armor of leather and bronze, and outfitted with weapons of every conceivable design. After they ate, the two were led to a training pit where they engaged other slaves in exercises of mortal combat. But by the late evening, fatigue was overtaking the two and even in his defiance, Amwe bowed to sleep and laid his head on a straw pallet and fell into a deep slumber where even his dreams of freedom were all but a distant memory.

* * *

It was the evening of the seventh day since Tulwryn and the Northman was sold into captivity when they were finally led to the arena. For the past week, the two had been fed the first choice of the field and the wine they drank was of the finest vintage; their weapons and armor was likewise the best they had ever seen or used, yet Tulwryn sighed for the Bloodsword, but did not know its whereabouts. Both men dreamed of escape, but yet had no plan of action to make that dream a reality.

Whilst Tulwryn was a strategist and a planner, Thegn Odinson preferred to use his brawn and berserker rage to win his freedom. Anyhow, Tulwryn's mind was drifting on a sea of melancholy and he knew of no way out of the pit other than death. But death was not an option, for he had given his word to Branjadom, crowned prince of Neturu, to find and rescue his royal sister and return her to the imperial palace in the City of the Gods. This he knew he must do, for his honor and his dignity depended on it.

In time, the two were stripped of their armor and weapons and led to a dark cell deep under the floor of the main arena. There they waited, along with a score of other combatants, awaiting their chance to face each other in mortal combat.

Tulwryn wondered why they had been stripped but asked naught a question, keeping his thoughts to himself. Each man was then chained to a heavy stake, which was pounded deep into the ground. There was enough slack in the chain to allow some freedom of movement, but still, they were prisoners awaiting a grim fate.

The stench in the cell was unbearable, and offal and stool was smeared across the length and breadth of the enclosure. Most of the men appeared in a state of lethargy, apparently devoid of all human hope. Only Tulwryn and the Northman appeared alive and alert, the heat of vengeance boiling in their savage veins.

Somewhere off in the distance a heavy gong sounded, and then stout guards in heavy armor entered the cell and began unlocking the fetters that bound the gladiators to their stakes. More than naught, the guards smote down a man with strong blows, and the men cowered before the violence. All but Tulwryn fell before the attacks. Even Thegn Odinson, mightiest of Gerdmor's valiant warriors, fell bloody upon the cold dark earthen floor of that vile cell.

As one of the guards reached for Tulwryn's chain to unlock him, another took a swing at his head with a heavy cudgel. Tulwryn saw the attack from the corner of his eye and ducked the blow. The man, swinging the weapon with all of his burly might, fell off balance as the club passed freely over the warrior's head without making contact. Tulwryn, seeing his chance for attack, sprang up with full force, kicked dirt up into the face of one guard with his free foot, and smote the other with the back of his clenched right fist. The first man fell to the ground, clutching his dirt filled eyes, whilst the other was laid unconscious from the blow, for it was dealt stoutly to his temple. Quickly, Tulwryn used the chain he was bound with to strangle both men dead.

The sounds from above were growing louder, and Tulwryn knew the games were commencing. Frantically, he searched the bodies of the dead guards and located the keys to freedom. Once liberated from his fetters, he likewise freed the Northman. The others he did not free since he believed them to be already dead and not worthy of his efforts.

After freeing themselves, Thegn and Tulwryn outfitted themselves using the armor and weapons of the dead guards. This Tulwryn found to his liking, but the Northman's size prevented him from using much of the armor save for only a steel cap and a bronze shield. Both warriors carried heavy short swords.

Alone, and with no knowledge of the underground tunnel system, Tulwryn and Thegn scampered down the long black corridors in hope of their freedom. On and on they ran, turning right and then left and then right again, for what seemed like an eternity. But still, no end to the tunnels could be found. Every now and again, a torch set in the wall illuminated the area, but for the most part, their trek was in bleak darkness.

As time drifted on, panic began to set in and they felt like rats in a maze, trapped by the hungry cat for its master's amusement. Finally, they came to a steep staircase, which at the top possessed a door made of thick slabs of oak bound by age-old iron. Cautiously, the two warriors climbed the stairs to the door.

"What think you of this," asked Thegn, sweat beading on his pale face.

"I don't know," answered Tulwryn, "This portal could be a blessing or a bane. It may lead to freedom, but by the way the gods have dealt with me in the past, I would venture to say it probably leads to the arena floor itself!"

The Northman glanced around, then answered: "Damn mine soul to Odhinn's seven hells and cook my guts in grease! I'm all for a straight fight to all this sneaking around; let's pass through this door and see what fate the gods have in store for us!" And with that, Tulwryn Bloodsword and Thegn Odinson broke the bonds of that great gate and passed from the darkness of the pit into the searing light of day.

* * *

Through squinted eyes, the two warriors espied their new world as they burst from the dark underground tunnels onto the arena floor. The sounds of the cheering Baezutuian crowd were deafening; men, women, and even bloodthirsty children, began screaming at the top of their lungs at the sight of the two foreign warriors as they entered the arena.

Thegn and his comrade glanced at each other only a moment before the first attack was launched. To Tulwryn's right, a burly warrior dressed in scale maile attacked him viscously with a long steel trident. The warrior from Heidmar parried the spear with a flick of his wrist, laying the flat of his blade heavily against the trident and then returning the strike full force to the attackers unarmored left arm. The arm was severed at the elbow and the man fell backwards holding his bleeding stump with his opposite hand.

Thegn was likewise attacked. Only a second lapsed ere he became enraged and counter attacked with the legendary fury of his northern people. On and on the two warriors battled throughout the long evening. Many warriors fell to their doom, and even Tulwryn and the Northman took dread wounds during the course of the battle. More than once, the Baezutuian officials that operated the games loosed wild beasts with the hopes of ending the onslaught being extracted by the two gladiators, but time and again, even the beasts fell to their deaths at the wrath of the warriors.

Sometime during the fighting, Tulwryn noticed a twinkling of gold and jewels in the stands and from the corner of his eye he espied his owner, the pit boss Lothar Dun'egain. Anger boiled up in him at seeing the man who possessed his freedom, and he ran straight for the wall beneath where the fat man sat. Many warriors tried to intercept the barbarian from Heidmar, but time and again they fell to their deaths, their bodies rent from Tulwryn's savage blade.

In a flash, Thegn paused in his slaughter to watch an amazing feat unfolding. He witnessed a great and heroic deed as Tulwryn leapt from the packed earthen ground of the arena floor and flew through the air to mount the arena wall. With bulging muscles, Tulwryn pulled his corded form atop the wall and jumped down into the stands where Lothar sat. The fat man had little time to scream, as Tulwryn's bloody blade severed his great stomach spilling the man's entrails in the isles. Seeing a chance for escape, Thegn followed suite and joined his comrade in the stands.

For many minutes, the two barbarians reeked havoc on the people of Baezutu and extracted a heavy toll. Men, women, and even children, fell under their wrath yet the two felt no guilt for these people were vile and a purging was a long time needed.

And so, as it is told in the chronicles of Phantasodyssea, Tulwryn Bloodsword, he who was called Amwe the Mighty, the Defiant One, cleansed the arenas of Baezutu in blood and won back his freedom at the center of a maelstrom of violence.

Thus ends Chapter Eleven of Book Three

TWELVE

The Bear Hunt

And so it was, that Thegn the Northman from Gerdmor and Tulwryn Bloodsword, after escaping the arena of Baezutu, made their way northeastward into the wilds of the Wastes, and there they came to a large river and thusly crossed over its dark waters and entered into the depths of the Azure Wood. It was there, in the stillness of that great forest, that Tulwryn finally told his friend about his mission and the charge that Branjadom of Neturu had given him. The Northman sat near Tulwryn and listened to his tale, but said naught, for it was not in his nature to be a crusader for the cause of another, even if the other be his friend.

In the days and weeks that followed, Tulwryn and the Northman traveled thusly, foraging the wilds for their sustenance but forever did Tulwryn bite his tongue and refrain from speaking of the princess thereafter knowing that the tale pained Thegn. Even so, he knew that soon he must part from his friend and strike out on his own, for he had given his oath to the prince of Neturu.

The days of his journey were long, but the nights longer, and the warrior from Heidmar was troubled and could not sleep. In truth, he was amazed that no longer was he plagued by the visions of his burden of the kinslaying, but rather a new burden, and that was of the princess, Octavia. Gone from his mind were the images of the kinslaying, and even the faces of his dead sons were but a memory; only now, he was obsessed by the princess and her rescue, even so he had never laid eyes on her beauty.

In time, Thegn the Northman began to rue the taste of wild herbs and fruit and the vegetation of the wood, and ever after did he crave the taste of meat, and so, being without ample weapons for felling game, he crafted himself a great bow of yew wood. And from bits of obsidian and flint did he work these stones into sharp arrowheads, which he affixed to the straight shafts of maple and hickory that he obtained from the wood.

One such morning, when his hunger moved him, he took up his bow and his arrows and went silently away from the camp in search of ready game. It was an auspicious morning indeed, and the air was heavy with melancholy for death lingered in the heart and mind of Thegn, the Northman from Gerdmor.

Upon stirring awake, Tulwryn noticed his friend's pallet empty and so he rose and left camp in search of his comrade. The day was still young when Tulwryn came upon Thegn on his hunt deep in the wood, and a strong feeling of uncertainty was heavy in his heart but he knew naught why.

And there was much excitement in Thegn's heart and he swallowed hard to hold down his thrill and steady his aim, for near him he espied a great bear foraging in the woods. Silently, the barbarian crept holding his bow and his arrows before him, and when he was within an arrow shot from his prey, he retrieved one arrow from the quiver and notched it. From a distance, Tulwryn witnessed the whole scene unfolding but shouted naught for he knew his friend to be in great danger had the beast seen him ere he took his shot.

The woods were still that day and not a bird chirped nor did any other wild sound enter the ears of the hunter, for he was in concentration on the kill and his mind was one with his quarry. Pulling the bowstring taught to his ear, Thegn aimed and loosed the shaft. The next few moments were as a blur, but the nightmare that unfolded would be ever etched in Tulwryn's brain forever.

In that moment, time stood still and the world fell away as did a life; and the shaft flew true and smote the great beast in the eye. And rocking back on its massive haunches, the bear screamed out in pain but it was not the scream of a beast but the cries of a man, and Tulwryn was moved to pity. Thegn knew naught of the pity that moved Tulwryn, for he was a barbarian of Gerdmor, but still, he knew that something was amiss in the world and he dropped his bow and ran off into the wood as a frightened child.

And from his place in the wood, Tulwryn watched the great beast as it groped at its face with mighty claws. The blooded shaft was still protruding from the wound and Tulwryn could see that the hurt was fatal and there was nothing more anyone could do, and the great beast died in pain and fell silent on the floor of the wood.

Tulwryn approached the massive carcass with cautious apprehension, appalled at the morning's murder. And looking up at the heavens he roared out a mighty roar that rent the firmament, and said:

"A great wrong has been committed this morning for only the greed of palate and stomach! Why must men kill when they need not flesh to live? As this mighty beast fell to the greed of man I am ashamed to be a man, even so it 'twas naught I that slayed him; and so from this day forward I vow never to hunt again nor eat of the flesh of any living thing." And so it was, that Tulwryn turned from the dead beast and walked silently away, his heart heavy with melancholy.

Never did he turn and wander to find his friend, for he knew Thegn to have been cursed with the madness of the hunt, and so he made his way eastward and resumed his quest to find the princess of Neturu. But every now and again, Tulwryn wondered if the spirit of the bear had possessed the warrior from Gerdmor, and he missed his friend, and grieved.

Thus ends Chapter Twelve of Book Three

THIRTEEN

A Meeting of Friends

For a day and a half Tulwryn trekked through the underbrush of the Azure Wood. The morning was cool and brisk, as was common in the wood, but the afternoon soon became humid and stifling, and his strength was sapped. Even so, the warrior from Nuvia kept up his pace eastward and trudged onward in his quest.

The Azure Wood was Tulwryn's old haunt and he knew it like the back of his hand even though he had not graced the forest with his presence in many years. Even with his heart heavy with melancholy at the loss of his friend, the theft of the Bloodsword, and the unknown whereabouts of the princess, Tulwryn smiled, for he loved these woods and the creatures that lived therein.

Along the journey, his mind wandered to the slaying of the great bear and the hideous madness of Thegn Odinson. Something was amiss in the world, but he knew not what it was; perhaps there was a change afoot, as with the dawning of a new age. Tulwryn knew quite well that Phantasodyssea was ancient beyond the count of mortal years, and with that age came change. Most likely, the recent events that shaped his life were also shaping the world. The prophecy foretold as much, he recalled, for it was written that he and the land were one.

"No," he thought to himself and shaking his head in disgust, "I will not allow myself to believe in these tales. I am a common man, not a savior! True, I have been subject to unforeseen circumstances, but as lately, the gods have abandoned me. Therefore, I am no hero; just a common man!"

And so, shaking the delusions of grandeur from his mind, Tulwryn walked on and thought no more of it. In time, he came upon a great lake, which he knew to be South Lake, and he laid down in the soft grasses of its banks and drank his fill from the clear waters of the lake, and was refreshed.

Tulwryn was only slightly familiar with this area of the forest for he seldom journeyed this far south. He knew that he was a few leagues south of the Obsidian River, and thus, many leagues to the north lay his home of Nuvia. There was no reason to journey there, since nothing of his former life remained in that village. The only logical idea that came to mind was to turn his attention southward and travel on toward the twin cities of Mok-Tor. In that vile cesspool of civilization, Tulwryn realized, that he could buy passage on a ship and possibly catch up with the slavers that had kidnapped the princess. It was not much of a plan, since he had no way of knowing the present location of the slavers, but it was all he had at the moment and he realized that even the worst plans sometimes prove their worth.

As the afternoon turned into evening, and evening into night, Tulwryn began to look for a suitable shelter amongst the willows and cattails of the lake whereas to make a comfortable camp. He had no possibles, no food, and no water skins, and therefore, he knew it best to remain near the lake for a few days. Here, he could forage for roots and other wild foods as well as take his fill of the sweet water of South Lake, and in time, replenish his strength.

The moon rose high in the heavens that night and Tulwryn's mind reeled in the nightmares of his burden. He was plagued with visions and sounds, and his heart was heavy with anguish and grief. Suddenly, there amongst the pine boughs of his camp he was not alone, and a shadow was with him.

A stirring in his belly brought him to his senses and the nape of his neck prickled as the shadow came closer. For a moment, Tulwryn thought the shadow to be that of the Bloodsword, but then he realized it to be much too short, and he grew restless, and worried.

"Who goes there and molests my camp," he cried out, but the intruder heeded him naught and continued his approach.

With a gruff laugh, the stranger spoke:

"Has it been so long that you have forgotten the familiar footfalls of your old friend?"

The sound of the voice was indeed familiar, thought Tulwryn, but the accent was strange, as was the man's dress. Short he was, but broad, and wearing a dark cloak with a heavy cowl that hid all but his face. Tulwryn searched his mind and his heart finally jumped for joy at the thought of being rejoined with his old comrade Dillwyn Anvilhand the dwarf, but then confusion overcame him.

"Dillwyn, is that you?"

"Aye," answered the dwarf, "'tis I indeed, in the flesh. Do you realize how hard you are to track in this wilderness?" And he gave another laugh from his robust belly.

"But what you here, so far from Covensted?"

"Are we not old friends," asked the dwarf. "Have we not been through much together?"

"Well, yes, but . . ."

Dillwyn interrupted with the wave of a hand. "Tulwryn, it has been five turnings of the great wheel of the seasons since we parted ways at Phaedron and I have missed you much. For these past years, as you know, I have studied with Mimir in Covensted. Much has the old sage taught me, yet much I still am destined to learn. Yet, in any case, you are in need of my aid and I am in need of adventure. Surely, thou must realize that a dwarf's heart is not content to be a recluse forever, and in time, I must return to my wanderings for it is in mine blood and mine soul."

Tulwryn bowed his head for he knew he was in the company of a great wizard, and moreso, a beloved friend.

"'Tis good to see you old friend. Have ye used thy craft to espy on me and learn of mine doom?"

"Indeed I have, Tulwryn. Mimir has taught me the art and

with that aid I saw that you had fell from your status. I then learned, by means of my craft, of all that befell you, of your battles with the Knobites, and of the charge of the Neturuians. After Mim gave me leave, I journeyed westward to find you, but alas, by then you had fallen in with the flesh merchants, and was on your way to the arenas of Baezutu. But enough said of such grim events and there is no need to waste time talking about the past. It is good that you are alive and without much hurt."

Tulwryn laughed. "'Twill take much to end mine days it seems. Even though the gods have abandoned me, they still leave me with the strength to best mine enemies, even without the blade."

The dwarf's brow furrowed deeply and a grave look overshadowed his fell eyes.

"What say you," he asked. "Where is the Bloodsword?"

Tulwryn shrugged his broad shoulders.

"I know naught. When I was overcome in the forest by the slavers they knocked my to the ground with heavy blows and bound me hand and foot like a wild thing. When I regained my senses I was all but naked and in a cage, without armor or my sword."

"And so again the Bloodsword has made its way into the hands of the enemy?"

"Perhaps, but methinks that the thieves know not what they possess. To them, the blade is merely an old relic and nothing more. It will turn up in the armories of the world sooner or later, of that much I am certain. Anyhow, my quest is to find the princess Octavia and reunite her with her people. I will search out the Bloodsword thereafter."

"But how wilt thou accomplish this task without the Sword?"

Tulwryn paused and thought long and hard about his words. The wild sounds of the woods seemed to grow in the silence of his thoughts, yet his heart moved toward his friend.

"Dillwyn," said he, "one eve, some nights past, I was visited once again by the Shadow of the Sword. It said that I was the Bloodsword and that I should not rely too heavily on the blade itself. Perhaps this is the working of the gods, that they take the blade from me so that I am forced to become that which I am destined to become."

"So, you have finally come to believe in the prophecies and your role in them?"

"I am not certain as to what I believe anymore," answered Tulwryn. "All I know is that once I smote great armies by the use of some celestial flame called forth from the blade you wrought, but in years past, that power has been denied me. Why, I know naught? Perhaps only time will tell."

The dwarf nodded his burly head and in the distance a wolf bayed at the rising moon. All about the camp, the wild things of the night were stirring and soon Tulwryn's lids became heavy.

"Yes, indeed," Dillwyn said, "perhaps only time will tell. Come my friend, let us get some rest this eve for we know naught what the future brings."

Thus ends Chapter Thirteen of Book Three

FOURTEEN

Dinner for Two

It was dark, and dank, in Octavia's cell. The mustiness of the air and the putrid surroundings of the room made existence most unbearable. Her hair, no longer clean and shiny, hung limp over her frail shoulders. Gone were the fragrant poppies that laced her once beautiful locks. Dirt and grime of the journey was smeared over her tiny face, yet in her eyes, there still remained a bit of Neturuian pride. Even her gown, the royal garment of a Neturuian princess, and the one she had been wearing on the night of her capture, was soiled and torn.

Octavia sighed. She looked down at her fingers and toes as she sat on the edge of her sleeping cot. All of her jewels, rings of amethyst and sapphire, ruby and diamonds, the brooch of black onyx given to her by her mother, and the necklace of fire opal and pearls that her grandmother gifted her years before, had been looted by the pirates. She thought quietly to herself, and she wondered at the theft. The jewels were from the Royal House of Neturu, worth more than a mortal king's ransom, so why were the buccaneers interested in her. But alas, she knew, a living goddess among mortals was a treasure beyond value. And she shuddered at the thought of what they had in store for her.

Shadows danced off the walls as the old slaver bucked at the waves and the timbers of the mighty ship groaned under the relentless pounding of the sea. To and fro went the great boat and more than once did Octavia feel the urge to vomit as she felt the sea sickness overtaking her at the rhythmic churning of her cell, but she fought back the urges and steeled herself for what lay ahead.

Then her mind drifted back to Neturu, and her magical pool. Octavia wondered about Tulwryn. It had been long since she gazed into the deep depths of the Pool of Neturu and watched her hero, and she wondered how he fared. She knew him to be strong beyond words, yet still, she yearned to see him, and a great melancholy overtook her and she cried.

Just then, the door to her cell creaked open and a large burly rogue walked across the threshold. A shiver ran up Octavia's spine as she feared that another attack on her virginity was in progress. Quickly, she pulled the soiled woolen blanket up about herself in a frail makeshift attempt at personal security. Through tear stained eyes she gazed daggers at the intruder, secretly wishing her delicate powers of magic were more suited for combat rather than mere foresight.

Seeing that the small child was frightened, Ulrich Mancrusher smiled, then gave a deep belly laugh as was his nature when he was in the company of weaker foes.

"I come to harm thee naught," laughed the haughty rouge at the child from Neturu. "Rather, I come hither to announce that you shall be molested no longer whilst aboard my ship, for the surly sea knave that attacked ye afore no longer lives."

Octavia dried her wet eyes with the back of her dirty hand and all but ceased her crying. Standing before her was a man of incredible size, his blue-black beard was long and unkempt, and a dark patch, as black as the gaping pit of hell, was covering his left eye, from under which a long pale scar wound its way, serpent-like, across his darkly lined face. The belly of the pirate was huge and round, and the fabric of his soiled surcoat was stretched to the limit. A great wide belt of darkly tanned leather embossed with strange markings wound about the man's thick waist, and through which, a large cutlass was thrust, and overwhich, his entire front was doused in fresh blood. And she wondered as to what manner her attacker was made to suffer and die.

"Who art thou," she asked, "and where art thou taking me?"

Ulrich smiled a great grin, his large yellow teeth clinched tight. Octavia could see the muscles of the pirate's jaws flexing even under his thick beard and she knew that his intentions were not good.

"My name is Ulrich Mancrusher," spouted the outlaw, waiting for a sign of terror to spring into the eyes of his cargo, but Octavia gave him so such satisfaction. In fact, she had never heard of him before being cloistered behind the mighty walls of the Neturuian Temple of the Cat all the days of her life. Even though the man standing before her was the most dread buccaneer in all the known world, his name meant nothing to her, and he frowned.

"So, then where art thou taking me? To which port are we bound for," she asked.

"The whereabouts of our destination are not important to ye, m'lady," replied the rouge, mocking her royal Neturuian accent with much contempt. "Just understand that you will not be harmed whilst in my care." And with that, the large man spun on a heel and exited the cell, slamming the door behind him. Octavia's heart sank deep as she heard the heavy bolt slide into place locking her in, and she knew that she was once again a prisoner and at the mercy of uncompassionate men.

For days, it seemed, the Malevolence tossed about on the relentless waves of the sea. The princess of Neturu grew weaker by the hour, for the pirates fed her only once a day, and that was nothing more than a thick paste-like curry or a bowl of porridge. How anyone could live on such fare, Octavia knew naught. She remembered her life back at the Temple, and the scrumptious feasts her brother would throw: Tables upon tables of ripe mangos and dates, pineapples and kiwi; the best of the Neturuian crop was brought before her in an attempt to spoil her with the cream of the land. Countless plates of stews and casseroles, endless bowls of sweet soups and delicious deserts, numberless loaves of warm breads, all these and more were at her fingertips. And then there was the wine, the fine Neturuian wine made from the choicest grapes in her brother's vineyards. Octavia relished in these memories, secretly wondering where Branjadom was and how he was doing. She wondered if he was using his powers as the High Prince of Neturu to devise a way to rescue her, and then her heart sunk once again.

She remembered their argument over Tulwryn only nights before her capture, and she feared that treachery was in the works. Perhaps, thought she, it was Branjadom himself that hired the pirates? Maybe this was his way of protecting her from herself; from Tulwryn? No! She angrily cursed under her breath. No matter how upset Branjadom was about her infatuation with the barbarian, Octavia could not bring herself to believe he was behind her kidnapping.

It was nearing the noon of the day and she knew that Ulrich would soon be bringing her some food, as was his nature to do. She could tell that he had taken a fond liking to her since the night of Burke's attack, and he made it routine to visit her at least once a day, usually bringing with him a small bowl of hot porridge and a hard loaf of bread. Her belly growled reminding her that he was late this day, and she wondered the reason.

Octavia gazed down at her dirty hands and feet, she looked with contempt on her torn and soiled dress, never in her life had she taken a fondness to filth and the rancid conditions of her cell and her own body moved her to pity. Her mind drifted back to Neturu and the Temple of the Cat. She remembered taking long, hot baths; she remembered the fragrant scents and the luscious lather of exotic soaps and oils. She remembered how it felt to be clean, yet she knew naught how long it had been since she felt such pleasures. Had it been a day or a year since she had been kidnapped? She had no way of knowing, locked in the belly of that great wooden beast. Octavia had lost track of time, for never had she been allowed to leave her quarters since the ship set sail.

Suddenly, and without warning, the door to her cell swung wide and three burly rogues entered, unannounced. The princess was taken aback with fear washing over her like a wave, yet the men entered too quickly for her to utter a single sound.

Behind the three pirates, and entering just as fast, was none other than Ulrich Mancrusher. His gaze landed upon Octavia and he could see that she was frightened.

"Be still," he called out to her, "we come not hither to harm ye." Then he bid her come near with a wave of his mighty hand.

"Come, I have prepared a bath for thee in my own stateroom. After you have washed yourself clean, you shall dine with me, and then, perhaps, I shall take you up on the poop so thee can have thy first taste of daylight in over a fortnight."

Many thoughts ran through Octavia's mind. First, there was an unreserved apprehension and the question as to why the buccaneer was eager to clean her up and feed her with a private feast in his company, since she had been treated as mere livestock since the onset of the journey. Then there was the excitement of seeing the daytime sun once again, afterwhich she had been forced to bask in the serene darkness of her cell since the night of her capture. Her emotions ran wild and she knew not whether to fear the pirate or love him. For certain, he was her kidnapper, the very man who stole her freedom, and yet he was also her protector, the one who extracted the price of death from any man who would do harm to her. And yet, her heart still pined for Tulwryn's touch. With these thoughts still swimming through her mind, she buried her feelings and followed the men out of her cell and into the darkness of the outer hall leading to Ulrich Mancrusher's stateroom.

* * *

The quarters of Ulrich Mancrusher was not what Octavia expected. The stateroom was meticulously clean, and there was a faint scent of sandalwood drifting in the air. The large room was petitioned off with a darkly stained bamboo screen to one side, behind which a steaming brass bathing vat had been prepared for her use. The hardwood floor was covered with deeply shag Phaedronian rugs, extravagantly dyed in the most exotic hues. Armoires full of exotic silks and linens, tables strewn with a king's ransom of perfumes and unguents, and priceless wall hangings adorned the room as well. All of this, and more, was apparently set up for the comfort of the rogue's new guest.

"I hope ye find these trappings fitting, m'lady," said the pirate to his captive. "Please, make yourself at home. Take as long as you like. When you have finished with your bath, I shall return and we shall dine together. A guard will be placed beyond yonder door. If you have need of anything, make it known to him and he will send for me at once. Dost thou understand?" The princess nodded.

"Very well," spoke Ulrich Mancrusher, tipping his hat. "Until we meet again." He thusly spun on a heel and exited the room.

Once again, alone with her thoughts, Octavia stripped off her soiled garments and slid into the hot waters of the bath. It had been so long since she felt the luxury of silken soaps upon her ivory skin and she drifted into an almost trance-like state. Her mind reeled under the many fragrances that were bombarding her senses; sandalwood and jasmine, Kiputu and lilac. Slightly intoxicating, they were, yet mentally stimulating as well. Her inner sight was heightened, and in her mind's eye, for only a brief moment, she say Tulwryn, and her heart leapt. But as quick as the vision arrived, it was lost. With a heavy sigh, the princess of Neturu finished her bath.

Leaving the tub, Octavia made her way across the room to the large mahogany bureau and wrapped herself with a soft robe of L'hoehnian wool. She then took up a burgundy colored brocade cushion and sat herself in front of an oaken table overloaded with luxurious toiletries. Exotic scents and fumes from the far corners of the known world. Liquid treasures that pleased the eyes and teased the senses, yet a thousand lucid thoughts danced through her mind as to why Ulrich Mancrusher, a burly rogue pirate would have her come hither to his stateroom. A shudder graced her spine and she pushed the rancid thoughts from her tormented brain.

One by one, Octavia picked up the small jars and vials of perfumes and creams. Everything was there, and then some, treasures from the east, exotics from the west. There, in a porcelain jar was the golden Crème of Golrin, a soft, silken powder whereby the damsels of Golrin would apply freely to their luscious skin giving themselves the hue of molten gold. And next to that, in a tall and slender vial of wrought turquoise, was the perfume of Kiputu, exceedingly stimulating yet slightly intoxicating.

When the buccaneer finally returned, he did not find what he expected. Rather than return to a freshly bathed yet frightened little girl, he found a goddess. As Ulrich Mancrusher entered the room, he himself adorned in splendor beyond imagination, his eyes beheld a vision of loveliness of which words cannot convey. The two stood motionless for some time, simply eyeing the other in an almost drunken stupor.

"Ah, I see that thou art beautiful beyond words m'lady," spoke the pirate. Octavia nodded and smiled, her petite mouth, whose lips were dyed a deep crimson from a paste made from the scented berries of Bain, curled in devilish innocence.

Taking the girl by the arm, he escorted her gently from the stateroom, down a long hall, to his private dining chamber. The fragrances of the feast assaulted her before they even entered the room. And once there, her eyes beheld such delicacies that even she had not experienced. The entire chamber was bathed in gold brocade, from the heavy curtains and tapestries adorning the walls and windows, to the carpets and rugs as well. Even the large walnut dining table was overlaid with hammered gold leaf. Even the plates, bowls, and flatware, were all wrought of fine gold. Octavia's eyes feasted on such treasures as even she had never seen.

Before she could speak, Ulrich gently led her to a comfortable chair, and then seated himself beside her. With a clap of his stout hands, a servant appeared with a flagon of wine and two crystal goblets.

"Have you ever tasted Nuvian wine," asked the pirate to his prize. She shook her head, all the while wondering why it was Nuvian wine onboard this ship. Of course, this buccaneer had been around the world a dozen times, looting the richest coffers around. This room alone proved as much was true. But Nuvian wine? Tulwryn was from Nuvia, she thought. It could have been wine from anywhere else in the world. Why did he have to say

Nuvia? Was there a connection, and if so, what did it mean? Or was it just some coincidence? Fate or no, her mind drifted to her warrior, and her heart pined for his touch.

"Nuvian wine is among the best in the world," boasted the rogue. "And, as you can see, I surround myself with nothing but the best." Smiling, he pointed at the two crystal goblets, now full of the sparkling liquid. "Ye see these drinking vessels? They are not mere crystal, but hewn from a large Golrin diamond! They alone are worth more than this entire ship."

"Then why risk them aboard?"

The question quickly turned his smile into a frown. "Why not? What have I to fear?"

"Dost thou naught fear anything, master butcher," retorted Octavia to her captor. "Why bring all this wealth onboard this floating barge? For certain, thy own men would fain to slit your thick neck to retain even a fraction of the treasures that I have seen hither."

Leaning back in his chair, the burly man let loose a laugh that shook the very walls of the ship, and then he quieted himself, and looking stern into the eyes of the princess, he spoke thus:

"Lass, I am Ulrich Mancrusher, and this is mine world. Hither, I am the god of the sea! There is not a ship, nor captain, nor crew, that dare to defile me. I am the high chief lord executioner and I fear no man. These treasures are safe here, that ye can bet on."

Again, the rogue clapped his hands and at once the feast was on. For some time, the two simply ate in silence, feasting on the exquisite fare set before them. From the bounty of earth, and air, and sea, nothing was spared. Many a thought traversed Octavia's mind: If this man was so rich and powerful, why had he not set himself up a kingdom; why all this masquerading on the high seas as a common murdering pirate? Ah, for true, the ways of men were unknown to the princess of Neturu. What comforts a man but adventure and violence, and Ulrich Mancrusher was a man among men. His life could not be spent in idle luxuries. No, he won his wealth at the end of a bloody cutlass, and certain enough, his days would end just the same.

"Why have thee brought me hither, and where are we going?"

Through his one good eye, the pirate gazed at the immortal beauty before him. Finishing on a heavy bone of mutton, the buccaneer tossed the scrap into a bowl, washed the morsel down with a hearty gulp of wine, and then spoke.

"M'lady, we are onboard the slave ship Malevolence, and bound for Kemet. Currently we have just sailed past the Cape of No Hope and have entered the Gulf of Misery. Once in the port city of Kemet, there I will abandon this large salver for a smaller Sloop and then sail onward, due east, for the Forbidden island. But do not trouble thyself with that."

The big man then pushed himself from the table. Extending a large and calloused hand, he helped the princess from her chair and, in silence, led her from the room and down a long dimly lit corridor. The hallway zigzagged left and right, and coupled with the ship's tossing about on the waves, Octavia lost all sense of direction. Finally they came to a staircase, of which they ascended to a quaint and cozy landing. Ulrich stopped just before the door and spoke.

"Shield thine eyes, m'lady, for beyond this door lies the outside world."

In an instant the door swung open and the light of day flooded the dark landing with blinding intensity. Octavia's pupils shrunk to pinpoints and the pain seared her as she had never known. Taking the blinded child by the hand, the pirate led her out onto the deck of the ship where she beheld the first daylight that she had seen in weeks.

Slowly and gently, the two of them made their way up the gangplanks and catwalks of the great galleon to the aft ladder that would eventually take them atop the high poop. After a while, Octavia's eyes regained their sight, and she beheld the wondrous world as can only be seen from high atop a tall ship.

Hugging the southern shores of Caiwryn, just south of the great twin city of Mok-Tor, yet at a distance to great to swim for freedom, the princess of Neturu gazed at the city's skyline, and the enormous Azure Wood as its backdrop. She wondered what kinds of fell beasts, and men, made their home in such a place. And then she remembered that somewhere deep in the heart of that hostile forest lay Nuvia, Tulwryn's home.

Turning her gaze to the south, her beautiful gown blowing in the breeze, the Crème of Golrin reflected in the glorious sunlight giving her ivory skin a divine luster, Octavia took a deep breath and hoped for freedom. But that hope was quickly thwarted, for as far as the eye could see, there was nothing but tossing and endless waves. Leaning on the rail, the princess lost her strength, yet was caught by the stout hand of her beau.

"Come now, m'lady. Ye don't want to cast thyself to the waters yet, and after so good a meal." The pirate boasted a hearty laugh.

"But what will become of me," she asked.

"Have I not protected ye, and bathed ye, and clothed ye, and even fed ye," he asked. "Why thou fear me and mine ways? But, if thou must have it, then so be it. Thou shalt know. Come hither."

Following the rogue to the far side of the deck, both leaned upon the rail. "You see yonder?"

Octavia glanced in the direction the man was pointing, yet shook her head.

"Of course not, we are still too far out. But it's out there, around the curve of the world."

"What's out there," she asked.

"Why, the Forbidden Island, that what."

Even though she had never even heard of such a place, just the name of it sent fear into her heart. She shuddered at what fate lay in such a destination. Ulrich continued:

"After we leave port in Kemet, onboard a sloop that already awaits for us thither, we will sail to the Forbidden Island."

"But why," she interrupted.

"To deliver the goods, m'lady. That's why."

Octavia did not like the look in the pirate's eyes, nor the smug grin on his harsh face. But she knew . . . deep in her being, she knew.

"Me," she spoke softly, almost as if she herself did not want to hear the words.

"Yes, m'lady . . . you. Thou art the precious cargo that I transport. Ye are to be a gift for the island king, Chief Talbod! You see, a man, mine employer, Yalad Munstur, has charged me to transport you to his highness. What his purpose is, I do not know. I am like you in this scheme, merely a pawn. People like us, you and me, do not understand the powers that run the world. We are merely existing to satisfy their desires."

"You do not believe that," she spat back at him in anger. While she had not known Ulrich long, she knew him to be no pawn for another man's use. He was to independent for that, this much she knew. Oh, thought she, he was simply trying to appease her and nothing more.

"Perhaps," he replied. "Perhaps not. But deliver ye I will. That much is certain."

Octavia glanced over the gunwale and gazed into the inky depths of the sea. Time seemed to stand still as she watched the waves crashing into the wooden hull of the *Malevolent.*

"So this is to be my fate: To be stolen from my ancestral home by a Kemetian outlaw, at the request of a hideous flesh merchant, and sent to who knows what kind of existence at the hands of a barbarian king. Perchance that I should just fall into these unforgiving waters and be lost forever."

Sorrow gripping her heart, the big man was moved to pity. Holding her tightly, not as a captor but as a lover, he pressed himself to her and spoke in confidence: "Octavia," said he, for the first time addressing her by her royal name, "I can tell thee, that I will let nothing harm you. Even as I am an outlaw by nature, I am not a barbarian. For certain, this king I know naught. Perhaps he is of royal blood, as are you, and you will live in splendor all your days? But as ye have my oath, I will deliver ye naught into the hands of death, or slavery. And think naught of sleeping under the waves, for there are creatures in these depths that hell hath naught know. Many a scary tale about monsters and serpents abound in these wretched waters, and I have witnessed many a fine sailor washed over the rail only to perish in the deep places of the world. But enough talk of this. Please, let us go below and rest. Use my cabin, for the bed is comfortable and the sheets warm."

He then escorted the princess below deck to his stateroom, and there he left her alone. In the silence of her solitude, again her mind dreams of Tulwryn, and her brother Branjadom.

"Yes, he will save me," Octavia tells herself. But then, hope turns to sadness and she knows fears in her heart that Branjadom may be right . . ."Tulwryn knows me naught," she whispers quietly to herself. "How can he save me when he does not even know I exist?"

Thus ends Chapter Fourteen of Book Three

FIFTEEN

The Savage King

Chief Talbod sat in his quarters, brooding. Candles flickered in the solemn atmosphere of the room, the scent of coconut and passionflower adrift on the air, as a thousand thoughts of heinous and cruel magic passed the transom of his dark mind. Just beyond the twin bronze doors of his palace, the inhabitants of the Forbidden Island joyously prepare for the annual celebration of Mokksbod, and the arrival of the princess. But the king had other plans.

For certain, it was a day like any other, and yet, it was different. This day was a long time in the making, and the world, he vowed, would soon learn of its mistake. Yes, thought he, the world would soon feel the wrath that had stirred in his veins for his entire life. But for what, five thousand years of exile since the great war? Certainly not, for had it not been that same exile that had eventually led to his enthronement? Surely, he would not have been born into royalty had his bloodline remained on the mainland. It was all a great mystery to him, and still, his heart burned for vengeance . . . but moreso, for power!

Yes, it had been a tricky undertaking, to utilize his royal influence and gain the confidence of a lowly flesh merchant to arrange for the kidnapping of the princess of Neturu. He knew quite well that the people of Neturu were nothing more than a myth to many of the races of Phantasodyssea, yet he knew different. By means of his cruel magic the king was able to extract information from the ethers for his own fell purposes, and this he did unceasingly. He realized that no one would search out a missing goddess that legend had bestowed into myth. Who would take such a charge? And so, knowing this, his prize was well chosen.

The king's heart stirred at the thought of young virgin flesh smothering under his great weight, and then he thought of the sacrifice itself. Slowly, he lifted himself from his great chair and stood on massive legs and walked to his private balcony. Chief Talbod then pushed open the double bamboo doors and passed over the threshold, stepping out into the view of his subjects, many stories below.

The king, a man in his sixties yet looking decades younger, was a terrible sight to behold. His skin was burned dark black from many seasons living under the hot tropic sun of Phantasodyssea. Around his head he wore the feathered plume of the Xlobyte, the native raptor and most deadly bird of prey in all of Caiwryn, as the sign of his sovereign lordship, and nothing more. While he was enormously heavy, his face was lovely to behold, yet his heart cruel. For centuries, the people of the Forbidden Island lived in peace and harmony in their exile, yet with his coronation, a great evil had come to Eden.

When the citizens of his kingdom saw him standing naked on the royal balcony they cheered, not out of love, but fear. They knew the day all too well, for Mokksbod was the day that the king would be celebrated, and with that celebration came death. In years past, the king would choose a virgin from among the poorest families of the tribe and sacrifice her to his cruel gods, thereby elevating the family from poverty to exceeding wealth. There were rumors that this wealth simply came from the king's own treasury and not from divine intervention, but no one questioned anything, for fear held them all at bay.

But this year it was to be different. Rumor had it that the through his bitter magics, the king had acquired a goddess of a foreign land and she was to be this year's sacrifice. There was some relief that no tribal virgin would die this day, but as to the reason behind such an atrocity that called for the kidnap of a goddess and then to slay her on an alter of evil, none could know.

But Chief Talbod knew. He knew in his cold, dark heart, his reasons, and these he kept to himself and no other. Yes, it was true that he disclosed his motives, rather vaguely, to the flesh merchant himself, yet that was merely to instill fear in the man's heart and nothing more.

And so it came to pass, that Chief Talbod, king of the Forbidden Island, would exhaust his royal fortunes to obtain the one thing that he was certain would guarantee omnipotent power and transform him from a king into a god. Thus laughing, a thousand thoughts of greed and domination running through his mind, the king turned and walked back to his chamber, and out of the view of his frightened subjects.

Thus ends Chapter Fifteen of Book Three

SIXTEEN

Ayndrian Aelfwine

It was late in the night when Dillwyn woke from his slumber. The sky was still black and many a star shone bright in the heavens, but he saw them naught for the eves of the forest hung thickly over his head. A warm glow was about the campfire, all but wasted into coals, and shadows flickered all about. In the distance, the dwarf could see that Tulwryn was still awake, standing guard near the edge of the clearing.

"Tulwryn, my friend," yelled Dillwyn, "come hither and get some rest. There is no need to stand watch. My magic is guarding this camp."

The warrior from Nuvia relaxed his guard and strode on heavy loins back toward the camp. Dillwyn sat up on his pallet, wrapped his coarse woolen blanket around himself, and then tossed another log on the fire. Tulwryn sat himself on a stump near the fire ring and gazed at the coals until they once again came alive and grew into a living flame. The wood burned, the sap crackled and popped, and the scent of oak and hickory hung heavy throughout the camp.

Breaking the silence, Tulwryn spoke: "So tell me, old friend, of thy adventures after we parted ways at Phaedron."

The dwarf sighed heavily. "There is not much to tell," he said. "After ye left the citadel, I likewise left, returning east with Mimir. We made our way back to his cottage in Covensted, and that's where I have called home for these past five summers."

"Five summers." Tulwryn paused, contemplating. "Has it been so long?"

"Aye," answered Dillwyn, "and longer."

"What do ye mean, longer? Has it been five turnings of the wheel of the seasons, or hasn't it?"

"What is time," answered the dwarf, "but the demon that steals all life. Days, months, years; who's counting? Only mortals concern themselves with linear measurements, not wizards."

"Riddles amuse me naught, dwarf," spate Tulwryn, growing agitated with his friend. "Many a year I have spent with thee, Dillwyn, yet now it seems I know thee naught. Ye have changed."

"As we all do, Tulwryn. That is the nature of time, it changes us. Do ye think that you are the same man ye were two years ago? Five years? Ten?"

"So, you mean to tell me that ye stayed all this time in Covensted?"

"For the most part, yes," answered Dillwyn, "but I did travel forth from time to time, although I never left Mim's cottage."

"Again with riddles?" Tulwryn sighed. He stood up and began to walk away, back toward the clearing, when Dillwyn rose and caught him by the arm. There was still strength in that old grip and Tulwryn grew amazed.

"You have gained in strength, old one."

"Tulwryn, do not be hasty. There is much to tell, for ye have much to learn, if ye would but listen and let thou mind be open."

"Speak then," spoke Tulwryn.

The two of them walked back to the campfire and sat themselves before its warmth.

"Strange, is it not, how the nights of the summer are so cold?"

Tulwryn simply gazed in confusion at the dwarven wizard. Strange, indeed, though he, at the thread of this odd conversation. But still, he bit his tongue and listened to his friend.

"Ye see," said Dillwyn, "Mim taught me the art of pathworking, of journeying forth from the physical body and visiting other places, other dimensions. Utilizing certain chants, transcendental vibrations, one can separate one's true being from the physical vehicle that most people identify as the self. Ha! What fools they are, for we are not this body!"

The dwarf paused, gazing deeply into Tulwryn's dark eyes. "You do understand, do ye naught," asked Dillwyn to his friend, "you who have walked with the shadow surely knows the truth of being."

"Aye," replied the warrior. "I know, but how, I cannot say. 'Tis all but a mystery to me."

"Then let me instruct ye. Tulwryn, you *have* a physical body, but you *are* an immortal spirit. 'Tis this spirit that it the real self. All else is a dream, an illusion. When I sit in deep meditation, I have learned to free my true self from the gross physical vehicle. In this manner, for instance, I can traverse thousands of miles without leaving the confines of Mim's cottage. Many times Mimir and myself have journeyed through the ethers to visit our friend Cohado, who likewise knows the art."

"The Fidelity? Ye have seen the Fidelity?"

"Aye, Tulwryn, I have," answered Dillwyn, "and yes, she still sails the skies above Caiwryn."

Tulwryn sat listening, trying to take it all in. The night grew long, yet the two wanderers knew it naught, and for them, time touched them naught as well. Over the course of many hours they relived past adventures and many quests; the two of them discussed philosophy and magic, war strategies and combat. Throughout the night they conversed, apparently catching up on old times, and looking toward a hopeful and possible future, but mirth was not in Tulwryn's voice, nor Dillwyn's.

After a time, the conversation turned to the present and Dillwyn boldly asked: "What plans have ye for gaining the princess? The Bloodsword?"

Pausing, Tulwryn answered thus: "My plan was to trek southward to Mok-Tor and then to buy passage via ship. With the right ship, I am certain I can catch the slavers before they reach the Forbidden Island."

"Hmmm," the dwarf sighed. "'Tis a plan, I suppose. Might I suggest high magic's aid?"

"Ye knows I have no love for sorcery, Dillwyn!"

"I know, but I was merely thinking about Cohado's windship; with the Fidelity we could catch that galleon with ease and dispatch her even quicker."

"Let me sleep on it, I have much on my mind."

"Your mind is troubled over the girl, is it naught?"

"Aye."

"Tulwryn, mine friend, the blade is thy priority, not that Neturuian lass."

"When I want your advice, old man, I shall ask for it," Tulwryn snapped. The dwarf sat quietly for a time.

Dillwyn removed his pipe from its ditty and quietly lit it. Leaning back, he took a long drag and slowly blew a gray ring of smoke into the crisp night air.

"Tulwryn," spoke the dwarf, "do ye know the tale of the lonely queen?'

The warrior from Nuvia shook his head. He was about to speak, then grew silent, for Dillwyn's glance held him in amaze.

"Once there was a beautiful queen, fair of skin and slight of build, who cast a great light about the entire world. Ayndrian Aelfwine was her name and elf friend she was, for her realm was vast and it encompassed all of the lands of Faery. But heavy was her heart for she knew no king and had no heir. And as the tale is told, the fair elf queen bound her golden tresses with an emerald veil, and over her slender shoulders she tossed her forest cloak, whereas she left the safety of her Hall to search the realm for love, and her king.

"And on that day, a great doom fell over the realm, for once on the trail alone, the Lonely Queen, unaided by steel or magic, fell prey to a grim dragon, who swept down upon her and carried her off to his lair.

"Now there are some who say that the Lonely Queen sacrificed herself to that worm, for centuries before she had known a king, but he was evil and cruel and failed to give her an heir, and in her distress she left him, but forgave him naught, nor even herself, and so, to punish herself, she cast herself upon the mercy of the worm, yet found not a sanctuary but a hell.

"Perhaps this is so, but truly I think naught, for out of loneliness and despair many a dread things happen. And even if the Queen of Elves exiled herself, she was guilty of no sin, but fell prey only to loneliness and sadness. Still, she became prisoner to that vile beast, and slowly the leech drained her of her vivid beauty and vibrant health.

"For many seasons the elves lamented the loss of their queen, and the land withered and died. Grey became the lands of Aelfwine, and all that traveled through the realm was moved to great sadness.

"But alas, now is where the tale takes a turn, for one day a great champion rode through the Grey Glen, as her magical lands came to be known in days of yore, and he stopped to water his steed by a tiny babbling brook. Great was his name, Iyengar the Strong he was called, dispatcher of vile beasts he was, and valiant. Heir to the Throne of Machthorr, and crown prince of the House of Yenengrad. Yet some knew him as Panyano-mortu or Suffering Death in the common tongue, for his wrath was great and his strength unmatched in all the world. But his dearest comrades guarded his true name, for he was Garthor, the king's son and that name carried a heavy price.

"On a red horse he did ride; a tall and powerful charger, yet no armor did he wear save a light shirt of maile and a steel cap. A heavy sword was his weapon and his shield, and before his arm no man could stand and hope to live.

"After dismounting from El-tiburon, his steed, he led the fair beast to the brook, but the water was dark. He noticed doom all about him and a great dread overshadowed his heart.

"'What vile evil has ensnared this land,' he whispered to himself, when suddenly afore him stood a vision of loveliness, and his heart was then moved to love, yet he was afraid for he thought the lady an evil sprite ready to theft his soul.

"'I am Ayndrian Aelfwine,' said the Lady. 'Rescue me.' And his heart leapt with joy and his fear left him.

"'Who are you m'lady,' he asked as he bowed deeply, then fell prostrate before her.

"'I am queen of these lands, but I have been taken prisoner by a grim dragon, and my realm wanes. Alas, so too do I slowly die, as you can see my beauty is fading.'

"But the warrior shook his head, for he saw only a wondrous sight, vast was her beauty, and her voice was like the sweetest music to his ears.

"'Nay,' said he, 'I see naught the fading of your beauty, but the fairness of your skin, the healthy gleam of your eyes, and the hue of radiance about your milky face. Say not your beauty fades, for truly, I have never seen the likes of you nor will I ever. Lovely Ayndrian Aelfwine, I take you as my queen from this day forward, and as long as you live I shall love no other!'

"'But alas, dear champion, even you cannot break the spell of this vile worm! How can you rescue me without destroying yourself? For his poison is dread, and his wrath deep.'

"And there Iyengar stood with a fell look in his dark eyes and a mood of melancholy washed over him. He removed his tall helm, a cap of polished silver, and his scalp shown like the radiance of the sun, for his head was shaved of every lock. A great gleam shown in his dark eyes, like the flashes of red fire seen in black diamonds, and he smiled a grim smile and spoke:

"'M' lady, I am your champion . . . and your king. From this vile beast I will liberate you, and even give you the ultimate treasure; an heiress of gold and lace who shall be known as Denali, the greatest Queen in all the world! But ere the deed be done ye must trust me as thou has trusted no other, and give to me unconditionally all your love. Can you do this?'

"And the lady sat afore him and was imprisoned by her own pride and mistrust, and across her beautiful face was etched a great sadness, and the apparition faded from his sight, and a great heavy tear fell from his dark eyes.

"Silently, he mounted his steed and brought the beast around, yet before he cantered off, he raised his eyes to the heavens and called out in a loud voice, and this is what he said:

"'I vow to thee, oh Ayndrian Aelfwine, my queen, that I shall search ye out and free thee from this self imposed exile, for

I love you as I have loved no other! But know this, even though my love is great, and my wrath against this fell worm is mighty, your strength is greater still. Call my name three times and I shall be there! But even ere my sword falls on the beast's throat, ye can destroy him by loving me . . . and this is true, for I am already yours, and all I have, yea, all I am, is yours! To love me unconditionally is to free yourself from this bondage, and the fetters of this poison can never touch thee again!'

"Then he fell silent and reigned El-tiburon through the fen and disappeared from sight, but in his heart he heard a small voice say, 'be patient father . . . mother loves you but she needs time.' And another tear fell from the dark eyes of the warrior as he rode away."

All was silent for a long time, and then Tulwryn spoke.

"So," asked Tulwryn, "did she trust the warrior? And did he free her?"

"None can say," answered Dillwyn, "if Iyengar the Strong slayed the worm, nor does anyone know if he freed the Queen from her prison and returned Ayndrian Aelfwine to her blessed Hall in Doerr L'oren. I would like to think that he did. I would like to think that she then wed her champion and made him king of all the realms of Faery, for I believe he loved her and would remain her husband, her protector, her lover, and her slave, but these tales are forgotten, and faded from the world."

"Then why tell me such a tragic yarn, Dillwyn," Tulwryn snapped back, angry at a tale of such gibberish, and angrier still, at himself, for listening to an old man's nursery riddle.

"I tell ye this tale to teach ye the folly of women and the tragedy when trust is not granted thereto. Guard thine heart, young warrior. For the lass ye hunt is not a mortal as ye know it. She is a goddess."

"Perchance ye know something that I do naught?"

"Only this," the dwarf continued," my art has shown me a glimpse of what is to come. Thine destiny and the destiny of the princess are along separate paths. Remember this when she asks for thine hand."

"My hand," Tulwryn exclaimed! "What nonsense ye speak, old one! If mine past has taught me anything, 'tis that I shall walk alone all my days. This I already know."

"Good, then remember this conversation when the time comes. Answer with your head and not your heart, for a wise man guards his senses well, yet the fool casts himself upon the mercy of the Lord of Death."

"It is late, old man, and I grow weary of your riddles and yarns. I am off to sleep, and ye better get some rest as well. We have a long day ahead of us, that is, if ye intend to join me in this quest."

The dwarf nodded, pulling his woolen blanket up around his wide shoulders.

"Aye, Tulwryn, where thee goes, so too will I follow." And the two companions rolled themselves in their bedrolls and drifted off to the realm of shadows and dreams.

Tulwryn was asleep no longer than a few moments when the dark hand of doom groped him from his slumber. Opening his eyes he woke in a surreal nightmare world. A cold rush of anxiety poured over his being, yet it vanished as quickly as it came. Looking around, he spied no dwarf, and he knew that he was alone. Even his mount was gone, and all of his worldly possessions as well. Standing, he glanced down at himself. He was not wearing his normal attire, but was clothed in the light grey raiment of the Shadow Elves. He had heard of these people before, but he thought them to be merely myth. Again, he thought of the Bloodsword, and of the Shadow of that accursed blade. Curiously, he was drawn southward with an eagerness to explore the terrible landscape that stretched out before him.

All about him were the greenest pastures that he have ever seen. The bright sun was shinning with an intensity he had never before experienced, and the skies were the deepest blue that Tulwryn's imagination had ever beheld. Far off in the distance, the warrior from Nuvia noticed a thick forest with tall dark trees, and while the atmosphere was beyond beauty, he could not help but feel a deep emotion of despair welling up inside his heart.

All of a sudden, the sound of many hooves beating the earth and the panting breath of a heavy horse blasted his ears. From behind him came a rider, and he turned quickly to gaze at that proud warrior, his breast maile streaked in crimson red. A lone wolf howled as the Shadow rode past like the wind; the demon horse's steel-shod hooves thundering loudly as they went their way. Deafening moaned the earth as the Shade rode to the Gate of the Seven Hells, and beyond.

"Come Tulwryn," whispered the Shadow, and Tulwryn heard it deep in his being. "Come, and find your destiny!"

For a moment, Tulwryn stood in amazement as he watched the rider vanish before his eyes into the distant forest. But soon he once again took up his spirit-journey southward, following the Shadow of the Blade.

Onwards he walked through the lush pasture, as wide as the horizon and as far as the eyes could see. Yet, in the far distance, Tulwryn espied the dark forest beyond the pasture's boundary, and towering over even the mightiest of trees was a lone Ash, and he knew this was where his journey lay. Forever green that mighty Ash stood, and it stood beside a sacred spring; a tall tree it was, throwing from its boughs sparkling drops of clear dew down into the valley below.

After some time, Tulwryn noticed the sky had darkened and a strange chilling wind was gently blowing up from the south. As he continue on his journey, far off in the distance, he noticed a lone herdsman tending sheep. The herdsman seemed old, yet stout, thought Tulwryn. He had a long gray beard and a worn and tattered cloak of the strangest hue of blue. A wide brimmed hat was pulled down over his right eye concealing his aged face.

It was then that Tulwryn saw through the masquerade, and at that instant, he saw not the herdsman's face, but his own.

"Only a fool would linger here to wander through these shadows of night," yelled the Shade with a roar, "Can you not see that the graves gape open and fires are rising? You have no business here . . . make haste!"

A terrible anxiety rushed over Tulwryn at the doom of the

Shadow's heavy words. "Why has thou brought me here to this accursed place," Tulwryn spat in anger. "How shall I extract the riddle of this realm if thee continues to plague me with this insanity? Speak to me like a man, or speak not at all. Do ye hear me, damn ye? Give me back my life!"

At once the Shade vanished, but Tulwryn woke naught from his nightmare. The sun began to sink low on the horizon, and even though it was clearly summer, an almost bitter cold rushed up from the ground into Tulwryn's very being. Onward he walked, pursuing the Shadow of the blade, even at the price of his own doom, until he finally entered the dark forest.

A few paces into that cold and foreboding forest, Tulwryn noticed that the floral and fauna had changed considerably. Nowhere did he see any plant that was recognizable; and the canopy overhead became so thick and entangled that not even a shard of sunlight penetrated to the forest floor.

Finally, he came to a great clearing in the forest where he fond a huge barrow mound. A thick fog began to send out its icy tendrils, and all about him a heavy sent of muskiness hung on the air. Suddenly, there arose a great flame, it roared high above the barrow mound, and the earth shook beneath Tulwryn's feet. The grave opened and once again the Shadow appeared before him.

Fierce was his gaze, and fiercer yet was his stern words. He was clothed in the armaments of a warrior king, with a great oaken shield and a long sword, wet with blood. Like a clasp of thunder his words roared, and Tulwryn's heart weakened as he spoke, for the voice he heard was his own.

"The Gate of the Seven Hells is down," spoke the Shade. "The graves are open and a great flame flickers over the land. Awesome it is to gaze upon it. Don't stay here, make hast while you still can!" And with those final words of warning, the Shadow vanished in a waft of smoke, as did the entire clearing.

Once again, Tulwryn was alone with his thoughts in the center of the great dark forest; no barrow mound could be seen, no heavy scent of musk could be smelled. The great flame was gone and he was alone. Somewhat weakened by the mental trauma of the onslaught of these visions, Tulwryn came upon a large Oak, and sat at its base for some time.

Rising from his seat at the base of the Oak, Tulwryn continued on his journey, stumbling through the forest in darkness. After much wandering, he came to a black stream laden with muck and thick sludge. The scent of pungent stench filled his lungs and he covered his face with a rag. To his right, there came a great splashing, and he crouched in the ferns to conceal himself.

Through the dense weeds Tulwryn saw men wading through the heavy stream. Oath breakers they were, yet others had murdered. How he knew these things, he knew naught, yet know them he did! Some had lured another man's love and basked in the pleasures of adultery, and there the serpent sucked on the corpses and the wolves rent dead men's flesh.

On his hands and knees Tulwryn crawled through this nightmare; he crawled through decaying earth to a clearing in the forest, and there he gazed in amazement, for the black stream was no longer black, but had grown to a deep turquoise blue. And in the stream was swimming a great fish, yet the fish was the color of a man's flesh, and no gills were to be seen anywhere on his body.

"My name is unimportant," spoke the great fish as it peered at Tulwryn though unblinking eyes. "The gods fixed my fate to spend my life swimming, but your destiny lies elsewhere, warrior." With those few words the great fish leapt from the waters and disappeared in a great shower of waves.

Tulwryn test the waters and crossed the stream; its wetness burned at his flesh, and singed his lungs. In his mind's eye, he saw a soot red cock in the halls of Hell, and he knew his fate was near.

Continuing on, many strange sights did Tulwryn see, and finally he came to the base of that dread Ash, its nine roots wound about a dark and foreboding cave. A lone wolf, tethered to an iron stake, moaned loudly, yet his rope will one day break and he will run free to consume the earth!

"Tulwryn," whispered a voice, echoes of a nameless fear, "can you clearly see the doom that awaits the gods?"

Tulwryn shook off the eldritch warning and entered the cave. Finding a stair going down deep into the womb of the earth, Tulwryn walked, feeling his way through the darkness by only touch of hand. The walls were wet with slime, and the stillness of the air was addictive. He fought the urge to abandon his quest, for he was tired and in need of rest.

"No," thought he, "my destiny is upon me, and yet its icy grip enthralls me, and even my strength must prevail. I must continue."

At the bottom of the stair was a chamber that opened to an immense space; at the south end of the chamber, far from sunlight, stood a hall. On the shores of the dead that hall stood. From its roof dripped deadly poison, and the rooms writhed with twisting snakes!

Cautiously, Tulwryn entered the hall yet was not ready for what he saw there. In the center of the room was a deep well and around the well stood four figures draped in darkness. Apprehensively, he approached the well and took his place beside the figures gazing into its still waters. The face of the Shadow stared back at him, and he fell to the ground groping for strength.

The four circled around him and he trembled with an unremembered fear. Slowly, one by one, the figures removed the cowls from their heads, and Tulwryn's fear abated, for he stared into the living eyes of Dillwyn the dwarf, Mimir the Covensted wizard, and Cohado the Long. The fourth figure removed naught his hood, for he and Tulwryn was one, and the Shadow beckoned him to stand.

"Now can you say where your fate lies hidden, Tulwryn Bloodsword, warrior from Nuvia, Amwe, Lion of Heidmar," asked the Shadow. Dillwyn helped his friend up, and Tulwryn staggered to his feet, his head swimming at the mystery unfolding before him. "Beneath this holy tree which hides the sun," spoke the Shadow, "this well will show you the answers ye seek. Come hither often and be naught a stranger to these realms. There will come a day when thee will travel the planes as easily as thou has traveled in the world of men."

Neither Cohado, nor Mimir, nor even Dillwyn, spoke a word. They were present only to witness this rite of passage and nothing more.

Summoning internal strength from he knew not where, Tulwryn stood before that ancient well, and once again peered into its inky depths. This time he did not see the face of the Shadow, nor did he see his own face, but rather, with a clairvoyant and omnipotent eye, Tulwryn saw the whole of the world laid out before him. He saw the past, present, and future, at once, and linear time lost all meaning for him. Then there was a huge galleon tossing about on stout waves, and a large rogue standing next to a beautiful maiden, and yet he knew naught her face. Tulwryn quickly snapped his gaze away from the well and confronted the four shadowy figures surrounding him.

"Why have ye brought me here," he asked in anger, his fear no longer present in his being, "and what would you ask of me? Do ye wish to torment me? Ye delay me from my quest, and I will have it no more!"

The Shadow raised a hand to silence the warrior, and he spoke thus: "Now it is your destiny to visit this well daily and drink from its fountain of wisdom. Good council will ye gain hither. Tulwryn, I have revealed in visions past that I am thee and thee art me, yet you believe me naught. Still, your destiny cannot be easily thwarted. Rise, oh warrior of the world from this well and take your worthy place in the Sage's chair! Drink daily from this sacred spring and contemplate the words of the wise when they speak in hidden runes."

"Far have I traveled," Tulwryn said, "and many wars have I waged. Against the gods have I proved my strength, yet you give me naught a moments peace!"

And the Shadow spoke his final say: "Remember this, oh warrior, every king enjoys his wealth until one destined day. Sooner or later every man surrenders his soul to death, yet your destiny lies beyond the Gate of the Seven Hells. Do not combat with thy destiny, and follow naught false paths. Come home Tulwryn, and take your place among us. Royal blood flows in thine veins!"

Tulwryn was about to answer when all his world went black. When he opened his eyes, he was once again rolled in his warm blankets by the glowing coals of his dying fire. Dillwyn was already up and breaking camp.

"Ye missed a fine sunrise, my friend."

"Oh?" Tulwryn scratched his troubled head. "A dream?"

"'Twas no dream, Tulwryn," answered the dwarf, "'twas the most brilliant sunrise I have seen in a long time. Very nice."

"No, I mean, last night. I had a dream. You were there, as was . . ."

Dillwyn interrupted saying: "As I said, 'twas no dream. Hear and understand this my friend, I foresee that this maid ye seek to rescue is in love with thee, yet it is in my power to know that your destiny lies naught on the same path as does hers. Beware of your feelings and hide them deep. The fate of the world lies on your shoulders."

"I am a sad choice of a savior."

"That may be so, but nonetheless, ye have been chosen. 'Tis your fate. Deal with it, yet say no more. We are wasting good daylight!" Tulwryn nodded and helped the dwarf break camp.

As they journeyed south, toward Mok-Tor, Tulwryn couldn't help but think about the past night's dream and visions, and about the galleon, the rogue, and the girl. Soon, his mind shifted to Dillwyn's tale of the lonely queen, and to Ayndrian Aelfwine. Then he saw her face, yet it was not the face of Ayndrian Aelfwine but the countenance of Octavia, princess of Neturu, yet he knew it naught. Tulwryn's mind then reeled in poem and song, and he felt a happiness that he hadn't felt in years, and he smiled . . .

From the stars that shine above
Tall white mountains that beam forth love
To my queen that I hold dear
Whisper words of love in her ear

Through damp mists and Faery dust
Dance moonbeams among the elms
A gown of yellow, green, and rust
Glides Ayndrian through her immortal realm

Queen of air, and land, and sea
The wee people of the forest love her still
Her breath gives life to all that be
From her font of love I shall drink my fill

She is my queen and I her king
Champion of her cause, and love
Defend her I will

To her, my treasures I shall bring
A golden child with sapphire eyes and golden locks
Lilacs and hollyhocks
Woven through her yellow hair

Happiness of uncounted days
We dance through groves of enchanted elms
Pleasures of unremembered years
Never showing signs of sadness' tears
And dancing forever through Ayndrian's immortal realms
Forever in love

In the glade, deep and shady
There stood an elfin lady
Smiling in the vale

Golden strands fell from her face
Green vines and elder lace
Tangled 'bout her neck

Eyes the color of the sea
Sparkled in the light of day
But the silver of the moon
Reflected in her gaze of steel grey

A smile etched across her face
Her gown of emerald gossamer billowed
in the breeze
My heart danced with joy at the sight of her
Dancing in the wind

Like a wisp of smoke, she moved
My heart shook with happiness
As she touched my face and hands

Lips of crimson ruby red
Parted in a soft warm kiss
As we sailed off to bed in the wooded glen
And a land of bliss

Thus ends Chapter Sixteen of Book Three

SEVENTEEN

A Voice from the Ethers

The sun was high in the heavens and the heat of the forest was stifling before Tulwryn and the dwarf even found themselves upon the main Phaedron Toll Road that wound its way south to Mok-Tor. The two adventurers abandoned their heavy forest cloaks for more comfortable raiment, paid the Phaedronian guards at the Toll gate, and continued afoot.

"At this pace," griped Tulwryn, angrily, "we will never make Mok-Tor in time." Dillwyn spoke no words but kept walking.

"What? Have you no comment, dwarf?"

"Tulwryn, old friend," answered Dillwyn, "what would ye have me do, wizard thee to Mok-Tor?"

"Well, is it naught in thine power?"

"Nay, 'tis naught. Mimir has taught me many things, and my abilities have indeed waxed these past five summers, but alas, I am still bound by the cumbersome vehicle of the flesh, as are you. Without horses or Cohado's windship, I fain we are destine to travel slowly."

"What good is thy damnable wizardry, then?"

The dwarf looked at his friend with contempt, a bitterness welled up in his throat that was difficult to swallow.

"Tulwryn, ye know naught if thy quest even lies in Mok-Tor. 'Tis only a hunch. For all we know, those blasted slavers could bypass the twin cities and make for the port of Kemet, or perchance, they will simply head due east and sally onward to the Forbidden Island itself without even making landfall."

"Perhaps," answered Tulwryn, "but at this pace we shall never know."

Dillwyn paused for a moment, looking deeply at his troubled friend. "What is it, old friend? I have never seen ye this way, except for times long past. 'Tis the girl, or the loss of the sword that troubles thee? Or perchance, does the burden of the kinslaying still weigh heavy on thy heart?"

"Perhaps a little of all."

"And . . ."

"Dillwyn," asked Tulwryn, "earlier afterday, thou spoke of summoning Cohado the Long and petitioning his aid in this matter. Is that still a possibility?"

"Aye," answered the dwarf, with a grim smile.

"Then let it be so. Ye said it yourself that we have no way of knowing the slaver's true route, and afoot we are neither a threat to the criminals nor a benefit to the lady of Neturu. Then let it be done as ye say. Please, for me, dear friend, summon the wizard of Rhyan and beg him come."

Looking up into the heavens, his physical sight obscured by the eves of the wood, Dillwyn peered into the etheric firmament for a moment. Tulwryn watched, knowing that his friend was using his inner sight rather than his two eyes, and was amazed. Suddenly, the dwarf broke his silence.

"This may take some time. Come and let us find a place to rest whereas I can do mine work."

"We haven't much time, Dillwyn," Tulwryn complained.

"Patience, mine child," answered the dwarven wizard, "one cannot be hasty when it comes to magic!"

In time, the two came upon a large oak grove, thick and tall. The area therein was dark and ominous, yet there was a small clearing within the center of the mighty trees. Dillwyn and the warrior from Nuvia entered thus to the clearing. Turning to his friend, the dwarf spoke:

"Tulwryn, find thyself a quiet spot and sit a while. This may take some time. I must prepare to send forth mine spirit, though the ethers, and rendezvous with our old friend via magical means.

There is some fresh fruit, hard bread, and a wineskin, in my pack. Please help yourself." Tulwryn nodded and walked away, seating himself at the base of an aged oak, its truck gnarled and twisted from the passage of time.

The dwarf walked to the center of the clearing and seated himself. Tulwryn watched in amazement as the old dwarf twisted his aged legs into a tight knot, and then, dropping his chin onto his chest, drifted off into an eldritch meditative state. Within a matter of seconds, the dwarf ceased breathing. Tulwryn rose from his place at the foot of the great tree and walked slowly to where his friend sat. Cautiously, he placed a finger upon Dillwyn's neck and fear possessed him, for there was no pulse and the body was cold as ice!

Tulwryn stumbled back as though struck by lightning, cursing the gods!

"Blast ye to hell, Athrum and all thine devilish kin! Blast ye to hell! Why didst ye deliver me into the hands of this wizard, mine friend, only to abandon me in the hour of mine last hope? Blast ye to hell!"

Kneeling at Dillwyn's aged feet, Tulwryn mourned. He mourned in rage, for the magic of Mimir would aid him naught this day; and he mourned in sorrow, for the loss of his dear friend. And even though his loss was great, no tear creased his cheek, but he was heavy of heart, and he sat in quiet for a very long time.

For the remainder of the afternoon, Tulwryn sat, and long into the night as well. He sat in vigil at the loss of his dear friend, now gone, and his mind drifted, and he lost all track of time, all hope in the future seemed lost.

Over barren landscapes, his mind wandered, and through deep canyons; he saw the world as an eagle sees it, yet he knew it to be a dream.

"Tulwryn," spoke a voice from the ethers, and the warrior's heart was stilled, for he remembered that voice, and he spoke naught.

And there, before him came the Shadow of the Bloodsword, and it spoke unto him with harsh words of bittersweet sorrow, and his heart was healed of its sadness.

"Tulwryn, suffer naught, for thy friend is not lost, but rather, he travels thither though the ethers by his will alone. He will return, and with glad tidings. But that is not why I am hither." The Shadow paused for a moment, allowing his words to seep into Tulwryn's being. But the warrior just sat there, cold and empty.

"Thine feelings for the child of Neturu is for naught. Know this, young warrior, that things are naught what they seem. Caiwryn is an ancient world, and the memories of men are short indeed. Tulwryn, thou art older than Mim . . . much older . . . and older than Cohado as well. Canst thou feel it naught in the dirt of the land? Canst ye smell it naught in the air? Much that once was is now forever lost, for none now live that remember it, yet I am hither with thee, to awaken thine memory unto thine true purpose."

Tulwryn looked up at the Shadow, but spoke naught. Too many times had he been visited by the shade, and too many riddles had plagued his brain. He cherished naught these celestial meetings, nor did he enjoy the ramblings of etheric prophecies. He was no savior, thought he, but a mere farmer whose life was destroyed by whimsical gods and manipulative wizards. Yet, he knew in his heart there was some truth to the fell words of the Shadow. And he listened.

"Ye have seen it Tulwryn, ye have felt it. When ye wax, the land waxes with thee. When ye wane, so does the world. Tulwryn, thou are one with Caiwryn and she with thee. This land, the sword, you, are all connected. Ah, but this thou already knows.

"Tulwryn, know this, you and the Bloodsword will be united ere ye even sets thine eyes to the flesh of the Neturuian girl. There is much bloodshed in thy future. Be strong, yet waver naught from your true path. Now awaken from this sleep, for thou friend arrives!"

Tulwryn stirred from his eldritch slumber and gazed into the dark eyes of Dillwyn the dwarf, kneeling before him.

"Me thought that thou was lost," spoke Dillwyn.

"And I you," answered Tulwryn.

"Aye, these days are filled with wonder and even I am not privy to the madness of the world. Ye were in trance! Ha! And I call myself the wizard," the dwarf threw his hands up in wonder. "The gods show favor on thee, mine friend, for what takes me great effort to achieve, thou are granted the gift without toil. So, what did the Shadow reveal?"

"Ah," answered Tulwryn, smiling, "ye first, old one."

Helping his friend to stand, Dillwyn began the telling of his etheric journey.

"Well, yes, I did make contact with Cohado the Long, and he has agreed to help us. Furthermore, he revealed to me his findings in these matters."

"Oh, you wizards are ever meddling in the affairs of men!"

"'Tis our duty, Tulwryn," Dillwyn said, "and our trade."

The two walked on for some time, discussing the matter, and still heading southbound toward Mok-Tor. Tulwryn's mood was somewhat lifted, yet he still drifted into the doldrums of melancholy, as was his nature.

"Cohado will rendezvous with us in Mok-Tor. This much he promised. A day or two further and we should make the city if we keep to this pace."

Tulwryn liked naught the thought of losing the slavers' trail, yet he bit his tongue. He knew the wizards were a wise lot and he valued their council, yet he could not but feel helpless at the moment. His mind thought of the princess in the company of rogue buccaneers, and his heart grew angry. Justice would be his, this much he knew, yet he knew naught why. Of course, he had been wronged by these very same men, his freedom stolen as well as his blade, but he knew naught the Neturuian girl. Yet, he owed Branjadom, her brother, his life. And the two quickened their pace southward.

* * *

Two days had passed since Tulwryn's dream and the dwarf's faring forth into the ethers, when they finally entered the gates of the twin city of Mok-Tor. Due to the nature of their visit, the two adventurers opted to enter the city after nightfall so as not to attract unwanted attention. Tulwryn had told Dillwyn of his exploits in the Baezutuian arena, and the dwarf agreed it best to keep a very low profile whilst in the city. Even though Baezutu was more than seventy leagues to the west, word of adventure and great feats of strength travels quickly in Phantasodyssea. The two knew the dangers if word of their exploits arrived in the city ere them.

A thousand lucid thoughts ran though Tulwryn's mind as he passed through the city gate. Even though his travels had taken him far and wide, he had never stepped foot here, in the southernmost town in Caiwryn, yet their legends he knew all too well.

The city, actually two towns, Mok and Tor, lay in the extreme south of the Azure Wood, merely forty leagues south of Nuvia, Tulwryn's native home. This treacherous strip of land, situated on the shores betwixt the wild South Sea and the tranquil, but dangerous, Gulf of Misery, was known as D'chiel na Bethlomein, the Cape of Hopelessness, in Tulwryn's Nuvian language. Many a sailor's yarn tells of shipwrecks and death in these foreboding black waters, yet the port is an active one at best, and lucrative, due to their extremely durable product, Bluewood, which is impervious to fire and saltwater damage making it essential to the area.

The people of Mok-Tor are a hardy folk and their main export is a composite mystical substance known as Bluewood. It is made through a secret process, believed to be composed of a bark-like substance from a magical tree found in the northeastern area of the Azure Wood combines with a secret mineral found in the caves of Akhrod. To insure a balance of power in the processing of Bluewood, the town of Mok regulates the activities in the caves and the village of Tor maintains timber activities in the forest. Only five people in the town know the manufacturing process of this product, therefore maintaining a strong balance between these two establishments. Neither can operate without the other. The Mokites, Tulwryn knew, were a moral and gentle people, but the Torites were extremely worldly, and violent.

"Tulwryn," spoke the dwarf, "we will wander the city until the late hours of the eve, and then make our way to the Tavern of Kismet. Once there, we shall wait for Cohado."

"Are ye certain he will arrive?"

"Have thee no faith," asked Dillwyn. Tulwryn dropped his head. "Come then, friend. Let us wander forth until the required hour." And the two of them strode down a dusky lane of the city and vanished into the inky darkness of the night.

Thus ends Chapter Seventeen of Book Three

EIGHTEEN

One Last Hope

The Malevolent sailed into the harbor at Kemet like a proud and conquering warrior, her decks were polished, her sails clean. Two grim figures stood high on the poop, their forms shrouded in dark mystery and melancholy, even though a bright Kemetian sun burned high in the heavens.

"I like this naught," spoke Dietrich Oarsbreaker to his captain. "Sailing into these dread waters during the light of day is not wise, I fear."

"Cease thou uneasiness, mine friend," replied Ulrich. "'Twould have brought more attention to us had we arrived after nightfall."

"Maybe so, but still, I like it naught. And the day of our fate draws near! Many a year have I sallied forth on the high seas, a pirate and an outlaw, yet never have I known fear as I do now. I shudder to think of our doom once the princess is in the hands of that barbarian savage."

"Aye," answered the captain, "perhaps our days are numbered? Yet, it matters naught. We have a job to do and do it we will, even at the cost of our own lives. That is the pact we have made."

"Folly, indeed, we made such a pact unknowingly."

"But made it we did, and now the consequences we will learn, be it wealth untold or the sharp end of a cutlass in the back. In time, all will reveal itself. Until then, there is no use in worrying about it. Go below and secure the cargo. Once we are docked, I will send Bollinger ashore to seek out Munster. With luck we can shove off ere the morrow."

"Aye," answered Dietrich, and quickly descended the stairs to the decks below. Ulrich Mancrusher stood in silence for a moment, his hawk-like eye scanning the harbor for anything unusual. "Ye are here, Yalad, I can feel thine filth in my bones," he said quietly to himself, "as Jang is my witness, I will slit your belly asunder for the curse you have set upon us, and the world."

* * *

The Tavern of Kismet was a dreadful place, dark and sullen, frequented only by the most contemptible patrons, truly it was a cesspool of villainy. The saloon lay on Barbary Street, down on the waterfront, near the harbor and shipyards. It was there, in that forsaken corner of the city, that Tulwryn and Dillwyn waited for Cohado's arrival.

"What thinks ye," asked Tulwryn to his friend? "Will Cohado arrive this eve?"

"Aye, Tulwryn, he will. Quickly, let us get a jack of dark ale and sit out yonder on the balcony whilst we wait." The warrior from Nuvia nodded in agreement.

After leaving the bar with two large tankards of that establishment's nasty swill, Tulwryn and the dwarf walked to the rear of the saloon and ascended a stair of roughly hewn maple to a dimly lit landing. There the two made their way down a long narrow hall and then to the door of a secluded balcony. Tulwryn noticed, upon entering the quaint balcony, the entire area was hidden by a thick arbor. This bowery, shielded from prying eyes, was the perfect place to wait for the wizard of Rhyan, since it offered a wondrous view of the entire harbor, and bay as well.

Dillwyn pulled a heavy stool to a stout table and seated himself thereon.

"Pull up a seat, Tulwryn. It may be a while ere Cohado arrives."

The warrior nodded, but did not like the feeling of waiting, sitting like ducks in a shooting gallery. He walked to the table and lowered himself onto a stool, then took a long drink from his Jack. "At least the ale is pleasant," he said to the dwarf, with a contemptible smile.

"'Tis like most everything in the world, Tulwryn. Ye must take the good with the bad."

Minutes passed into hours, and in time, Tulwryn grew agitated. He was a wanderer, an adventurer, and all this creeping around pleased him little. Then suddenly, Dillwyn stood and pointed south with a stubby finger, yet saying nothing. Tulwryn's gazed followed that finger, and his heart stirred at the sight of the Fidelity sailing calmly into the bay.

"By Athrum, he arrives! Cohado arrives!"

"Aye, my friend," answered Dillwyn, "did ye have any doubt?"

The two men stood there in awe as the great ship cruised into the harbor. A sight she was, thought Tulwryn, for she was even larger and more spectacular than he had remembered. Yet, they were the only ones that Cohado had allowed to see her in all her majesty, for he had cloaked her in illusion to all else.

"Come, let us be off," Tulwryn said in haste, but Dillwyn caught him by the arm.

"Nay, Tulwryn," said the dwarf. "We shall wait hither. It is Cohado's request that we wait hither. He will come to us."

"But he is here already, in the harbor. Why should we wait hither, when we can sally forth and meet him at the dock?"

"Because it is his will. He has some business to attend to ere he comes to meet us. I am certain that his business is his own and does not want us to interfere. I can respect that. Now sit and wait. He will be hither ere ye know it."

And wait they did, for three hours the two sat on that accursed balcony and waited. Tulwryn lost track of the number of tankards of ale he consumed, yet his wits were not impeded. His stomach began to grumble and he called for a barhop to bring a menu, but ere his meal was brought, Cohado arrived.

"Greetings friends," spoke Cohado to the travelers.

"Is this how ye greets friends," snapped Tulwryn? "Ye have kept us waiting for hours, yet the Fidelity has been docked for the better part of three hours!"

"Indeed, master Tulwryn," nodded Cohado. "Many apologies for my tardiness, but I had business to attend to."

"What nature of business does a priest of Rhyan have in this seedy town?

"Tulwryn!" Dillwyn raised his voice, apparently angered at the warrior's rude comments. "What business is it of yours what Cohado does hither. It is enough that he has come to aid thee."

"I was not born yesterday, Dillwyn," spat Tulwryn. "Cohado would have come naught unless there is something in it for him. And now his greed proves true. Are ye to sell us out to the authorities of this god forsaken cesspool?"

"Tulwryn," answered Cohado, "after all we have been through, and thee still doubts me? Very well, if ye must know. I was merely making a purchase of a substantial quantity of Bluewood. The Fidelity, among other windships, are in need of repair. The mystical product of Mok-Tor, as you may know, is extremely durable and is also impervious to fire and saltwater damage, making it excellent in windship construction. It is extremely expensive, the most sought after ship building material in the whole of Phantasodyssea, but I am not without my resources." The wizard smiled. "Come, my friends, let us leave this pub and board the Fidelity. We can dine in splendor this eve and after the repairs are made, we can sail forth on thine quest, even unto the ends of the world."

The three of them left the Tavern of Kismet, still under the cover of darkness, and strolled down the waterfront to where the ship was anchored. Again, Tulwryn was in awe of the immenseness of the Fidelity. He also wondered how such a grand ship did not attract the attention of noisy onlookers. The warrior noticed that the few people that were present near the docks acted as if they didn't even notice the majestic galleon floating in their harbor.

"Master Tulwryn," Cohado said, "rest easy, dear friend. Magic is surrounding the ship. No one can see it, except for the few Mok-Torian deckhands loading my shipment of Bluewood into the hold, and to them the ship appears as a rickety old barge, unthreatening in its appearance and size."

The warrior nodded his head, yet grimaced, his question answered, but he liked it naught that the wizard of Rhyan was quick to read his thoughts.

Quickly, the three boarded the Fidelity and made their way to the lower decks. First, Cohado showed the travelers to their private quarters, and then instructed them to come to the dining hall at the top of the hour. "There will be much feasting ere this eve is done," said Cohado, "for on the marrow a great undertaking is before us and we will need much strength. But for now, rest a while in thine cabins. There are a clean change of raiment in the bureaus. Please, help yourselves to whatsoever you find pleasing." He bid them go and he likewise took leave and parted, vanishing down the corridor like a wraith in the night.

"So, again we find ourselves alone." Tulwryn spoke these words, not out of contempt, but as fact. Wizards, he knew, were a strange lot; always showing up when you didn't expect them, and disappearing when you thought that you needed them the most. It was all very aggravating, to say the least.

Time passed quickly and much commotion could be heard above deck. Tulwryn, laying on a bed of burgundy dyed fine silks, listened to the footfalls of the deck crew for the better part of an hour. He closed his eyes and yet, could almost see the non-stop activities of the men as they worked at a breakneck pace to load Cohado's precious Bluewood onto the main deck and then move it again, to deep within the ship's cargo hold. He wondered if these men were undead creations like the mystical warriors he beheld so many years before. Too many questions and not enough answers, he thought to himself. And then he quieted his thoughts for fear that the wizard was once again eavesdropping on the privacy of his mind.

At the top of the hour, Tulwryn and the dwarf was escorted to Cohado's dining hall by a slender mate wearing a saffron dhoti and kurta. The lad, not more than seventeen seasons old, held himself proudly. It was quite clear that such a honorable duty was high on his list of priorities. The boy's head, like Cohado's, sported the typical topknot of the priests of Rhyan. The long braid of dark brown hair fell loosely down his neck and over his left shoulder.

Upon entering the hall, the lad led them to the table where they took their seats across from Cohado, who was already seated. The two bowed to the old priest and he smiled back. Cohado looked at the two travelers before him. Both men had opted to remain in their own clothes rather than utilize the wizard's hospitality of fresh attire.

"Ye did not find the clothes appealing," Cohado asked?

Dillwyn simply smiled, but Tulwryn spoke first. "Sir," said Tulwryn, "whilst thou hospitality is mighty, I will prefer to fight this battle in mine own raiment."

Cohado lifted an eyebrow. "Fight? Who said anything about a fight?"

"Are ye naught taking us into battle?" Tulwryn took his eyes off the priest and glanced at Dillwyn. The dwarf smiled naught, and spoke even less.

"Master Tulwryn," said Cohado, "I give thee the use of the Fidelity, this is true. But she is not ready for any battles. The craft is old, as am I. We are at thy service only until we find the galleon ye seeks. After that, I must leave thee, for this shipment of Bluewood must needs get back to Rhyan. There is much work to do yonder and very little time . . ." The old wizard's words drifted off and his sight turned inwards. Once again, Tulwryn was at a loss.

Dillwyn quickly changed the subject to food, and Cohado clapped his hand loudly. Quickly, ten lean servants appeared, all wearing the priestly attire of Rhyan divinity, and catering to the visitors every whim. The table was set for a king. Plates of silver, bowls of gold, and goblets of carved ruby were laid out before them. Rhyan casseroles, savory breads, plates of cheeses and flagons of sweet milk graced the table as well. For the better part of an hour the three ate in silence, and Tulwryn did his best to quell his many suspicions.

Finally, nearing the end of the meal, Cohado spoke to Dillwyn in a strange tongue that Tulwryn did not know. The dwarf then, in turn, looked at the warrior and spoke.

"Tulwryn," ye can go to your cabin and rest, if it be thy desire. There are some things that Cohado and I must discuss ere we set sail on the morrow."

"To hell I will," answered Tulwryn, quickly coming to his feet and slamming a thick fist down onto the table. "This is my quest, not thine! You will speak thy peace before me, and in a common tongue. I have had enough of these damn riddles and wizard's games!"

Cohado rocked back in his chair laughing.

"Truly ye do your namesake justice, Master Tulwryn, for certainly thou are the Lion of Heidmar!" He then looked at the dwarf. "Oh, alright Dillwyn, let the lad stay. It will be alright."

Tulwryn, calming the rage in his heart, slowly seated himself.

"My two dear friends," spoke Cohado, "the world is once again in grim peril. I have learned, though the means of my art, that a great evil is amassing in the east. Master Tulwryn, your very quest is woven into this dark scenario as ye may never know. But I will now tell thee, so that thou can know everything."

Cohado the Long, high priest of Rhyan, then disclosed everything he knew about the plans of Chief Talbod and Yalad Munster.

"At first," he said, "the plan seemed to be nothing more than a desperate attempt at seizing power.

"Two men, Chief Talbod, a king ruling the Forbidden Island, and Yalad Munster, a notorious flesh merchant, struck a deal some time ago to abduct the princess of Neturu. Of this, you already know. But the reason of this abduction, ye know naught."

Tulwryn was not liking the flow of the conversation, but he listened keenly to all what was said. Anger welled up in his Nuvian veins when Cohado revealed the king's plan.

"Octavia is to be sacrificed to Chief Talbod's bloodthirsty deity on the eve of Mokksbod, less than a fortnight away. Whilst it is possible to catch the slavers ere they reach the island, due to the speed of this craft, overtaking them and rescuing the princess may be another matter."

"Why," asked Tulwryn? "Have ye naught battled more vile creatures than this flesh merchant?" He looked anxiously at Dillwyn, remembering the dwarf's tale concerning the gorkon that was dispatched years ago by this very ship.

"If it would be that simple," answered the priest, "but it is naught."

"And again I ask thee why?"

"Because Yalad Munster carries thine blade!"

"What?"

"Yes, 'tis true, Master Tulwryn," Cohado said. "After ye were captured by the slavers, yet ere ye graced the arenas of Baezutu, thine blade was given to Yalad Munster by the men that ambushed thee. And he is not a mere slaver. Indeed, this trader of living flesh is a menace most evil. He trafficks in the dark arts. If anyone can manipulate the Bloodsword for evil, it is he. Yet, stop him we must. I have foreseen that he plans to take the princess to the Forbidden Island, and, betraying the king, he will proceed with the sacrifice himself. We must thwart his plan, for if he is not destroyed, and the princess rescued, an evil will be released over the whole of the land that has slept undisturbed since the dawn of the world."

"So, it is as if the dragon has awoke already," answered Tulwryn.

"Nay," Cohado replied. "This evil is many times greater than that of Darkoth; and even the dark powers of Kimark Khan knows naught the rage of the god of the Black Death that Yalad Munster seeks to wield. But unbeknownst to even him, the bloodthirsty deity that he must awaken through the sacrifice is utterly uncontrollable. No one can barter with this demon! No one can dare to control its hideous power. Only the ancient magics that have sealed him into his prison dimension, at the cost of many lives, can hold him at bay. And this ignorant mortal, swimming with lustful dreams of power, dares to open the portal with the sacred blood of the virgin goddess of Neturu. Yes, he must be stopped!"

"So," said Tulwryn, "if what ye say is true, there is a double-cross in the works? Chief Talbod wants the girl for his own fell purpose, yet the flesh merchant will betray him to his death. If we miss the mark, then the girl will die and the portal of doom opened, allowing the god of the Black Death freedom to enter and ransack our world. And ye say there will be no battle?"

Tulwryn, clearly angered at the recent turn of events, pushed himself away from the table and paced the length of the room. Dillwyn and Cohado remained seated, watching the unpredictability of their comrade.

"Cohado," Tulwryn's voice was soft and caring. He knelt at the priest's feet, gazing into Cohado's caring and compassionate eyes. "Conjure me two hundred grim warriors ere we assault the slavers on the high sea. With thine powers, and Dillwyn's too, I can end this madness."

"Have ye naught heard a word that has passed mine lips? This man possesses the Bloodsword! He can use it against us."

"Cures the day I ever forged the blade," spat Dillwyn, rising from his chair.

"Nay," answered Tulwryn, "ye forget that I am Amwe, the Lion of Heidmar. It is our Wyrd, our Orlog! Can ye naught see that our fate is interwoven with that of the world? I am the chosen one, and with or without the crimson sword, I shall fulfill mine destiny!" Tulwryn spun on his heel, the feeling of exhilaration washing over his being, most intoxicating. He was on the threshold of the berserker rage, and his gloom was lifted.

"Ah, for only when thou kills is the curse of the kinslaying lifted, even for a moment," spoke the Keeper of Lies. And Cohado understood. "Ye travel under a heavy burden, Lord Tulwryn. If thou seeks a battle who am I to thwart that prophecy? Thine battle has already been written into the history of the world, yet even I know naught the outcome. Very well, let us sleep on this. We shall set sail in the morn."

Tulwryn nodded, a smile etched across his grim countenance, and left the hall. Cohado waited a few moments, making certain that the Lion of Heidmar was out of earshot, and spoke thusly to Dillwyn the dwarf:

"I feel that boy will be the downfall of us all."

"Nay, Cohado," answered the dwarf, "Tulwryn is our only hope."

Thus ends Chapter Eighteen of Book Three

NINETEEN

Honor Amongst Thieves

The Malevolent had not been docked at the Port of Kemet for more than a few minutes when Ulrich Mancrusher noticed the flamboyant figure standing on the dock. A frown creased the pirate's face and his brow furrowed deep. In all his days, Ulrich despised the sight of Yalad Munster. It was something in the man's personality, most likely, for he was an arrogant cur and yielded no respect to anyone, but demanded it from everyone. And for all of his silks, and leathers, and lace, for all of his gaudy perfumes and ostentatious attitudes, he was still nothing more than a damnable slave trader. Ulrich Mancrusher knew this and loathed him. Yet now, he had become what he most hated, a trafficker in human flesh, and the thought of it sickened him.

One of the Malevolent's crew came running up the catwalk and yelled up to his captain, who was then still standing on the high poop.

"Captain, Lord Munster desires to come aboard sir."

Ulrich nodded to the deckhand and waved him off. The man turned and ran back to the port gunwale's landing and instructed two other crewmen to lower the ramp. It was a matter of minutes ere Yalad Munster, the most notorious flesh merchant in all of the known world, was striding down the Malevolent's long deck toward her captain, Ulrich Mancrusher.

All eyes were on the figure, arrogantly strutting towards the aft of the ship. Yalad's burgundy doublet was well tailored, and his long black velvet cape billowed in the breeze. He was wearing thigh high round toe boots that were polished to an immaculate luster, and his pantaloons were clean and pressed. A heavy broadsword hung loosely at his hip, and an oversized slouch beret, shadowing his face, completed the ensemble. For an outlaw, he was truly a magnificent sight to behold, yet this meeting did not please Ulrich Mancrusher and he was eager to get the man off his ship as soon as the necessities of his visit where complete.

"Aye," bellowed Yalad, "It's about time ye arrived. I was beginning to wonder if ye had second thoughts about this job."

"I told you I would be here, and here I am. Ulrich Mancrusher is a man of his word." The large pirate paused for a moment to look at the man standing before him. "What respectable corsair wears a broadsword rather than a cutlass? Methinks ye have been too long selling barbarians on the mainland!"

Insulted to the point of blood, Yalad snapped back hard: "Never ye mind mine blade! Ye may seek to guard your own life with mere trinkets. I do naught! This blade be wrought of powerful magic, as ye will soon see." Yalad then paused and scanned the deck of the ship with his eagle eyes. Changing the subject, he said: "Well, I can see that it is a miracle you made it here at all, given the shape of this barge."

"She's sea worthy, even if she's old. Concern yourself naught about this ship, but about my pay. And where's the sloop ye promised. I see none in the harbor."

"There has been a change of plans," replied the flesh merchant. "There seems to be enemy ships in the area, or so I am told. We shall stay aboard this vessel. It is a galleon, with cannon to spare, is it naught?"

"Aye, we have guns, and enough crew to man them. Sea worthy she is, but I am not certain as to her mettle in a fair fight. 'Tis been a long day gone since she's blasted her way through an enemy armada."

"No one said anything of a fair fight," Yalad Munster said with a smiled.

"What are ye talking about then, old fool!"

The flesh merchant frowned, not taking a liking to being

insulted by a lowly buccaneer. His first reaction was to reach for his sword and teach this rogue a lesson, but he realized there would be time enough for killing Ulrich later, and so he pushed the offence to the back of his mind and continued on with the business at hand.

"I am not without my resources," Yalad said. "I, too, have employed the aid of high magic, being somewhat of a sorcerer in my own right. Anyhow, I have foreseen the possibility of a rival foe in the vicinity. We should hoist anchor and set sail at once. In a day or two the Mokksbod prison barge will depart for the Forbidden Island carrying a shipment of Kemetian curs to be marooned on the island. We should quit this harbor now and get ourselves few days ahead of them. The barge will have a military escort. Our enemies may have already contacted the Kemetian authorities. If they catch us here in the bay, we are dead. But on the high seas, well, that is another matter."

Ulrich did wonder as to who the flesh merchant was talking about, but nonetheless, he bit his tongue for the time being. He did not like all this talk about magic. Soon enough there would be time to skewer the rogue on the end of his cutlass and feed his flesh to the sharks, but for now there was business to attend to, and above all else, Ulrich Mancrusher was a businessman. Still, a double-cross was in his mind and he intended to kill the flesh merchant ere they reach the Forbidden Island.

The two men continued their conversation for some time, discussing details and possible battle plans. Double-crosses and triple-crosses were in the air, and the tension was pulled as tight as a L'hoehnian bowstring. After the talk was finished, Yalad Munster disappeared down the stairs to his private quarters, and Ulrich Mancrusher began shouting orders to the crew. In moments, the anchor was drawn up, the moorings were loosed, the sails were unfurled, and the large ship was underway, cruising for the dread shores of the Forbidden Island.

* * *

It was a beautiful morning, thought Tulwryn, as he languidly strolled the fore deck of the Fidelity. The sun was blazing high in the heavens and the azure blue of the sky was reflected brilliantly in the waters of the Mok-Torian harbor. Normally Tulwryn was not moved by the wonder and beauty of nature, but for some reason, today was different. Today, more than any other day in his memory, he felt alive. The air tasted cleaner, the sun, brighter. Tulwryn took it all in, and smiled. His gaze scanned first, the dock and seaport, then the harbor and bay itself. Lastly, he looked out to sea, and his eyes fell on the distant horizon. Watching wave after endless wave, almost as if in a hypnotic trance, Tulwryn's mind drifted over the Gulf of Misery and then, far out to the Ocean of No Return. The sky melted into the sea and everything became a creamy grayish haze. Tulwryn looked up into the ship's rigging, and then at the crewman sitting as lookout from the eyrie high atop the main mast, his eyes fixed on out at the horizon. He wondered how far or how clear the man could see on a day like this.

"He's out there," said a gruff voice, and Tulwryn spun around quickly.

"Yes," replied Tulwryn to his friend, "he's out there, somewhere. But the sea is a large place to hide, Dillwyn. I was thinking. If the galleon left port at Kemet and was put on course for the Forbidden Island, she may take a southeasterly heading? In this foreboding god-cursed ocean the ship could lay just off the horizon and still be invisible from our deck. On the other hand, if our crow's nest lookouts are lucky enough to be scanning the sea in her direction, from our mastheads they might get a glimpse of the tops of her rigging as the ship rises on the swells. But it's a long shot. The sea is large. So tell me, old friend, how do ye suppose we find them?"

"Things look differently from the heavens," replied the dwarf. "Or have you forgotten?"

"I remember all too well, dwarf. When do we set sail?"

"We are hoisting the anchor even as we speak. See, up there

on the high poop! Cohado the Long is already giving the command to shove off and sail with the tide."

And sure enough, there he was in all his divine splendor. High on the quarterdeck, Cohado the Long, high priest of Rhyan and senior captain of the Fidelity, Rhyan's flagship, was barking orders like an old sea dog, his sacred garments fluttering in the salty air. Sixty crewmen hustled under the command of their captain, yet Tulwryn knew it all to be a masquerade, for he realized the entire ship was nothing more than illusion. Everything, from the tallest mast and silk sails, to the smallest detail, was a figment of Cohado's dreamtime imagination and brought to life through the wizard's sheer willpower. You only saw what he wanted you to see; the outsiders on the peer saw one thing, Tulwryn and the dwarf, another.

Yet, it was a truly majestic thing to see, illusion or no, as the Fidelity's anchor was raised and its sails were lowered, her reddish-golden hull and decks reflecting the sun's rays off millions of shimmering dragon scales. But alas, no one saw the true magnificence of the ship, for Cohado's magic was hiding her glory from all that looked at her. From the docks, those that gazed in her direction saw nothing more than a old, dark hulled, triple masted merchantman.

In no time at all, the Fidelity's sails were full of wind and the ship was cruising steadily for the mouth of the harbor. Cohado motioned to Tulwryn and the dwarf to come and the two obeyed quickly.

Once atop the high poop, Cohado spoke thus to his two friends: "We will cruise out of the harbor under the power of the wind. Once we clear the harbor, we will circle northwest out of the bay. After I am certain that there are no prying eyes on us, then and only then, will I employ magic. Understood?" Both men nodded.

"Good. Go and wander about, Master Tulwryn. 'Tis been a long time since your presence has graced my ship. I am certain that ye will enjoy the modification I have made in her."

"Thank ye," answered Tulwryn, and he excused himself and disappeared down the stair and strode to the forward deck.

Dillwyn then turned to Cohado and spoke: "What thinks ye?"

"I conversed with Mimir earlier this morn, old friend," answered Cohado. "He tells me grave news."

"Yes?"

"Seems that Yalad Munster has been trafficking in the dark arts."

"Why should that concern us," replied Dillwyn, "We are not neophyte apprentices. Surely this rouge cannot have the strength of seasoned wizards?"

"Do not underestimate thine enemies, Master Dillwyn. Years do not a strong wizard make. We must needs be on our guard, indeed. And it is imperative that we overtake the Malevolent at sea. Of this, I have no doubt. We cannot allow the galleon to make landfall on the Forbidden Island. No, we must fight these battles separately, for if Yalad Munster and Chief Talbod were to both fight against us at the same time, our odds of survival would be nil."

Dillwyn's face turned ashen and his heart sunk at this news. "What is thy plan then, dear friend?"

Cohado smiled a grim smile. "This old priest has a surprise or two still left in him, I can assure ye." And he patted the dwarf on his thick shoulder with a tender hand. But Cohado's show of confidence lifted naught Dillwyn's heart. "Master Tulwryn still has little confidence in his own abilities. He will be of little aid to us unless he quickly develops a change of heart."

"Aye," answered Dillwyn. "But he is lost without the blade."

"Lost or no, he must believe. There is no other way. I leave that lesson to be taught by ye, old friend."

Less than a hour had passed since the Fidelity had left the port at Mok-Tor. The ship was just nearing the bend in the coastline, the area Tulwryn knew that Cohado was aiming for whereas the craft would be out of the view of prying eyes and he would then employ his magic.

The warrior from Nuvia wandered over to the port gunwale and leaned on the rail. The smooth to and fro motion of the mighty ship was soothing to him. Gently, the huge ship cut through the waves and Tulwryn smiled. He then glanced up into the rigging and still was amazed at the immensity of the ship, and at Cohado's powers. Normally it would take eight hundred and seventy-five able bodied men to sail a ship the size of the Fidelity, yet the wizard of Rhyan did it all himself, through high magic's aid. Even the sixty crewmembers, Tulwryn knew, was nothing more than illusion. He shook his head in amazement.

Then came suddenly a deafening roar and a high pitched hissing sound from below deck, and Tulwryn realized that the illusion was about to end.

"We are out of sight's range from the harbor," yelled Dillwyn, from across the deck. "and we will be ascending, for Cohado has already engaged the Levititium drive! Hold on until we climb to cruising altitude."

Tulwryn shot a glance toward the dwarf and smiled. A thousand memories came rushing back into his mind at once, for Dillwyn was no longer wearing the traditional dark robes of a Covensted cenobite. Standing proudly on the Fidelity's main, the dwarf from Carthus was fully clothed from head to foot in the golden maile of his people, dressed for war.

"How long will it take to reach altitude," Tulwryn screamed back to the dwarf trying to be heard over the roar over the ship's engines.

"Not long. Cohado tells me that he has made some modifications since our last voyage. At any measure . . . hold on tight!"

Just then the entire ship bucked and groaned, and then the rocking stopped. Tulwryn quickly grabbed the gunwale's rail tightly and looked up into the rigging. Before his startled eyes, all three masts and the entire rigging, sails and all, vanished into thin air. The ship's engines were now screaming at a pitch that even his mighty ears could barely stand, the sound reaching a painful volume. The Fidelity's bow surged high and then left the water altogether. In the next moment the entire ship lifted itself from the waves and began her climb skyward through the air at an alarming rate.

Tulwryn, still clutching the rail, glanced around quickly. Abruptly, he noticed that he was alone. Nowhere could any of Cohado's mystic crew be seen. Even Dillwyn had vanished. A cold menace gripped the warrior's strong heart. Tulwryn was no weakling, and he was afraid of no man or beast. Yet magic troubled him greatly, and he liked it naught. But it was the magic of the Bloodsword that surged through his veins, he told himself. Still, the thought comforted him naught and he held on for dear life as the ship, all three leagues of her, rocketed skyward like a comet.

For a moment his mind was a jumbled mess of memories and painful images. He thought of the lost Bloodsword, and then of the kidnapped princess. Visions of terror overwhelmed his troubled mind as he saw the goddess of Neturu among desperate men on board their pirate galleon, and then he thought of the hideous sacrificial rite that was to be her destiny. Rage washed over the warrior like a tidal wave and anger became his intimate friend once again.

Then unexpectedly, the ship leveled itself and the hissing quieted to an agreeable timbre. Tulwryn released the rail, looked about, and then made his way toward the poop deck.

Upon reaching the high quarterdeck, he was greeted by Dillwyn and Cohado. Yet he was amazed, for Cohado was not wearing his usual attire. Instead, he was clothed in shining red armor that resembled heavy dragon scales.

"What's the matter, Tulwryn," asked the wizard of Rhyan. "Have ye never seen a priest clothed for battle?"

"But I thought ye said . . ."

"Never mind what I said," Cohado snapped back. "Wizards are prone to make mistakes just as anybody. There has been some complications since we last spoke and I feel that a battle, if not an entire war, will be fought ere this adventure is done." Tulwryn nodded in agreement and his heart smiled a grim smile.

"But enough talk for now," said Cohado. "Now we have a galleon to catch, and a princess to rescue."

"And my sword?" Tulwryn looked first at Cohado, and then to Dillwyn.

"Aye," answered Cohado. "Methinks ye sword will come to thee. At any rate, go below to the quartermaster's chamber. I am certain ye will find a suitable blade 'til ye can regain your own." The wizard motioned to Dillwyn and the dwarf understood.

"Come, Tulwryn," he said, then he descended the stair and led Tulwryn below to the armory.

Cohado the Long stood steadfast on the poop, a firm hand on the helm and a keen eye on the horizon. "We'll find ye, Yalad Munster, we'll find ye," Cohado whispered to himself. "And when we do, all the demons in hell won't be able to save your filthy hide. Not if I can help it!"

Thus ends Chapter Nineteen of Book Three

TWENTY

The Tempest

A faint grey line marked the location of the horizon far off in the distance and Roth, the bowsprit lookout, knew the storm up ahead would be a bad one. The night was as black as a Vodmarian tomb, and the sea as still as glass, but the peace was not to last.

"The quiet ere the storm," Roth mumbled to himself, ruefully. He had been sent to pull bowsprit duty early in the eve, ordered by the captain himself, against his own wishes. But no one argues with the captain, especially one as mean and as violent as Ulrich Mancrusher. His mind raced to Burke and his horrible end. Again he grimaced and cursed an oath under his breath, fearing one of his back stabbing mates might overhear his discontent and spread a rumor of mutiny back to the captain.

"Go forward and check the forestays, he says. Check with the Bo's'n mate if the equipment needs repair, he says. Keep an eye open for reefs and storms and such, he says. And now look, for sure 'tis I'm a dead man breathin', there's a squall ahead, an' a bad one too." Roth immediately called out to the nearest deckhand. It was Johan, a lithe, tall man in his early twenties. They picked him up shortly ere they shoved off from Kemet, as was Ulrich Mancrusher's custom when beginning a long voyage. More to use the men as an example than for the extra hands, Roth knew, since when times got bad, and the crew bickered amongst themselves, his grim captain never hesitated to use a newcomer as living proof of his short temper and relentless demand for unconditional obedience. Any show of defiance would bring the wrath of Ulrich Mancrusher down upon the crew. Many times had Roth seen Ulrich send a man to his watery grave, whether by keelhauling, walking the plank in shark infested waters, or hauling the cur aloft and hanging them from the yardarm. No, he thought to himself, I shall naught end my days as such. He cared not if Johan or any of the others died, yet he knew the treachery of his mates, so he quieted his grumbling in their presence.

"Johan, go aft and let the captain know there's a squall ahead. Looks like it might be a bad one too!" The tall man nodded his head and disappeared in the darkness.

In a matter of minuets, Ulrich was barking commands at his men and the main and foresails were hoisted and furled. Dietrich Oarsbreaker was ringing the bell hard, calling for all hands on deck. The commotion was deafening as the sleeping crew rolled from their bunks, and stormed their way onto the main. With sleep still in their eyes, they all took up their allotted posts.

Cold raindrops splattered Roth's face as the storm finally blew in. He was still maintaining his vigilant watch in the bowsprit, teeth clenched and jaw set, waiting to fight the tempest that was about to assault them.

Ulrich Mancrusher gazed at the ship's binnacle and took note of the heading. He trimmed the mizzen and then lashed himself tightly into his seachair and called for Dietrich Oarsbreaker, his First Mate.

"I have the rudder," the captain yelled to the other as he approached the quarterdeck, "ye go forward and command the crew from the forecastle deck. Make certain the main and foresails stay furled or the storm will rip us to pieces!"

"Aye, aye, cap'in!" The man was gone as fast as he had appeared.

Ulrich watched in the gloom as the storm rolled in. His mind wandered over the vast Ocean of No-Return and his heart lurched at the thought of being caught at its mercy. Many a sailor's yarn told of the rough seas and violent winds far off from the coastal waters of the main. And then he remembered the tales of the many deadly beasts that lurked in those black waters, and other deep places of the world.

Trying to take his mind off of the melancholy thoughts that were plaguing him, Ulrich glanced across the deck of his ship. He felt a sense of pride well up inside of him, for she was a tall, square rigged galleon, high prowed and broad waited, with three tall masts and billowing sails propelled by two hundred and forty-eight thousand square feet of sail area. A mighty ship to say the least, even if she was old and heavily worn.

They were running with only storm topsails when the storm finally hit. The sail's canvas stretched to the breaking point and the ropes groaned under the stress of the violent storm's sudden blast of high winds.

Roth held on for dear life to the bowsprit rail, as did many of the other mates when the tempest hit them with full force. Lightning flashed and lit up the night sky, the thunder roared, and the first mate's commands could barely be heard over the din.

The wind was violent and the decks were awash with the sea. Time and again, the great galleon rose high on the swells, only to have a wall of water crash down upon them as they descended from the tall wave.

"God curses us, captain," screamed a terrified deckhand, "for this stinking voyage and it's damned living cargo! We'll all die tonight!" Ulrich heard the cry, but the night and the storm kept him from knowing who it was that spoke those mutinous words. He clenched his teeth in anger, and his fists as well.

A bolt of lightning struck the main mast but she stayed. Fire and sparks sprayed forth, covering the main deck and the crew scurried like rats trying to hide from the falling timbers and the splintering mast. Yet the wood was strong even for her age, and it held. Then suddenly the rope that secured the main sail in place was burned in twain by the blast. Within seconds the huge sail was unfurling.

Horror seized Ulrich Mancrusher as he watched the vast mainsail fill to the breaking point by the storm's livid fury. The ship reeled under the relentless pounding of the sea, and for a moment he thought she might flounder and be lost.

"Get aloft," cried the captain to the nearest deckhand. "Tend the mainsail now ere we flounder and capsize!" A dozen soaked crew members raced skywards into the rigging at their captain's behest. One man grabbed a broken line but the wind caught the sail and the block and tackle sprung forth. The rope whizzed through the man's grip with such speed it burned the skin away within seconds. Blood sprayed from the wound, but he clenched his teeth and held tight. A second gust caught the sail and took it high, with the man still holding on to the bloody line. Like a dangling spider on a silken thread, the man was lifted from the deck and sent high over the port gunwale into oblivion.

Then came the cry that turned every man's marrow to ice. It was Roth, still in the bowsprit, barely alive and waterlogged. He belched forth a mouthful of warm sea water and ere he took in another breath, and more water assaulted him. How he could even yell, no one knew, for he was nearly drowned. But yell he did, and at the top of his sea drenched lungs.

"Reef ahead," he cried, as if his life depended on it. "Hard to starboard, captain! Now!" His knuckles tightened and his fingers dug into the wood of the rail. Blood spurted from his fingers, but was instantly washed away by the roaring sea.

Ulrich heard the cry and leaned hard into the rudder with all his strength. Still lashed to the seachair but now almost standing, the burly pirate strained with all his might against the fury of the storm. The mighty ship lurched starboard.

Roth choked up another mouthful of the salty water and was about to give another warning cry when he saw his doom. It was a giant comber, the largest he had ever saw, and it was coming straight for the ship!

The huge wave hit the Malevolence's bow hard and with such force that Roth was knocked unconscious. Johan saw the impact ere he felt it. For a second he thought he saw Roth, still in the bowsprit and hanging on. He shook sheets of water from his hair and took another look forward, his eyes searching hard for the man in the bow. There he is, he told himself! And he smiled at the strength of the buccaneer. Then came a second comber, as large as the first if not larger. After the spray of water abated, Johan looked again for Roth. Holding on tight to the foresail's rigging, he watched in horror as he saw Roth washed overboard. First he was there, and then he was gone. And the sea took him, and he was lost forever. A sick feeling welled up in Johan's guts, yet he knew there was nothing he could have done.

"Go forward and take his place!" Johan turned to see the face that gave the command. It was Dietrich Oarsbreaker. He was standing on the forecastle deck and shouting orders. "Take his place, Johan! Do it now ere we are all lost in this gale!"

Obeying without question, Johan inched his way forward into the bowsprit even though he knew he would not survive the night.

The sea roared, lightning streaked the black sky, and the thunder crashed ominously, but the Malevolence sailed on. Her topsails were still holding, but the foresail and main where lost. The wind changed direction and the large ship struggled past the reef with nary a scratch. It was nearly three hours when the storm finally subsided, and all hands, exhausted to the point of death, were mustered for a head count.

Once again the sea was quiet and the blue haze of morning was beginning to show itself far off to the east. Ulrich unstrapped himself from his captain's seachair and descended the poop's stairs in two bounds. Landing firmly on the main deck, he strode to where the crew had lined up. He was as exhausted as them, yet he would not let it show.

Slowly his eye wandered the deck. He glanced up into the damaged rigging and at the sails hanging like ghostly grey shrouds from their yardarms. He then turned his attention to Dietrich Oarsbreaker, who was already standing with the crew.

"How many did we lose," he asked his first mate.

"Ten, sir."

The big man nodded and then remembered the scream in the night that had angered him so. He searched the faces of the remaining crew looking for the coward that had cursed his command. It may have been the first big storm ere they reached the Forbidden Island, but Ulrich Mancrusher knew it would not be their last.

Thus ends Chapter Twenty of Book Three

TWENTY-ONE

Death from Above

The Fidelity had been aloft the better part of a fortnight and still there was no sign the Malevolent, or any ship for that matter, sailing toward the Forbidden Island. Life on the ship was quiet, to say the least, except for the constant droning and hissing of the Levititium drive. Cohado kept mostly to himself nearly all of the time, as did his mystical crew. It was all very unnerving for Tulwryn, who longed for the action of combat and the joy of wetting his blade in the guts of his foes.

Tulwryn was out of the forecastle deck, gazing off in the distance, his hawk eyes straining hard to see though the cloudy haze to the waters below. He had been standing there all night, and the better part of the morning. Tulwryn remembered the peace and tranquility of soaring majestically through the cool star-lit night and knowing that the ocean was fleeing beneath the keel of Cohado's mighty ship. It was a long time since the warrior from Heidmar had known such peace. It was not to last. Instantly, Dillwyn appeared behind him.

"Any sign of them," asked the dwarf?

"Nay."

"Then it comes to this." Dillwyn paused, lost to his own thoughts.

"Comes to what," asked Tulwryn.

The dwarf smiled, and grasped the warrior's thick shoulder with a firm hand.

"Never mind, dear friend. It's an old man's dream, and

nothing more. I would rather end my days in bloody combat that skulk around up here in the ethers searching for a ship we may never find."

"Bite thy tongue, Dillwyn," Tulwryn replied. "Ye have many seasons left ere ye give up the ghost. And we will find them, I know. The two best wizards in all of Caiwryn fly the skies searching them. How can they elude us?"

"Tulwryn, mine friend," Dillwyn said. "I have seen more than ninety snows. Surely thou realizes this? Dwarves live long indeed, yet we are not immortal. I can feel my strength waning even as we speak. The end of my adventures grows near. But alas, it may very well be as you say. Perhaps we will be lucky enough to catch these cutthroats ere I draw mine last breath."

Before Tulwryn had a chance to protest his friend's melancholy attitude, the Fidelity's great horn of Rhyan blew loudly from the crow's nest. Tulwryn and the dwarf looked up at the buccaneer, who was then leaning over the edge of his lookout, nestled high on the main mast.

"What sees ye," hollered Tulwryn at the man. The man merely pointed a long and gnarled index finger starboard. And behold, a glorious sight, for through the clouds of that overcast morning, the warrior from Nuvia espied a great war ship heading due east, and his blood boiled.

And again, another blast of the horn! But this time, the two realized that the sound came naught from the crow's nest, but from the poop.

"Come Tulwryn," yelled the dwarf, as he was already on the run aft ward to the poop deck. "Come, the captain calls!"

Tulwryn and the dwarf scurried down the ladder from the forecastle deck and hit the main deck running hard. Dressed for battle they were, but their barbarous instincts, tempered in the untamed lands of the Heidmarian wilderness years before, gave them inhuman strength. Despite their armor, their speed was blinding. In a matter of minutes they were on the poop and standing before Cohado, neither out of breath nor exhausted.

"Now the game begins," said the Rhyan priest. "We shall

assault the ship below at once. Once we have boarded the vessel, give no quarter! We must fight our way through the curs and find the princess. Once we have her in our possession, the battle is half won. Remember, no mercy!"

At once, the wizard turned from the two warrior before him and looked over the quarterdeck's rail to the main deck below. One clap of his hands and instantly one hundred and sixty crewmen materialized out of thin air, fully clothed in battle raiment, and mustered themselves quicker than any crack troops Tulwryn had ever seen. He was impressed.

Cohado turned back to Tulwryn and the dwarf. "Hold on, my friends. Our descent will be more violent that our ascent! Those in yonder ship whilst naught know what hit them." Laughing, the wizard of Rhyan clapped his hands once again, and vanished in a cloud of blue smoke.

"Dillwyn," screamed Tulwryn, yet the warrior's words were cut off by a huge roar from below deck.

"No time for discussion, Tulwryn," Dillwyn yelled, as he turned and ran for the helm. "Hold on to something! Cohado has returned to the wheelhouse. We are in for the ride of our lives!"

* * *

The storm was past, yet it was still an overcast day, when Dietrich Oarsbreaker saw the sight that caused his strength to leave him in a flash. He was strolling along the Malevolent's main deck, attending to the business at hand, commanding the ships crew in their daily chores as they cut their way through the Ocean of No Return, due east, toward the Forbidden Island. Suddenly, high in the heavens, and descending upon them like a thunderbolt of savage violence, he saw a huge fiery dragon, hungry with wrath.

"Sound the main alarm! All hands on deck," he screamed at the top of his lungs as he ran toward the stern, "we are under attack from above! Look! Yonder dragon descends upon us!"

Terrified men scrambled upon the decks and the warning bells were rung loudly. Yalad Munster and Ulrich Mancrusher came up from below to asses the assault, yet they were not ready for what they beheld. Beyond the sunset lies the Forbidden Island, Ulrich thought to himself as he gazed upon the fiery horror that was descending upon them, and beyond that, no man knows. In the few dread seconds before the great beast impacted the great war galleon, a thousand thoughts traveled across the Ulrich Mancrusher's mind.

Throughout the long centuries, buccaneers heard no yarns to spur them on to higher, bolder adventure than that which set their tall ships out across the vast Ocean of No Return. Nowhere, throughout the whole of Phantasodyssea, was there a theater of such proportions, so fit for vivid pageantry; whereupon that watery stage, before the background of a sea that stretched onward to eternity! Many a proud pirate, and Ulrich was no different, threw caution to the wind and led their tiny caravels across the endless sea, free-booting with the hope of finding the plunder of a mystic continent lying somewhere out there, on the edge of reality. How many sought out pristine islands of undreamed peace and loveliness, only to never be heard or seen again? Courageous buccaneers, great men of war, bold men of the sea, dipped in and out of forbidden ports, whose lust for plunder fueled their quest to discover the magic lands that lay hid behind the sunset. Tall-masted ships, with billowing sails and decks awash with the sun, raced onward into oblivion seeking the fabled richness of the exotic Faraway Land.

And then the big pirate laughed. Who has never dreamed of seeing the Faraway Land, that treasure house of wonder that no one who has ever lived upon the world should fail to see? But no, there has never been an ocean map charted. No ship has ever returned, it's hull laden with gold, and silver, and plunder beyond all imagination. And why? Ulrich now knew that answer! For high above the Malevolent that answer came in the form of a fiery wrathful dragon. How many times had this beast sailed through the trackless leagues of the never ending sky searching for its prey, and only then to sweep down from the heavens in a hailstorm of flames and brimstone to forever remove the proud tall ships from the seas? Fate, it seemed; fate or destiny, would remove the Malevolent and its crew from the world this day, and again the rogue captain laughed the grim laugh of a doomed man.

* * *

Tulwryn held tight to the rail, and Dillwyn did likewise, as the Fidelity dove from the heavens like a falling star. From his position, near the forward forecastle deck, Tulwryn could see the flames licking up from under the ship's hull. Seconds later he felt the intensity of their heat.

"What is this Dillwyn," screamed the warrior over the din of the craft's engines. "The ship is bursting aflame!"

"Nay," replied the dwarf, yelling loud enough to be barely heard over the rush of wind that whistled past their tormented ears. "This is another of Cohado's illusions."

"Seems real enough to me," answered Tulwryn.

"Just thank the gods that ye are on this ship rather than naught. Methinks the sight of this falling fiery beast is enough to fell the strongest cutthroat onboard yonder ship by fear alone!"

"That may be true, but still, this is no way for a warrior to travel!"

"Fear naught, Tulwryn," proclaimed the dwarf, "this battle shall be over ere it begins!"

Tulwryn, carefully and step by step, still grasping hard on the fore rail, moved toward the bow of the Fidelity. Through the orange blaze of flames he could clearly see half a dozen burly sea dogs, bare chested and browned from the burning sun, standing dazed on the main deck of the Malevolent. Doomed men, they were, and looking into the face of eternity! Tulwryn saw the fear behind their hollow eyes and was moved to pity, yet mercy was not in his nature to give, this day or any other. His blood boiled for the battle that would soon ensnare them all.

Within seconds, the Fidelity, all three leagues of her flaming glory, crashed head on into the sea a mere hundred yards from the Malevolent's starboard bow. The mighty ship dove down deep into the green water of the sea and shot like a torpedo under the heavy galleon, coming asurface just on the port side of the large vessel.

The Fidelity's impact caused such an immense wave, it snapped the Malevolent's foremast like a twig and nearly topsided the great ship. The foresail hung loosely from its broken home and clothed more than half the forecastle deck in darkness. Fires began to blaze all about as many of the ships lanterns were broken in the attack. The crew scrambled like mad rabbits caught in a flaming barn and the entire deck was awash with their screams.

Ulrich Mancrusher began shouting commands to his disoriented crew and then disappeared below to check on Octavia. Confusion engulfed the Malevolent like a storm. The crew was working frantically to extinguish the fires and clear the deck of the broken mast and sails when they saw the mighty Fidelity, still appearing like a huge fiery dragon, materialized just yards off their port stern. The Fidelity was close enough now for Tulwryn to see the defeat in the eyes of the Malevolent's crew. Surely, the galleon was a huge and impressive ship of war, but sitting dead in the water next to the gigantic Fidelity the men knew they were dead ere the battle begin.

Terror seized the burly rogues when Yalad Munster appeared atop deck and yelled: "To guns, ye dogs! Blast that beast back to the hell whence it came!"

At once, the mighty ship's twenty-five port side cannon doors swung open in one last great act of defiance, but ere a single shot could be loosed, a blast of dragonfire and brimstone was belched forth from the mouth of the great beast. The blast impacted the galleon's port hull in a bone shattering explosion melting cannon and incinerating men. Dietrich Oarsbreaker fought his way to the poop deck through the inferno.

"Where is the captain," he cried out to no one in particular.

"He went below to see to our precious cargo," answered the flesh merchant.

"To hell with the bitch from Neturu," screamed the first mate in a fit of fury, "and to hell with you and your accursed plans of devilry!" In a flash, Dietrich's cutlass leapt from its scabbard and he was upon Yalad Munster, and seething with rage. With the blinding speed of an angry cobra, the Bloodsword was in the flesh merchant's hand and blocking the first mate's cutlass slash.

"Ye dog," yelled Yalad over the din and confusion of the Fidelity's first attack, "ye mean to mutiny on me? Death to you now!" And faster than the eye could see, the mighty broadsword licked out like the tongue of an angry serpent and severed Dietrich's arm at the wrist. Ere the massive pirate had time to scream, a second blow of that heavy sword cleaved him in twain.

Yalad Munster looked bitterly at the three pieces of dead meat lying on the high poop that was once the Malevolent's first mate and laughed bitterly. Kicking one chunk of the dead man overboard, he then turned back to the fray. Suddenly, using his own sorcery, he saw through Cohado's illusion, as if a ripple in the fabric of time and space had somehow been sheered away, and he saw the Fidelity in all her true glory. True enough, she was a mighty craft, but a craft she was, and naught a fiery beast. This revelation gave the flesh merchant hope and he yelled to his ravished crew:

"Blades men! This is no dragon but a dragon ship. 'Tis illusion and nothing more. To blades! These demons mean to board us!"

Blades leapt from scabbards and the crew mustered to arms at the behest of their master, but fear was in their hearts and they knew that before the sun set that day they would be feeding the sharks rather than enjoying plunder and grog.

The Fidelity swung closer for a boarding pass, and Cohado, still high on the captain's quarterdeck, gave the command to launch the grappling hooks. Tulwryn and the dwarf, still on the forecastle deck, watched in awe at the precision of Cohado's mystic warriors. Eight score of red eyed buccaneers worked through the control of one man, yet they were all as individual as any living man. But Tulwryn knew they were not alive, but extensions of the Rhyan priest's high magic. Even Dillwyn, trained for the past five years in the secrets of magic, was amazed at the powers of his friend.

From powerful catapults, three dozen grappling hooks were fired at the large galleon, now sitting dead in the water. More than half the hooks hit their mark and Cohado's mighty sea dogs pulled hard on the cords, closing the distance from ship to ship.

"Put your backs into it, ye dogs," yelled Cohado, and the warriors strained under his command. Inch by inch, the two ships crept closer together.

Tulwryn could see the Malevolent's crew waiting on the far side of their ship's gunwale, anticipating the boarding. His heart leapt for the coming battle, just seconds away. And then his excitement turned to rage as he espied Yalad Munster, the flesh merchant that had stolen his blade and sold him into slavery, striding arrogantly among the confusion on the galleon's main deck. The Bloodsword was in his hand, still dripping with the blood of his first mate.

Rage clouded his mind and he could not wait any longer. Tulwryn climbed high into the Fidelity's rigging and loosed a heavy lead rope.

"Die ye god forsaken son of a lice infested whore," screamed the warrior from the top of his lungs. In a flash, he was airborne, swing from his lofty perch and landing with both feet firmly on the Malevolent's main deck.

When Cohado's crew saw Tulwryn's daring act, they followed his lead. In a matter of seconds after the Lion of Heidmar had boarded the galleon, one hundred and sixty surly buccaneers launched themselves from ship to ship in like manner. The sky above the two ships were filled with the silhouettes of seamen, dangling from their lines like spiders on silken threads, and hungry for blood.

For many minutes, the battle was fierce. Many a pirate was tossed overboard, and Cohado, from his post on the high poop, could see the water frothing with the angry rage of feeding sharks. The eerie green waters of the sea were red that day with the blood of dying men.

With cutlass in hand, Tulwryn cut a wide and bloody path through the Malevolent's sea dogs, fighting his way to Yalad Munster. Seeing the flesh merchant with the Bloodsword gave Tulwryn a strength he never knew. Suddenly, the two men came face to face. Like the eye of a hurricane, the tension was tight, but time and space had ceased to exist, and reality was nil. All around them, men fought and died, yet for these two combatants, time stood still.

"Ye have a thing of mine, dog," snapped Tulwryn.

"Come and take it back," answered Yalad, "if ye can!"

Tulwryn felt his palms blaze red, and he instinctively dropped his cutlass. Standing apparently helpless before Yalad Munster, the flesh merchant began to laugh. He raised the Bloodsword high over his head and advanced toward the helpless barbarian for a first and final death blow. Yet, ere the flesh merchant could traverse even one step, Tulwryn raised his hands. A flash of celestial fire shot forth from Tulwryn's blazing palms and smote his attacker forthwith. The flesh merchant died instantly in a blast of white flame ere he could even scream, turned to ashes by Tulwryn's Will alone.

In that fiery second, the intensity of the blast blinded many of the men onboard the galleon. Even Tulwryn's buccaneers lost their sight to the flame of his rage.

Dillwyn, who was knee deep in blood and offal, was knocked off his feet by the impact. Shaking stars from his head, and trying to stand, he peered through squinted eyes at the Lion of Heidmar. Hazily, he saw Tulwryn, through a cloud of white smoke. The warrior walked to the stain on the deck that was once Yalad Munster and knelt. In a moment of serene reverence amidst the confusion of battle, Tulwryn retrieved his blade. The dwarf smiled, for he knew this battle was won, but still, there was the matter of Chief Talbod and the Forbidden Island.

At once, Tulwryn raised his mighty blade high overhead and

then slammed its thick point down into the wood of the deck. A blinding flash shot forth from that crimson blade and the celestial fire danced along the Malevolent's deck, stealing the life of her crew. In one blazing second of intense heat and fury, all of the Galleon's crew lay dead, burnt to cinders.

Dillwyn held back the urge to vomit, for the stench of the burnt human bodies was more than he could stand. He felt a firm hand grip his thick shoulder as Cohado helped him to his feet.

"How long have ye been onboard," Dillwyn asked his captain.

"Long enough," replied the wizard of Rhyan. "Ye fought boldly, dear friend. The world is a safer place this day because of ye."

"Nay," answered Dillwyn. "Tulwryn is the real hero, for he has regained the Bloodsword whereby he smote our enemies with his heavenly flame."

The two made their way toward the hero, still standing midship surrounded by the burnt bodies of his foes. Tulwryn turned to his two friends, the Bloodsword still glowing a bright crimson, and he smiled.

"Our work here is finished," Tulwryn said to the two wizards standing before him.

"But what about the Forbidden Island," asked Dillwyn?

Without answering, Tulwryn pointed to the heavy figure walking towards them. Through the clouds of billowing smoke came a burly pirate, unscathed by the recent battle. It was Ulrich Mancrusher, the pilot-navigator of the Malevolent, and he was lovingly carrying the princess, Octavia. No one knew why the once bloodthirsty pirate showed no signs of violence, nor why he surrendered so tenderly. Certainly, it was not in his nature. Perhaps he had somehow fallen in love with the princess? Or maybe, her magic had consumed him. None will know, that is for certain. But return her, he did. And submit to his captors, this he also did as well.

The princess showed no emotion as her physical eyes looked for the first time on Tulwryn, the man she called her savior, yet her heart stirred for the love of him. Ulrich set the princess down before the three warriors and knelt at their feet like a beaten dog.

Dillwyn stepped forward, blade in hand, ready to dispatch the rogue, but Tulwryn caught the dwarf's mighty wrist in a grip of steel.

"Nay," spoke Tulwryn, "this man has had a change of heart. Can ye naught see in his eyes that he is a beaten man? Slay him naught, for he will now do our bidding."

Dillwyn looked at Tulwryn, confused. Cohado stood silent. Tulwryn looked into the eyes of his friend, and then turned his attention to Cohado. "There is still work to be done on the Island, no?"

"Aye," answered the Rhyan priest. "Whilst Chief Talbod lives, the princess will never be safe."

"So be it," spoke Tulwryn. And turning back to Ulrich Mancrusher, he spoke thus: "I thank ye for safeguarding this lass, and I shall spare thine miserable life. But still, t'was ye that stole her from her ancestral home in the first place, and that is a crime most grievous. For your punishment, ye shall be marooned upon the Forbidden Island for the rest of thy life. But methinks this is not such a bad punishment for a rogue such as you." Tulwryn smiled. "With your ingenuity, I foresee ye murdering that vile king and taking his throne for yourself. For true, ye shall never sail again, but the Forbidden Island shall be yours. Do you understand?"

Ulrich Mancrusher nodded his head. Deep in his blackened soul he knew that Tulwryn had spared his life for the sole purpose of killing Chief Talbod. He thanked Jang, the god of sea rogues for this pleasant turn of events. Certainly, his heart sank at the thought of never sailing again. But then again, being the king of the Forbidden Island wasn't such a bad destiny. He bowed deeply to his captors.

Cohado snapped his fingers and four mystic warriors appeared, surrounding the princess Octavia. "Take the princess back to our ship and put her in my quarters for safe keeping," he said, and without hesitation, the four led the girl away.

Again, the wizard of Rhyan snapped his long fingers, yet this time a dozen of his mystic rogues materialized out of thin air and surrounded Ulrich Mancrusher. With a wave of the wizard's hand, almost as if reading his mind, they escorted the pirate to the starboard gunwale. Tulwryn and the others watched as Ulrich, once the mighty captain of the Malevolent, but now nothing more than a helpless castaway, was set in a small dingy and lowered into the shark infested waters of the Ocean of No Return.

"Do ye think this is the right thing to do," asked Dillwyn.

"Aye," answered Tulwryn. "We needs get the princess back to Neturu, and ye heard Cohado. She will never be safe as long as Chief Talbod lives. Even with all of your magic, we cannot be in two places at once. So, this is as it should be. The rogue will slay the savage king, this I feel in me bones."

"Still, t'would have been nice to slit his damnable belly from crotch to eyebrow!"

"Aye, Dillwyn," replied Tulwryn, "but some pleasures are left un-tasted for the betterment of the world." The two laughed a hearty laugh, yet Cohado did naught. He merely gazed steadfast into the dark eyes of the barbarian.

"What?"

"'Tis nice to know that with power comes wisdom," answered Cohado. "Come, let us be away from this barge. She'll float no longer. See, the flames consume her. Come, we have work to do." And with that, the three warriors abandoned ship for their own.

* * *

Ulrich Mancrusher rowed hard, for he knew that making landfall on the shores of the Forbidden Island was his only hope of survival. As he rowed, he watched in amazement as the great ship transformed itself once again into the form of a fiery dragon before his very eyes. And then suddenly, it lifted its great body from the waters of the sea. Shaking his head in confusion, he continued his rowing.

The great beast ascended high into the firmament and was lost from his sight, yet just when Ulrich thought he was rid of the accursed thing, his ears were assaulted by a terrible noise. From the heavens, streaking across the sky like a fiery comet, came a hoary blast from the far side of eternity. The blazing missile smote the hull of the Malevolent directly and rent her to bits. Red flame and black smoke painted the sky, and Ulrich cast down his oars and huddled low in his boat, hoping to ride out the shock wave that was coming his way.

The small craft tossed on the waves, yet it was swamped naught. Ulrich breathed a sigh of relief, for in the distance he could see hundreds of fins breaking the rough surface of the sea as hungry sharks filled their bellies on the bodies of his dead crew.

Once again, pushing the grisly scene from his mind, Ulrich turned his thoughts toward the murder of Chief Talbod, and the glorious throne of the Forbidden Island.

Thus ends Chapter Twenty-one of Book Three

TWENTY-TWO

The Crimson Citadel

Five days had passed since Tulwryn had rescued the princess and regained his crimson blade. The morning was pleasant and cool, and the warrior was leisurely strolling the decks of the Fidelity, enjoying the peace of the quiet morning. The sun was burning brightly, yet his heart was heavy, for the burden of the kinslaying was once again upon him.

"Can ye never know peace," said a small voice from yonder, and Tulwryn turned with a jolt as if struck by lightning.

"What knows ye of my plight," said he.

"I know more than ye think, Master Tulwryn," answered Octavia. Tulwryn looked at the girl. She was a vision of loveliness, and he remembered Dillwyn's tale of Ayndrian Aelfwine, the lonely queen.

"T'was thine face I have seen in mine dreams," he said. And she nodded.

"Thine face has graced mine dreams as well." The girl smiled. She examined her thoughts and realized that she had not yet thanked him for her rescue, and so she began to speak, but Tulwryn placed a finger upon her lips ere she spoke.

"Speak naught," he said, "for I know what thou would have of me, and it cannot be. I must return ye to Neturu, and thine brother. Your destiny lies on a different road than mine."

The princess dropped her head heavily, for her sorrow was great. Tulwryn then turned and gazed off into the distance, his mind wandering the ethers for the words he would now speak.

As if in a hypnotic dream, he began to tell Octavia about his burden:

"Once, it seems to me, long ago, that an ancient wizard, Mimir, showed me the face of my own guilt in that of my dead wife. Yet, his face I saw naught! He hid his very essence from me, and my guilt consumed me. But it was her undoing that set this burden on me, and I cannot bring them back! Oh, too look on the faces of my sons one last time. But my heart grows cold and bitter, and it is wrath, not guilt, that fuels the fires of my passions!"

He paused a moment and looked into her glassy eyes.

"Had I the wealth, I would ride in like a conquering hero and sweep ye off your feet. I would take you to my castle and make you my queen. I would worship you as my Goddess, forsaking all others, be they Gods or mortals, in lieu of you, my one and only Divine Queen!

"If it were in my power, I would give thee the world. But alas, I am a poor man, and the world is not mine to give. Therefore, I give ye all that I have, which is all I am free to give, and that is merely myself and my unconditional love, for I own no wealth of gold, nor estate, nor any other thing of worldly value. All I have is myself and my love, and these I freely give ye if you would have them. Yet, it is because of this love, I can have ye naught, for I am a vile and undeserving thing. And this is why I must return ye thither to your brother's house."

Octavia dropped her tiny head once again, for she knew to argue would be meaningless. Her warrior had made up his mind and she would not be able to convince him otherwise. She accepted her fate and the terrible fact that her destiny would not be shared with him. Silently, she turned and left him, walking back to her lonely cabin, tears of rejection pooling in her beautiful star-like eyes.

* * *

The sun burned brightly over the Golrin prairie as a lone horseman trekked his way eastward through that bleak expanse of that barren land. Once, long ago, the beauty of the prairie of Golrin was legendary, but now its ground was dead. Only a day earlier he had been in the glorious presence of the gods, the high royalty of the Neturuian court, surrounded by wealth and pleasures untold. Cohado and Dillwyn could not understand why Tulwryn had refused the treasures that prince Branjadom was prepared to heap upon him. Likewise, they were confused as to his reasons for abandoning them. Rather than stay aboard the Fidelity, Tulwryn asked the prince of Neturu merely for one horse and a days ration of food and water. He then took his leave of the wizards and set out on his own. He even refused Cohado's request that he should take a hundred of his mystic warriors with him. He merely said: "Where I am going, none shall follow. This is mine destiny."

Perhaps it was because the night before, unbeknownst to anyone, that Tulwryn received one last visit from the shadow of the Bloodsword. The shadow was vague in his words, yet Tulwryn knew well what he meant when he said: "Ye must surrender yourself to yourself, Tulwryn, and come through the dark night of your Soul."

Yes, knew Tulwryn, that he had come full circle. He finally realized the full magnitude of his destiny. He and the shadow were one, and the Bloodsword was him as well. There was a power at work that was to unite his soul with the spirit of the land. Ha! Laughed the warrior to himself, under his breath; his soul was the soul of the world, and a grim world it had become. This he knew.

It took Tulwryn the better part of a week to reach the battlefield of Golrin. As he walked amongst the bones of the dead, stretching as far as the eye could see, a thousand memories washed over his being. He relived that gruesome battle, for many of the dead here were slayed by his own hand. He remembered his fight with the savage Knobites as well. His hands moved softly over the scars of his darkened body, and he smiled.

"So, I must yet fulfill another prophecy?" He quietly whispered the words to himself: "During the dark times, his wrath had become great and entire nations rose and fell at the wave of his hand, and so it seemed that he was of the land and the land was of him, for their two destinies had merged and become one. And he shall forge a kingdom, and his house shall be built from the bones of his foes."

Looking high into the heavens, he yelled an oath to his grim gods for the curse they heaped upon him.

"So be it," he yelled, "if this be my destiny, then so be it!"

And his palms once again blazed with the power of the Bloodsword, and so he gripped the crimson blade and swung it high overhead. With one mighty grunt, Tulwryn slammed the sword, point first, into the dry and parched earth. The power of the gods surged through his mighty veins and a crimson arc of celestial flame leapt forth from the Bloodsword's gleaming blade. Dancing like living fire, the celestial flame lashed out and singed the bones of the dead, and they became as stone. Suddenly, there grew a huge mountain from the midst of those grim stones, and atop that mountain was a crimson castle, whose bricks were the bones of dead warriors and whose mortar was the blood that once pumped through their living veins, and by spells and the strength of dark magic was the stones of Tulwryn's house held together. Yet that begins another tale, and its memory is lost from the minds of men and gods alike.

Here ends Book Three

APPENDIX

MAIN CHARACTERS OF BOOK ONE

Atli the Terrible: Atli is the old, but strong and valiant chieftain of the clan of Gerdmor. He was slain in the war against Darkoth, the frost dragon.

Darkoth: Darkoth is an evil frost dragon that hails from the frozen wastes of Phantasodyssea. He sits in a great ice castle, upon a dark throne, and commands his minions by way of evil magic, and through fear. His greatest dream is to crush the many kingdoms of Phantasodyssea and bring the world's people under his complete tyranny. His greatest fear is that of the wrath of the Bloodsword.

Dillwyn Anvilhand: Dillwyn was a dwarven smith, short and stout and incredibly powerful. He is always dressed in the golden chainmaile and battle gear of the western dwarves of Carthus, his home, unless he is working in his smithy, then he wears the garb of a smith. He has a full beard the color of tanned leather and his face is criss crossed with deep age lines. On his head he wears a heavy helm of gilded steel, yet he carries no weapons that can be seen; his hands always being covered with heavy bronze gauntlets that are studded with large round steel bolts; these alone are his weapons.

Grimthor the Strong: Grimthor the Strong was chieftain of the clan of Heidmar, and a mighty warrior from the house of Rexor. He took Halgr Manslayer as his wife and she bore him only one heir, a female: Halgi Mansbane. Grimthor was murdered by sorcery, but the slaying was made to look like the work of a Rodmarian assassin with the hope of bringing the two clans together in war.

Gunnar Trollsbane: Gunnar Trollsbane was a mighty warrior from the clan of Heidmar. He is brother to Uther the Courageous, Luther the Daring, and Omar Giantslayer. Gunnar was slain in the war against Darkoth, the frost dragon.

Halgi Mansbane: Halgi Mansbane was the only child of Grimthor the Strong. Like her mother, she was quick to anger and would slay rather than argue with words. She received her title after a fight with an L'hoehnian slaver who had stolen into the Heidmarian camp under the cover of night and tried to make off with her. Ere the bandit could escape her tent, he lay dead in a pool of his own blood, her dagger still lodged betwixt his black eyes. Halgi was in love with Tulwryn, but was slain by evil sorcery woven by the Volva whilst she was in the service of Darkoth.

Halgr Manslayer: The wife of Grimthor the Strong was Halgr Manslayer. She was a strong woman, quick to anger and heavy of wrath, yet her countenance was fair and pleasant to look on. She became chieftain of the Heidmarian clan two days after her husband was slain.

Hem: The god Hem is a minor deity honored by the dwarves of Carthus. He is said to live in the rocks and ore of the land. His aid is sought when seeking new areas to mine.

Ian the Eager: Ian was a young Heidmarian boy whose parents fell during the battle of Volsung. Since the boy is small for his age, he has been placed under the watchful eye of Dillwyn Anvilhand, the clan's smith, rather than be allowed to learn combat skills with others of his winters. Someday Dillwyn plans to teach Ian how to wield the weapons he forges. Ian fell in the war against Darkoth; he was the youngest warrior to be slain in the war.

Lectite: The god Lectite is a major deity honored by the dwarves of Carthus. He is the patron god of smiths and presides over all activities related to iron and steel.

Luther the Daring: Luther the Daring was a mighty warrior from the clan of Heidmar. He is brother to Uther the Courageous, Gunnar Trollsbane, and Omar Giantslayer.

Mimir: Mimir is an old he-witch currently living in Covensted. He is the Keeper of the Dragon Shield, and the one who bestows the shield to Urgan the Brave, who in turn, delivers it to Tulwryn Bloodsword ere the final battle of the tale.

Morab: The god Morab is another deity honored by the dwarves of Carthus. This land god presides over all elements concerning dirt, rock, ore, iron, and steel.

Odhinn: The patron deity of the Heidmarian kindred is Odhinn. He is a grim war-like god.

Omar Giantslayer: Omar Giantslayer was a mighty warrior from the clan of Heidmar. He is brother to Uther the Courageous, Gunnar Trollsbane, and Luther the Daring. Whilst on a mission with Tulwryn Bloodsword, he was slain by Vogelmir the Bold under a vile spell of sorcery, which the traitor assassin was disguised as a mighty war wolf.

Thorfinn: A mighty Gerdmorian warrior.

Tuc: The god Tuc is a deity honored by the dwarves of Carthus. Little is known about this old god, as he is a very quiet and unresponsive deity. It is believed that he is as old as the world, if not older.

Tulwryn Bloodsword: Born to a family of alfalfa farmers in the tiny village of Nuvia, Tulwryn was a bright and cheerful lad, and grew into a strong and resilient man with high moral virtues and a strict code of honor more akin to a soldier than a farmer. But a farmer he was through and through, and a family man as well.

Nuvia was located just south of the Plain of Kem, east of the River Phaedron, and on the main trade route that criss-crossed the length and breadth of Phantasodyssea. Yet, Tulwryn established his farm far to the south of the village, deep within the Azure Wood, to protect his family from the marauding bands of Kemite river pirates and plains bandits that constantly plagued the area.

The village of Nuvia's main export was agriculture in the form of alfalfa, barely, corn, oats, and wheat, but some of its inhabitants farmed the illegal herb Wormwood, used in the manufacture of Absynth, a highly addictive and toxic social drug, for it demanded an extremely high price in places like Covensted and Baezutu.

Being of black hair and medium build, with the olive skin and the dark eyes of his people, Tulwryn prided himself on an honest days toil. He trafficked naught in the growing of illegal poisons, as did those around him, but worked hard to provide for his growing family, his wife Durayn and his four young sons. Tulwryn was always light of mood and in good cheer, even though he was but a poor farmer, for his family gave him much joy. But alas, this was to change, for a dark cloud of doom would soon settle over his life and his heart would darken and become grim.

As a farmer, he was an unlikely candidate for warriorhood, yet a warrior he did become, and a strong one at that. Perhaps it was the doom that over shadowed his life, or perhaps it was the will of the gods, who often twisted the fates of men for their own fell purposes. Perhaps none will know for certain, for all that remains of Tulwryn's life is this account, a mere collection of his travels and adventures across the whole of Phantasodyssea.

During the dark times, his wrath had become great and entire nations rose and fell at the wave of his hand, and so it seemed that he was of the land and the land was of him, for their two destinies had merged and become one. Yet, through all the wars and the bloodshed, his heart had hardened and he wanted none of it, save only to throw down his sword and return to the simple life of a farmer, and his to family. But that was not his destiny.

Urgan the Brave: Urgan is a young warrior of the clan of Heidmar. He is a splendid example of his people, sturdy and tall, with light skin and pale yellow hair. He wears the furs of his tribe, and carries a broadsword as well as a long pole of ash topped with a slender spear of bright polished steel. On his left arm, he wears the Circlet of Bravery, a golden torque of polished brass that terminates with the interlocking heads of the mighty ice boar, which he earned during the battle of Volsung when he was but fifteen winters grown. The Circlet, as it is called by the tribe, is a symbol of great courage and only the most skilled fighters can boast such honors; Urgan wears the badge with great pride.

Uther the Courageous: Uther the Courageous was a mighty warrior from the clan of Heidmar. He is brother to Gunnar Trollsbane, Luther the Daring, and Omar Giantslayer.

Vogelmir the Bold: Vogelmir was a strong warrior from the clan of Heidmar. He was a rival of Tulwryn Bloodsword, and constantly worked to usurp his place within the structure of the clan. By sorcery, he was transformed into a mighty war wolf and murdered Omar Giantslayer, and in turn, was slain by Tulwryn Bloodsword.

Volva: For sixty winters, the Volva has been the loyal sorceress of the Heidmarian clan, but unbeknownst to the tribe, she is actually an evil minion of Darkoth, the dread frost dragon. Darkoth created the witch from the seething entrails of dying Gerdmorian infants, babies he stole from their dead mothers soon after slaying the women. Over the vile gore, he cast a horrendous enchantment, empowering it to breathe life and lust for the death of others. From this mass of blood and offal came the Volva; he then clothed it in mortal flesh and set it within the womb of Kath, a Heidmarian girl. The dragon then wove a false prophecy about the primitive minds of the Heidmarian people, and when the child was born, they revered her as a great seer, and appointed her Volva. Kath perished in childbirth, unable to survive the dread venom stirring within her womb. The Volva lived a secret life amongst the clan until her sixtieth winter, where then she betrayed her people and unleashed a terrible evil upon the world.

Walter the Horrible: A grim old war veteran from the clan of Heidmar.

Ymir: The god Ymir is the major sky deity honored by the dwarves of Carthus. He is the god which controls the actions of fire and wind.

MAIN CHARACTERS OF BOOK TWO

Adivarapupeta: Adivarapupeta was a Baezutuian girl that was taken prisoner by a band of L'hoehnian silk merchants. After making a formidable escape from her captives while its caravan was passing through the Helheim Plateau, she wandered the wastes until falling unconscious from the heat of the Phaedronian sun. Tulwryn and the dwarf found her and nursed her back to health whereas she accompanied them on their current adventure.

Athrum: The patron god of Nuvia. He sometimes takes on the physical form of a raven to travel among the world of men and espy their heroic deeds. Athrum is a grim god, more akin to warriors than to farmers, and it is anybody's guess why the agricultural society of Nuvia venerates such a deity.

Beck: A Woodling from the village of Bain.

Cohado the Long (The Keeper of Lies): Cohado the Long is a banished priest, living in seclusion in the hidden village of Rhyan. He is called the *Keeper of Lies* because he discovered secret untruths that his priestly brotherhood, the Order of the Crystal Sphere, swore to keep hidden from the eyes of men. Angered that such evils could be kept under wraps, he threatened the security of the brotherhood by exposing the Order and its lies. Cohado was forced to flee for fear of death. He is still being sought by the brotherhood, which will stop at nothing to silence him forever. Cohado has long been the voice of Truth in Phantasodyssea and his magic is powerful indeed; he has always helped those in need, especially those pursued by evil.

Daithi Mac Bhurrais: Daithi Mac Bhurrais is an elderly gentleman who is usually found smoking a long pipe. He wears a forest green cloak and keeps his head hooded most of the time. He is completely bald save for a long strand of braided gray hair, which gently falls from under his hood, down onto his right shoulder. Not much is know about him, but many believe him to be an old wizard. He is usually friendly and in good cheer. Some call him the Green Wanderer, for none know whence he hails.

Dillwyn Anvilhand: Please see character list for Book One.

Kaine Obel: After murdering Nimrod the Just and usurping his crown and throne, Obel changed his name to Zulanmalh I, thus creating the Dynasty of the House of Zula.

Kimark Khan: Kimark Khan is the infamous Warrior-wizard that resides atop of Mt. Malador. He originally hailed from Covensted, but centuries ago, after mastering the intricacies of magic, he left the Village of Witches to seek his fortunes in the west. After coming upon the Phaedron Citadel, he was employed for some time as a seer for the High Elder but soon fell out of favor with the King and had to flee for his life. He has vowed to return one day to Phaedron, and extracting his vengeance, has promised to usurp the throne and take the crown for himself. Most in Phaedron despise Kimark Khan, yet there are a few factions of rebels that constantly pray for his return.

Lord Jerrod Balor: Lord Jerrod Balor was originally of noble blood, and at one time was heir to the throne of Phaedron. After his father, the High Elder Nimrod the Just, was murdered, the throne was assumed by his assassin, the evil cleric Kaine Obel. Fearing for his life, Jerrod left Phaedron and became an explorer and adventurer. Even though he was not in the service of the High Elder, since he was originally of royal Phaedron blood, his achievement of discovering the pass through the Ymir Mountains was heralded as a great Phaedronian achievement.

Maztaque: Maztaque was the leader of a renegade band of L'hoehnian marauders. His cruelty won him a fell reputation through the whole of Phantasodyssea, and even as far south as the wastes there were bounty hunters seeking the fortune that had been place on his head.

Mimir: Please see character list for Book One.

Rog: Tall, swarthy, and extremely good with a L'hoehn blade, Rog was Maztaque's man-at-arms.

Tulwryn Bloodsword: Please see character list for Book One.

Zulanmalh IV: Zulanmalh is the fourth Phaedron ruler from the house of Zula. He is the High Elder of Phaedron, crowned King of the known world, although most city-states lying beyond the reach of the Phaedron army do not recognize his omnipotent authority.

MAIN CHARACTERS OF BOOK THREE

Bast: The main deity that the Neturuians worship. The worship of Bast takes place in the Temple of the Cat on the banks of the Great Pool of Neturu.

Branjadom: Eldest heir to the Neturuian throne and the god-man that charged Tulwryn to locate and rescue his sister, kidnapped by Yalad Munster, the flesh merchant.

Chief Talbod: King of the exiled society on the Forbidden Island. He has put into effect an evil scheme for world domination, and will stop at nothing to see it executed.

Cohado the Long (The Keeper of Lies): Please see character list for Book Two.

Dietrich Oarsbreaker: Kemetian outlaw and a rough contemporary of the buccaneer Ulrich Mancrusher. While not quite as large as his companion, he was equally deadly with steel as well as his bare hands.

Dillwyn Anvilhand: Please see character list for Book One.

Jang: The patron god of sea rogues. Many pirates pray to this deity for blood and plunder on the high seas.

Lothar Dun'egain: Lothar Dun'egain is the last heir of the House of Hudlthem. He is a pit boss for the Baezutu Arena.

Mimir: Please see character list for Book One.

Octavia: Branjadom's younger sister and a pawn in the power struggle of the evil Chief Talbod.

Thegn Odinson: Gerdmorian barbarian that befriended Tulwryn in the slave camp of Yalad Munster.

Tulwryn Bloodsword: Please see character list for Book One.

Ulrich Mancrusher: Ulrich Mancrusher, was a Kemetian outlaw that was wanted in half a dozen cities throughout the whole of Phantasodyssea as well as for crimes committed on the high seas. His blue-black beard was long and unkempt, and a patch was covering his left eye, from under which a long pale scar wound its way, serpent-like, across his darkly lined face.

Yalad Munstur: A flesh merchant of unknown origin. He is rumored to be of Kemite blood, but his features are dark, more akin to that of the L'hoehnians, and he is tall like the wizards of Covensted. No one knows the place wherein he dwells, yet there are tales that he calls the swamp of the Black Delta his home.

IMPORTANT PLACES OF *PHANTASODYSSEA*

1 league= 3 miles.

A

Akhrod, Caves of: The caves of Akhrod are not natural, but are rather deep, maze-like tunnels that are thought to have been quarried by an ancient race of desert dwellers, long forgotten. The city of Mok controls all mining in the caves and unrestricted travel is highly frowned upon. A secret mineral is mined here, by the Mokites, indispensable to the production of their chief export, Bluewood.

Azazel Plain: The Azazel Plain is a seemingly endless expanse of dry, parched, high desert located in the northern reaches of Phantasodyssea. There is no plant life in this region to speak of, and the only animals that call this desolate place home are the many poisonous sandworms that constantly plague unsuspecting travelers.

Azure Wood: Although being located in a most distasteful area, having the Obsidian River pour through its center, and the Black Delta directly to its south, the Azure Wood is practically the most beautiful place in Phantasodyssea. The East Wood, located on the east side of the Obsidian River, is the most peaceful of the wooded area, being located in the temporal zone between the Plain of Kem and the Grasslands of Kemet. The West Wood is a little warmer in summer and very cold at night all year long. The wood is home to many fairy beings, some extremely curious but none harmful.

B

Baezutu: The town of Baezutu is found near the eastern border of The Wastes. It is made up of mostly sand pirates and desert bandits. Phaedron has maintained a garrison in Baezutu for many years, aiming to guarantee the smooth operation and safe passage of caravans traveling on the trade routes in that area, but due to internal corruption within its ranks, there are still many problems and dangers in Baezutu and the surrounding area.

Bain: Bain is a small village of Woodlings nestled in the Forest of Bain. Woodlings are small elf-like creatures with large yellow eyes and light brown skin. While they are friendly, they are also highly mischievous. They have no real export to speak of, and mainly hire themselves out as trackers and guides. They are the best woodsmen in Phantasodyssea.

Bain, Forest of: The Forest of Bain is an extremely old forest surrounding the village of Bain, surrounded by the Golrin Prairie. It is one of the oldest forests in Phantasodyssea.

Balor Pass: As one leaves the northern boundary of Darkwood on the trade route one directly enters the Ymir Mountains. After many miles of treacherous trails into the mountains one advances onto the Balor Pass, the only sure way through this otherwise impassable mountain barrier. It was named after Lord Jerrod Balor. Lord Balor was originally of noble blood, and at one time heir to the throne of Phaedron. After his father, the High Elder Nimrod the Just, was murdered, the throne was assumed by his assassin, the evil cleric Kaine Obel. Fearing for his life, Jerrod left Phaedron and became an explorer and adventurer. Even though he was not in the service of the High Elder, since he was originally of royal Phaedron blood, his achievement of discovering the pass through the un-named mountains was heralded as a great Phaedronian achievement.

Basalt River: The Basalt River is a shallow, semi-salt/semi-fresh water river that cuts across the northern area of the Seething Swamp.

Bluewood: Bluewood is a mystical product of Mok-Tor. The substance is extremely durable and is impervious to fire and salt-water damage. Even though it is extremely expensive, it is the most sought after ship building material in Phantasodyssea.

Brine: Brine is a tiny bayou town located on the south western most tip of the Seething Swamp. Its main exports are roots and herbs, which are collected for medicinal purposes. Although the area and climate is extremely hostile, the people of Brine are exceptionally friendly.

C

Caiwryn: Phantasodyssea.

Carthus: A medium sized town located in the northwest reaches of the Golrin Prairie, just south of the Sea of Fire, and a stone's throw from the Lower Crimson Forest. The town is peopled by a mighty race of Dwarf engineers and warriors. It is said that many centuries ago when the Dragon's Needle began to rumble, the mystics of Golrin employed the Carthusians to build a Fire Wall Dam at the southern rim of the Rhyan Valley. Even though the Dwarves didn't believe the story that the mystics told, that the Dragon's Needle would spew so much fire and brimstone that the whole of the Golrin Prairie would be flooded, they nevertheless took the job and built the dam. With the finances from the job, Carthus was able to expand into the thriving city it is today. Needless to say, those ancient mystics were correct, for the Dragon's Needle did erupt and flood the entire Rhyan Valley!

This event did not happen though, for about six hundred and eighty years after the Great Dam was built. Almost seven centuries after being built, and with practically no maintenance or upkeep to speak of, the dam held. This has put the town of Carthus on the map, and now the town is heralded as the foremost place of learning for those interested in engineering and architecture. At last count, the lava flow from the Dragon's Needle continues to fill the Sea of Fire even to this day!

Chete: At the western-most border of a vast expanse known only as The Wastes lies the small village of Chete. Surrounded by nameless mountains and burning desert sands, Chete is a peaceful place of contemplation. Mystics come from miles around to study in its many underground temples and monasteries, searching for the seeds of wisdom and enlightenment. It is believed that the old teachers of Chete are the very same priests that once occupied the Holy City of Vodmar in the Golrin Prairie. Legend has it that after these priests fled Vodmar from a fierce band of Knobite raiders, they traveled south into The Wastes. Here, they discovered the secrets of immortality and ultimate knowledge. Chete is dedicated to peace and compassion.

Covensted: Covensted is a village of witches located on the eastern border of Darkwood. No roads lead to Covensted, and visitors are discouraged from travel within its city limits. Covensted has no exports to speak of, although the village maintains a fairly large and competent array of professional sorcerers.

Crimson Forest: On the western shore of the Sea of Fire, extending from the southern border of the Sulphur Mountains to the northern border of the Forest of Neturu, and eastward all the way to the Golrin Prairie is the majestic Crimson Forest. The many colors seen here are absolutely spectacular. Towering Ironwood trees glow red from the continuous blasts of heat from the Sea of Fire and many armored creatures, such as dragons and gorkons, live within this amazing forest.

D

Darkwood: Darkwood is a vast stretch of densely canopied forest. It is believed to be inhabited by beasts created by the witches of Covensted. Only one safe passage cuts through this expanse of wilderness, the Phaedron trade route. This is one of the most expensive roads in Phantasodyssea, mainly due to the risk and expense Phaedron puts forth in trying to keep it safe for travelers.

Dead Man's Reef: Dead man's Reef is a large and foreboding reef of razor coral located off the western shore of Kemet's Forbidden Island. The reef is not only sharp enough to tear the most sea worthy vessel to splinters, it is said to be the home of some of imaginations most deadly creatures.

Devil's Anvil: The Devil's Anvil is a slang term for the Phaedron Desert.

Dragon's Needle: The Dragon's Needle is an active volcano in the Sulphur Mountains.

E

East Lake: The East Lake is a large lake in the northern area of the Grasslands of Kemet.

Enchanted Forest: A magical expanse of flora and fauna containing many tens of millions of magical plants and wildlife is known as the Enchanted Forest. It is located in the northeastern most reaches of Phantasodyssea. No roads or settlements are found within its boarders and the Phaedrons do not even trespass here, for it is under the control of Kimark Khan, the most powerful warlock in Phantasodyssea.

Enchanted Mountains: The mountain range known as the Enchanted Mountains are located in the northeastern area of the Enchanted Forest. Comprised of extremely foreboding mountains, and home of Phantasodyssea's tallest mountain, Mt. Malador, they are a remnant of the Ice Times, which occurred 80,000 years ago.

Endless Mountains: Stretching westward from Neturu are the Endless Mountains. Many wondrous splendors can be found here, although the terrain is treacherous. There are no known passes, and if there were, the Neturuians would surely keep them a secret as they do with all their territory. The entire range is inhabited by various mythical beasts of ancient legends.

F

Flaming River: The Flaming River is a large body of forever flowing lava pouring forth from the Dragon's Needle into the Sea of Fire.

Foothills of Insanity: These rolling hills are so named for the mental condition of those hardy souls who did not perish in the Phaedron desert. For one who has survived the countless horrors of the desert, upon reaching this far, one would surely be mad!

Forbidden Island: Over five thousand years ago the people of Kem split violently in a bloody civil war. Those that came south established the city of Kemet. With them, they brought slaves, Kemites who were taken as prisoners in the war. After these slaves outlived their usefulness they were banished to the then un-named, Forbidden Island. In time, Kemet declared sole ownership of this piece of rock in the southern corner of the Ocean of No Return; for the past four thousand years it has been a place of exile; a prison colony. Most Kemetians believe that one condemned to exile on the island is guaranteed a certain and heinous death. But on the contrary, the island is a virtual paradise, and is inhabited by the decedents of long banished prisoners. They have a primitive tribal society and are quite self sufficient in their existence. The tribe has but four sacred holidays: Ekksbod, Mokksbod, Nemsbod, and Jukksbod.

Fords of Doom: The Fords of Doom are a hazardous array of inlets and fords north east of the Enchanted Mountain Range.

Frozen Lake: The Frozen Lake is a large lake in the Northern Territories. It remains frozen most of the year.

Frozen River: The Frozen River is actually the headwaters of the Basalt River, yet most do not know it, for not many explorers have ever journeyed upstream that far north. It originates from a spring near the Frozen Lake in the Northern Territories.

G

Golrin: The second largest metropolis in Phantasodyssea is Golrin, yet it is the richest. Its people are very friendly, but extremely wary of outsiders due to the vast amounts of wealth they protect in their underground vaults. The city Magistrate has employed, for the last few centuries, an extremely powerful crack unit of Kemetian Mercenaries to act as Guardians of Golrin. Golrin has no export since its wealth has made it financially independent from all other establishments in Phantasodyssea. The city gets its wealth from the many mines it operates in the Golrin Prairie. These mines are said to contain Black Diamonds, Red Gold, and Liquid Steel. The location of these mines has never been shown on any map, and their parameters are heavily guarded.

Gulf of Misery: The infamous Gulf of Misery is a southern gulf in the Ocean of No Return located on the shored of the Black Delta and the Azure Wood. Many ships have been lost in this area, and many islands dot the coasts, especially near the southern reaches of the Grasslands of Kemet, which harbor pirates and other dregs of Phantasodyssea.

H

Helheim Plateau: The Helheim plateau is one of the most forbidding places in Phantasodyssea. During the height of the day, surface temperatures soar high enough to melt lead, and at night, plummet low enough to freeze quicksilver!

Hidden Lake: Hidden Lake is a large lake located in the northern reaches of the Forest of Neturu.

K

Kem: Kem is a medium sized bowery town located on the banks of the River Phaedron. It is made up of mostly fishermen and river pirates. Bandits occupy the Plain of Kem, usually robbing and killing any bold enough to travel unprotected. Occasionally, they invade the Grasslands of Kemet. Even though the inhabitants of Kem and Kemet are from the same ancestral line, there is no love between these two peoples, and bloody skirmishes in the borderlands are common. (*The symbol of the Kemite river pirates is the Kemite cutlass, a stout single edged curved sword*).

Kem, Plain of: Surrounding the village of Kem is the Plain of Kem. It is mainly a large expanse of open savannah and sage fields. In the spring, the whole area comes alive with the cornucopia of colorful wildflowers, and is truly an amazing sight. The plain is home to many large herbivores and some predators.

Kemet, Grasslands of: This grassland is a large rolling field that stretches north and west of Kemet; it is made up of mostly wild grasses, some being taller than the tallest Kemetian. It is a great hiding place for venomous snakes. Bandits make it is a highly dangerous area to travel, and even the protected trade route has its risks.

Kemet, Village of: Kemet is a small port community on the southeastern shores of the Ocean of No Return. Shipbuilding and sea faring are the main jobs in Kemet, although the village does have a seedy red-light district where taverns and brothels abound. Many mercenaries and pirates come to this area looking for work. The main export is seafood, seaweed, and sea salt. The Forbidden Island is under Kemet's control. Kemet is linked to the civilized world via the trade route, which is controlled and maintained by Phaedron. All trade routes are toll routes. They are the safest means of travel throughout Phantasodyssea, and the most expensive.

The King's Wood: The King's Wood is an area, made up actually of gardens, woods, and beautiful architecture; it is the High Elder's private place of contemplation. Only those of royal blood are permitted, all else are strictly forbidden.

Knob: Knob is a small village of extremely vicious cannibals. They are extremely skillful in hunting and tracking. They are believed to be distantly related to the Woodlings of Bain, but not as skilled in general woodsmanship. What they lack in woodsmanship skills they make up for in savagery. They have no known export for they take what they want. They are considered the plague of the western reaches of the Golrin Prairie. (*Knobites are black skinned with hair dyed bright yellow. They have glowing red eyes and upon reaching adulthood, their teeth are ceremonially filed into sharp points*).

Kra River: At the junction of the Xu River and the River Phaedron is the Kra River. Winding southwest it reaches the desolate hills of The Wastes. Great beasts are said to inhabit these deep and foreboding waters.

L

L'hoehn: L'hoehn is a large tent village of nomads located in the southeastern area of the Azazel Plain, many leagues east of the main trade route to Phaedron. A rough and unruly lot of cut-throats and bandits populate this village. Their two main exports are L'hoehn magical silk, made from the silken cocoons of Ningham Silkworms, and the root of the Kiputu Cactus, said to be extremely toxic. It is used as a medicine, a social drug, and a poison.

M

Mok-Tor, The Twin Cities of: The southern-most town in Phantasodyssea is actually two towns, the twin cities of Mok-Tor, which lies in the extreme south of the Azure Wood. They are a hardy folk and their main export is a composite substance known as Bluewood. It is made through a secret process, believed to be composed of a bark-like substance from a magical tree found in the northeastern area of the Azure Wood and a secret mineral found in the caves of Akhrod. To insure a balance in the processing of Bluewood, the town of Mok regulates the activities in the caves and the village of Tor maintains timber activities in the forest. Only five people in the town know the manufacturing process of this substance, therefore maintaining a strong balance between these two establishments. Neither can operate without the other. The Mokites are a moral people, but the Torites are extremely worldly.

Mt. Malador: In the northern reaches of the Enchanted Forest and completely surrounded by the Enchanted Mountain Range Mt. Malador raises its lofty head high over the canopy of the forest. Easily the realm's highest mountain, and from its peak, it is said that one can observe every corner of the land in a single glance. It is here, atop Mt. Malador, that it is believed the mage Kimark Khan makes his home.

N

Neturu: This metropolis is mistakenly called The City of the

Gods after the giant-like race that dwells there. Because the city is cleverly located on the banks of the Xu River, nestled between the Forest of Neturu and the Endless Mountains, they are completely self-sufficient. They take from the bounty of the waters, the forest, and the mountains, and have neither need of import or export. They are a fairly agreeable race, although they are not to be toyed with. Of all the races in Phantasodyssea, the Neturuians are the only tribe that the Knobites fear.

Neturu, Forest of: The Forest of Neturu is an immeasurable forest at the western end of the Golrin Prairie. The forest totally surrounds the endless mountains and is impassable due to the many thousands of thorny, briar-like undergrowth.

Neturu, Sea of: The Sea of Neturu is the ocean on the west coast of Phantasodyssea.

Northern Territories: Bleak frozen wasteland in the northern most reaches of Phantasodyssea comprised of mountains, forests, lakes, rivers, and vast plains; home to many war loving barbarian tribes (*All the northern barbarian tribes are of the same race and are tall, with a large build. Their skin is pale and they have blonde hair with blue or grey eyes*).

Nuvia: This small farm village is located just south of the Plain of Kem and east of the River Phaedron, near the main trade route. Their main export is agriculture, but some of its inhabitants farm Wormwood illegally, for it demands an extremely high price in places like Covensted and Baezutu. (*Nuvians are of medium build with olive color skin, dark eyes and black hair*).

O

Obsidian River: The Obsidian River is so named because of the black, crushed glass-like sand found along its banks. It stretches from north to south, from the River Phaedron, south through the Plain of Kem, all the way through the Azure Wood to the Black Delta, and emptying into the Gulf of Misery. The river abounds with twenty-six foot long armored razor eels and eighty-two foot long lizard-like flesh eating amphibians.

Ocean of No Return: East of the Golden Shores of Kemet lie the unspeakable horrors of the Ocean of No Return. This ocean is an extremely vast, uncharted and hostile sea. The Kemetians alone possess the seamanship to navigate these waters, and even then, only hug the coastline. The only ship that ventures out into the deep reaches of the Ocean of No Return is the Kemetian prison bark. Twice a year the prison barge takes those condemned to exile on Kemet's Forbidden Island. There is only one way to pass safely through Dead Man's Reef, and the senior barge master is the only one trusted with that secret.

P

Phaedron: Within the massive stone walls of Phaedron lives the High Elder, King of Phaedron, and originally lord and master of Phantasodyssea. Those who choose to live under his watchful, yet often times tyrannically protective eye, do so within the walls of the city. It is by far the largest metropolis in Phantasodyssea, housing well over five hundred thousand people. Due to the vast area of the continent, and the relatively small size of the Phaedron Army, taxes are somewhat difficult to collect from the many outlying towns and villages. This was why the system of the toll trade routes was created. It is also why substances such as Nuvian Absynth, L'hoehn magical silk, and L'hoehn Kiputu are illegal.

Phaedron Desert: The Phaedron Desert is the most forbidding place in Phantasodyssea; the Helheim Plateau stands as a paradise in comparison. The Phaedrons use this desert as a tool of execution for its condemned prisoners. The condemned are exiled to this wasteland with no food, water, or gear of any kind. It is said that this desert sparkles white in the searing brilliance of the midday sun, a reflection of the many bones, bleached white by the intense heat, left behind by the countless dead.

Phaedron Wood: The Phaedron Wood is a large expanse of beautiful forest surrounding the walled city-state of Phaedron.

R

Rhyan: On the west side of the Sea of Fire, located atop a high ridge in the Crimson Forest, just on the southern most border of the Sulphur Mountains lies the mystical city of Rhyan. No one has had contact with the inhabitants of Rhyan in over seven centuries, and so the city is not believed to exist, although it does appear on a few old maps. Most think this is due to folklore and not really factual. As legend goes, the Rhyans were a strong race of powerful wizards that understood the deep mysteries of the natural world. They discovered, and extracted from the Sulphur Mountains, a mineral known as Levititium; this rare and magical mineral has an anti-magnetic property and is used in Rhyan Windship engineering. If the city and its people still exist to the present day, they live obscure, reclusive lives, safely out of reach behind the wall of molten lava that is the Sea of Fire.

River Adronn: The only river in the realm that flows north is the River Adronn. It is believed that there are strange metallic properties within the river's water, probably a by-product run-off from the Crimson Forest, that give it the resistance needed to defy gravity and flow up-stream. No one has successfully explored this region, and nothing is known of the extent of this mysterious river.

River Agu: The River Agu is a shallow, salt-water river emptying into the Ocean of No Return on the east bank of the Seething Swamp. It is believed to be laden with gemstones of unlimited magical value, as well as vast schools of flesh eating fish, which makes excavation of these gems almost an impossibility, save for the most experienced and bold diver.

River Phaedron: The Phaedron River is a mighty river that stretches the entire length of Phantasodyssea; it is deep, swift, violent, and in most places, un-navigatable.

S

Sea of Fire: Pouring forth from the mouth of the Dragon's Needle is the Flaming River. From this river opens the Sea of Fire, a vast ocean of brimstone and molten rock.

Seething Swamp: The Seething Swamp is a vast marsh, and gets its name from the sound that is produced from its depths. The swamp sounds as if it is breathing, and indeed, many believe it to be a living entity in and of itself. There are many dangerous creatures that inhabit the swamp, although the people of Brine seem to survive in a relatively peaceful co-existence within its borders.

South Lake: The South Lake is a large lake located in the northern area of the Azure Wood.

Sulphur Mountains: This northwestern mountain range is a desolate and unforgiving realm of death. It is home to the Dragon's Needle, the most violent volcano in the realm. No vegetation of any kind grows here. The ground is charred rock and ash. The air is saturated with sulphurous fumes. There are no known passes; the region has never successfully been charted.

T

Temple of the Cat: The Temple of the Cat is a Neturuian sanctuary and holy place of worship for the Neturuians. Within its marble halls stands their most holy relic, the Neter, a mummified feline believed to be the physical embodiment of the Neturuians ancient cat deity.

U

Un-named Mountains: In the central region of the Northern Territories rises the Un-named Mountains. They are an ancient mountain chain and are one of the last remaining pristine examples of the forgotten Ice Times. The fierce Gerdmorians call the region home.

V

Valley of the Tombs: Directly cut through the center of the Endless Mountains is a vast valley, the Valley of the Tombs. It was believed to have been carved by an ancient race of gods for the burial of the past kings of Neturu. There are said to be more than one thousand kings and royalty buried within this valley, making it the richest place in Phantasodyssea for archeological findings. However, due to extensive grave robbing and desecration by looters and treasure hunters, the Neturuians have declared excavation forbidden and punishable by death.

Vodmar, Ruins of: Old ruins, decaying temples, and crumbling monuments litter the entire area of the ancient city of Vodmar. Most of their history is lost. The city is thought to be currently inhabited by outcasts, fugitives, and ghosts.

W

Wastes, The: The wastes are a large expanse of barren lands more than twice as large as the Plain of Kem. It is most inhospitable. Only but the most hardy desert dwellers live here. Contrary to popular belief, there is a wide array of edible, non-poisonous flora and fauna to be found in this region.

West Lake: The West Lake is the largest lake in Phantasodyssea, located in the northwestern corner of the vast Golrin Prairie.

X

Xu River: The Xu River is a small, pristine river branching off from the River Phaedron. It terminates at the Great Pool of Neturu in the Temple of the Cat. It is here that the Neturuians come to pay homage to their sacred deity. All activity in and around the Xu River is extremely forbidden.

Y

Ymir Mountains: Along the northern boundary of Darkwood lies the Ymir Mountains. Many miles of treacherous trails criss-cross these foreboding mountains, and the Balor Pass is the only sure way through this otherwise impassable mountain barrier.

The Preview of

THE BLOODSWORD SAGA
BOOK IV:

The Voidmaster

ONE

Memories of Pain

It was a humid morning. The tropical sun was burning brightly and the wetness of his surroundings made Ulrich Mancrusher ill. Or was it the stability of the land that made his stomach lurch? For as long as he could remember, every morning was the same. First he was visited by nausea, then the headaches. Ulrich remembered his old sailing master, Logan Michaels, who often told him about the land sickness that old sailors often experienced when they were beached for any length of time. Ulrich was young then, and he would laugh, telling the old shipwright that he would grow to be stronger than most. Yet now, he did not feel strong. He hadn't felt strong for a very long time. Perhaps the royal life had made him soft, he thought to himself? How long had he been king of the Forbidden Island, one year? Five years? No! It had been over eight turnings of the great wheel of the seasons since he rowed to the island, broke into the imperial palace, and killed Chief Talbod in his own stateroom, taking the crown and the throne for himself. But it had been a curse, not a blessing! The damnable non-movement of the land constantly made him ill. He longed for a heaving deck under his feet; he ached for the sea!

"What doom have I allowed myself to fall in to," he quietly asked himself for the millionth time. Sweat ran down his back in a thick stream. He removed his soaked shirt and tossed it onto the floor of his room. It quickly disappeared, snatched by the dark hand of one of his many servants. The scent of coconut and passionflower was adrift on the air, but still, this gave him no pleasure.

"How could I have let this happen? I should have died gloriously on the decks of the Malevolent like Dietrich did. Jang rest his filthy soul. And curse mine!"

He pushed open the double bamboo doors and passed over the threshold, stepping out onto the king's balcony. Glancing over the balcony's rail he espied his many subjects, far below, groveling in the dirt of the Forbidden Island. A Xlobyte called loudly overhead, and at once Ulrich's mind was adrift. He remembered how the dwarf wanted to slay him, and how the barbarian had interceded.

"Why did I hand over the girl? Why not use her as a hostage?" But he knew the answer all too well. Octavia was beautiful. From the first day he set his eyes on her, he was held captive by her beauty. He was spellbound. And he cursed himself for his weakness.

"A bloody pirate has no use for those types of tender feelings," he had told himself time and again. "And look, this life's proof of the pudding! Letting me guard down landed mine sorry bones on this god-forsaken lice infested rock!" His anger was overwhelming, and he slammed a huge fist down on the balcony rail sending splinters flying. A tiny thread of blood trickled from his large knuckles and stained the aged wood.

He remembered how Tulwryn had marooned him on the island. No! He wasn't marooned on an island, he was marooned in a rowboat! Made to shove off in that tiny dingy, with no food or water. His ship destroyed. Ulrich remembered how the Fidelity destroyed his ship with a blast of hell fire.

"Curse the day I set mine one good eye on that god-forsaken dragonship!"

He remembered thinking to himself how many leagues was it to the island? And his shoulders and back ached at the thought of reliving his torture. How many days had he rowed, non-stop, through shark infested waters? Look at the sharks, all the sharks! Fins everywhere! His heart leapt at the dark memory.

Then his mind drifted to other memories. His mind was a tangled web of lore, and he could not ascertain reality from fiction. So many stories had he heard about the Forbidden Island; how it was guarded by a deadly razor sharp reef and peopled by criminals.

"I should fit right in then," he said, laughing. And true it was, that over five thousand years ago the people of Kem split violently in a bloody civil war. Those that came south established the city of Kemet. With them, they brought slaves, Kemites who were taken as prisoners in the war. After these slaves outlived their usefulness they were banished to the then un-named, Forbidden Island. In time, Kemet declared sole ownership of that piece of rock in the southern corner of the Ocean of No Return. For the past four thousand years it had been a place of exile. A prison colony. Most Kemetians believed that anyone condemned to exile on the island is guaranteed a certain and heinous death do to the harshness of the island, and the many ferocious beasts that live thereon. But there were other legends too, legends that say the island is a virtual paradise, and is inhabited by the decedents of those long banished prisoners. He remembered how Yalad Munster told him that the inhabitants of the island had set themselves up a primitive tribal society and were quite self sufficient in their existence. It was for the annual celebration of Mokksbod that the princess was kidnapped.

"We shall see," Ulrich remembered thinking to himself as he rowed his small life craft to the Forbidden Island. Of course, he didn't want to discover the island this way. He had hoped for success in his one last venture, cruising into the hidden bay whilst standing proud high on the captain's quarterdeck. He dreamed of riches beyond imagination. But of course, he had been deceived by the flesh merchant. He spit at the thought of doing business with that vile slave trader.

"Ye stooped pretty low this time," he told himself. "Perhaps this is mine just reward?" And how is the princess faring these days, he wondered?

"Not sweating her pretty self to death on a rock, marooned

with plague infested savages!" Again, he slammed his huge fist into the rail, this time driving splinters deep into his skin. He did not flinch at the pain.

"But I did it, didn't I?" Ulrich was a survivor, and he knew it. Straining his back to the point of breaking, he rowed his tiny boat to the dread beaches of the Forbidden Island. Since the northwestern shores of the island were blocked by the razor sharp Deadman's Reef he was forced to row around the island. He discovered a southern beachhead and made landfall. Pulling the tiny craft from the sea with all his might, he hid it in the scrub, well out of sight of prying eyes.

There were no tracks, no signs of life anywhere, so he instinctively began his journey inland, seeking to find the main settlement. If it truly existed.

Every day he wandered, he realized many of the legends were true. Even though the beaches were bleak, the interior of the island was beautiful. Most of the island was tropical, majestic palm trees grew in abundance, as well as other jungle-like flora and fauna that he had never seen. Huge leafed plants with stalks as large as a man's thigh and lovely scented flowers were everywhere. Many intoxicating fragrances drifted on the air, yet the intense heat was stifling. And there was no game to speak of, he remembered. Then he laughed at the memory, for even had he found a beast to slay, there would have been no way to slay it, for the barbarian cast him from the ship without a weapon.

After a few days of wandering, growing thin from the want of meat, Ulrich stumbled on a small grove of broad leaf trees south of a sparkling lake. The trees were tall and their trunks thick. They were covered with a shaggy type of rough bark and had vines growing from them in all directions. He soon noticed a strange lavender hued fruit hanging from the vines, about as big as a man's fist, and his hunger drove him to taste one. A smile wormed its way across the old pirate's aged face at this delicious memory. He could almost taste the sweetness of the fruit, and he remembered the vitality that came rushing back to his exhausted muscles. It was as if the fruit gave him immediate strength. Perhaps a drug was present within its sweet nectar? He had no way of knowing, nor did he care. And for two days he remained under the eves of those strange trees, growing strong from their forbidden fruit.

In time, he once again began his search for the native settlement, and for Chief Talbod. Again, he spat at the memory.

"If ye are here, king, and I know ye are, I will find you. And when I do, I shall kill you." He remember his words as if they were just spoken. But that was a long time ago. Over eight turnings of the great wheel of the seasons had passed since he landed on the Forbidden Island, and a lot had happened since then. At least he thought it was eight. There was no way of knowing, for in the remote tropics of Phantasodyssea, the seasons changed naught. At least not as he was used to. There were rainy seasons, and there were dry seasons. This was all he knew, yet he tried to keep track all the same.

What kept the pirate going on his quest to find the settlement that Yalad Munster had told him about was the simple idea that the flesh merchant had to have known first hand of the island's inhabitants. At first, he thought it was just a hoax to taunt him and his men into kidnapping the princess. But after the kidnapping, and after the girl was brought across the continent to Kemet, Yalad Munster had him shove off and proceed as planned.

It was insane, he knew. To take a ship as old as the Malevolent into uncharted waters. Hell, it would be madness to take any ship over the horizon on a whim. No! The flesh merchant had been there and back. That was the only possible truth. So, deep in his heart, Ulrich knew the settlement was there. He knew that Chief Talbod existed. And he knew that when he found him, he would kill him and become king. The idea of undreamed of wealth drove him on.

He finally discovered the settlement on the eastern bank of small river. It was a quaint village. The buildings were a mixture of log and stone, with thickly thatched roofs of palm leaves. The inhabitants were short, dark, and naked. They bore a striking resemblance to the people of Kem, and again he knew the legends were true.

Ulrich took one last glance at the people below him, and then turned and walked from the balcony back into his private quarters. His servants were still there, and there was a clean shirt laid out for him on his settee.

He looked around the room, the room where it happened. Smiling, he relived those glorious moments where a marooned pirate could become a king in one act of bloody violence.

It had been a day like any other, and yet, it was different. He remembered waiting until nightfall, and then skulking in the shadows, listening to the natives talk. Fortunately, their language had not evolved much over the past four thousand years and he was able to understand bits and pieces of their conversations. By this, Ulrich Mancrusher was able to learn the whereabouts of the imperial palace. Quickly, he made his way to that very building.

The palace guards were easy to dispatch, and in seconds he had access to the interior of the building. Room by room he searched, like a hungry panther stalking its prey, until finally, he came to a room. This room.

Chief Talbod was entering the room from his private balcony, laughing. Ulrich knew naught the reason why the king laughed, but he remembered the sound of his laughing, and the hideous sight of the fat naked king standing before him. In a flash he was across the room, his massive hands fastened tightly around the thick blubber of the king's throat. Bones snapped like twigs. The laughing ceased, and so did the life of the king.

As the huge carcass fell to the floor, Ulrich remembered the overwhelming joy of crushing the life out of a man. He hadn't killed in such a long time. He hadn't needed to. He was king now.

Ulrich's mind then reeled and he remembered how he removed the feathered plume of the Xlobyte from the head of the dead king, and how he placed the crown on his own head. He remembered how majestic he felt, his head adorned with the feathered crown of the native raptor, most deadly bird of prey in all of Caiwryn, a sign of his sovereign lordship as the newly crowned king of the Forbidden Island. And then he frowned hard.

"Damn mine black soul to Jang's eternal depths," he cursed under his breath. And again, more memories flooded his mind. Over and over he relived the past, and grew angry at his punishment.

"Damn that barbarian for this sentence, and damn me for mine greed! How was I to know that the fat fool of a king would exhaust his own royal fortunes to obtain the princess, the one thing that he was certain would guarantee him omnipotent power and transform him from a king into a god? What a fool he was! And what a fool I am as well."

Then suddenly, he got an idea. Clapping his hands, he summoned a servant. Immediately one appeared. The girl was a dark beauty, naked but for the tiny shell anklet she wore about her left ankle. As she entered the room, she bowed low. Ulrich's eyes danced over her ebony flesh. Shining black hair hung down past her waist, and the soft patch of sparkling hair between her legs gave away her age. The girl's full breasts were pleasing to the eye, and her slender waist and wide hips were lovely as well. Her fingernails and toenails were neatly trimmed and painted, and she wore bright yellow flowers in her hair. Instantly, he remembered Octavia, and he was saddened. Pushing the thoughts of passion from his mind he called out to the girl in a graven tone.

"Where is Umi," he asked? The girl told him that the priest was in the temple. Ulrich gave the girl orders for him to be brought to his quarters immediately. She disappeared as quickly as she arrived.

Ulrich Mancrusher put on his clean shirt and lowered himself onto the settee. He sat in his room, brooding. There was already a gloomy atmosphere present in the room. You could almost smell the fear in the sweat of his servants even though the fragrance of coconut and passionflower was adrift on the air. A thousand dark thoughts passed the transom of his mind.

"Damn him! Damn me! Damn the annual celebration of Mokksbod! Damn this accursed island and the day I made the deal with that flesh merchant!" His hand was still bleeding, and had begun to swell. Still, he paid it no heed.

An hour later Umi arrived. Ulrich's anger had not subsided. The priest entered and bowed low.

"Tell me something, priest," Ulrich said to Umi, "I have been your king for eight seasons now, but yet ye have naught been truthful with me. Tell me why your dead king wanted the goddess of Neturu. Tell me of the ritual of power! Speak quickly and with the truth or I will send ye to meet thy doom!"

Sweat beaded on the priest's brow yet somehow in the back of his mind, he knew this day would come. And he feared it. Time and again, he had tried to dissuade Chief Talbod from attempting to summon Tikupitu, the vile god of the Void. But the king would listen naught to his words of wisdom. And for the past eight turnings of the great wheel of the seasons he had hoped to keep this secret hidden from the mind of his new king. But he knew that the power of Tikupitu was strong, and that somehow, one way or another, he would break free from the Void and enter this world. And fear washed over him.

"Sire," spoke the high priest, in a very shaky voice, "I have always been loyal to ye. Even when the whole of the kingdom was against you, I was there. Please, for your own protection, ask me naught this thing. For it was my dead Lord's undoing and his plan was madness."

"My patience grows thin, Umi. I was Talbod's undoing! He died by mine hands, not by some plan that went awry."

"Nay, Lord," Umi said, bowing low and showing complete submissiveness. "King Talbod died because of the will of Tikupitu. Ye were just an instrument of His will." Umi dropped once again to his knees and bowed low, for he knew this information would anger his new king.

Ulrich screamed at the top of his lungs, his anger growing like a hurricane. He grabbed the groveling priest by the scruff of his neck and hoisted him high into the air and then dashed him to the hard teakwood floor. The man slammed hard onto the floor and painted the wood with his blood.

"Ulrich is no pawn, damn ye! Now tell me what I seek or I shall send thee to meet thy dead king this very day!"

The priest looked up at Ulrich, spit and blood streaming from his broken face, and wept. Ulrich motioned for a servant to help the priest to a low bench and another aid produced a small wet towel in which he dabbed the blood from the priest's mouth and nose. Umi's breathing was quick and choppy and it was apparent that he was in great pain. He took a deep breath trying to calm himself, then coughed and spit out a few teeth. After a few moments he regained some of his composure and he began speaking once again.

"Against my judgment, m'lord, I shall tell ye what you wish to hear. Although it pleases me naught, for I know it shall be your downfall. And mine."

Ulrich sat on his settee and relaxed a bit, readying himself to hear the high priest's words. He stared daggers at the man with his one good eye. Never had he hated anyone as much as he had hated the man now standing before him. Even Yalad Munster, the vile slave trader whose dreadful plan to kidnap a goddess and which eventually landed him in his present loathsome situation, he didn't even hate as much. Ulrich's eye studied the priest's face. Why did he hate this man so much? What had he ever done to deserve such contempt? He did not know. All he knew is the hatred he felt, and that someday, perhaps today, he would kill him. But not before he knew Talbod's dark secret. He had to know the details of the ritual. So he sat there quietly, and listened.

"Sire," spoke Umi, yet it pained him much for his mouth was broken. "'Tis no secret that Chief Talbod desired power more than wealth, more than women, more than worldly pleasures. Aye, he trafficked in the dark arts. That also is no secret. The reason why he sought the goddess of Neturu was for sacrifice.

"Somehow, and this I know naught how, he was able to contact someone on the mainland. Perhaps it was by his art? I know naught. But somehow he contacted the mainland, yet this apparently ye already know. And how ye know, again, I know naught. Maybe ye traffick in the dark arts too? This is not my business, sire. Ye are king. And rightly so, for ye attained the throne by the strength of your thews!" Umi paused for a moment, allowing a servant to dab his bleeding face with the warm wet towel.

"Yes, it had been a tricky undertaking, to arrange for the kidnapping of the goddess of Neturu. But he was mad with power. Every year since he came into power, at Mokksbod, Chief Talbod would choose a virgin from among the poorest families of the tribe and sacrifice her to his cruel gods. In all our tribe's history, never had such atrocities been committed, yet our savage king extracted blood and made it law. We are a weak and beaten people. How were we to combat this evil? Aye, with his coronation, a great evil had come to Eden.

"There had been rumors that through his bitter magics, the king had acquired a goddess and that she was to be the year's sacrifice. No one knew why such a sin was to be committed, for who could sacrifice a goddess? Yet there was some relief among the people that no tribal virgin would die that day, but as to the reason behind such an atrocity that called for the kidnap of a goddess and then to slay her on an alter of evil, none could know. So, as high priest, I took it on myself to find the answers to these dark questions. What I discovered was more terrifying than death itself.

"Somehow, through the practice of his dark art, Chief Talbod had made contact with Tikupitu. 'Twas this god that ordered our king to arrange the sacrifice. Tikupitu promised our king powers beyond imagination, and twisted the king's greedy heart to do His own bidding.

"Tikupitu wanted the virgin blood of the goddess of Neturu, and our king had become a slave of the dark powers of the Voidmaster, yet he knew it naught. Eventually, he thought he could betray the dark god, yet, as ye now know, that did not happen. Somehow his plans were thwarted. No princess came. And then ye arrived and slew our king, taking the throne for yourself. That is all I know, sire. Ye must believe me. I know nothing of the details of the ritual. Please believe me."

Ulrich stood up and wandered around the room, thinking. He turned the scenes over and over in his mind; from the meeting with Yalad Munster at the Silver Saber to the final battle in the Ocean of No Return, and everything in between. Where had that dragonship come from? Who were those sky pirates? Too many questions. Not enough answers.

"There is too much madness hither. I must get off this island," he thought quietly to himself. "There is no wealth hither anyway. I am a prisoner, marooned on an island of savages by a no good stinking maggot eating barbarian. The next time I meet him, and I will meet him again ere I throw mine life away, I will not bow in submission. I will slice him wide with the bloody blade of me cutlass and boil his guts in whale blubber!"

Without taking another glance at Umi, Ulrich Mancrusher, the king of the Forbidden Island, simply turned and left the room, leaving the high priest and his servants wondering.

* * *

Tulwryn paced the floor of the immense throne room, his mind a jumbled mess of emotions. His blood red cape billowed as he walked revealing his shining vermillion chainmaile byrnie underneath. The great wheel of the seasons had turned eight times since he had built, some say summoned, the Crimson Citadel. Forever was the face of the Golrin Prairie changed by the dark power of his Bloodsword. And even though his tower of bones cast an eerie mood over the whole of the land, there came a peace to Phantasodyssea that had become legendary.

He had now seen fifty-one summers, and with that age, came wisdom and knowledge. Yet, his heart was still heavy and a gloom was on him as never before. It puzzled him though. Why, thought he, had his powers not destroyed the burden that troubled him? He looked around the large room. Beautiful tapestries hung from the cold stone walls and all about the entire castle there hung the appearance of great wealth. Thus far the prophecies had been true. When he prospered, so did the land. And there had been peace and prosperity throughout the whole of the world since the raising of Tulwrynhof, as his Citadel had come to be known.

Yet, something was wrong. He felt it in his bones. But no answer came from the world beyond. The Shadow had been quiet for many seasons, and there had been no word from Dillwyn, Cohado, or Mimir. And this troubled him.

He often thought about the old days, the northern territories, Halgi sleeping eternally in that shallow grave under a bed of stones, Halgr her mother, and the child he gave her.

Yes, he had known his seed had taken hold in the womb of Halgr, Grimthor's widow. How he knew this, he could not say, but know it he did.

Many times he pondered about such things. What would his life had been like, had he stayed in the north with the Heidmarians? How would he have fared, had he fulfilled the prophecy completely, assuming the throne of the House of Rexor for himself?

"Nonsense," he said to himself angrily. "There was no more Heidmar. There were no more clans in the north! Those days were over." And besides, he was naught of their true blood. He was a southerner, through and through. No! His destiny was not to spend his days wandering the eternal frozen wastes of Caiwryn. His destiny lay elsewhere.

Tulwryn looked around the room. It was large and empty save for a few well hewn chairs of heavy oak and a long table of Bluewood. The memories gave him a nauseating feeling in the pit of his stomach. He thought often of his son.

"It was a boy, right? Halgr had a son, right? By me? Yes! The lad would have seen thirteen snows by now."

Instantly, his mind was transported back to Nuvia and his farm. He saw his wife, and his four young sons. How old would they have been by now? He tried to remember? Belwyn was the eldest, twenty-three, maybe. And Hailwryn, the second son, wouldst naught he now be twenty-two? Wrynthor, his favorite; he tried to remember the boy's face, his dark hair, his beautiful smile, the mirror image of his father. He would be around twenty now, he told himself, right? And Rayn, named after his wife. Nineteen? He could not remember. Why could he not remember? Has it been so long that the lives of his sons were wiped from his living memory?

What evil was this, he wondered, that could erase fond memories, and put the painful ones in their place. He could not get the face of his wife from his mind. Not a day passed where he didn't see Durayn lying dead in a pool of her own blood, her face smashed by his axe. Likewise, he was also tormented by the daily visions of Halgi impaled on the point of the Bloodsword.

Angered beyond words by this treachery, Tulwryn screamed an oath at the top of his lungs.

"What do ye want from me," he cried out to his grim gods. "Why am I to be tormented thus?" No answer came.

At once Tulwryn stood and walked over to the balcony door. He paused, and then stepped out into the heat of the Golrin summer. The Crimson Citadel was nestled high atop a mountain of bones and the view was quite impressive. For league after league, as far as the eye could see, there was nothing but wasteland. Not a tree nor shrub grew, just the endless expanse of the vast Golrin prairie and its beautiful golden grasslands shimmering in the heat of the noonday sun.

Then he looked to the north. Carthus is there, Tulwryn told himself. Just over the horizon. And beyond that, Golrin itself. He thought of those two rich and amazing cities teeming with people who had no clue as to the fragility of their world.

"Oh, those sleeping masses," Tulwryn mumbled to himself. "Perhaps ignorance is bliss?"

He then turned his attention to the south, and the city of Neturu. Ah, he remembered the princess and he smiled. But the smile left him, and his heart became cold once again. His hand dropped to the hilt of the great crimson blade, aching for combat. It had been a long time since his sword tasted blood. The thought of combat pleased him and his burden was lifted, if only for a moment.

Perhaps there was another evil brewing on the mountain of Malador? Or maybe in Phaedron? No. That was not it. There was something left undone. And then his sight suddenly turned to the east. The very far away east. And he knew that the evil he felt was once again present just over the horizon, on the far side of the rising sun. On the Forbidden Island.

"I must go to Covensted," Tulwryn told himself. "I must consult the wizards!"

In a flash, the lord of the Crimson Citadel had quit his throne room, left the main Keep, and made his way to the stables. There, he saddled Blackthorn for the long ride east. The mighty horse whinnied with excitement, for he was a beast of war and he could smell the adrenaline in Tulwryn's veins.

Like the wind, Blackthorn ran, his corded muscles catapulting his heavy form down the side of the mountain and across the flat expanse of the prairie. Tulwryn held fast to the reins but did not hold the animal back. It had been a long time since he had ridden Blackthorn into combat. It felt good to once again be on his back, thought Tulwryn, as he clinched his teeth and spurred the great beast onward.

Far in the distance, on the other side of the vast unknown, a nightmare had spawned a terrible evil and the fabric of dreams were rent in twain. And a high priest died painfully.

Thus ends the First Chapter of Book Four

ABOUT THE AUTHOR

Mark Ventimiglia was born on July 15th, 1965 in the sleepy little river town of Alton, Illinois, on the eastern banks of the Mississippi River. He has been an avid fan of fantasy fiction all of his life and spends many hours reading the novels of his favorite authors, as well as writing his own stories for publication. He is also a professional artist and his expressionistic paintings grace some of the covers of his novels.

Mr. Ventimiglia currently lives in Illinois.

OTHER BOOKS BY THE AUTHOR

Fiction:

The Residence, Whitechapel, 1999.
The Adventures of Tulwryn Bloodsword, Xlibris, 2002.
10 Minutes of Forever, Xlibris, 2004.

BVG